Izzaldin Alzain is a management consultant, who studied at the universities of Khartoum, Manchester, and Grenoble. He lives with his family in Dubai.

"A haunting cerebral novel with a perfect balance of thrills coupled with dark musings on what would motivate a thoroughly charming person to commit chilling crimes. *Going to Cameroon* is an interesting book from a variety of perspectives – a psychological analysis of homicide, a reflection on the nature of human motivation, and an action packed story that will leave the reader with questions and ideas to be explored."

Dr. Francine Pinnuck, Ph.D.
Consultant, Writer and Film Producer

# GOING TO CAMEROON

## A NOVEL

## IZZALDIN ALZAIN

This is a work of fiction. Any resemblance between its characters and any persons, living or dead, is purely coincidental.

*To*

**D., K., and L.**

The world would be a better place with more people like you.

"We are what we think. All that we are arises with our thoughts. With our thoughts we perceive the world."

*Buddha*

"What is called freedom of the will is, therefore, an absurdity."

*Schopenhauer*

# PROLOGUE

In the darkness of the night, an outwardly calm and unruffled young man—who was inwardly furious and resentful—awaited a woman's return home, unwavering in his resolve to murder her. Pierre Boucher was a university student, and his intended victim was Brigitte, the wife of Jean-Paul Villard. There was a long and close friendship between their two families.

He had come two nights before, but Brigitte was out, and after waiting for more than two hours he had left, feeling disappointed. When he came back the following night, she was at home, but again he had to leave because he knew that the house had an ultramodern electronic security system fitted to all the windows and doors, except for the four-car garage attached to the large house. Anyone could easily break into the garage, remain in hiding, and then eliminate any of the Villards. Small lapses such as this could prove to be Achilles' heels, precipitating disaster in the best strategies or plans, he reflected. The master strategist, Napoleon Bonaparte, was soundly defeated in 1812 because he overlooked the Russian winter.

The Villards ignored connecting the garage to their ultra-modern security system, which was connected to the nearest police station. However, his plan excluded stepping into the garage, for he was intent on leaving not even a speck of evidence for the police. In fact, his three murders would not involve any break-in—whether into a house, a bedroom, or a garage.

Now he was sitting silently on one of the six chairs surrounding a white garden table, hidden behind a shrubbery on the spacious and manicured front lawn of the house. The high pink walls, of specially-made brick, of the mansion added to its impressiveness. With his customary composure, he was as calm and peaceful as the night that settled upon the premises, yet somehow his relaxed demeanor surprised him, for he was about to commit his first murder. He had never thought he could or would kill anyone in his life.

As he sat silently and patiently, he was taking in all the details that the semidarkness allowed. From where he was sitting in the corner of the yard, he could see different parts of the house. The opulent house was dark except for a dim light in the foyer downstairs, a light in one of the six bedrooms on the upper floor that he knew was Anna Marr's room, and the single light in the open, four-car garage. The lamps on the two pillars of the main gate shone brightly at the entrance to the mansion. The small, detached, one-bedroom apartment occupied by the Moretti couple—the Villards' elderly, Italian cook and gardener—was in pitch-black darkness.

He affirmed to himself that he was ready to await Brigitte's return until four or five o'clock in the morning, for he was determined to eliminate her tonight. He hoped she was not spending the night with a secret lover, since her husband, Jean-Paul Villard, was away on a long business trip in Asia, according to the local newspapers. At forty-five, Brigitte retained the slim body of her modeling days in Paris, Milan, and London. Her husband, who was in his early sixties, looked very fit for his age. Pierre knew that the couple regularly used the small gym on the first floor of their mansion.

Pierre turned his face to the right, glancing at the upper part of the main gate. The Villards' house was not only large but also splendid by any standard. His parents' house, with its three bedrooms, was simply a middle-class villa, but the Villards' house was a mansion, and a magnificent one at that. Suddenly, he saw the light in Anna Marr's room on the second floor go off. Anna was the daughter of a multimillionaire German friend of Jean-Paul Villard, and the Villards had invited her to stay with them for a year to polish up her French.

The large garage, on top of which there was a terrace, was attached to the left side of the house. He stared at the now wide open garage—with a Mercedes, a Volvo, and a Bentley parked in it—and estimated the distance from where he sat to the garage was six to seven meters. To access the main house from the garage, one had to enter a digital code in a small, white box fixed on the wall next to the door leading into the family TV room. This would deactivate the security system in that part of the house only. This is what Brigitte would have to do after she left her car in the garage. He knew he had to shoot her before she started the automatic mechanism of closing the garage's sliding door.

Few, if any, people in this city thought they could be murdered; most of them, perhaps, never thought about such an eventuality. Pierre reflected that since his childhood, there had been few murders committed in this city. The last one had occurred almost one year ago when a young, married schoolteacher persuaded her eighteen-year-old pupil to kill her husband, who was a schoolteacher in another local school. She had enjoyed a two-year affair with her then-minor lover before they decided to eliminate the hapless husband. Within a week, the police managed to get confessions from them both. The murder had generated a lot of interest in the local and national media. The city was stunned when the woman told the court that her motive was to have more stimulating sex. She had found her sex life with her husband dull and boring, while sex with her pupil was much more exciting and invigorating. Her foolish lawyer, who insisted it was a *crime passionnel*, had thought that the fact that it was the pupil, when he was sixteen, who had seduced his client, plus the contention that a sex life that was lousy and stale could be insufferable, would be mitigating factors. The court differed and gave the two culprits stiff prison sentences. The media dubbed the murder 'The Duval Case', Duval being the family name of the libidinous schoolteacher.

His silent waiting coupled with his unwavering determination conjured up the image of a resolute predator awaiting an unsuspecting prey that had no way of escaping. A prey whose doom is a foregone conclusion, he thought. He gently tapped the grass with his shoes; he could feel the bounciness of the lush lawn.

After tonight's murder, he said to himself, I have to carry out two other murders. Then there will be no further bloodshed. I will kill, in retribution, three lusty, deceitful women, and them only. It is restitution. It is nemesis. Clear, pure, and simple. One cannot measure retribution with a ruler. The emotional state one is in when dispensing retribution dictates its magnitude and intensity. Yet the decision to mete out retribution was due to his reflection and free will, he mused. Then his mind drifted to Martine Aubert. He told himself he had to reciprocate her generosity and guileless trust. He had known her for about a month, but she had been, unwittingly, of immense help to him, though she did not know his real name or identity. Recalling their fortuitous encounter, he believed that his daring and free will had turned it into a singular opportunity. He had transformed it into a timely and rewarding encounter. It was a lucky day because he had made it so. A spineless man would have cowered and squandered that priceless opportunity.

His imaginings came to an abrupt end at the sound of Brigitte's BMW coupé easing through the main gate. Its headlights flooded the garage, making the Mercedes and the Volvo shine brightly. He adjusted his synthetic, black mask, which had two gaps for his eyes—and covered both his head and face—and stood up, holding the pistol with its attached silencer. There was no need to use his flashlight. Adrenaline started pumping through his body. He stepped in a measured way toward the garage, as Brigitte slowed her car to insert it between the Mercedes and the Volvo. Now two meters separated him from the threshold of the garage, as Brigitte switched off the engine and emerged from the car. He decided not to cross the threshold and stepped forward, leaving a meter between him and the garage. She was wearing a chic, light-pink, clingy evening dress. As she clicked her key to lock the car, with her back still toward Pierre, he shot her in the back of the head. The bullet penetrated her brain with a muffled sound, an almost inaudible thud. Her slim body hit her car and then bounced, hitting the Volvo before it fell facedown. Her car keys flew, hitting the garage wall in front of her, then ricocheted and settled on the cement floor.

She emitted a pitiful whimper.

Pierre took two steps forward and fired another bullet into her neck. There was a gurgling sound as blood gushed to the garage floor. Pierre remained where he was, outside the garage, and then fired a third bullet into the upper part of her body. A strong smell of cordite filled his nostrils.

It surprised him that she did not utter a loud scream after the first bullet, but only a heartbreaking whimper, like a creature that had resignedly accepted its sudden and inevitable end. He stared down at the dead woman, sprawled between the two cars with her left arm underneath her body and her right arm extended toward the wall of the garage. He never imagined that the human body could release so much blood. Brigitte's elegantly set hair and the top of her dress were drenched in dark-red blood, and a lot of blood seeped to the floor. There was a splash of blood on the front tire of her car. A lot of blood ran down, forming a red pool in the small space between her body and her car. More blood seeped under her lifeless body, and some of it ran toward the Volvo. Her legs were set apart, as if someone had deliberately separated them. While the shoe on her right foot remained in place, the left shoe had slipped off and now rested on its side with its six-centimeter heel pointing to the Volvo. As Pierre stared down, he thought the whole scene was messy, very messy. It was macabre. The fetid smell of raw blood, which reached him through his mask, nauseated him. He put his left, gloved hand to his nose, holding his breath for a few moments, before he stepped back further from the garage.

He turned his head and glanced at the shadowy garden, and then slipped agilely to the back of the house. After leaving the grounds through the small back gate, he removed the mask, and stuffed it into the right pocket of his jeans before detaching the silencer from the Beretta. Then he removed his black, thin, leather gloves and put each item in a separate pocket in his black leather jacket. A voice deep inside him whispered, "Brigitte, forgive me. Jean-Paul, forgive me." With his right hand, he touched the flashlight in the right pocket of his jeans to make sure it was still in its place; he did not want to leave anything behind, not any trace of evidence.

As Pierre crossed the two streets to retrieve his bicycle, he did not see anyone around; it must be past midnight, he thought. A traffic light to his right blinked yellow in the quietude of this upscale residential area. When he walked into the alley where he had hidden his bike, a fat tomcat swaggered across his path without caring to look at Pierre.

The arrogant cat proceeded to the end of the alley and turned to the right. Pierre took out the small key for the loop lock and mounted his bicycle.

It took him more than half an hour of steady cycling through the deserted streets to reach the apartment at 144 rue Karl Marx, in a derelict part of the city. A large number of stray dogs were fighting and copulating noisily in an empty plot of land next to the abandoned, four-story apartment building. His apartment was on the third floor. He opened the front door of the building, took his bicycle inside, closed and locked the door, and then switched on his flashlight to dispel the darkness in the building, which had had no electricity for some years.

Leaving his bike leaning against a wall in the small lobby, he ascended the stairs with the beam of the flashlight. He felt a strong sense of relief that Brigitte Villard had not seen who had snuffed out her life. Her final moments of life would have been filled with immense horror and profound sadness if she had realized that it was Pierre Boucher—the son of her close friend, Jacqueline Boucher, and her secret lover, Christian Boucher— who had shot her.

He craved a cigarette.

I need two cigarettes, he told himself.

# CHAPTER 1

One Friday evening, about a month earlier, Pierre had gone to the campus room of his girlfriend, Catherine Derome, a second-year law student. He had carried with him the draft of a course paper on how a constitution could restrain 'majoritarian authoritarianism'. She had asked him two weeks before to help her with it, and the deadline for its submission to her professor was looming. He had found the topic very interesting and had gone to the trouble of writing a full draft of the essay over four days of serious research. He'd cited fifteen references though her professor had required a minimum of eight.

He gave Catherine a kiss. "This is the essay, Cathy. I do not think your professor can do better. I have used four references in English and translated the quotes from them into French."

"Thanks, Pierre," said Catherine, who sat on a chair at her desk, and immediately started reading the draft.

Pierre lay down on the small bed with his hands clasped under his head, staring up at the poster of Guevara on the back of the door. He found Guevara's eyes fixed on something far distant, eternal, and impenetrable.

Suddenly, Catherine jumped from the chair, knelt near the bed, and planted a hot kiss on his lips. "Pierre, you are not only my boyfriend, you are my elder brother. This is an excellent essay."

She stood up and poured red wine in a glass up to the brim, and handed it to Pierre, and then poured some wine in another glass and added water to it as she usually did. Pierre found Cathy's habit of adding water to her wine intriguing, but he accepted it just like other things Cathy did, such as spending more time playing her guitar than studying, and always wearing long, casual dresses, mostly of cotton. She abhorred makeup and perfume, and never shaved her pubic or body hair, though she shaved her armpits, showered daily, and used deodorant. She was a full-blown, post-hippy-era hippy; she went to parties, meetings, and lectures in her long cotton dresses, sometimes without underwear.

"I will be spending the weekend at home," Pierre said, sighing. He propped his head with two pillows and sipped his wine. He told himself that he actually spent his weekends at home for the sake of his sensitive and emotionally crippled mother. He had no doubt that there was not a flicker of hope for a meaningful and tenable détente between his parents.

They had more wine, and as Catherine was jotting some remarks in the margins of the draft, Pierre debated whether or not to tell her about his plan to go to Cameroon. He felt sure she would shoot it down. But I could easily persuade her to swallow my overt reasons. I would tell no one my covert reasons of my plan, for it was a cover-up for something extremely sinister and horrendous.

He decided not to tell her for the time being, took a gulp of his wine, and stared up at Guevara's face on the back of the door. Now he thought that Guevara's unblinking and eternal eyes were somehow friendly and benign.

He recalled how he had decided on Cameroon. His late maternal uncle, Marcel Dillon, had told him how Africa was fascinating and enticing and had encouraged Pierre to plan a visit to Africa sometime; that was always in the back of Pierre's mind. One day when he was fine-tuning his murderous plan, it occurred to him to announce that he was going to an African country as a cover. He was working in the main library. He picked up a large atlas, put it on a table, opened it to a page with a map of Africa, and closed his eyes. He rotated the atlas seven times, and then put his index finger on the map. Opening his eyes, he found his finger resting on Cameroon and its capital, Yaoundé. That settled it. It would not be any other African country.

Pierre started unbuttoning his shirt. "Come here, Cathy."

"You are arrogant, bossy, and horny." She stood up and took off her long dress; she was nude underneath, and on her lithe, white body, the only dark spots were the two nipples on her small breasts and her bushy pubic hair. She was petite and slim but was endowed with wide hips, which were the first thing that had attracted Pierre to her when she had been a new student at the university. As their relationship blossomed, Pierre, who was attracted to women who possessed stimulating intellect, discovered that she had a vibrant mind and could sustain an argument. Catherine thrived on debates and her catholic reading on almost any subject served her well in her fierce, cut-and-thrust debating style.

Now Cathy, stark naked, sat astride his burning, nude body—to be impaled as she used to say playfully—, and at once started moaning and cursing until she climaxed. Before her erratic gasping subsided, she slid under Pierre, who continued their lustful lovemaking. The small bed shook and rattled under their vigorous, erotic tango. Cathy climaxed again, shouting and howling. When Pierre orgasmed, he rolled next to her, and they cuddled until their heavy breathing petered out. As Pierre kneaded her soft back, breasts, and the side of her torso, he mused that over the course of their relationship, Cathy had honed their lovemaking into a torrid carnal ritual whereby she enjoyed two or three orgasms for his one orgasm. Cathy had assured him a female of the human species can have two to three climaxes within twenty minutes, something no male can achieve. And who could argue with Cathy, he asked himself. Anyway, she had proved it again and again.

They snuggled in the small bed. Soon they both fell asleep. It was approaching ten o'clock when Pierre awoke and gently disentangled himself from Catherine; he carefully covered her with a light blanket, like a parent—or as she said, an elder brother—covering a child in her sleep. Noiselessly, he dressed and closed the door behind him.

As he walked to his nearby campus dormitory, he mused that he and Cathy shared almost identical dysfunctional and pathological upbringings; it was one of the things that seemed to glue them together. Cathy and her father lived in a perpetual war of abuse and degradation waged by her draconian mother. In his case, it was Pierre and his mother who were on the receiving end of his father's persistent abuse and humiliation. Yet in both situations, there were quiet truces, sometimes for long periods. But the truces were unpredictably aborted by scolding, yelling, and degradation. While Cathy's father and Pierre's mother lived with their tails between their legs, he and Cathy rebelled, though in different ways and styles. While Cathy, despite her joviality and congeniality, was overtly combative, he was covertly enraged but outwardly gregarious and self-possessed.

Then his mind shifted to his plan, which had germinated over the past year, ever since he had read his mother's secret diary and discovered the names of three of his father's mistresses—the three women and their spouses were very close friends of the Bouchers. Hence, his assassination list was short. Only three women who betrayed their friendship with his refined mother, and cheated on their husbands—husbands who were gracious and trusting. Pierre truly admired and liked each of the three husbands; sometimes he wondered if killing the three cheating wives also arose from a subconscious desire to avenge their respectable husbands, who equally admired and liked him. Though the prime motives for his retribution was his rage over the three women's indecent and brazen betrayal of the friendship of his long-suffering mother, coupled with a strong urge to defile the stately public persona of his rotten, abusive, and lecherous father. Following the shocking discovery, Pierre felt his world falling apart and he wanted to take prompt action. In the heat of the moment, he had decided to confront his father and his three whores, but he realized that the four would vehemently deny everything. It would have been his word against theirs. Nobody would have believed him; he could have been labeled a raving lunatic. Hence, he had opted for soberly considering other avenues of retaliatory action.

He had not immediately reached the conclusion to execute them, but over the months, he toyed with many scenarios of how to expose his father. One by one, he eliminated most of these scenarios and settled upon killing them, but he was not going to kill his father. That was unthinkable. It was the ultimate taboo.

In fact, these three women and their spouses, together with Pierre's parents, a few other couples, and two or three bachelors, formed the most glittering social circle in the city. The husbands were all highly regarded in their professions: entrepreneurs, bankers, lawyers, executives, university professors, and medical doctors. They considered themselves—and were considered by others—to be the upper crust of the local society. They threw parties at their respective homes, or wined and dined at the exclusive and sprawling Le Club Bellecour, entirely owned by Jean-Paul Villard, the only billionaire in the city, as far as the media was concerned.

Pierre was preoccupied for a long time with destroying his abusive father's charade and shattering his façade, even before the discovery of the names of his three mistresses. The discovery of his father's despicable cheating on his mother added fuel to his long simmering hate and rage, sending him into a seething frenzy. When he killed his father's three mistresses, he thought, the police or the media were bound to see the connection, and consequently his father's professional and social standing would be wiped out.

Pierre was going to buy a good, second-hand car, and rent—under a false name—an apartment in a nearby town or village, and then drop out of the university and tell everyone he was going to Cameroon to join a humanitarian nongovernmental organization, operating in the north of that country. He would commute from the nearby apartment to eliminate his father's mistresses. He was well acquainted with them, their houses, and their patterns of daily life. He had the pistol, the silencer, the ammunition, and the money. Over the last few months, he had gradually withdrawn eighty-five thousand euros from the €250,000 left to him by his late maternal uncle, Marcel, and he had stashed most of the money in a small, solid safe in a cupboard in his bedroom at home.

Reaching his campus room, he took a small bag containing some shirts and underwear for laundering at home. Then he put on his leather jacket and cycled home. When he entered the house, his parents had already retired to their bedroom. Deciding not to eat anything, he proceeded to his bedroom noiselessly, brushed his teeth, put on his red-striped pajamas, and turned off the light. He slept soundly and awoke shortly before seven in the morning. While showering, he decided to tell his parents that he was going to Cameroon; that would be the tip of the iceberg, a destructive and malicious iceberg. He put on dark-brown corduroy trousers, and a brown T-Shirt, and went downstairs to the kitchen where the family ate breakfast. "*Bonjour,*" he said before taking a chair. He surveyed the croissants, toast, butter, marmalade, and the mushroom-tomato-green-pepper omelet his mother usually prepared for their Saturday breakfast.

His father, Christian, mumbled a cold 'good morning' from behind the newspaper he was reading. In contrast, his mother was obviously pleased to see him. "*Bonjour*, Pierre. How good of you to come," Jacqueline said warmly.

"Merci, *Maman.*"

Jacqueline poured coffee into a cup, added some milk and two spoons of sugar, stirred it, and handed it to Pierre. "Did you have a good night's sleep?" she asked, with an angelic smile. She was always, without ever bragging about it, proud that her only child was taller and more handsome than his father was. She was sure that Pierre had inherited his muscular physique from her paternal family, the Dillons, and had inherited his thick, brown hair and his long, almost feminine, eyelashes from her maternal family, the Rollins.

They all fell silent as Pierre devoured his omelet, took another portion on his plate, and took a gulp of his *café au lait*. He looked at his father's newspaper and then gave his mother a knowing look. His mother did not grasp its message but opted to remain quiet. Then he cleared his throat and declared in a calm, almost casual tone, "I have to tell you something important. I am planning to go to Cameroon."

His mother's heart jumped to her throat, but she decided to let Pierre explain this inconceivable idea. She was petrified. What Pierre said would cause her husband to see red and explode. She knew there had been a long and bitter, though undeclared, war between her husband and their only offspring ever since Pierre was a teenager. A war that was interrupted, sometimes, by long and undeclared truces, but erupted whenever her husband was in a bad mood, or Pierre deliberately uttered something unsettling that her husband considered as being a hand grenade tossed at him.

Now his father lowered his newspaper, took off his reading glasses, and inserted them in his shirt pocket, before staring menacingly at his son, obviously reluctant to listen, let alone digest, what his son had declared. Yet Pierre could detect some agony and misery laced with disappointment and anger in his father's face. He decided to maintain his calm and restraint; he would not budge, regardless of what his father thought, said, or did.

Jacqueline looked at her son genuinely dumbfounded. "Why are you going to Cameroon?" Her voice was broken. She feared that all hell would break loose, for she knew there would be no way to placate her husband.

Before Pierre could reply, his father raised his voice in a hostile tone. "Cameroon!" Then he gave Pierre a condescending look. "Going to Cameroon? Is this one of your many juvenile and irresponsible ideas?"

"Dad, let me explain, please." Pierre managed to retain his serenity.

"Explain! There is nothing to explain," his father retorted with finality, folding the newspaper and banging it on the table. "Cameroon!"

Jacqueline winced and felt a knot in her stomach. Then she pleaded in a pitiful tone, "Christian, please let him explain himself."

"Damn it! So explain. Go ahead and explain." Bristling with hostility, his complexion scarlet with fury, Christian stared at his son.

Pierre glanced at his mother and then turned his eyes to his father. "I am going to work with a humanitarian NGO in Cameroon."

Before her husband could respond belligerently, Jacqueline asked, "Pierre, what about your master's studies?"

"I have decided to drop out of the university." Pierre's eyes and voice displayed his well-honed, imperturbable, calm demeanor.

"Why don't you get your degree and then go to Cameroon?" his mother pleaded in a tentative tone.

"I am no longer interested in my studies. They are boring and meaningless. Anyway, a master's degree will not add anything to my personal, intellectual, or real life development. My first degree is enough."

"You must finish your second degree first and then you can talk to me about doing humanitarian work," his father commanded sternly.

"Dad, I don't need a master's degree to do humanitarian work." Pierre looked his father in the eye in an unruffled way, though he hoped the confrontation would not escalate.

His father's fury was surging. "What is this nonsense? You don't need a master's degree because of the quarter of a million euros your uncle left you?"

"No, Dad. It has nothing to do with the money I have inherited." As he had learned over the years, the best way to deal with enraged people was to be firm but blasé, yet he knew that his blasé tone and bearing always incensed his father.

"So what is it then?" snapped his father. "What is it then?"

Jacqueline covered her face with her trembling hands, her elbows resting on the table, and decided to mitigate the unbridled hostility of her husband. She raised her face and said in a quavering voice, "Christian, please, let Pierre tell us more about his plan and the logic behind it." My son and I have been living for too long in a hell created by this brutish man, she reflected.

"Logic? What logic? This is sheer irresponsibility. This is complete madness," said Christian, looking harshly at his wife.

As he turned his steely stare at his son, Pierre stated, "Dad, this is not irresponsibility. I have been considering the idea for more than a year. Now I have come to a firm decision."

His father went ballistic. "You are as stupid as your late, mercenary uncle who ended up killed in the Congo and buried in an unknown grave. I hope you meet the same end in a God-forsaken African village or jungle. I have spent most of my life providing you with the very best things in life. Is this what I get in repayment, you idiot?"

Jacqueline flinched and clasped her hands tightly in a futile attempt to repress their trembling. "Christian, please—" Her voice was tentative, and she knew any attempt to neutralize the situation was futile.

Her husband interrupted her brusquely. "Don't 'please' me, Jacqueline. You have spoiled this brat beyond redemption. And now, it is obvious you don't mind if he goes to Cameroon, Timbuktu, or Patagonia." Then he thrust his hand toward at her and added in a highly accusatory voice, "You have spoiled him beyond salvation."

"No, I have not spoiled him." The unfair accusation provoked her, yet she did her utmost not to shout back. She uttered her words in a flat voice.

"Damn it. You have spoiled him rotten."

Jacqueline found the courage to respond, though in a feeble voice. "Christian, don't say that. You are being very unfair to me and to Pierre."

"And going to Cameroon is good for him?" asked Christian, before adding, "I will not be surprised if the two of you have already discussed this, and as usual you gave him your blessing for his bizarre idea."

Jacqueline felt herself retreat into the hole from which she had ventured out for a fleeting moment.

"Dad, it is not bizarre. And we have not discussed it at all." Pierre spoke in a nonchalant tone, and that exacerbated his father's fury even more.

"Listen to me, you bastard—"

"Yes, Dad?" his son deliberately interrupted him, making it sound calmly deferential.

"Don't you ever call me 'Dad' again," thundered Christian, pounding the table with his fist. He stared at his son and Pierre stared back, defiantly and nonchalantly. When it came to staring, Pierre knew he was capable of staring down the devil, let alone his father.

His father, still staring at him, gave a sarcastic snigger. "Are you trying to browbeat me?"

"How could I browbeat my father?" asked Pierre.

"You are being sarcastic. You are adding insult to injury." Christian was livid, yet the blank and glassy look in his son's eyes momentarily intimidated him.

"No, I am not. I am just listening to you," answered Pierre.

Jacqueline was distressed, but not surprised, by her son's calmness; she knew he was capable of confronting anyone head on and yet remaining unruffled. He reminded her of her late brother, Marcel, but sometimes she was worried that her son's hubris exceeded his. She reflected that was not always the appropriate way to deal with one's opponents.

Christian stood up, picked up his empty coffee cup, and threw it in fury at his son. It missed Pierre's face and landed on his plate, and then bounced, hitting the glass coffee pot in front of Jacqueline. The remains of Pierre's omelet slid onto the table. The pepper mill landed on the floor with a crash. Jacqueline closed her eyes and shivered.

"Frankly, I don't give a damn if you go to hell," shouted Christian, staring fiercely at his son. "You can damn well do whatever you want, you moron."

As he strode out of the kitchen, he landed a powerful slap on the back of Pierre's head, and as a parting shot, he hissed like an enraged cobra, "I wish we never had you. I wish we never had you." It was a painful slap, yet Pierre did not wince or show any sign of being hurt.

Jacqueline heard that and thought it was too gross, too foul. It grated on her ears and nerves. As if whispering to herself, she said, "I can't believe it. Oh my God, I can't believe it."

Pierre heard her words, grasped her hand, and said, "Never mind, *Maman*."

"This is too callous," she said, looking at her son with tearful blue eyes.

"Never mind, *Maman*. There is nothing surprising in what he did and said."

She shook her head. "No, Pierre. That was too gross."

He tenderly patted her hand. "I know. Let it slide."

"Pierre, you are too precious to be treated like that."

"I don't care about what he said or says," Pierre assured her.

Jacqueline exhaled heavily and tenderly patted his hand. "That is the right attitude, Pierre."

Pierre stood up and put his hand on the spot on his head where his father had slapped him. This degrading verbal and physical abuse conjured up memories of his childhood helplessness, but also of his sudden internal resolution, when he was only seven, never to capitulate, never to cave in; and his teens' resolve never to show his rage, yet calmly do whatever he deemed necessary, come hell or high water. He collected the shattered remains of the broken pepper mill and threw them in the trash can in the kitchen. He put his hand on his mother's shoulder. "*Maman*, his childish tantrums will not sway me from my plans."

Jacqueline tenderly and reassuringly patted his hand. "Now I fully endorse your plan, Pierre. You don't need to explain it to me. Just do it."

"Thanks, *Maman*. I am going to my room now."

When Pierre left the kitchen, Jacqueline felt confused, lonely, and miserable, like an abandoned child, but she remained in her chair, lost in a morass of conflicting emotions.

Pierre walked into his bedroom, locked the door, and went to the bathroom. Since his teens, he had discovered that he could relieve his internal, seething rage against his father by either masturbating or shoplifting. The urge to do either—or both—was irresistible, and beyond his control. He found these secret compulsions distressingly shameful. It had occurred to him a number of times to consult a psychologist about the matter, but he had always dismissed the idea, telling himself that the two urges—given time—would dwindle and disappear. The repression of his internal fury left him prey to the grip of these two compulsive urges, which had proved time and again to dissipate his rage. He preferred masturbation because it provided quick gratification and swift relief from his fury. Shoplifting took a long time to accomplish, if he were to avoid being caught in the act.

As he was masturbating in his bathroom, his father's mean words 'I wish we never had you' resonated in his mind, and he repeated angrily and loudly, "I wish you were never my father, you monster." After he relieved himself and cleansed his body, he left the bathroom and slumped onto his bed. He felt calm and quiet but as he ruminated about what had happened that morning, and what he and his mother had suffered over the years, his ire seeped into every fiber of his being. The three bitches must be eliminated, and his father's self-serving façade must be smashed—there were no other viable options.

Then he decided there was no point in these depressive ruminations. He stood up, decided to go shoplifting, and put on his black leather jacket, which he always used— regardless of the weather—for this purpose; with its internal as well as external pockets, it was very practical for hiding more than one item in his shoplifting ventures.

With a sardonic smile, he told himself if—and this is a big if, he mused—he returned safely, he would make his bed.

# CHAPTER 2

Pierre emerged onto the street with forty euros in an inside pocket of his jacket; his cellphone in the top right, outside pocket; and his cigarettes and lighter in the left. It was a sunny but mild morning. For a few moments, he stood on a sidewalk to breathe in some clean air. A hint of the aftershave he had put on before having breakfast reached his nose; it gave him a pleasurable sense of contentment.

His venture was hazardous and adrenaline-filled, yet he felt eager for the risk. He was confident, very confident, but not overconfident. Uncle Marcel had told him that overconfidence, over planning, and overtraining could work against one.

Crossing a number of streets, he reached a shopping area in the city center. He was looking for a suitable shop to steal anything he could get his hands on. While he continued his search, he pondered why the local media considered his father a pillar of society. If Dr. Christian Boucher was a pillar of society, then there was something wrong with society. It was a sick society with rotten and hollow pillars. Perhaps the other so-called pillars of society were also fake and rotten like his father. Pierre had attended many parties thrown by these pillars of society, some at their homes, and some at Le Club Bellecour—where membership was permitted to *la crème de la crème* only. All he saw was sickening deception, pompous vanity, and superficial friendships.

His hand reached the back of his head where his father had hit him. It felt sore. He rubbed the stinging spot gently, telling himself that in a few days the soreness would vanish, though he would not forget or forgive the degradation it had caused him.

Walking down the street, he could smell the stench of car exhaust. He glanced at the shops on the other side of the street. He walked a few meters farther then decided to cross the street and go into the shop of the Genet sisters: Janine and Jeannette, who were twin sisters in their mid or late seventies. They sold cigarettes, tobacco, lighters, pipes, newspapers, assorted sweets, cookies, umbrellas, scarves, flashlights, cosmetics, and second-hand books. Though he had managed to shoplift a number of items from the old Genet sisters, he knew they were always very vigilant. Despite their wrinkled faces and hands they were still in full command of their faculties—the type of people destined to live robustly for more than one hundred years, he reckoned. Any shoplifting attempt at their shop would be a touch-and-go experience.

So he changed his mind and decided to walk to the end of the street, turn right, and go to La Librairie Stendhal, one of the largest bookshops in the city. It was always crowded with customers and browsers, particularly on Saturdays like today, and it had no closed-circuit TV system. He had stolen, over the last four or five years, at least ten books from it. When he entered the bookshop, he felt at ease as he noticed there were thirty or more customers scattered around the place. The aroma of books—the smell of paper, ink, and dust—always gave him a heartfelt and palpable sense of affinity. He was delighted; momentarily forgetting what brought him here.

As usual, there were four staff helping the customers apart from the cashier: an elderly, bespectacled man, who always wore a jacket and necktie; a young woman, who wore jeans and had a boyish haircut; a smiling, lanky man in his late twenties, wearing a white shirt and gray trousers; and the stunning young woman who had been working in the bookshop as long as Pierre could remember. She moved around the bookshop silently and with an air of authority about her. Her face was well chiseled, with strikingly captivating green eyes, and a small scar running from the bottom of her right temple to the top of her cheek. It was three to four centimeters away from her right eye. She was slim with beautiful, delicate hands and long, feminine fingers. Sometimes her hair concealed the scar. She always seemed melancholy and aloof, unless a customer or one of the other staff spoke to her. Sometimes she exuded a haughty and standoffish air, but there was always about her a subtle radiance of feminine mystique coupled with an aura of authority. Somehow, Pierre felt there was something mystical about her aside from her sensual attractiveness.

Every time Pierre saw her, she was wearing black trousers with a soft, silk blouse or shirt in a different color. Now she looked elegant in her black trousers and a soft-blue, long-sleeved blouse.

Pierre told himself to take his time, so he browsed through French novels unhurriedly. He found a book by an Alain Marchand and thought about stealing it later on. He read the titles and the names of some other French novels. Then he moved to the shelves of foreign-language books at the back of the bookshop. It occurred to him to steal a German book for Anna Marr, the young German woman living with the Villards, and he discarded the idea of stealing the French book by Marchand. Though Anna never appealed to him sexually, he found her personable. After a few minutes, he picked up a German book, which appeared to be a novel, and swiftly inserted it into one of his inside pockets. It fitted perfectly.

Now Pierre turned his attention to the young, effeminate cashier, who was now distracted by customers standing in a queue. So Pierre walked unhurriedly, with his head up and adrenaline coursing through his veins, toward the entrance. As he was about to step outside the bookshop, he heard a feminine voice behind him.

"Would you come with me, sir?"

He froze.

The feminine voice politely repeated, "Would you come with me, sir?"

He turned around and saw the young woman with the large, green eyes, looking at him in a benign manner. "What is it?" Pierre asked in a casual tone.

"Just follow me and bring the book you took, please," she said, and added almost in a whisper, "I don't want to make a scene."

"*D'accord*," Pierre said with a twinge of shame. But he told himself to handle the situation with nonchalance. She struck him as a well-bred and refined person.

His mouth was dry as he followed her through the bookshop into a small office in a corner of the place. He cleared his throat before stepping into the office. There was a desk with a PC and a pile of what seemed to Pierre to be invoices, another pile of printouts, a large calculator, and about twenty five books divided into two stacks. There were two plastic chairs in front of the desk. It was a small and cozy office, he thought. On the wall to his left there was a framed color photo of this woman, smiling proudly, with her hands around the shoulders of a distinguished-looking, elderly gentleman, with thoughtful eyes, sitting in a wheelchair.

The young woman closed the door and politely ordered, "Please take out the book in your jacket pocket."

She stood facing him, and he, as an obedient pupil or thief, took out the book and handed it to her. She glanced at the book. "So you read German?"

"No, I don't."

There was a fleeting look of surprise on her face, and then she put the book on the desk and fell silent, thinking.

Pierre studied her face and physique. She oozed alluring femininity. Her large, green eyes had tiny touches of sparkling yellow around them; the tiny yellow streaks accentuated the green, making her eyes lush, like those of a rare, mysterious, and exquisite cat. He had never seen such dazzling eyes before. Her full lips were sexy, with the lower one protruding in an erotic and enticing way. He thought the scar on her face emphasized the fineness and delicacy of her nose, chin, and cheekbones.

Pierre feared he would be sexually aroused, an involuntary reaction that he could not control whenever he gazed into the face of a beautiful woman who happened to stand in front of him, face-to-face. So he averted his eyes. He had had this reflexive reaction since he was fifteen, whenever he stood face-to-face with Dr. Isabelle Bourdin, the clinical psychologist friend of his mother, to whom his mother had sent him when he had problems with the school authorities.

"What's your name?" she asked in a soft voice.

Without missing a beat, he replied, "Jean-Claude Marchand." He had responded spontaneously and with some élan. The name he gave her was a combination of the names of two authors that had stuck in his mind while he browsed through the French books.

"Mr. Marchand, this is not the first time I have seen you stealing books from my bookshop."

He looked into her eyes and gently said, "You are the owner of the bookshop." He delivered the words like a statement but it was obviously a question.

"No, I am the manager, not the owner. But that is beside the point." She held her hands behind her back, but she seemed temptingly vulnerable to Pierre as he looked into her green eyes.

"What do you do?" she asked.

"I don't work. I am a university student." He gazed into her eyes seductively, deciding to take the initiative.

The fact that he was a student with a handsome face seemed to quell her anger. She stood with her buttocks touching the edge of the desk, and said, "Mr. Marchand, when we catch a thief red-handed, it is not our policy to call the police. The amount of time and energy spent prosecuting a shoplifting case is a great waste of money. It will cost much more than the ten or twenty euros that are the cost of an average book." Now as she looked at him, she was shifting her weight from one foot to the other. Pierre attributed that to some nervousness on her part, as he imagined her buttocks provocatively rubbing the edge of the desk with every shift her body made.

As they faced each other, Pierre found himself sexually aroused. He felt somewhat embarrassed but he knew that this was something beyond his control. "I understand. I am sorry. I am very sorry indeed. I promise I will never do it again." He paused before asking, "What's your name?"

"Martine. But why do you want to know my name?"

He had been expecting her to refuse to give him her name. So she was a reasonable and flexible person, Pierre deduced; he decided to ladle out some charm on her. "I am impressed by your politeness and managerial wisdom. One does not come across someone with such great attributes every day. In fact, it is very rare to come across someone like you."

She knew that he was flattering her, yet somehow she liked his nonchalant and audacious approach.

"So, please, let me know your full name," he asked with what seemed to Martine a measured but assured imploring tone. She liked his voice. It had an appealing quality to it.

"Martine Aubert." Now she fully rested her buttocks against the edge of the desk, her left hand holding the desk and her right hand on her thigh. "I hope this is the last time you steal from our shop. And if you steal from other bookshops and you are caught, you might very well end up in prison."

Without a moment's hesitation, he said, "You are an angel, Martine Aubert." His voice was seductive and assertive, as he felt his erection was thickening. "You are a beautiful woman with a beautiful name. I like your name, Martine Aubert." He pretended to savor each syllable of her name.

She said, "I like it too," while an inner voice whispered, I like your face too, Jean-Claude Marchand.

He persisted in his enticing offensive. "I am very lucky to have met such a gentle soul as you." He gazed at her, full in the eye, in a lustful way. He could see a repressed, sex-starved soul.

In her mind, Martine relished his flattery but decided to deflect the dialogue. "What are you studying?"

Pierre sensed that her voice was somewhat faltering, though she made an effort to keep it composed. She looked at his erection, quickly averted her eyes, and then gazed at the wall behind him. She couldn't help swallowing audibly.

"Political science."

"Political science!" she exclaimed. "Why then did you steal a German novel?"

"I don't know, Martine. Believe me, I don't know." He sensed somehow that she believed him.

Pierre extended his hand and gently took her right hand. She did not object. She looked at him as her knees started to sag; she found his eyes sensual and hypnotic. "Why are you doing this?" she asked in a quavering voice, without withdrawing her hand. Her heart was thumping, her hand was quivering, and her palm was seating. Her body was melting. He looked into her eyes in an openly libidinous way. "I find you adorable, Martine." He could see her face flush with desire.

She breathed heavily and her voice abandoned her. She cast her eyes to the floor as her heavy breathing became more and more audible. Stepping closer to her, he could see her reserve was gone. He put his hands firmly around her slim waist, planted a hot kiss on her scar, then grabbed her face before taking her lower lip in his lips, sucking it. Sliding his tongue into her mouth, he found it wet, warm, and sweet. She managed to say weakly, "No, please. No, please. Stop this."

Pierre embraced her tightly, fervently kissing her eyes, face, scar, and lips. Suddenly, she put her feverish hands around his shoulders, and started kissing him passionately. Her kisses tasted like honey to Pierre, and he felt her whole body trembling with sexually charged hunger.

She gasped for air, then in a quivering voice managed to say, "Lock the door." She had cast away all resistance and decided to surrender her trembling body to her burning desire. Swiftly Pierre locked the door, and then removed his jacket, throwing it aside on a pile of books on the floor. They both started shedding their clothes. Pierre did so in a frantic way, which heightened Martine's excitement. He took all the books, printouts, and invoices from the desk and put them on the floor near the wall. Martine, despite her rising desire, took off her clothes and put them in an orderly manner on the large chair behind the desk. Yet her whole body shivered with mounting anticipation.

Pierre—now Jean-Claude—gently lifted the naked Martine, like a sensual divine being, and eased her onto the desk. Their lovemaking was a frenzied animalistic copulation. He felt the fire of desire oozing from every pore of her youthful, supple, hot body. When she climaxed she put her hand on her mouth firmly to stifle her wild shrieks, but she could not control her frenzied convulsions.

Jean-Claude/Pierre, also aware that people outside might hear the sounds of their feverish copulation, forced himself to grunt his orgasmic howls, grinding his teeth and pursing his lips. He gently rested his body on top of Martine's, and she wrapped her legs around his back as they both gasped for air. It took a few moments before they regained their normal breathing; sweat still clung to their sated bodies.

To Martine their feverish sex was thrillingly animalistic and immensely gratifying. Pierre kissed her tenderly, and then sat naked on one of the plastic chairs in front of the desk. He craved a cigarette, but he noticed a NO SMOKING PLEASE sign fixed to the wall behind the desk. So he stood up and put on his clothes, leaving his leather jacket on the other chair. Then he started returning to the desk the books, invoices, and printouts that he had moved to the floor. Martine said, "No need for that, Jean-Claude. I can do it later." He persisted, putting every item in its proper place on the desk, and resumed his chair.

Martine put on her clothes then sat in her large, blue chair behind the desk, reflecting on the reckless audacity of this young student; how had he managed to change the situation from what was supposed to be a confrontational scolding over stealing a book to a frenzied copulation? Her mind was filled with a confluence of delightful thoughts. She wondered how she had allowed him to seduce her in what seemed to be the blink of an eye and make love to her in her own office. She felt relieved that none of her staff had come to talk to her while she enjoyed this wild and feverish sex. She had never experienced such frenzied sex. In fact, she had not had sex for a long time. It seemed to her that Jean-Claude had detected in her eyes her sexual starvation and brazenly decided to seduce her.

She stood up and unlocked the door, leaving it closed. "Just in case," she said and returned to her chair. Pierre extended his hand across the desk and held her hand affectionately. "That was good, Martine," he said as he looked into her eyes.

She smiled and pressed his hand. "That was crazy, crazy, very crazy—but very good," she assured him, though she seemed to be addressing the words to herself. Pierre, aka Jean-Claude, pondered that under Martine's air of authority and aloofness, there was a hot volcano of desire.

After a while, Pierre, who had remained silent to give her enough space to think, asked, "Do you care to have dinner with me sometime?"

She found herself saying, "Anytime, Jean-Claude."

"Would tomorrow be fine with you?" Pierre wanted to settle the matter here and now.

"*Parfait.*"

"How about seven thirty?" he asked.

"That is fine with me. Which place?"

"Do you know the Algerian restaurant near the Place de la Poste? Not far from here."

"Yes. I have been to it a few times. They serve very good couscous."

"I know it is cheap, but the atmosphere is relaxed."

"Since you are a student, Jean-Claude, I will foot the bill."

"No way. I am a student but a rich student." He stood up and put on his leather jacket.

"Why do you steal books if you are a rich student?" she asked teasingly.

"That is a long story. I might tell you more about it tomorrow evening."

"I shouldn't have asked such a question," she said in an apologetic tone.

"Why not? You were simply teasing me. But, honestly, it is something compulsive that grips me from time to time."

She smiled tenderly. "And who hasn't got compulsive urges? It is only human, only too human, Jean-Claude."

"You are a dazzling and gracious angel, Martine."

"I suspect I will soon be addicted to your flattery." She stood up, walked to him, and hugged him.

"It is not flattery. I think the more you know me, the more you will be aware of your great qualities." He sounded convincing to Martine, and she was delighted by what he pronounced.

She kissed him. "I think I need that. It seems they teach you in political science how to seduce women." They both laughed. Then she added, "Anyway, very few students have faces as handsome as yours."

"Thanks, Martine," he said. "So see you tomorrow evening at seven thirty."

"*Bien sûr.*"

He kissed her scar. "I am already beginning to fall in love with your scar."

She planted a mock punch on his taut stomach. "Don't bullshit me."

"I am serious. Apart from the occasional shoplifting, I am a 100 percent straightforward person."

"I don't think there are 100-percent-straightforward human beings." Her tone was devoid of any flippancy.

"Maybe I am 99 percent straightforward."

"Let us settle on 60 or 70 percent. That will be good enough. Don't you think?"

"I fully agree, Martine," he said and kissed her.

After they exchanged their cellphone numbers and saved them, they kissed passionately for a long time. Then he winked at her, opened the door, and left.

Martine settled in her chair, her mind going through all that had just happened. It all seemed unbelievable. It was like one of her occasional, pleasurable sexual fantasies; but this was for real. It had been immensely fulfilling and wildly erotic. She'd never thought a shoplifter, caught red-handed, could seduce her in such a daring and uplifting way. Yet she hugely enjoyed it. It had been a long time since she'd had sex, and never like today's rejuvenating sex.

She was glad that she had stopped him before he disappeared with the book.

# CHAPTER 3

It was drizzling as Pierre arrived at the Algerian restaurant in a light-blue jacket and a white shirt, about seven fifteen the following evening. He dismounted from his bicycle and flipped the kickstand to keep it standing upright, secured it with its loop lock, and then put its small key in one of his pockets. He had selected this restaurant because he did not frequent it; he had come here only three or four times before with Amanda Jenkins, a very wild, verbose, and giggling Welsh exchange student. He believed that none of the people who worked in the restaurant knew his real name, and if any one of them happened to hear Martine calling him Jean-Claude, he would be none the wiser.

He entered the place, which was almost empty. Two young women were engrossed in an inaudible conversation over their plates of couscous. A thin, Algerian waiter rushed to greet Pierre, saying, "Good evening, sir, where would you like to sit?" The polite young waiter bore a strong resemblance to the stern, heavily mustached man standing behind the counter, who could be his father or uncle.

Pierre replied, "Good evening." He glanced at the tables and selected one with four chairs in the corner to the left, at the rear of the place. He walked slowly, with the service counter to his right, behind which there was a small opening for passing dishes from the kitchen. He sat in the chair next to the corner, to face the entrance of the restaurant. The table was covered with a red-and-white-checkered cloth. Touching it, he found it had a soft texture as if made of pure cotton, which he doubted. The young Algerian brought a small, overused menu card, and then produced a lighter and lit the medium-sized candle in the middle of the table. Pierre glanced at the menu and put it down. He looked at the young Algerian. "I am expecting a friend so we shall order our food later. Now bring me a bottle of the best Algerian red wine you have, please."

"Of course, sir." The Algerian bent his head, jotted the order in a tiny notebook, and walked away.

Within a minute or so, the young Algerian brought a bottle of wine. Pierre indicated that he should open the bottle, and then gestured to him not to fill his glass. Pierre lit a cigarette and stared up at an enlarged, color poster pinned on the wall to his right, which added some liveliness to the off-white walls. It showed a beautiful, white horse with brilliant yellow eyes, darkish flaring nostrils, a magnificent luxuriant tail, and large bird wings fixed to the tops of its forelegs, soaring in space. He had asked an Algerian here, some time ago, about this horse; he had told him it is called in Arabic *Al Buraq*, the heavenly horse on which Prophet Muhammad traveled to Jerusalem at night before he ascended to the seventh sky, where it was revealed to him that Muslims should perform five prayers a day. At the time, Pierre had wondered how a Muslim could display such a religious picture in a place where alcohol was served.

He kept his eye on the entrance.

A few minutes passed before he saw Martine walking in, wearing an elegant, green, sleeveless dress. Perfect taste, Pierre thought, befitting much superior restaurants. He could see that the Algerian waiter and his father, or uncle, were stunned by Martine's beauty and elegance. One of the two young French women ogled her, and then said something to her companion, who turned her head and gaped at Martine. Pierre stood up and kissed her on the cheeks when she reached the table. They sat in their chairs, facing each other. Pierre looked into her eyes; the light of the candle added a titillating radiance to their deep-green color.

"How gorgeous, Martine! You are dressed to kill."

"I am dressed to kill you, Jean-Claude. Not anybody else," she said with a sweet smile.

"I am an easy prey. You already killed me yesterday."

She gently slapped his hand. "I was the one who was killed."

"Anyway, thanks for coming."

"So, you thought I would stand you up, Jean-Claude?"

He looked her at her reassuringly. "No, not at all. I am a very trusting person, Martine."

As he poured some wine into their two glasses, he remarked, "I asked for the best Algerian wine in the establishment."

They raised their glasses and clicked them. Martine, after tasting and swallowing her first sip, announced, "It is good. I like it."

"I like it too. It has a different taste from French wines."

The young Algerian approached their table with decorum and jotted down their orders in his tiny notebook: two green salads and two couscouses with mutton. Pierre moved the candle to his left on the table so that they could be closer to each other. As he moved the candle, its light made the thin and sweet saliva on Martine's white, healthy teeth glisten with animal magnetism, giving her—in his mind—a palpable erotic intensity and allure.

"You have very seductive teeth, Martine," he said.

She chuckled. "My teeth?"

"Yes, your teeth, and your sweet saliva glittering on them. The thin layer of your saliva makes them like pearls emitting a heavenly light."

"That is utterly original, Jean-Claude. I have read a lot of fiction and poetry and I don't recall anyone saying this. It is delightful to hear something so original."

"You have to believe it," Pierre gently insisted.

"I do believe it." She closed her fist and brought it down to the table in jestful affirmation.

She held his hand and stroked it with her long and delicate fingers, and he put his other hand on top of her hand and pressed it firmly. Suddenly, she realized that part of his animal magnetism had to do with his melodious voice. It occurred to her that she now recognized what she'd always found appealing in Françoise Lépine, her ex-nanny and current assistant to her father. It was her melodious voice. Since Françoise had lived with them for many years, Martine had failed to pinpoint this alluring and elusive appeal—a subtle libidinous appeal—in her. Few people are blessed with such a seductive, melodious voice; Jean-Claude and Françoise are among those few, she reflected.

"Jean-Claude, do you know you are crazy?"

"Maybe. A crazy person doesn't know he is crazy."

Martine winked at him with her left eye. "How did you dredge up the courage to seduce me after I caught you red-handed stealing a book from my bookshop?"

"I didn't dredge up any courage." He paused, thinking. "I think it was a situation where both of us did the natural thing. As you were talking to me face-to-face I was admiring your eyes, your lips, your scar, your physique, and I was involuntarily sexually aroused. Isn't that natural?"

"No. It is natural to have an erection, but if every man who has an erection decides to ravish the woman facing him, we would have complete chaos in society."

"I agree with that. But, honestly, I found you irresistible and I could see in your eyes a burning desire. When I held your hand, I found it sweating. It would have been cowardly and unbecoming of me not to fulfill your desire."

"It would have been cowardly and unbecoming of me," she mimicked him. "I like that. It makes you sound like a chivalrous knight from a past era."

Pierre was not going to reveal to Martine, not now, that he had discovered—since he was fifteen—he would always be sexually aroused whenever he found himself standing face-to-face with a beautiful woman. However, he did not always proceed to have sex with every woman who triggered this spontaneous reflex. He raised the empty wine bottle and indicated to the waiter to bring them another bottle. "But, tell me, Martine, why did you give in to my advances?"

"I don't know."

"You are being evasive, Martine."

When the waiter opened the second bottle of wine and refilled their glasses, Pierre reflected that the wine had already made him exuberant, and more wine would make him exultant. Martine remained silent, pondering whether to be candid with him or not.

"Come on, Martine. You did not give me a good answer to my question." He wanted to tease her but at the same time he was interested in hearing a candid reply.

Martine, emboldened by the wine, decided to be open with him. She looked into his eyes and said with no hesitancy in her tone, "Because I had not had sex for more than five years."

"You are pulling my leg."

"No. I am serious, Jean-Claude," she said. Her tone was calm and sincere, yet Pierre found the statement difficult to swallow.

"How can a young, healthy woman with stunning eyes, provocative lips, and a dazzling figure not have sex for so long?" he asked before adding, "I bet you have a long string of hidden lovers."

She took a gulp of wine and gazed into his eyes. "What I am telling you is true, though it may seem to you unbelievable."

Looking into her eyes, he could perceive deep sadness and tenderness. He brought his face closer to hers and gave her a reassuring peck on the lips, and then took her hands. "But why?"

Martine clasped his hands and sensed that his persistence in getting a frank answer was well intentioned. "It is simply the ugly scar on my face. It puts a lot of people off, particularly men, Jean-Claude."

Pierre Boucher, alias Jean-Claude Marchand, whispered, "Let me lick this beautiful scar." He did not wait for a response; he proceeded to lick her scar, and then softly kissed her lips. "I hope you don't find my licking your scar off-putting, Martine?"

She raised his hand and kissed it with appreciation. "On the contrary. I do like it. If the two Algerians here will not be offended, you can do it again."

He held her face again and let his tongue sensuously probe her scar up and down, and then planted a long kiss on it.

"I bet it was not your scar that put people off, but your being overly self-conscious about it. Whenever I visited your bookshop, you struck me as someone who was aloof and somewhat stand-offish."

She nodded. "Maybe you are right."

"There is no maybe about it, Martine." His melodious voice seemed to disarm her further.

"Honestly, I have always felt detached from people. I have been inhibited in my thoughts, words, and deeds."

"Most people are put off by anyone who is shy and stand-offish, while deep inside, that person craves human affection and bonding."

They fell silent. Martine fought her tears and then managed to say, "I think you are spot on. Very much spot on, Jean-Claude. I have always craved human bonding."

"Are you aware that this scar adds to your feminine mystique?"

"I don't know about my mystique. I have always avoided engaging people I do not know well, and withdraw from any attempt by them to engage me. I am highly sensitive to rejection so I don't put myself in any situation unless I am very sure I will not be rejected."

Pierre felt empathy for her and held her hand tightly and reassuringly. "You have put yourself in a very destructive mind-set. Rejection is part of human existence. No one can go through life without being rejected now and then." Pierre paused, pondering. "You know, Martine, a lot of people cripple themselves with self-imposed emotional shackles. As a result, they miss a lot in life."

Martine felt as if she was listening to a therapist or a guru. She wondered if it was sheer luck or some angel that had sent Jean-Claude to steal a book from her bookshop, and made her stop him and confront him in a refined way. "I fully agree with that, Jean-Claude."

After she drowned most of her wine glass, she decided to be more open with him. "My external scar has caused me many agonizing internal scars." She paused for a few moments. "I have always felt defective," she added in a wavering voice.

He raised his two hands, gesturing his incredulity. "Oh my God! Defective? You can't be serious. Martine, it is all in your mind. I, for one, find you strikingly beautiful, with a charming personality. I am sure there are a lot of others who would find you attractive if you worked hard to demolish your shackles." He paused and smiled, before adding in a hurry, "But hey, I am not trying to convince you to start sleeping around. I am talking about human bonding, not sex."

She chuckled, took the bottle, and topped off the two glasses.

"Sleeping around!" she exclaimed, laughing heartily. Then she said teasingly, "Maybe I should try it for a few weeks. Or a few months."

Immediately, he countered in a mocking tone, "I will kill you for that."

Perhaps their fortuitous sexual encounter meant a quick physical gratification for Jean-Claude and nothing more than that, she thought. However, to her it meant much more. It was a sudden opening of her carnal floodgates, an unexpected awaking that shed light on some of the shackles she had imposed upon herself through fear of rejection, fear of ridicule, and fear of intimacy.

As Pierre put a cigarette to his lips, Martine took his lighter from his hand, lit the cigarette, and said, "You see, Jean-Claude, I am an accomplice in all your vices."

They both chuckled like old friends or lovers. Then he asked casually, "Does your father have green eyes?"

"No. He has dark-brown eyes. I inherited my green eyes from my mother. Most of my maternal relatives have green eyes, but in different shades. And a few of them have predominantly yellow eyes with a few streaks of green. They call themselves, with some egotism, 'the cat family."

The young waiter, who did his utmost not to ogle blatantly at Martine, brought them the two green salads and a small basket of baguette slices. As they started tucking into their salads, Pierre kept reminding himself that to Martine he was 'Jean-Claude Marchand', not 'Pierre Boucher'.

"Do all the women in your maternal family also possess striking figures?"

"Of course not all of them. I doubt that all the men in your family are as strikingly handsome and attractive as you are. You have a manly, animal magnetism, Jean-Claude."

"Such a compliment coming from you is something I deeply cherish." He paused, and then said in a low, slow, yet assertive voice, "Martine, we only live one life. Therefore, we have to take care of our needs, desires, and dreams without being encumbered by what society or our families dictate. Society is the devil incarnate, and those who conform to the devil's dictates live diminished lives. Yet we have to respect others, care for them, and bond with them. I think when we liberate ourselves from society's constraints, we can help others to liberate themselves. We have to care for ourselves first, and care for others as much as we can, and then face oblivion with courage. We can stare death in the eye."

"This comes so closely to what my father is fond of preaching, if I remember it correctly. 'Of all who went to the end of this road, has anyone returned to tell us the secret? Take care of your needs on this one-ended way. You will not be coming back."' She paused and added, "Or something to that effect."

"That is splendid. So your father is a poet and a philosopher!"

"No, he is neither. These are verses by Omar Khayyam."

"Excuse my ignorance. But the name doesn't ring a bell, Martine."

"Omar Khayyam was a Persian poet who lived in the twelfth century. He wrote very moving and philosophical stanzas, which formed a book entitled, *The Ruba'iyat of Omar Khayyam*. So far it has been translated into almost every major language, and within each language there are a number of translations because of the nuances of Khayyam's words and ideas."

"I am glad I am learning something entirely new to me."

"My father owns different translations of the *Ruba'iyat* in French, English, Arabic, and Spanish."

"Your father reads in all these languages?"

"Yes, he does," she said, with evident pride. "His library contains more than six thousand books in these four languages."

"It must have cost him a fortune."

"Yes. However, he is comfortably well-off. Not rich or filthy rich like you," she said with a smile. "He is an avid reader. Jokingly, he says, he is suffering from a chronic case of moderate to severe bibliomania."

"Wow, more than six thousand books! That is staggering," he said, and then decided to tease her. "Don't tell me that half of them were shoplifted by you from La Librairie Stendhal."

She lightly slapped his hand. "Never. Never. But if I keep going out with you, I will soon start shoplifting."

Pierre smiled. "I am sure you will."

At that moment, he saw two middle-aged couples, led by a man who looked slightly younger, enter the restaurant; the waiter ushered them to a table with six chairs near Pierre and Martine's table. The younger man was pontificating loudly about the dismal state of French football and how to rescue it, but it was obvious that his docile companions had no clue about what he was talking about. Pierre turned his attention back to Martine. He reckoned that asking her about her scar would induce more openness between them; he was not driven by curiosity or pity. "Could I ask what caused this charming scar?" He put the question in a casual tone.

She clasped her glass with her hands and showed no hesitation. "It was a very tragic accident. A head-on car collision when I was eleven years old. That was twenty years ago. Our family had spent two weeks vacationing on the Cote d'Azur, and my father was driving us back home. My late mother was sitting next to him in the passenger seat. I was sitting between my brother, Jacques, and our nanny, Françoise, in the back seat. It was a long journey, and I fell asleep. Suddenly, a car crashed head on into our car."

She paused and could see that Jean-Claude was listening with rapt attention. She continued, "Both cars were wrecked. The two passengers in the other car, which was driving in the wrong direction, died on the spot. Later on, the police found out they were intoxicated. One of them was nineteen and the other twenty-one." She took another sip of her wine. "My mother was pronounced dead upon arrival at the hospital. My father was paralyzed from his hips to his feet. The impact of the collision threw me between the two front seats, my face hit the dashboard, and I got this permanent scar. Miraculously, my brother, who is five years older than I am, and our nanny escaped unscathed. They were released from the hospital after two days of observation."

"That is very tragic. Very sad, indeed," said Pierre in a soft tone.

"Yes, it just destroyed our family. My father was supposed to go to Morocco within two months as the French ambassador. After the accident, the Ministry of Foreign Affairs offered him a position in Paris, but he turned it down. Therefore, his diplomatic career ended. At the time, he was forty-five and a distinguished diplomat. My mother was forty-two. Poor Mum."

She paused with choked-back tears in her eyes. Then she added in a lamenting voice, "I still miss her. I think Dad still misses her, though he is a real stoic. She was always cheerful, loving, outgoing, and very positive."

"I am sure something so tragic would leave any family scarred for a long time," said Pierre, and held her hand in a consoling and reassuring gesture.

Martine felt he was sincere; somehow, she sensed he was someone she could trust. "This small external scar remained after three operations. The surgeons did an excellent job because it was almost from my temple to my chin. I think this tragedy and the scar made me crawl into a shell."

"I can understand that, Martine."

"I am glad to find someone who can understand my internal scars. You will be surprised to know that you are the first person ever to ask me about my facial scar."

Pierre decided to change the subject, sensing it was too painful for Martine. "Now you, your father, and brother live here?"

"Only my father and me. Jacques is a journalist in Paris working with *Le Figaro*. He started his journalistic career here with *Le Quotidien* for three years. Then he moved to a paper in Lyon, where he spent five years, two of them as its correspondent in Berlin. After his return from Germany, he spent one more year in Lyon before joining *Le Figaro*."

"He has obviously made very good career moves. Tell me more about him."

"Jacques has always been ambitious, not like me." Martine fell silent and took a sip of her wine.

"Go on, please. I am fascinated by your family because there is nothing fascinating about mine."

She grinned. "I beg to disagree. Every family is fascinating in its own way."

"My family is an exception," he emphasized and assumed the countenance of someone who was ready to listen attentively.

"My father has, ever since, stayed at home in a wheelchair. Françoise Lépine, who was our nanny, stayed with us. All of us consider her a family member. She is now about forty-one, and she and I are taking care of the well-being of my father. She and

I have developed a strong friendship. My father is very content and happy with her. Moreover, he is very happy with his books and writing. And an old yellow Labrador that he adores and pampers. He named him after Neruda, the famous Chilean poet."

Pierre laughed. "You are determined to expose my ignorance. First Omar Khayyam, now Neruda."

"Maybe poetry is not your cup of tea."

"I have to admit that besides political science, I love fiction, as well as European and world current affairs. No poetry for me," said Pierre. Then he asked, "Your father has friends despite his reclusive life?"

"Plenty of friends. His friendships are cosmopolitan. Because he attended *L'école Normale Supérieure* in Paris, he has a lot of friends in the upper echelons of the French government."

"So he did not go to a run-of-the-mill university. He must have a brilliant mind to be among the select few."

"Yes," she replied, doing her best to conceal her pride.

"Very interesting. Very interesting," responded Pierre.

"Before his diplomatic career was cut short, he had worked in Egypt, Argentina, and Britain. He loves all these countries and their peoples. He is nostalgic about his time in these countries. He loves and respects the Argentineans, the Arabs, and the British—even the English!"

"It is somewhat strange that a Frenchman loves and respects the English, Martine," he said with a smile. "I must admit I also like the English." Unbidden, a few names came to his mind:

Mrs. Mary McGregor, Mr. Richard Naylor and Mr. Bill Miller. And the sexy and wild Amanda Jenkins. He found himself saying, "In fact, the British in general."

"He is fond of the English. He always says to know is to understand and to understand is to love."

The waiter came to their table and politely took away their empty salad plates. Pierre, sensing that Martine was very proud of her father, asked, "How does your father spend his time?"

"Françoise takes him in his old Citroën for a morning or afternoon drive by the river almost every day. Otherwise, he spends most of his time in his library. Dinner is an important ritual in his day. He takes it with Françoise and me. Otherwise, with his friends; and he loves having friends around. Perhaps one day you can join us for dinner."

"I would love to meet him," Pierre lied. He would not, for he feared the old diplomat would see through his camouflage.

The waiter brought them their meat couscous. "*Bon appétit*," he said and left them to their conversation.

Martine looked at her steaming plate. "I love couscous."

"Your father is a fascinating man. Tell me more about him."

That delighted Martine. "He loves people and is capable of influencing them in a subtle and disarming way. Now Françoise is a passionate lover of jazz, as he is, and an avid reader of French novels. He is also teaching her English. My father thinks English is an easy language, particularly for the French. He asserts that 50 percent of English words were originally French."

"Is that so!" exclaimed Pierre, genuinely surprised.

"Yes. My father is fond of telling the story of the great French writer, Dumas, who was persuaded by some of his friends to learn English. So Dumas attended one or two English lessons and abandoned the idea. He declared that English is nothing but French wrongly pronounced."

Pierre laughed heartily before declaring, "Very interesting. That never occurred to me, though my English isn't bad." As he topped their two glasses of wine, he repeated, "Very interesting."

"My father loves to tell this story, especially to his English friends," said Martine before taking a sip of wine.

Pierre swallowed another spoonful of couscous, and said wistfully, "You know, Martine, I've seen you a number of times at La Librairie Stendhal, but I never thought you were the manageress."

"I began working—"

Pierre interrupted her with a mischievous smile on his face. "Excuse me. I want to make a confession."

"A confession! Go ahead!"

"I have stolen about ten books from your bookshop. All in French. So I plead guilty and ask for forgiveness."

"How many books did you buy from us over the years?" she spontaneously asked.

"About sixty or seventy."

"That more than compensates for the stolen books, or at least breaks even, Jean-Claude."

"I still ask for forgiveness, Martine."

"As I always condemn the sin, not the sinner, you are granted full forgiveness. Do you know that large bookshops expect about 1 to 2 percent of their books to be stolen? They budget for that."

"I didn't know that. So I should have stolen more books."

"In fact, I saw you stealing books on two occasions and I turned a blind eye. It is my policy to allow a customer to steal once or twice, but if I see him doing it for the third time I will stop him, retrieve the book, and politely tell him never to come to our bookshop again. People who steal compulsively are said to be suffering from kleptomania. One has to treat them with compassion."

Pierre grinned. "*Sainte Martine*, I don't think I am suffering from kleptomania."

"This is denial, sheer denial, Jean-Claude. Just like a paranoid saying, I am not paranoid but everyone is harboring malicious feelings or scheming against me," she said with a sweet smile.

"OK. Perhaps I am suffering from kleptomania."

"Perhaps not. You can't tell."

"That is kind of you, *Sainte Martine*," he teasingly assured her.

"Don't use the word saint lightly with me. Perhaps I am a true saint." She laughed.

"I think you are. You treated me with touching dignity and compassion when you stopped me with the book in my pocket." He paused then asked, "Did you stop me because it was a German book?"

She cast a teasing eye at him. "No. Because you were a repeat offender."

He held her hand and squeezed it. "I am glad you stopped me."

In a tender voice, she remarked, "I am more than glad that I stopped you. I think the joy of the crazy sex we had exceeds by far the cost of all the books in La Librairie Stendhal."

"The way I see it, our relationship will not be about sex. I am positive we are going to have an affectionate and warm friendship." There was conviction in his voice, but he wanted to gauge her reaction to what he said.

Martine raised her glass and announced, "Let us drink to our friendship." He joined her in the toast and said earnestly, "I am confident we shall have a great friendship."

Though Pierre sensed that she was sincere about having a meaningful friendship, he guessed she was not infatuated like a teenager. She was a sensible and mature woman, and he liked it that way. Martine sensed he was a man who knew what he wanted but she felt disarmed further and further by his warmth, openness, and attentiveness.

"Martine, I haven't started on a career yet. So tell me about your career so far. I may learn a few things from your experience."

"I don't know if you can call it a career, Jean-Claude. When I graduated from university, my father suggested that I go into journalism, but I opted for teaching. I started teaching in a large school and I had a terrible time. It was hell."

"How come?" Pierre hastened to ask.

"The pupils gave me a very miserable time, harassing me and openly making jokes about my facial scar. A number of times, I found drawings on the blackboard of women with large scars in different parts of her face. It really hurt me, yet I forced myself to carry on, telling myself they are just kids. But I found that a few teachers, who ought to know better, were taunting me, particularly female teachers."

"How beastly!" exclaimed Pierre.

"Of course, some of them were very nice and supportive. However, my fragile self-esteem plummeted and I was heading toward a nervous breakdown. Therefore, I quit teaching. I could not take it anymore, although teaching was my dream. After a few months, I joined La Librairie Stendhal as an assistant salesperson." She smiled in a sardonic way and said, "After two years, I was promoted to the cashier position. One year later, I became a full salesperson, then after another two years, a senior salesperson. How about that for career progress? Brilliant, isn't it?" She laughed, and Pierre thought her laugh was cute—self-mocking but without bitterness. It delighted him, and he joined her laughing.

"You have a charming laugh, Martine. Do you know that?"

"Nobody has ever told me that. But to be honest I do not laugh with people who are not close to me. I laugh with my father, Jacques, and Françoise."

Pierre could now understand why Martine looked aloof, haughty and standoffish whenever he had seen her in the bookshop. She had allowed a few uncouth pupils and cruel teachers to undermine her self-esteem and then gradually instill in her psyche a harmful and negative self-image despite her beauty and intelligence. "You shouldn't laugh at your progress in the bookshop. You are the manageress now, Martine."

"I know. After one year as a senior salesperson, I was promoted to deputy manager, a position I held for a few years. But that position does not exist anymore."

As they tucked into their couscous, now a voice in her head told her she was as good and loveable as anyone else. Instantaneously, her mind rejected what the voice said. No, no, and no, she declared to herself. She corrected it by telling herself, "I am more gorgeous than many women. I am far better than many people." This silent dialogue left her glowing inside. A sense of liberation and elation enveloped her. She felt grateful to Jean-Claude and wanted to know more about him. She gazed into his eyes with an endearing smile on her face. "Now you know everything about me."

"Not everything," said Pierre. He turned his head to the left so as not to blow his cigarette smoke into her face.

"There is nothing left to know about me. Nothing worth telling. So tell me something about you."

Pierre reflected. "What do you want to know about me?"

"Everything. Do not think I have been open with you because of the wine. I truly felt I could trust you. And maybe because you are the first person who was ready to listen to me so attentively."

"I do appreciate your trust, Martine. So I will tell you about all my skeletons," he said, knowing he had to lie through his teeth.

# CHAPTER 4

"**I** have many skeletons. A lot of them will frighten you, Martine." Pierre looked into her eyes and fell silent.

"I am not easily frightened. Just try me," said Martine in a challenging tone.

Pierre averted his eyes and remained silent deliberately— not out of hesitation but for effect. He intended to impress upon her that what he was about to say was grave, painful, and true, and to bring her to the conclusion that he had not said it to anyone before, and would not say it to anyone in the future. He slowly stubbed out his cigarette in the small ashtray in front of him. "Where should I start?"

"Start anywhere. When did you lose your virginity? When did you start your unsuccessful shoplifting career? Or when did you become aware you are an attractive son-of-a-bitch?"

Pierre laughed.

"I am making it easy for you, Jean-Claude."

"I come from Toulouse. I came to the university here because I wanted to escape from my family. I want to stay as far away as possible away from my parents. My mother, to be exact."

"Why do you want to escape from your mother?"

"She is what you could rightly describe as a mother from hell." Now he decided to adopt his girlfriend Catherine Derome's parents exactly the way she described them, including their professions. He thought that when he said he came from Toulouse, his mind was subconsciously nudging him to transpose Catherine's family story to the imagined Jean-Claude Marchand character. The words 'a mother from hell', he realized, were the words Catherine used to describe her mother.

Pierre heaved a feigned sigh. "Mind you, I am their only child. My father is a successful banker, and my mother is a geography schoolteacher. She is the most domineering human being I have ever met. She treats my father and me like trash. And my father is a cowering, submissive coward. He takes any tongue-lashing from my mother without raising even an eyebrow. In my battle against my mother, he has been not only a bystander but also an accomplice. If she wanted to administer a physical punishment to me, she would always order him to do it." He clasped his hands firmly and moved them forward and backward as if in subtle lamentation.

"How could your father cope with this sustained degradation from your mother?"

"I think he finds solace in his work. He is a workaholic. He finds his job a convenient escape from my mother's nagging and domination. She is severely neurotic and unhinged. That is why she has been using psychiatric drugs for more than a decade. And with those, she functions effectively as a teacher."

"Perhaps she has the capability to compartmentalize the different roles in her life. Some people have this capacity," stated Martine.

"I don't know if she has that capacity or not. I think the medical drugs are effectively keeping her functioning instead of turning her into a zombie."

"Why didn't your father seek a divorce?"

"I think he has resigned himself to a meaningless marriage. Around the house, he moves as if walking on eggshells. He is using alcohol as medication but not in excess. Just the right daily dose of Scotch. Without it, he would not cope."

"This is sad, very sad, Jean-Claude. You don't need to tell me more. I fully understand your anger and pain."

"Martine, the rotten thing is that the three of us, my parents and I, always pretended to the world to be a picture-perfect family. And this ongoing charade of a solid and loving family has always been eating my insides."

She patted his hand. "Now you are an adult and free to do what you want."

"I know. However, I feel badly for my father, who is really a gentle, loving person. I do adore him and pity him. The only person who knew the true dynamics of our family was my late, beloved, paternal uncle, Pierre Marchand, who was a sea captain."

"Let us talk about something else, Jean-Claude," said Martine in a sympathetic tone.

"No. You have been very candid with me, and I have to be as candid with you." He paused for effect and then continued in a grave and measured way. "You are a gentle soul and an empathetic spirit. You and I are soul mates that fate decided at last to bring together. So give me the chance to unburden my pain and rage."

Feeling touched and flattered, she held his two hands in hers. "If you want to do that, I am more than glad to listen, Jean-Claude." Then she hastened to add, "Jean-Claude, you are an educated and strong man. Why don't you stand up to your abusive mother?"

"I do stand up to her but in my own way. With nonchalance, and that infuriates her. I never insult her or hit her because, after all, she is my mother. But I am going to escape from all of this very soon."

"No one can blame you for distancing yourself from her. But tell me, how can you maintain an exterior of calmness and cheerfulness despite all of these family horrors?"

"It goes back to the time when I was seven. It is an incident that I will never forget. I was seven, and the three of us were having dinner. I refused to eat some steamed broccoli, and my mother was adamant that I should eat it. Gently, my father told her there was no need for me to eat something I didn't like. She shouted at him, 'You are always spoiling this brat!' Then she yelled at me, 'You are going to eat it, or I will force it down your throat.' I found myself throwing the plate, with its steak, broccoli, and carrots to the floor, and yelling, 'No. No. I am not going to eat it.' She lost it and dragged me into a dark closet and locked it, telling my father not to let me out until the next morning when I had to go to school. Just remember, I was only seven years old." There was great conviction in his tone because this had really happened to him.

Martine could see the pain in Jean-Claude's eyes, which were brimming with tears. "Jean-Claude, this is too painful for you and for me. So you don't need to continue flagellating yourself."

"You asked me how I have a calm and cheerful personality despite my deep internal wounds." He brushed his tears. "It is all related to this incident."

"How?" asked Martine, with a mixture of puzzlement and expectancy.

"After I had been cowering, sobbing and frightened, in the closet for an hour or so, my father came stealthily to the closet door and whispered, 'Jean-Claude, you are a brave boy. Don't be frightened of the darkness. My heart is with you. And God is with you.' Then he left. But I continued whimpering like a gravely wounded animal and I sobbed my heart out until I fell asleep. Then I woke up around four in the morning and to my utter surprise, I found myself enfolded in a strange calmness. A blissful calmness I had never experienced before. In my mind, I went over what happened as though it had happened to someone else, not me. I felt a thorough detachment from the incident. It was as though the whole experience had happened to someone else or to another being inside me. You could call it a complete disassociation."

Pierre paused and took a sip of his wine. Looking into Martine's green eyes, he could sense that she was entranced by this story. She was waiting for him to continue. He knew that he told the story with vividness because it really happened to him, but the culprit was his father, not his mother. And it had happened here, not in Toulouse.

"Suddenly, Martine, I was gripped with a strange certitude that I would never again be scared. Never be terrified by darkness; never be intimidated by my mother—or anything or anyone. It was like a spiritual awakening or a divine revelation. It was a metamorphosis into a fearless soul. Nevertheless, I felt I could be like my paternal uncle, Captain Pierre Marchand. He was a fearless man, never ruffled by anyone or anything. Yet he was always courteous and polite to a fault. He called courage with finesse *la force tranquille*. Since I was a child, I have looked up to him as a role model."

Martine rested her chin on her palm, thoroughly absorbed. "That is the right disposition. Courage and finesse. I wish that all human beings were like that. The world would certainly be a much better place." She looked at Jean-Claude with undisguised adoration; she reflected that she had the finesse but lacked the courage; finesse without courage is a sign of weakness, and courage without finesse is a sign of coarseness.

"So I came out of that closet when I was seven, not a submissive or a cowering person, but an invincible and unbreakable human being," stated Pierre in a calm and impressive tone. "It seemed that my spirit, or my soul, had hit rock bottom.

Then, perhaps my subconscious, or my soul, rebelled in that dark closet."

"Like a spiritual resurrection," Martine suggested.

"That is it. You hit the nail on the head, Martine."

She held his hand with one hand and caressed it with the other. "What about your paternal uncle? Your role model."

Pierre took a sip from his wine before saying in a sad tone, "He was a great man. We had great mutual love, respect, and fondness. Unfortunately, he went down with his ship in the Indian Ocean one year ago." Fabrication? No. Inventiveness is the word, he thought.

"I am so sorry to hear that, Jean-Claude."

"Thanks, Martine, but *c'est la vie*."

"I know, but it must have been devastating to you."

"It was a terrible blow for me. However, to honor his spirit and what he embedded in my soul, I don't wallow in sorrow or bitterness. I am sure this is what he expects from me, to take life's blows with fortitude despite all the pain and existential angst."

Now Martine held his hand in a gesture of consolation and admiration.

"Uncle Pierre never married so he looked to me as his son." He paused before adding, "He insisted that I should learn the English language. So during the summer break after my first year at the university, he sent me to an English institute in Bristol in England. During the summer break of my second year, he sent me to live with the family of one of his English friends, Captain Richard Naylor, in Norwich." Actually, Richard Naylor was not a sea captain, but a comrade of his late maternal uncle, Marcel Dillon—in South Africa.

"This is what one could call a real uncle, Jean-Claude," Martine said with evident warmth.

"One of the things that I also admired about him is that he was never judgmental. He always politely indicated to me never to say my father is submissive, or to say my mother is a demonic sadist. He impressed upon me that if I judge people, my mental house will fester with disharmony, anger, and bitterness."

"How true! How wise!" Martine exclaimed in an animated voice.

"He was the wisest man, at least, in my life. He used to tell me that a child cannot find his own way if his parents pave a path for him." In fact, this was what Pierre's maternal uncle, Marcel Dillon, used to tell him; he transposed that wisdom to his imaginary paternal uncle, Captain Marchand.

"Wow! Wow!" exclaimed Martine. "I love that. It is a great insight."

"I was surprised when I discovered he had left me in his will an apartment in Toulouse plus one hundred thousand euros. He also left my father an apartment in Marseilles."

Teasingly, Martine said, "You are not rich. You are filthy rich."

"For a twenty-three-old student, I am bloody, filthy rich. Therefore, I have decided to go to Ethiopia to work with a humanitarian organization called ADPA, *Action Directe Pour l'Afrique*, for a few years." Something inside him made him change Cameroon to Ethiopia.

"What about your university studies? Are you going to drop out?" asked Martine.

"Yes. I have my bachelor's degree in political science. Now I am working for my master's degree. I have decided that I do not need it. I will drop out and go to Africa. But if my mother gets wind of this, she will bundle my father with her on the first train from Toulouse and do her best to obstruct my plans." He smiled. "Sometimes I think I am going to Africa just to be as far away as possible from her."

"Why don't you get your master's degree first before going to Ethiopia?"

"I don't need a master's degree to do humanitarian work. I think a spell of administrative work with a humanitarian NGO in Africa will provide me with an experience more valuable than a master's degree." He chuckled. "And it will enhance my CV when I plunge into political life. I believe we should not let France stagnate for long. The main trouble with France is the persistent failure of leadership. When I return to France, I want to join a party with socialist leanings and agenda and work my way up to be a member of *L'Assemblée Nationale*."

Martine grinned. Her admiration for Jean-Claude was soaring.

"I believe in having dreams, Martine. I also believe that one has to take action to realize one's dreams. Otherwise, you will be a perpetual armchair dreamer."

"I like that. It is inspiring," said Martine. She told herself that Jean-Claude was not simply a daring seducer but someone who was practical and caring. And he was a man with aspirations. Her father would love to meet him.

"Martine, we Europeans robbed and plundered Africa for centuries. Don't you think we owe it to Africa to give something back, however small? My take on my humanitarian work in Ethiopia is that it will be a tiny restitution."

"So what are you going to do now, Jean-Claude?"

"I need a couple of months to finalize my arrangements while I wait for instructions from the ADPA head office in Paris as to when to fly to Addis Ababa." The assurance with which he uttered these words was convincing to Martine and to him in equal measure. "In the meantime, I will rent an apartment in any nearby town to hide from my mother and colleagues. Many students in the university here come from Toulouse. If anyone hears of my plan to go to Ethiopia, the information will definitely reach my neurotic mother. So I have to stay under the radar, away from my university colleagues, until I fly to Addis Ababa." He paused, pondering what to add. "I have already discussed my plan with my father, and he has given me his blessing. However, he earnestly advised me to hide until I fly to Addis Ababa."

"You really need to hide from your mother?" asked Martine in a low voice, almost conspiratorially.

"Yes, I do. I don't want any crazy scenes from her at the university. Can you imagine what my friends and colleagues would think if they saw my mother reducing my father and me to cowering, blithering idiots in my dormitory or one of the university cafeterias? Even if she gets wind of my plans while I am in Paris, preparing to fly to Addis Ababa, she will do everything at her disposal to sabotage my plans."

"This is horrible, Jean-Claude." Her eyes radiated empathy. "Have you found an apartment yet?"

"No. But I am working on it. I want a small, furnished apartment."

Martine rested her chin on her left hand, and Pierre could sense she was contemplating something. Then she mustered the courage to ask him, "Would you be willing to live in an old and derelict apartment in an abandoned area of the city?"

Pierre managed to conceal his enthusiasm at the suggestion. "What do you mean by an abandoned area?"

"An old area of the city that was previously inhabited by the well-to-do, but nobody lives there anymore. It is in the southern part of the city, this side of the river. As you know, for the last few decades, the development programs have been concentrated in the northern part of the city on both sides of the river. In a way, the city center, with its old and new parts, separates the developed area in the north from the neglected area in the south. And nobody lives in the abandoned area to which I am referring." She gazed at his eyes to gauge his reaction to her suggestion, which she feared could hurt his feelings. "If you really want to hide from your mother or the world, it could be—I am not sure—the ideal place."

Pierre was listening attentively without showing any discernible sign of aversion or eagerness. He nodded his head, indicating that she should go on. "My father owns an apartment that he inherited from his father in an abandoned building in this deserted area. His apartment, though abandoned, is in a very good shape. Strong doors. Sturdy furniture. Great kitchen. I go there every two or three months to check on it. Of course, it needs a lot of cleaning and dusting before anyone could move in. Surprisingly, it has tap water. The municipality either deliberately or through an oversight kept the water supply on. But with no electricity or gas, one has to use candles."

"Why not? Let me see it, Martine," he said in a neutral tone.

"I am not sure you could consent to live in such an apartment, Jean-Claude."

"Well, I have to see it and then decide." He disguised his enthusiasm for this unexpected option. It was a far better proposition than renting an apartment in a nearby town and buying a car to commute to commit the three murders. It would be a handy sanctuary from which he could carry out his plans, using his bicycle.

"All right. I will take you to inspect it, and we'll see what you think," replied Martine.

He thought Martine was a God-sent angel. He squeezed her hand in appreciation. "So, if I like it, how much should I pay for rent?"

She laughed. "What rent? The apartment has not been used for almost two decades. My father doesn't want to sell it because he was brought up there. So we don't expect any rent."

"Why not? I am ready to pay rent," he insisted.

"Don't jump to conclusions. First, I have to ask my father's permission—though I don't expect him to object to letting an aspiring politician use it." She was sure her father would not object to a student using it, particularly one who is going to make some restitution to Africa.

"Anyway, I have to thank you, Martine, for your generosity of spirit whether your father gives you permission or not. It is very thoughtful of you."

She laughed heartily. "Don't be ridiculous. If everything goes well, you will need to undertake the mammoth task of cleaning it. We should be paying you for cleaning the apartment instead of asking you for rent."

Before they left the restaurant, Martine's generosity of spirit, which she had viscerally assimilated from her munificent father over the years, had made her unwittingly offer a man she hardly knew a haven from which he would be committing atrocious acts.

# CHAPTER 5

The next morning, shortly after ten, Pierre received a cellphone call from Martine telling him that her father had agreed that he could use the abandoned apartment.

"Many thanks to you and your father, Martine," said Pierre in a tone that betrayed his excitement.

"Cool down, Jean-Claude. I'm warning you. Don't get your hopes up. I have a strong feeling it may not be up to your standards, as a filthy rich student." She stressed the last three words in a winsome way.

"Why? Is it rat-infested, Martine?"

"There are no rats because the area around the building is crawling with stray cats and dogs. They have pushed the rats out to the riverbank."

"I can tolerate anything else."

"Fine, Jean-Claude. So come to the bookshop before one and we can drive to your new palace," she said.

A few minutes before one, Pierre climbed into the passenger seat of Martine's gray Peugeot, and said, "*Merci*, Martine."

"*Pas de quoi.*"

"Let's buy some cleaning materials."

Martine smiled benignly. "Don't be impatient. Have a look at the place first. It may not be up to your expectations."

"Martine, I am sure I will like it." He smiled and added, "It is an Auberts' apartment. So how could it be below my expectations?"

"I like the way you mix stubbornness with teasing."

"Oh, yes. I am stubborn," he replied with a grin.

"I think you are a diehard optimist. So let's buy some cleaning stuff." Martine yielded with a sweet smile.

She drove to a supermarket two blocks away from the bookshop. She parked the car in front of it, and told Jean-Claude that while he was buying some cleaning stuff, she would buy some bread, cheese, a few bottles of wine, and a corkscrew. He gave her three hundred euros, which she tried to refuse. But he insisted, telling her she could return to him whatever remained after her purchases.

Before he entered the supermarket, she called him, "Jean-Claude, don't forget to buy lots of candles and two or three flashlights." A half an hour later they drove, with their purchases bundled on the back seat, to the abandoned apartment. They had driven for about ten minutes, when Martine mischievously announced, "Now we are approaching your holy hermitage, Jean-Claude."

The slum area looked as if nobody had cared to rehabilitate it since the Second World War, thought Pierre, as he gazed out the window, surveying the old buildings. Some had already fallen apart; some were about to collapse; yet some stood intact, defying the elements. He was glad that the area had a lot of large, green trees, and haphazardly scattered shrubs.

After a few minutes, Martine turned to Jean-Claude. "We are about to enter what some people call the 'ghost city', Jean-Claude."

"Fortunately, I don't believe in ghosts."

"Unfortunately, ghosts don't care what you think about them. You may soon change your mind about ghosts." Martine chuckled, before stating, "This area is three to four square kilometers. You can read, fornicate, get drunk, or meditate without a single soul disturbing you. If you focus on meditation, you might emerge as a new prophet with a new scripture."

"Why not? I might do that," replied Pierre in mock earnestness.

"But don't expect me to believe a single word in your scripture because I know you are a fake prophet."

"Instead of a prophet, I might emerge as a true saint, a blessed and blessing saint, Martine. A true saint, pure and without a sin." He glanced at her beautiful face, wondering how she would respond to his flippant words.

"They say a saint is an ex-sinner, and a sinner is a future saint."

"So as an out-and-out sinner, I am a strong candidate for sainthood, Martine."

"You bet." Martine slapped his thigh and laughed jovially. "Do you have enough books to read?"

"Yes. I have eight novels by literary giants. Tolstoy, Stendhal, and others. That reminds me, could you lend me the book by Omar Khayyam that you told me about?"

"I will lend you my copy of his *Ruba'iyat* in French. I can also lend you two books by Rumi."

"I know about Rumi. There was a Canadian student and her Bolivian boyfriend at the university two years ago. You could not have a conversation with either of them without having a Rumi quote thrown at you. The Canadian woman made one think Rumi was a Canadian. So I read about Rumi and I read a few of his works. Of course, he was neither a Canadian nor a Bolivian."

As she was about to turn left, she glanced at him and pointed to a tattered sign on the corner of a decayed, four-story building to her left. "Now pay attention, Jean-Claude. You have to remember your route to the apartment building. Straight from the city center, through the slum area, up to this old building with the faded, wooden sign. See the remaining letters—'*rasser*'—in faint blue? It was a *brasserie*. Here you have to turn left. After three buildings, you turn right. Then after six buildings, our apartment building will be on your left."

"I got it. Turn left at the old *brasserie*; then after three buildings, I have to turn right. Go straight and the sixth building will be opposite your apartment building."

"*Exactement*," Martine said.

Five minutes later, Martine parked the car in front of a four-story building and looked at Jean-Claude. "Here we are. It is 144 rue Karl Marx."

Pierre could see a few trees and wild shrubs here and there in the street. There was a thick shrub in an empty plot of land next to the building, very close to it. Then he stared up at the street sign on the corner of the building, which read 'Rue Karl Marx', the words somewhat eroded by the elements. "I never thought this city, crawling with greedy capitalists, would have a street named after Karl Marx, Martine."

"This was named in the old days when the city was crawling with socialists and communists. It was a bastion of socialism and Marxism. It had a long succession of socialist mayors."

Pierre repeated the address to himself—144 rue Karl Marx, 144 rue Karl Marx. A fitting address, he thought. He was as angry as the old man had been. Marx never concealed his rage at any establishment, religion, or person who disagreed with him. He was even angry with his wealthy friend, Friedrich Engels, the first champagne communist, who supported Marx and his family financially from Manchester, because Engels kept exhorting him to stop his endless research and start writing. Marx never disguised his rage, but I know how to conceal my rage: under a disarming and tranquil exterior. Marx was furious at the world; I am furious at my father and his mistresses. Not the world. Not anybody else.

Martine handed Pierre two keys on a small chain. "This is your set of keys. The large one is for the main door to the building and the small one is for the apartment door on the third floor. Apartment 303."

"Many thanks, Martine," said Pierre enthusiastically.

"You sound as if you have already made up your mind." She gazed at his face and smiled.

"Oh, yes. No turning back for me."

Martine said, "Fine." Then she reached into the back seat for a paper bag containing three baguettes and three pieces of different types of cheese, and a plastic bag containing two bottles of merlot, a corkscrew, four small bottles of mineral water, and a copy of the day's Le Quotidien. She opened the main door, and Pierre followed her with his bags and the broom. "You'll need a lot of stamina, Jean-Claude. The old elevator has been out of use for ages."

The apartment reeked with a stale and fusty odor, but Pierre told himself he would soon change this.

"We took away all the carpets years ago, so you have this light-beige ceramic in all the rooms, Jean-Claude."

"This is better. It is easier to mop and clean," replied Pierre.

Some dim light seemed to come from the windows. Pierre took out a flashlight, moved its beam around the room, and then raised it to a framed, black-and-white photo of a distinguished-looking man in his fifties with a large moustache, a trimmed beard, and abundant hair crowning his head. He wore a pince-nez.

All of the furniture was protected with thick, blue coverings except the round, marble table in the middle of the large room. Martine removed the blue covering from the dining table and asked Jean-Claude to put his bags and broom on the table.

"I think you should use the master bedroom with its en suite bathroom. You can use the other two bedrooms to store anything you want," she said as she started removing the blue coverings from the eight chairs around the dining table. Pierre removed the blue coverings from the couch and four arm-chairs. He liked the light-yellow, mustard, and green stripes of the upholstery of the couch and the four armchairs. They were made of sturdy wood and elegant, enduring cloth. The walls were painted a light, rosy shade of beige. He immensely liked the large living room.

"Do you have another flashlight?" asked Martine.

"Yes, I have." He retrieved the other flashlight from one of the bags and handed it to her.

"I will open the inner windows, which are made of glass, to let in fresh air. The outer windows are made of small, fixed, wooden slats to allow the sunlight and air in. The old design, you know. However, you have to keep the outer win-dows closed all the time so as not to draw the attention of any human or a ghost. You can close the inner glass windows whenever you like, if you find the noise of the fighting dogs too loud."

The keenly observant Pierre, aka Jean-Claude, was taking in many details. Now he nodded, and commented, "This is a very spacious apartment, not like the small apartments they build today."

"Yes, of course," said Martine, who then went into the kitchen and the three bedrooms, briskly opening all of the inner, glass-paned windows. Immediately, fresh air flooded the apartment. Pierre could smell it as he carefully folded the blue furniture covers.

Martine saw him folding the covers and suggested that he store them in one of the two small bedrooms. She entered the kitchen and opened the tap, and then went into the master bedroom and opened the shower and basin taps. The water that gushed from the taps was dark brown. She came into the living room and told Jean-Claude, "In ten to fifteen minutes we will have clean water in this place."

"Fantastic, Martine. I will start piling the dust in one corner. "

"Fine. I will see what I can do about the kitchen."

When she disappeared into the kitchen, Pierre tore a piece from one of the brown paper bags and wrote at the top with a ball-point pen, "To Buy List." He jotted down some items Martine had mentioned, and added bed sheets, pillows, duvet, and sofa cushions. Then he put the brown piece of paper and the pen on the round, marble table. He took all the folded furniture covers into the bedroom next to the kitchen and placed them on the covered bed.

Noticing some dust on his shirt sleeve, he took the shirt and undershirt off and draped them on one of the dining-table chairs. Then he took the list and the pen, meaning to jot down any other necessary items, and sat on the couch. He found it comfortable. As he tried to add more items to the list, he decided that he would remember many items once he went to a shopping mall. He stood up, took the broom, and started sweeping the dust toward the corner between the master bedroom and the bedroom adjacent to it.

After some fifteen minutes, Martine came into the living room and said with a triumphant voice, "The water is now clear and clean, Jean-Claude."

Pierre yelled enthusiastically, "Bravo. Bravo, Martine."

They embraced like two young children who had done something remarkable. Then Pierre said, "You'd better take off your silk shirt before you stain it or spoil it."

"No, I am not taking it off. I have simply rolled up my sleeves."

"Why not?" asked Pierre.

"Because I'm not wearing a bra."

"The other day in the bookshop you were wearing a bra. So, you occasionally go braless?"

Martine hesitated before saying, "I have always been tempted not to wear a bra, but my inhibitions have always overridden my temptation."

"So what happened today?"

"I think you are to blame." She gazed at him, smiling. "The way we had sex in the bookshop and our long conversation in the restaurant made me override my inhibitions. At least some of them."

"That is good for you, Martine. Your motto should always be, 'Down with all inhibitions and down with all society's dictates'. I have already taken off my cheap shirt and undershirt. So take off your expensive shirt. Or I will take it off for you." He stepped toward her.

"OK. I will take it off." She looked at Pierre's naked torso; she thought he had a dazzling abdomen—hairless, muscular, and taut, like that of an athletic teenager. He also possessed muscular shoulders and arms. Very sexy, very erotic, she thought, and found herself almost gaping. She took off her shirt and carefully draped it on another chair at the dining table. He could see her breasts with their firm, pink, enticing nipples. Martine possessed a lean abdomen and enthralling curves, and her breasts would drive any man crazy—they were large, supple, yet firm.

"I think we will need at least a week to clean this place and put it in proper order befitting a rich student and a future politician."

"Please, say a down-to-earth future politician," responded Pierre.

"I doubt if there are any down-to-earth politicians. Why don't you hire one or two workers to help you clean the apartment, Jean-Claude?"

He replied, "I don't want anyone to help me clean the apartment. If I bring in a worker, then it will not be a secret sanctuary."

"I see. You are right, Jean-Claude."

"I can clean and scrub the whole place within a few days without any help. But I need to buy some other cleaning materials."

When Martine decided to open one of the bottles of merlot, it dawned on her that she had forgotten to buy wineglasses. As she was opening the bottle, she said, "Please write on your list, wineglasses, cups, knives, forks, spoons, and mugs."

"Oh, yes. Thanks, Martine. I also need plates, a teapot..." He paused, thinking, what else? "Aha, a cooking stove. One of those camping stoves that use bottled kerosene. I am sure when I go into a shopping mall I will see more items to buy."

Spreading some inner pages of *Le Quotidien* on the dining table, Martine said, "Now let's eat something."

"Good. I have to wash my hands," he said before adding: soap, dish liquid, toilet paper, and Kleenex to his list. Then he went into the kitchen to wash his hands. It was spacious, with cream-colored marble counters. He was delighted to have such an apartment at his disposal.

As he walked back to the dining table, he noticed on the wall next to the table an antique pendulum clock that had stopped, perhaps many years ago, at four seventeen. He looked at Martine's firm and voluptuous breasts as she took a sip of wine and passed the bottle to him. He held the bottle while he kept staring at Martine's voluptuous breasts. The image of Catherine Derome's breasts came to his mind; they were small, and her nipples were tiny.

Martine said in deadpan, "I am sure you haven't seen a woman's breasts before."

He whistled. "I have, but I haven't seen such breathtaking breasts."

"Do you expect me to believe that, Jean-Claude?"

"No. The important thing is that I believe it."

"I am ready to believe it." She smiled mischievously, "Just to please you."

They used their hands to eat the cheese and bread, and now and then sipped from the wine bottle. Pierre took a swig of the wine, kept it in his mouth and stood up, then held Martine's face in his hands, pressed his lips against hers, slowly opened her mouth, and passed the wine into her mouth. She swallowed it with great delight.

"You see, Martine, we don't need wineglasses."

"Yes," she said, standing up, taking some wine in her mouth, and passing it into Pierre's mouth.

He did not resist and swallowed it with relish. "The wine when mixed with your saliva becomes divine. Don't tell me Rumi or Khayyam said that."

She gave him a playful look, and replied, "Maybe they both said it centuries before you."

"Even if they said it, they didn't taste your saliva. Your saliva is heavenly and angelic." He kissed her, kneading her white, firm, and provocative breasts. He extended his hand to unzip her trousers. She smiled and said sweetly, "I'll do it."

Pierre started taking off his shoes, socks, trousers, and boxer shorts, and throwing them in all directions. Martine, who was taking off her black trousers and red panties unhurriedly, looked at him. "Why do you throw your clothes like that?"

"I think it is something I do subconsciously against the way I was brought up. My tyrannical mother is so fastidious about everything, and I am subconsciously rebelling against her maddening perfectionism."

Martine, now stark naked, said, "That doesn't sound like anything to do with the subconscious. You are consciously rebelling against everything about her."

"I think you are right. Let's forget about her," he said, feigning mild irritation.

She kissed him and said, "I think you are rebelling consciously and subconsciously against mama, poor child." She sucked his lips and inserted her tongue in his mouth, hotly probing it.

He put his right arm under her head and his left under her knees, and gently placed her on the couch. As he started gently making love to her, she felt intense, successive waves of pleasure spreading throughout her body. Her eyes were closed and her mouth was open. The erotic waves, though intensely carnal, seemed to her to be coming from the realm of fantasy. Her passionate moans were euphoric and delirious. Pierre did his best not to climax before Martine had an orgasm. When she reached her climax, she was howling with pleasure, gasping for air, her legs thrusting into the air in a frenzy of involuntary jolts. He let her calm down before he resumed his passionate lovemaking, until he climaxed. Then, breathless and spent, he squeezed himself next to her on the couch and brushed the beads of sweat from her forehead. Their silence was saturated with blissful warmth and tenderness. Martine closed her eyes and, silently, let herself be transported out of this world and time, into a heavenly and divine universe. Neither of them was concerned about what the future concealed for their relationship. It was a time for affection and bonding, not a time for reflection or prediction.

After a while, Pierre whispered, "You are more than lovely, Martine."

With her eyes closed, she tenderly put her finger to her lips and said in a soft and deep voice, "Let me savor the bliss that is embracing me."

Her soft voice filled him with a sense of peacefulness, and he decided to defer to her request. He could see that her face was still flushed with the glow of carnal and soulful rapture. After a few minutes, Martine whispered, "You will be surprised that I slept with six or eight men, a number of times, before meeting you, but I did not achieve an orgasm with any of them."

"I can't believe that!"

"You'd better believe it."

"You didn't even masturbate until you climaxed?" he asked.

She opened her eyes and looked at him, more puzzled than embarrassed. "I don't masturbate."

"Do you know women have more orgasms through masturbation than through normal sexual intercourse?"

"Is that true?" she asked, searching his eyes for a moment or two. Then she closed her eyes and inquired, "Who said that?"

"A lot of research has proved it." It was his girlfriend, or ex-girlfriend, Catherine Derome, who had revealed to him this research finding, he remembered. "If you want, one day I can teach you how to masturbate until you have an orgasm."

Martine opened her eyes and smiled. "I think with you I want to stick to natural sexual intercourse."

"At your disposal, Martine, anytime."

"Do you masturbate?" she asked tentatively.

"Yes, I do. But not regularly."

"How often?" she asked as she caressed his thigh, amazed by the smoothness of his skin.

He paused for a few moments, debating whether to tell her the truth or not; then he decided to be candid, yet stick to his Jean-Claude Marchand story. "Not very often, but whenever I am humiliated and insulted by my mother, I am gripped by an urge to masturbate." He decided not to tell her that his repressed rage also drove him to shoplift.

She kissed his cheek. "I admire your openness. I wish I could be as candid as you are."

He raised her hand and kissed it. "Martine, don't forget that you have been very open with me."

"I never imagined that I would be as open with anyone as I have been with you," she said and then paused before declaring, "I have to go back to work. I am already late. I should be a good model for my staff."

"That is real leadership. Your staff and customers are lucky to have a ravishing, gorgeous, and conscientious woman like you managing the bookshop."

"If for any reason you quit your humanitarian work in Ethiopia, I will offer you a job for a few years before you start your political career." She stood up and started dressing. She chuckled. "It could also enhance your political CV."

When she dropped him near La Librairie Stendhal to pick up his bicycle, it was almost four o'clock in the afternoon. Before leaving the car, Pierre put his hand behind her head and kissed her passionately. She feared that one of her staff might see them; looking around and seeing no one, she planted a quick kiss on his lips.

As she walked into the bookshop, she was still glowing with the gratification and bliss of her orgasm. And what an orgasm! It occurred to her that perhaps the fact that Jean-Claude was eight years younger than she was made him more erotic and more ardent. She decided to advise Françoise to go for a much younger man than she is if she wanted some volcanic orgasms.

# CHAPTER 6

In his campus room, Pierre took a long shower to get rid of the dust that had clung to his body from cleaning the apartment. He left the bathroom rubbing his back, chest, abdomen, and thighs with a large, blue towel, then slumped into his bed with the towel on top of him. He closed his eyes and felt very relaxed. It occurred to him that he was nicely settling into the character of Jean-Claude Marchand of Toulouse, with his fictitious, bestial mother; his henpecked father; and his late paternal uncle, Captain Pierre Marchand—the brave and wise man who was claimed by the Indian Ocean.

He decided he had to go to sleep early so that he could be fresh to resume cleaning the Karl Marx apartment the next morning. Since he had not turned on a light, the room was dark now, and his mind drifted into his uncomfortable memory lane. His late Uncle Marcel came to mind; he always remembered Marcel with great fondness and deep sadness. It was Marcel who had sent him twice to England to sharpen his English. It was Marcel who had patiently taught him to use a pistol and Kalashnikov when he came to visit them during his semiannual breaks from South Africa. He had repeatedly told Pierre that a man's education is incomplete if he can't effectively handle lethal weapons to defend himself. Marcel, as a true professional, had taken Pierre's training seriously—teaching him not only how to shoot and where to shoot an adversary but also how to disassemble and assemble a Beretta and a Kalashnikov. They had carried out the training in the deserted, rocky hills on the eastern side of the city. And during his last visit, as though he'd had a premonition, he had given Pierre a spare key to the large and well-crafted trunk in the brick storage shed behind the Bouchers' villa. Marcel had cached in his trunk assorted weapons, different types of ammunition, two expensive cameras, eight photo albums, and his hardcover diaries. No one, including Pierre's parents, had seen the contents of Marcel's trunk. It was a well-guarded secret between the uncle and his nephew. If Pierre's parents came to know about the contents of the trunk, they would have the shock of their lives.

One year ago, Marcel, the brave and true gentleman, and Pierre's dear friend, met his end in an ambush in the Congo. When the sad news of his demise reached them, Pierre and his mother were devastated. Jacqueline fell apart. She was inconsolable and plunged into a severe depression. Professor Bernard Lacan, a friend of Pierre's parents, decided to augment the antidepressant—a selective serotonin reuptake inhibitor— she had been using for some time with another antidepressant, a serotonin norepinephrine reuptake inhibitor; plus a strong antianxiety tranquilizer. Lacan had pronounced that Jacqueline was suffering from a double depression. She had been battling for years with dysthymia, a chronic, low-grade depression yet a debilitating malady. But with the death of her brother, a major depression was superimposed on her dysthymia, hence the paralyzing double depression. However, within one month of Lacan's aggressive treatment, she managed to function normally, though with difficulty. Pierre, as usual, put on a brave front for the sake of his mother, while he silently loathed his father's thoughtless and mean insistence that Marcel was a mercenary whose death in that way was something to be expected.

The words of his insensitive father still resonated in Pierre's mind: 'That is the way most mercenaries end up—buried in an unmarked grave in a God-forsaken place in Africa.' His father was so uncouth that he uttered those coarse words just a few minutes after his wife told him the sad news, upon his return from the hospital. At first, he had declared that he was sorry to hear the sad news. Then he poured himself a tumbler of his favorite malt and fell silent as he nursed it. After about five minutes and for no discernible reason, he blasted out his insulting judgment on the death of his brother-in-law, a man well above him in bravery and magnanimity.

Without hesitation, Pierre had told his father, "You should respect the memory of Uncle Marcel, at least for the sake of my mother. This brave man was her only bother."

Jacqueline, sobbing, shot out of the living room and rushed upstairs. Pierre stared fiercely at his father and calmly announced, "How gracious of you, Dad."

"Pierre, don't spoil my evening with your rudeness and sarcasm. I have told you repeatedly to speak to me with all the respect I deserve or just shut up. Don't you get it?" asked Christian.

Pierre stood up and left the living room without responding, just to annoy his father. He went upstairs and discovered that his mother was not in the master bedroom she shared with his father. He found her stretched on a bed in the guest room, with the lower half of her body covered with a blue-and-red-checkered duvet and her face covered with a cotton pillow. He noticed her prescribed tranquilizers on the bedside table. When he gently lifted the pillow, he could see she was already asleep with anger and sadness contorting her face. He had immediately decided to return to campus, for he feared that if he remained in the house, his fury would lead him to give his father a bloody thrashing. All the way to his dormitory, his emotions lurched from deep grief at the loss of his beloved uncle to profound resentment for his father's crassness.

Surprisingly, his rage against his father's blatant rudeness evoked the resolve and certitude he had experienced when his father had locked him in the dark closet when he was seven. Until this day, he couldn't find a rational explanation for his metamorphosis from a frightened child into a fearless one. His father had intended to teach him a lesson and break his spirit. Nevertheless, whatever happened to Pierre's soul in that closet, the result was flagrantly opposite of his father's intention; the certitude that descended upon the seven-year-old Pierre still puzzled him at twenty-three. It also continued to confound his father and mother, for neither of them was aware of what had happened to him in that closet. Sometimes, Pierre thought that it had happened to him because he was a very special person, and he had a significant role to play in life.

His late Uncle Marcel abhorred lying; he was an upright and incorruptible man. He had been discharged from the army when he was a major for gross insubordination because he had defiantly refused to participate in the cover-up of a serious case of embezzlement that involved a number of his superiors. Within a few months, he was hired by a Belgian company paid by the Congolese government to conduct a war against insurgents. Two years later, he was hired away by a British-South African security company for much better pay and generous bonuses. This company fought in a number of African countries. He lived in luxury between assignments, spending his two twenty-one-day leaves a year in France.

Marcel had been generous to Pierre and Jacqueline, his friends, and his girlfriends with his money. He was a true gentleman who treated his women as proper and veritable ladies.

Nonetheless, Pierre never expected his uncle to be so rich from sixteen years of mercenary work after all his lavish largesse during his life. In his will, he left Pierre and Jacqueline €250,000 each. He left fifty thousand euros to his girlfriend, Christina Amado, a Brazilian divorcée and a Harvard graduate working for an international organization in Paris; and twenty-five thousand euros to one of his ex-girlfriends, Yasmine AlWakeel, a Lebanese. Pierre recalled that Marcel spoke with great fondness of her sense of humor and superb cooking. Marcel did not forget the seventy-nine-year old Aunt Marie-Hélène, who had been his and Jacqueline's childhood nanny, and who was now spending her twilight years in Aix-en-Provence. He left her twenty-five thousand euros.

On top of the money Marcel had left him, Pierre's mother gave him one hundred thousand dollars of the two-hundred-thousand-dollar ex-gratia payment sent to her by Bill Miller, the CEO of the security company for which Marcel worked in South Africa, COMCO—Cromwell Operations Management Consulting Organization. Miller had enclosed the ex-gratia check with a typed letter to Jacqueline expressing his commiseration and those of all COMCO personnel at the loss of a gallant comrade and the epitome of unpretentious leadership. Miller also sent her a personal letter in longhand assuring her that Marcel's loss was a personal loss to him; his wife, Emily; his sons, Peter and Charles; and his daughter, Sandra; for they considered Marcel not only a friend but also a family member. To Pierre's mind, this confirmed what Marcel had told him: there is a cohesive camaraderie among these men whom the wimps call mercenaries—men who dearly love their families; men who play an important role in shaping the geopolitics of the post-colonial era.

Marcel was magnanimous enough to leave two paintings to his brother-in-law, Dr. Christian Boucher, though he hated him. The two men had lived in a long and simmering undeclared war; a war of mutual animosity and disdain that they both managed somehow to keep shrouded under the carpet of de rigueur civility. Christian, with his unbounded arrogance, decided not to keep the two paintings. He gave one to Jean-Paul Villard and the other to another family friend, Paul Roget, an investment banker. Jacqueline found her husband's refusal to retain the two paintings an outright insult to her and to the memory of her beloved brother.

Paul Roget and Jean-Paul Villard had agreed to send their two paintings to Paris for professional evaluation. Christian kept his shock and regret to himself when the market value of the two paintings was conveyed to him by the immensely grateful Paul Roget. The painting given to Villard was valued at between sixty-five thousand and seventy thousand euros; and that given to Roget, at between fifty-five thousand and sixty thousand euros. Of course, Mrs. Villard and Mrs. Roget phoned Jacqueline to thank her and her husband profusely for the precious gifts. Mrs. Roget revealed the market price for each of the two paintings to Jacqueline, who was appalled and perturbed by her husband's foolishness. Seeing her husband unsettled and melancholy when he discovered his reckless rashness, she kept silent, but her bitterness at his foolishness smoldered and simmered.

One evening, when Pierre was having dinner with his parents at home, his mother, fortified and emboldened by too much vodka, let her anger erupt like a volcano. They were having their meal in complete silence, when she suddenly hit the table with her clenched fist and blurted out, "Christian, your animosity to Marcel led you to think he left you two paintings that will fetch only three or four thousand euros. And your naivety led you to throw away more than one hundred thousand euros to people who are much richer than you."

His father continued eating his sirloin steak, steamed carrots, and Brussels sprouts, pretending he did not hear her remarks. He played dumb. That simply added fuel to Jacqueline's irritation, and she snapped, "How stupid of you, Christian. We have been talking for years of buying a country villa in Provence. My brother gave you two paintings that could have bought us a decent villa but your hatred for—"

Christian interrupted her, yelling, "You drunk, crazy woman, you better shut up. Do you think I will stoop to keep a gift from a professional killer who, I now suspect, also dealt in stolen diamonds or some other sinister business? Even if the two paintings could fetch two million euros, I would not have kept them."

"You are talking out of the top of your head," retorted Jacqueline.

"After twenty-five years of marriage, I thought you would know I will never stoop to accept anything from a mercenary," snapped Christian.

Jacqueline, utterly infuriated, stood up and shouted, "I know you stoop to do the most immoral things that no man worth his salt would ever do."

At the time, Pierre did not fully comprehend what his mother meant by that, but he was gladdened that his mother was throwing all caution to the wind and brazenly insulting his father. At last, he told himself, the daring Dillons' genes that had lain dormant deep within her for so long had resurfaced. She had cast away the chains of her sullen despair and resignation.

"What do you mean by that?" asked his father, stunned.

"You know very well what I mean," she yelled. Then she stormed from the dining room. Pierre decided to add insult to injury to his father, so he stood up, pushed his chair back, threw his napkin on the table with undisguised disgust, and walked out of the room without uttering a word.

Though he found his mother's rebuke to his father—I know you stoop to do the most immoral things that no man worth his salt would ever do—a bit perplexing, he hoped that her brave stand would not be a one-off incident, but a sustained attitude. Pierre went upstairs, opened the door of the master bedroom, and entered. His mother was sitting in one of the two armchairs in the room, holding a half-empty glass of vodka. Knowing that his mother would not tell him what she meant by what she'd flung at his father, he refrained from asking her; she was always a stickler for doing the right thing, the decent thing; she would not compromise her husband despite his bestiality.

He knelt in front of her and held her hand, reassuringly. "You have done the right thing, *Maman.*" She nodded her head silently. He brushed the tears from her cheeks and stood up. "I am going to the campus."

"Why don't you spend the night here?"

"I have a lot of work to do in the library very early tomorrow morning." He bent and kissed her forehead. "Take care of yourself. Don't let him destroy your spirit, *Maman.*"

"He has already destroyed my spirit and soul. Nevertheless, I will slog on as long as I have you. My life without you would not be worth living, Pierre."

Her words tugged at his heart and he found himself declaring, "One day, I will make him pay dearly for the way he is treating you. Mark my words."

"Don't say that, Pierre. He is your father, after all. I don't want you to worry about the occasional flare-ups between us."

All the way to campus, he reflected upon the sorry emotional and mental state of his beleaguered mother. He vowed that he would do everything he could to ease his mother's pain and misery. But I should not have told her that I would make him pay, he reflected. I should have kept that to myself.

His mother had stood by him and done her utmost to protect him from his father's tyranny ever since he was a kid. As he recalled his childhood bedwetting, he felt a tingle of shame. He had wet his bed until he was six or seven. His father had wanted to refer him to a medical doctor, but his mother had adamantly rejected the idea, insisting his bedwetting would cease as he grew up, which had proved to be correct. He could still remember very vividly some of the shouting matches between his parents over his embarrassing, involuntary habit. His mother had concealed many incidents of bedwetting from his heartless father; she had wanted the whole thing to be kept a secret between her and her son, hurriedly changing his clothes and bed sheets and kissing him reassuringly.

Pierre had resented his father since he was a child. When he was fourteen or fifteen, he took out his resentment on his school colleagues and his teachers, beating the bullies who tried to bully their weaker peers and defying teachers whom he thought were talking nonsense or not showing enough respect to the fragile among their charges. The school authorities contacted his mother, telling her that the school would expel him if he didn't stop bullying his peers and treating some of the teachers with insolence. His mother, without telling his father, met with the school's headmaster, who recommended that she take him to a Dr. Gaston Cloutier, a psychotherapist who specialized in helping adolescents with serious behavioral problems. The headmaster told her that Cloutier had worked, when he was young, under a path-breaking British consultant, Dr. R. D. Laing.

Pierre and his mother attended the first session with Dr. Cloutier, and then Pierre went to two sessions on his own. Cloutier was a giant of a man, with a towering body, large hands, and large feet. He had dark, mysterious eyes, a white mustache, and a thick, well-trimmed beard. His voice was deep and hypnotic. As he smoked his pipe, he listened attentively to Pierre. Pierre recalled how he liked the aroma of Dr. Cloutier's tobacco. Cloutier sat in a comfortable armchair and asked Pierre to sit in a similar armchair facing him. From the first session, his features and bearing reminded Pierre of Rasputin, though Cloutier was a Rasputin with an elegant pipe, a trimmed beard, and a necktie. At the time Pierre wondered if the Russian Rasputin had a slow-pace manner of speech and movement like the French one.

After the two one-on-one sessions, Cloutier held the fourth and final session with both Pierre and Jacqueline, and delivered his verdict: Pierre had signs of a mild defiant, oppositional disorder, with clear tendencies of resistance and opposition to authority. It was a phase in Pierre's development and he would outgrow it within a few years if the family showed him more respect and unfailing support.

Dr. Cloutier's manner of speaking—despite its mildness and slow pace—made his views sound like proclamations delivered by a soft-spoken giant. He removed his pipe, held it in his left hand, and fixed his hypnotic gaze on Jacqueline. "The good news is that Pierre has two healthy aspects to his personality. First, he is not suffering from what is called identification with the aggressor. Secondly, he has a very healthy degree of individuation."

Jacqueline interposed, "What's—"

Cloutier ignored her question and continued with his proclamations. "Both are indicative of a healthy personality, particularly at his age. If he had identification with the aggressor or poor individuation, he would have shown an impaired self-assertive aggression.

"Those who suffer from an impaired self-assertive aggression are afflicted with shyness, over obedience, and submissiveness. And Pierre has none of these maladaptive and neurotic defenses. In fact, Pierre has a sound, self-assertive aggression, which is vital for success in life, in both love and work. It is also indicative of strong social intelligence. So I don't recommend any psychoanalysis or psychiatric treatment for him."

Toward the end of the session, the French Rasputin gazed at Jacqueline and said, "Mrs. Boucher, if an individual is adversely shaped by the dynamics of his family, then it is necessary to reshape the family dynamics to serve the interests of the individual. This is elementary, isn't it?"

Jacqueline almost submissively nodded her head.

Dr. Cloutier briefly glanced at Pierre, and then held Jacqueline's eyes with his hypnotic gaze and announced in a measured way, "Mrs. Boucher, you and your husband have the choice of either continuing to be the source of Pierre's problems or becoming a catalyst for their solution." When he stood up, indicating that the session was over, he added, "The family is always the culprit." Then he advised her in a mild but lecturing tone, "You and your husband should never lose sight of this fundamental fact, Mrs. Boucher."

In the car, Jacqueline expressed her displeasure with Dr. Cloutier, describing what he said as nonsensical rubbish, and saying that she had never heard of a defiant oppositional disorder. She said Dr. Cloutier did not look like a professional therapist but rather an opinionated giant vagabond. "I have never heard about Cloutier's teacher, this Dr. R. D. Laing. Who is this R. D. Laing?"

"I am not sure. But I saw in one of Dr. Cloutier's bookcases French and Japanese translations of his English books. He seems to be a famous British psychiatrist or philosopher," responded Pierre, who was immensely delighted by Dr. Cloutier's verdict and advice. He admired the wisdom of both Cloutier and Laing, whoever he was.

"The British have no idea about philosophy and psychiatry. They never made any significant contribution in either field," his mother asserted with exasperated conviction.

# CHAPTER 7

Pierre recalled that his mother, Jacqueline, after Dr. Cloutier's exasperating positive diagnosis and prognosis of his case, had immediately resolved to take him to her college friend, Dr. Isabelle Bourdin, a private clinical psychologist. However, his father, who had no faith in talk therapists, psychologists in general, and Dr. Isabelle Bourdin in particular—personally and professionally—insisted that Pierre should see a family friend, Professor Bernard Lacan, the preeminent psychiatrist. So Pierre ended up seeing three highly-experienced professionals, Dr. Cloutier, Professor Lacan, and Dr. Bourdin, at the tender age of fifteen.

Dr. Isabelle Bourdin still held a very prominent place in Pierre's mind and heart. He still vividly recalled the first time his eyes fell on her stunning beauty. His mother had accompanied him to the first session. Isabelle hugged Jacqueline warmly, and then gave her cheek to Pierre to kiss it in a civil way. But it sent an electric charge through his whole body. Pierre did not experience a sexual arousal, which happened in subsequent sessions, because of the presence of his mother. Moreover, the three of them were seated in armchairs, with Isabelle holding a pen and a notebook in her lap. In that first session, Isabelle never stood up and faced him long enough. In later sessions, whenever she stood up facing him, he found himself spontaneously sexually aroused. Since then he had become conditioned to have a reflexive erection whenever he found himself standing face-to-face with a gorgeous woman, and he had been hoping for years to outgrow it.

Pierre attended five sessions with Professor Lacan and found him a cheerful and cheering man, warm and affable. In the first session, Lacan put a fatherly hand on Pierre's shoulder and led him to a comfortable chair at his elegant and expensive desk. He said jovially that God had taken good care of Pierre by bestowing on him Jacqueline's looks, rather than his father's. Then he sat behind his desk in a cream-colored leather chair. The balding professor was not a tall man, but he looked big and tall nonetheless and had a boyish face despite his sixty-something years.

In the first session, Pierre related to the professor some of his traumatic childhood incidents: how his father had thrown him into a public swimming pool to swim or sink, and how he was saved from drowning by a muscular man who had wanted to teach his father a lesson, but Jacqueline smoothed things over, sparing his father a humiliating public thrashing; how his father had slapped him on the face when he refused to go to school on the first day of school; and how he had given him a brutal hiding with his belt when Pierre escaped from school in the third grade. Pierre could see that Lacan failed to maintain his professional composure, for his face betrayed a mixture of dismay and revulsion. He averted his eyes, opened his mouth to say something but refrained, and then gazed at the notebook on the top of his desk for a few moments before saying in a composed and solemn tone, "Pierre, you must be proud of yourself. I think you are unbreakable. Any sane father would be proud to have you as a son." At the end of the session, he put his hand on Pierre's shoulder with sincere warmth, as he walked with him to the reception area and bid him a warm farewell.

At the time, Pierre decided not to tell Lacan about the closet incident, for he did not want to tarnish his father's image further in the eyes of his close friend, Bernard Lacan.

During another session, Lacan leaned back in his chair and asked in a casual tone, "Have you ever experienced hallucinations, Pierre?"

"Never," Pierre responded emphatically.

"Have you ever heard voices in your head?"

"Not in my head," answered Pierre. And a bit confused, he added, "I don't know how to describe this. Perhaps in my head. Over the last five years, something happened to me eight or ten times." He paused, and the professor waited for a few moments before saying, "Go on. Say it in any way you want. You don't need to be perfect."

"On these eight or ten occasions, I heard someone calling my name in a soft voice, Pierre Boucher or just Pierre, from behind. But when I turned, I found no one."

"Was it a male or female voice, Pierre?"

"Always a male voice," Pierre replied. "Always a male voice, Bernard." He used the name Bernard because the professor had told him from the outset that it was advisable to use their first names.

"Did it sound like your father's voice?"

"No. It was always a soft and friendly voice."

"You shouldn't be worried about that. It is either a sign of episodic anxiety or a mild sense of abandonment. You don't have any indication of acute anxiety or a disturbing need for love. And you have no history of anxiety or panic attacks. So I don't recommend resorting to antianxiety medication, particularly at your age. However, if you ever experience an anxiety attack, which I don't foresee, just come to my clinic as a walk-in patient. You don't need to make an appointment."

At the end of the last session, Professor Lacan pronounced, "I can honestly tell you that you don't have any serious psychiatric problems, though you have some normal teenage rebellion issues. And I think they are bound to disappear in a few years, bearing in mind your strong self-confidence. This is indicative of resilience, Pierre. And with resilience, one can meet life's challenges with courage and resourcefulness. Some clear indications of that are the facts that you have weathered horrific abuse, you are performing well at school, and you are capable of standing up to authority figures."

"Thanks, Bernard."

"I do mean it, Pierre." Lacan clasped his hands in front of him and looked at Pierre. "It is my considered opinion that you don't need psychiatric intervention. I recommend talk therapy with a good professional. The two of you could work on the normal rebellion issues you have." The professor paused before adding, "If you give me your consent, Pierre, I could phone Jacqueline about my recommendation."

Pierre could perceive that Lacan was appalled by his father's behavior and he did not want to contact him. Pierre was very pleased by that. At once, he replied, "Of course, you have my consent." He was thrilled by Professor Lacan's recommendation, for it meant more sessions with the ravishing Isabelle Bourdin.

Pierre found Dr. Isabelle Bourdin dazzlingly attractive and articulate, but she had a somewhat authoritative professional bearing that seemed to make her more alluring to him. She was always elegantly dressed in skirts short enough to show her comely legs and erotic knees. He had never known before that a woman's knees could be downright sexual. He thought she should have been a cinema star not a clinical psychologist.

He told her all he had told Professor Lacan but added the barbaric closet incident when he was seven. He thought that mentioning it to Isabelle would endear him to her. He had always been proud of his almost metaphysical childhood metamorphosis.

Isabelle did not label him as depressive, anxious, or having any particular personality disorder. She focused on what she called schemas—negative maladaptive, adaptive, and positive adaptive schemas—which are usually developed in childhood. They are coping styles adopted by a child to cope with his world. She emphasized to him, "Nobody can blame himself or his parents for negative maladaptive schemas, Pierre. They can be caused by an amalgam of things. An inherited disposition, a certain gene, the lack of a nurturing home environment, something acquired from one's peers or teachers at school, or simply an unfortunate circumstance or experience. Or a cocktail of some of these elements."

"I see, Isabelle." The very name still tantalized him to this day.

"Pierre, psychiatry, psychology, and neurology have a long way to go to pinpoint with certainty how some people develop a certain schema," she said in her seductive voice. She paused to see if he was digesting what she said. She clasped her elegant hands, looking at Pierre, who gazed daringly at her large blue eyes. "Even siblings raised in the same home and school environment adopt different coping styles. And psychological schemas are coping responses to our environment, to other people, and to the unfortunate blows that life deals to us regardless of family environment, gender or intelligence," she asserted in her sexy voice.

He felt a strong urge to stand up and suck her delicious lips but managed to control himself. The very idea frightened him, but he assured himself that he was in full control of his senses and would never try to seduce, or sexually assault, her.

In another session, she told him that maladaptive schemas might remain dormant for a long time until they are triggered by adverse events or circumstances. She explained to him that the healing process requires three steps: first, identifying the maladaptive schema; second, gradually eliminating or mitigating its negative components; and third, trying to replace the maladaptive schema with a healthy and positive schema. She said this was a long process but assured him that working together they would succeed. Whenever a session ended, she walked toward him and stood talking to him face to face, and he found himself instinctively sexually aroused. He usually put his left hand in his trousers pocket, deflected his erect penis to the side, and held it firmly until he left the building.

Pierre recalled that after his sessions with Dr. Isabelle Bourdin, he kept trying to recapture her face and voice at night in the darkness of his room. Sometimes, her beautiful face and seductive voice eluded him. Sometimes they were vivid and titillating.

After twelve sessions, Isabelle gave him a copy of an academic paper that she had authored on cognitive behavioral therapy. To his regret, she told him he didn't need further therapy, but he should digest all the insights that they had produced during the sessions. She advised him to read her academic paper. Over the following days, he read and reread Isabelle's eight pages like a zealot reading scripture. He committed some parts of the paper to memory, particularly a quote from William James, who, according to Isabelle, was the father of American psychology: 'If we wish to conquer undesirable emotional tendencies in ourselves, we must assiduously, and in the first instant cold-bloodedly, go through the outward motions of those contrary dispositions we prefer to cultivate.'

Pierre not only committed the words of the father of American psychology to memory but he acted on them. From that time, eight years ago, he adopted William James' advice. He decided that if the world wanted something, so be it. Just give it. Give people what they expect from you yet do your own bidding without causing outward ripples or aggravations. He took James' words as a personal message from Isabelle. Following Isabelle's intimation, he assiduously and cold-bloodedly stopped bullying other pupils and arguing with his teachers. He was amazed by how his popularity shot up among his peers, and how his teachers and the school administrators looked at him as an exemplary pupil. He even started engaging his father in conversations, and became even calmer, in the face of his father's unpredictable outbursts. That simply served to confound his father even further concerning his son's blasé insolence and sangfroid.

Now he fell asleep in his dormitory room as he was repeating William James' words, which he had memorized eight years ago because they had been passed to him from Isabelle Bourdin. Since then, they had become the guiding tenet in his life. They meant a lot to him—it was as though they were the words of Isabelle Bourdin and not William James. James had meant little, if anything, to the teenage Pierre.

The words were his silent and secret, but practical and enduring mantra.

# CHAPTER 8

Pierre slaved tirelessly over the following days putting the Auberts' apartment into a pristine condition after all its years of dereliction. Each morning before he went to the apartment, he went shopping for items such as cutlery, utensils, kerosene cooking stove and lamps, small kerosene containers, bedding, cushions for the sofa, and covers of different sizes for the tables. After depositing them in the apartment, he immediately started his taxing cleaning task and worked until four or five in the afternoon, with a short break for some cheese, bread, and wine. When he returned to his campus room, he showered, had some more bread, cheese and red wine, and lay on his bed physically exhausted, letting his ruminations crowd his mind. He shunned going out with his friends and spending evenings with his girlfriend, Catherine Derome.

One evening, as he lay on his bed after he showered, he recalled with striking vividness the day, about a year ago, when he stumbled on his mother's secret diary. It had happened a few weeks after Uncle Marcel's demise. Reading his mother's diary put him firmly on the path to his murderous plan. With his long-simmering but veiled resentment and fury at his father, Pierre was a time bomb that might explode anytime, though he was not consciously aware of it. And even if he had been, he would have had no clue when, how, or where it would go off. Jacqueline had returned to her job at the bank after her two-week compassionate leave, and Pierre had resumed his academic and social life with adequate interest, if not with his usual vigor.

It was a sunny day with a light-blue sky dotted with small, fluffy clouds. Pierre attended two lectures from ten to twelve and then hurried to the main library to catch up on the work he had missed while he mourned the death of his uncle. He stood on the steps of the three-story building, lit a cigarette, and decided to phone his mother on her cellphone, as he had done every day since she had returned to work, to nudge her spirits.

"Hello, *Maman.* How are you doing today?" he asked warmly.

"Thanks, Pierre. I am fine. And how are you doing?" asked his mother in a feeble, broken voice.

"I am working hard to catch up on the lecture material I missed. I am sure your colleagues are glad you are back."

"Oh, not today. I have taken the day off because I have a very bad bout of flu."

"You have to drink a lot of hot drinks. And ask Maryse to make you chicken soup. By the way, I have vitamin C tablets in my medicine cabinet. They are very effective in fighting the flu."

"I will do those things, Pierre. Take care."

"You too, *Maman*."

After working in the library for about an hour, it suddenly dawned on him that his mother never took a day off however bad her flu was. She was more than a conscientious bank executive; she was overly conscientious. Her taking a day off was a cry for help, he reflected. At once, he left the library with his small black case and raced home on his bike to check on his mother. At the time, he did not know he had made a momentous decision. A decision that would culminate in grave consequences—not immediately, but within a year.

When he reached home, he decided to be calm and collected so as not to ruffle his mother with his unexpected appearance. Maryse Gasnier, having completed her cooking and cleaning chores, had gone home. A heavy, ominous silence pervaded the house. He went upstairs and took his small zippered case to his bedroom before going to the master bedroom. He knocked gently for some time and there was no response. Not a sound. He opened the door, and his mother was not there. Obviously, his mother would be in the guest room, he decided; she had been withdrawn, in fact unequivocally detached, from his father since Marcel's death.

He knocked gently on the guest room door, which stood slightly ajar, for a few moments, telling himself to be patient. He knocked on the door again, but when there was no response, he gently opened the door and noiselessly entered the room. In the dim room, with its curtains still drawn, he could see his mother lying motionless in bed in a fetal position. On the bedside table, there was an almost empty bottle of vodka and her medication.

Next to his mother, there was an old studio portrait of Marcel in the uniform of a captain, obviously taken during his army days when he was in his prime. Marcel looked splendid and his eyes beamed with an undisguised youthful cockiness, a cockiness that had mellowed over the years and had been replaced with a harmonious balance of strength and gentleness that Marcel had called *la force tranquille*.

Then Pierre's eyes rested on a blue diary with a small, silver lock, lying open in front of her, and a small ball-point pen next to it. He picked up the diary and read the last entry: 'I have lost my only brother and now my life has little meaning, if it ever had any meaning at all. Life seems pointless. But I have to slog on for the sake of my dear son, the apple of—' She had not finished the sentence. He found himself quietly holding the blue diary and picking up the small key lying next to it. He paused, contemplating whether to read his mother's diary or not. I have to read it, he decided. Then he picked up the ball-point pen as well. As he left the room silently, he pulled the door behind him, leaving it slightly ajar.

As he read her diary entry by entry, in his bedroom, he felt like an overheating pressure cooker. His mother sporadically disclosed her marital tribulations, her depression and anxiety, changes made by Professor Lacan in her medication, and how she responded to each type of tablet and capsule. More stunning were her suspicions of her husband's affairs with women who, with their husbands, were very close family friends. She used the first letters in the names of these women, and she used 'C.' to refer to her husband, Christian. It was not difficult for Pierre to decipher the initials B.V. and N.G., Brigitte Villard and Nicole Gautier. Jacqueline was certain about her husband's affair with Mrs. Villard, and a number of incidents supported her suspicions about his affairs with Mrs. Gautier, and 'M.R.', Monique Roget. A few pages before the end of her entries, his mother wrote: 'C. is a filthy dog. Now he is fornicating with B.V., a whore with the mask of an angel; N.G., a bitch in heat; and M.R., a sweet but conniving slut. How could these women cheat on their decent and loving husbands?'

This entry gashed a hole in his heart. He stared through the page without seeing it. He sensed that dark clouds were gathering around him. After a few minutes in which fury smoldered within him, he heaved a deep sigh of profound resentment. As he glanced around the room, he took a few slow and deep breaths. He felt dazed and detached as he held the diary in his hand. This could not be happening in his family. It should not be happening. His mind seemed to have stopped functioning. He stared at the white cupboard in front of him; he could not see it. His mind was somewhere else—in a place that was not accessible to reason.

Presently, he closed the explosive diary in disgust. His senses were flooded with a miasma of filth and baseness, arising from the morass of adultery, infidelity, and duplicity. He decided to keep the diary and take it to campus lest it fell into the hands of his father while Jacqueline was still asleep. He locked it with its tiny key and put them and the ball-point pen in his black case, telling himself that since his mother resorted to writing in her diary only sporadically, she may not miss it for weeks. And if she did miss it, her suspicions would settle squarely on her grisly husband. He was glad that he had decided to come home today; otherwise his father could have found the diary and read it while his mother was still asleep.

Retribution. Retribution and retribution, he mused. Nothing but retribution. But retaliatory retribution in the heat of the moment would be rash and premature, he cautioned himself. I am no longer the hotheaded adolescent I used to be. If my retribution is to emanate from my free will, it ought to be well conceived, well planned, and well timed.

Back in his campus room, Pierre opened a bottle of red wine, took a swig, and lay on his bed, putting the bottle on the floor next to the bed. He went through his mother's diary again with undiminished rage and disgust. When he came to the end of the entries, he closed the diary and placed it on the floor next to the wine bottle.

He stared up at the ceiling, then closed his eyes. A strange sensation took hold of him. With his eyes closed, he felt detached from his body. He could see himself in a separate body, standing not far from his bed. It was another Pierre Boucher, silent and unruffled, yet his bearing was amiable. With his eyes still closed, Pierre experienced an undeniable affinity to the silent, impassive, but warm Pierre. He admired him and wanted to emulate his unruffled calm. As he kept his mind's eye on the other Pierre Boucher, who stood not far from his bed for a long time, he sensed that this Pierre Boucher was saying many things to him despite—or perhaps because of—his serenity. He was telling him to have the guts to take aggressive action, not to retreat in front of obstacles, not to let down his mother. Pierre opened his eyes. The other Pierre was not there. He had simply vanished.

He was left perplexed by this confounding experience. What did it mean? From where did the other Pierre materialize? Did he come from another universe? Did he come from a nonhuman domain though he seemed very human? Although he could not answer these questions, he did not feel unsettled by the experience. In fact, he felt that silent and composed Pierre's thoughts were identical to his own thoughts. He closed his eyes again, and again he could see the other Pierre standing near his bed, silent, cool, and collected. Opening his eyes, the other Pierre was not there.

What is happening to my mind? Reflecting deeply for a long time and recalling the image of the other Pierre at will, he decided there was nothing wrong with his mind.

Perhaps there is another human being inside every human being, he reflected. Is this what some people call 'one's double'? Sometimes the two are poles apart in their thinking, sometimes they are at odds to different degrees, and sometimes they are congruent in their thinking. Just like my double, the other Pierre, and me. He is not in conflict with me; on the contrary, he supports me and backs my resolve. We are thoroughly compatible.

He wondered if this other Pierre was the one who used to call his name softly in his teen years. It had happened a number of times; he'd occasionally heard someone softly calling, 'Pierre. Pierre Boucher', behind his back and when he turned toward the source of the gentle voice, he had found no one. These isolated incidents stopped when he reached the age of seventeen or eighteen. However, he always found the voice somewhat soothing rather than disturbing. There was affinity and warmth about that voice. Now this other Pierre struck him as warm and supportive. Both the soft voice and now this other Pierre seemed comforting and heartwarming. If I have a double, he is on my side, he reflected. We are not in conflict or dissension. My double and I are standing side by side. We are on the same wavelength. We are standing up for each other.

It had taken Pierre almost a year to settle on the irreversible decision to eliminate his father's three mistresses. After reading and rereading his mother's diary, he had mulled over many options, such as challenging his father with the facts, confronting one or all three women, talking to their cuckolded husbands, sending unsigned poison-pen letters to the husbands, hiring a private detective to capture photos of at least one of his father's affairs as irrefutable evidence, starting a fire in Nicole Gautier's beauty salon, and tampering with the brakes on Monique Roget's car. Each idea had gotten him worked up. He'd gone as far as writing unsigned letters to the cuckolded husbands but he did not send them. He researched the best accelerants to use to start an uncontrollable fire in Nicole's beauty salon. Each time, he abandoned the idea. He was floundering in a swamp of consuming but conflicting solutions and alternatives. For instance, he got the telephone numbers of two private detective agencies. But then he worried that if he sent incriminating photos to the sleazy newspaper *Le Matin* and it published them, that would embarrass and crush his mother.

Since that fateful day, vengeful scenarios kept percolating in his mind: changing, converging, diverging, and calibrating on their own accord. After scrutinizing one scenario and discarding it, another leaped into his mind, only to meet the same fate. Finally, they condensed into one course of action pregnant with profound certainty: eliminating his filthy father's three mistresses.

After that long restive period of fermentation, the idea of eliminating the three mistresses gripped him. He brooded over it for weeks, and though he discarded it a number of times, it kept returning with more force. Then one day, the die was cast and the battle lines were drawn clearly in his heart and mind. With that firm resolution, details of how to carry out the plan started to spring into his mind almost unbidden, setting the irreversible course of events leading to tragic consequences. Actually, he had reached the point of no-return in his plan, before he fortuitously met Martine Aubert at La Librairie Stendhal.

Was it the devil that proffered the mélange of vengeful scenarios? No. He did not believe in the devil or in angels. He believed in God only. God gave us a large and complex brain and the freedom to make our own decisions. God does not interfere in our free will, he believed. Or was it his double— the other, silent, amiable Pierre? Probably, he thought. The other Pierre is planting ideas in my mind from his unearthly universe. However, my double's ideas are completely congruent with my own free-will decisions.

He knew he had to do a lot of planning. He needed money for purchasing a used car, and renting an apartment, so he started withdrawing small amounts from his bank account: five thousand euros, then eight thousand, then seven thousand, and so on. All in all, he withdrew eighty-five thousand euros. He hid part of it in the large briefcase in his campus bedroom, but he stashed most of it in the small safe in his bedroom at home.

Now, lying on his dormitory bed, he glanced around his small campus room with its desk, two small chairs, a small washbasin, and four shelves packed with books, and then he looked at his wristwatch. It was almost midnight. He decided to stop reviewing the past. I need some sleep, since I have to resume work at the rue Karl Marx apartment tomorrow morning. It is hard work but it is worth it, he reflected. The Auberts' apartment is a God-sent sanctuary to carry out my plan, meticulously and stealthy. Thanks to Martine and her father. I must ensure that their reputation will not be compromised by a single blunder or faux pas on my part.

He switched off the bedside lamp. As he started to drift into sleep he sensed a soft spot for Martine gently and deeply planting itself in his heart.

# CHAPTER 9

As Pierre labored to restore the dusty and stuffy apartment to its lost glory, he kept in touch with both Martine and Catherine by phone. One afternoon, Martine called and told him she had the copy of Omar Khayyam's book in her office at La Librairie Stendhal; he promised to stop by and collect it the next day. After a few hours of unflagging work, he reached a point at which he decided that the apartment was now in a pristine and fragrant condition. It was ready for him to move into.

In his dormitory, he showered, alternating the water between cold and hot, and then he put on clean underwear, a blue shirt, and jeans. He was not sure if he would be able to see Catherine again after this evening, when he would disappear into the rue Karl Marx apartment, though he hoped he would. However, tonight he had to tell her about his plan to go to Cameroon and he knew he had to come up with a plausible and well-presented explanation, for Catherine had an incisive mind.

Carrying a bottle of red wine, he crossed the green lawn between his dormitory and hers. The streetlamps on campus were already on, and the birds had settled in the trees for a peaceful night. He knocked on the door and waited a few moments before knocking harder. Catherine, slim and petite, opened the door wearing a long, beige, cotton dress with thin shoulder straps. With her large eyes, oval face, and long, unkempt hair, she radiated a bohemian feminine appeal. She gave him a big, warm smile before embracing him, and then bit his lower lip. They kissed, and as Pierre closed the door with the back of his right shoe, she complained, teasingly, "You just disappear for ages and then resurface when you want to. How cruel of you, Pierre!"

"I do apologize, Cathy. I have been so busy working on my damned dissertation," he lied.

He placed the bottle on her desk, held her closely, and maneuvered her to the small bed. They tumbled onto it and started kissing and cuddling. Then she jumped up and said, with a charming smile, "Horny Pierre, let us first have some wine before you impale me."

"Cathy, I adore everything about you. So the moment I see you I get very hot."

As she filled two glasses with wine, she teased him, "I know that, Pierre. You are a sex maniac."

"May be. But your physique will turn any man into a sex maniac."

She handed him his glass of wine and took a swig from her wine, mixed with water. "You know I love everything about myself except my tiny breasts. I am sure men always prefer large breasts."

"Cathy, I am not the type of person who loves a woman depending on the size of her breasts."

"I know, my Pierre. But I always wished to have larger breasts," she said, then lit two cigarettes and gave one to Pierre.

"Thanks," he mumbled.

"I am going to Toulouse this weekend to attend the wedding of one of my first cousins to a gorgeous Russian girl who is a software engineer."

"Oh, that's lovely, Cathy. It will be a nice family reunion, I presume." Pierre sounded as though he was posing a question.

"Well, our family reunions are not always nice, but I still enjoy them. There is lots of laughter, catching up, and gossip, but the usual family put-downs and backstabbing. And of course, I will be playing my guitar. I'll be taking the one you gave me. I am sure my mother will interrogate me. 'Where did you get this new guitar? How much did it cost? You already own a guitar, why buy another one? Am I concentrating on my studies or wasting my time playing my guitar?' She is a domineering lunatic."

"Why should she ask such questions, Cathy?" he asked from the bed, puffing on his cigarette.

"You'd better ask her. I will take you one weekend to Toulouse to see how she criticizes my father and me about almost anything. I think it was mother who gave me an inferiority complex about my breasts. She has been critical of them since I was sixteen. 'Where did you get those mini breasts from, Cathy? Your chances of getting a suitable man are as tiny as your breasts, Cathy."' She paused and then asked, "Can you imagine that?"

"Of course I can imagine it. There are a lot of people like your mother. You know my father is much worse than your mother is. Abusive, draconian, and arrogant."

"My mother is a neurotic, obsessive-compulsive maniac. Poor Dad is living in hell. After I graduate, my mother will be lucky if she sees me even at Christmas. I will arrange to meet my father as often as I can without her knowledge," she said, adding in a pensive voice, "Poor Dad. He has always supported me and encouraged me behind my mother's back."

"If your mother is a lunatic, my father is Lucifer incarnate."

She stubbed out her cigarette, stood up, and took off her long dress. Pierre could see that, as usual, she was not wearing anything under her dress. He always approved of the way she flouted many of the conventions and norms of society. He unbuckled his belt but Catherine hastily ordered in mock seriousness, "Don't move. Don't touch anything. Let me undress you, *mon petit Pierre*. With the pressure of your dissertation, I doubt you can have a solid erection.

"I will do my best for *ma petite Cathy.*"

She undressed him hurriedly before she straddled his naked body, in her full nudity. As usual, they enjoyed their torrid carnal ritual where she climaxed twice for his sole orgasm. When Pierre shrieked with ecstasy, he collapsed on top of her before rolling to her side. With her back touching the wall next to the bed, her mind was still blown out with the spasms of her two giddy orgasms. They nuzzled tenderly and remained silent, savoring the rapture of their fulfilling and gratifying sex.

He stared up at the poster of Guevara, with his handsomely bearded face and eternally haunting gaze. Few people even remember Guevara now, Pierre reflected, but this is the rebellious Cathy's bedroom. He was debating how to tell her about his plan to go to Cameroon; he was not debating *whether* to tell her because that was already a settled issue.

After a while, Cathy whispered, "Why are you so silent, Pierre?"

"Oh, nothing," he said casually.

"I sense you are preoccupied. Is it your dissertation, a family problem, or something else? Just tell me."

Pierre took a deep breath and remained silent.

"Just tell your Cathy." She playfully slapped his shoulder twice. "If you have any problem, I can help you. Don't forget, I am the lawyer here. Lawyers can fix any problem, not like you political scientists who are always creating problems, and more problems."

Pierre turned his face toward her as they lay in bed and answered, "I don't have a problem, Cathy. But I have decided to drop out of the university."

"What!" exclaimed Catherine. She propped herself up on her elbow and looked into his eyes. "There must be something wrong with you. You should see a shrink," she said in a serious tone, then climbed out of bed and sat on the desk chair, stark naked.

From the bed came Pierre's voice, calm and matter-of-fact. "I have decided to go to Cameroon—"

"What?" she interrupted him. She stood up, donned her long dress, and then sat on the chair with palpable bafflement on her face. "Going to Cameroon!" she exclaimed in a low voice, unable to believe what he declared. "Are you kidding me?"

"No, I am not kidding you, Cathy. I intend to do humanitarian work. I find my studies meaningless. Not difficult or boring, but meaningless and useless."

Catherine nervously lit a cigarette. "What a story. Humanitarian work!" She puffed heavily at her cigarette and exhaled a long stream of smoke. "For how long?" she asked, fixing her eyes on his face.

For a moment or two, he avoided looking at her. Then he returned her gaze. "Two to three years."

"I don't understand you, Pierre. What about us?" Resentment was evident in her tone.

Pierre looked at her with hurt and concern on his face. "Let me explain my plan to you, Cathy."

"You have never discussed this crazy plan with me. Now, after you have made your decision, you want to explain it to me." Her voice was bristling with hostility. She was like a provoked lioness. Pierre was taken aback. He had expected some questions and even reservations from her, but not immediate out-and-out antagonism.

"You are the first person I am discussing this matter with." He was lying, but he thought he had to. He wanted to appease her if she gave him the opportunity to do so.

"I don't care. You go to Cameroon for two to three years. What do you expect? Do you want me to join you in Cameroon, or do you want me to wait for *Your Majesty* to return, and then resume our relationship as if nothing had happened?" she asked, thrusting her index finger aggressively toward him. He sat up. "Please, let me—"

Still incredulous, she interrupted him in a low voice. It was the voice of someone who has not given up all hope. "Tell me you are not serious. Tell me you are simply pulling my leg."

Pierre stood up, put on his T-shirt and boxer shorts, and assumed his blasé demeanor.

"Cathy, I am very serious. And we should not allow this to destroy our relationship."

"What does your family think about your dropping out of the university and your crusade to save the Cameroonians?"

"I don't care about their views. They can't run my life or overrule my decisions." He paused, looking at Catherine, and immediately sensed that his response had rekindled her hostility. He continued in a calm but very emphatic tone, "The decision is mine. I make my own decisions and bear the consequences. I thought that while I am in Cameroon—"

She stood up with a defiant and belligerent look in her eyes. "So you make your own decisions and bear the consequences! That is fine with me. I will not allow you or anybody else to make decisions for me either."

He interposed, "Cathy, let me—"

She disregarded what he wanted to say, pointed her index finger at him, and yelled, "Don't you ever call me Cathy. Now leave my room and go to Cameroon or the South Pole. It is a matter of complete indifference to me."

He looked into her eyes and realized she was deeply hurt. He decided to try to mollify her, and as he was mulling over what to say, she blurted, "Don't look at me like an idiot. Put on your damned clothes and leave at once." There was an undisguised finality in her tone.

As he started putting on his trousers, he said, "Catherine, I want to—"

She interrupted him instantly. "You'd better forget about me and our relationship at once and forever. You are a big fake, and I am glad that I discovered it early." The swiftness of her response reminded him of the cut-throat technique she effectively utilized in political debates; she was capable of making mincemeat of any opponent.

After he put on his shoes, still hoping to appease her, he tried to put his hand gently on her shoulder. She immediately stepped back and shouted, "Don't touch me. Don't you ever touch me." She strode to the door, flung it open, and gestured with her hand for him to leave.

Pierre was stunned. He had never expected anything like this. As he walked toward the door, a sense of remorse descended upon him. Yet he was not going to reveal to her, or to anyone, that the whole thing was a temporary ruse. At the open door, he stopped, looked at her, and softly said, "I will send you an e-mail to explain everything."

"Don't waste my time with your explanations. You suck. Just get lost," she shouted and slammed the door with a resounding bang behind him. He could hear her locking the door with violent force.

Cathy, her fury mounting, moved a few steps from the locked door and started screeching, "Damn you, Pierre Boucher! Damn you, you bastard!" She fell silent and took a deep breath, moving to the middle of her room. Planting her spread feet on the floor, she raised her clenched fists toward the ceiling and yelled at the top of her voice, "You bastard. You son-of-a-bitch." She kept yelling until she felt drained. She fell onto her bed, filled with burning anger rather than sadness. Being a plucky and hard-boiled woman, she told herself that she had to move on with her life. Good riddance, Pierre; you would have derailed my life if I had married you.

Pierre shuffled back to his dormitory downcast and dispirited. He knew Catherine was a fiercely independent and ambitious woman, yet he had not expected such an explosive and irrational reaction from her. She must be nuts, he thought. He had never seen this dark side of her during their two-year relationship. What a wildcat she'd turned out to be. Yet, it pained him that he still loved her, and worse, he was not actually going to Cameroon.

In his room, he sat on the chair at his desk, reflecting for some time on Catherine's wildness and acrimony. Then he stood up, switched off the light, walked to his bed, and, touching its edge in the darkness, collapsed into it without undressing or taking off his shoes. The darkness seemed to soothe him; it fit his mood. Human life is sheer angst and anguish, he thought, but he would slog on. His father's barbaric abuse of him and his mother must be met with formidable force. Casanova's words, which he'd memorized a year earlier, came to his mind: 'In the physical world anything that strikes is subjected to the same force in reaction; but in the moral world the reaction is stronger than the action. The reaction from being imposed upon is scorn; the reaction from hatred is murder.'

He mulled over Casanova's words. He found them true, very much true, and flawless. Few people think of Casanova as a wise man, but Pierre found these words not only wise but also therapeutic. He recalled that he had these words by Casanova recorded in one of his literary journals.

Whatever Catherine decided to do, he was not going to abandon his plans. He consoled himself with the thought that once his plans were successfully executed and the dust had settled, he could find a way to resume his relationship with Catherine. After three months. After six months. Or even after one year. Who knows?

At last, he fell asleep.

# CHAPTER 10

Pierre spent almost a week before moving into the Auberts' apartment, saying goodbye to his university friends and colleagues, and attending boisterous farewell parties thrown by them. He distributed all his textbooks and most of his novels to various friends. He felt very sentimental about his leaving his friends, and knew he would forever keep fond memories of them, his university days, and his city.

He steadily and secretly moved all the belongings that he decided to keep into the apartment: the thousands of euros he had kept at home and at campus, his clothes, shoes, novels, laptop; and also new purchases, including three cheap cellphones and cushions for the sofa set. He took the Beretta, the silencer, and the Winchester bullets from Uncle Marcel's trunk, and kept them with the rest of his murder kit in the large brief case, which he placed in the cupboard of the master bedroom of the apartment. He also retained the keys to the trunk, the store where it was kept, and the keys to his family house. Inside the large briefcase, he put his two passports on top of the bundles of banknotes. One passport for Pierre

Boucher, and the other for Martin Lavoie. He recalled that the latter passport was sent to him by Marcel two years ago, after he kept inviting Pierre to visit him in South Africa to meet his friends, especially Bill Miller's family. Marcel had assured him that he would love Africa and the Africans, particularly the women. The name Martin Lavoie was fictitious, conjured up by Pierre at the time, as he wanted to upset his father by not telling him if he ever decided to go to Africa. However, the passport itself was authentic, with Pierre's photo. Marcel had acquired it for him through one of his government cronies.

I am like an animal hoarding things for a long period of hibernation, quiet and peaceful hibernation, but my hibernation will be loaded with vicious, though justified, acts. Anyway, now I don't need to venture into the city; I have to keep my outings to the shabby tobacconists, newspaper shops, brasseries, groceries, laundry and dry cleaning places in the poor and sorry edge of the city—nearest to my hideout.

On the day he decided to move into the apartment, he bought a compact radio/CD player, and double the number of the batteries necessary to operate the set. He also bought classic music CDs for Beethoven, Mozart and Brahms, as well as jazz music CDs for Duke Ellington, Ella Fitzgerald, and Louis Armstrong, and an Edith Piaf CD. Then he went to Martine's office. She was hugely delighted that he was moving into the apartment that evening. He tantalized her by refusing to describe to her the new condition of the apartment. And it took him a lot of persuasion to convince her to accept one thousand euros, which she could use whenever he asked her to buy food, wine or anything for the apartment—to reduce his need to venture out of the apartment.

She gave him back two of the three cellphones, which he had bought under the name of Jean-Claude Marchand, and asked her to charge their batteries, then she gave him the copy of *The Ruba'iyat of Omar Khayyam*, which she had promised him. After kissing passionately, Martine agreed she would be coming tomorrow evening to the apartment. "I am excited about seeing you and the effort you put into transforming the apartment," she said enthusiastically.

He cycled to the apartment, where he left all his purchases, Omar Khayyam's book, and one of the new cellphones, then cycled home to tell his parents one more lie: that he would be going to Paris early the next morning.

He took a shower in his bedroom, and felt very excited by the fact that the time for action was upon him. After taking a short nap, he dressed and went downstairs to see his parents. He found them sitting in the living room in armchairs separated by about two meters, and, as usual, not communicating but emitting vibes of resignation to a hopelessly dysfunctional marriage. They were silently nursing their aperitifs before consuming their dinner, which was usually prepared by their skillful cook and cleaner, Mrs. Maryse Gasnier.

Pierre said with some cheer, "*Bon soir.*"

His mother responded with evident delight, "How good to see you, Pierre."

His father gave a drab, "*Bon soir.*"

Pierre decided to be brief and direct. He stood a few steps from his pitiable parents with his hands in his pockets. "I have to travel to Paris tomorrow to spend a few days with the staff of the NGO before flying to Cameroon. So tomorrow morning, I will be going to the railway station from the university." He glanced at each one of them before adding, "You don't need to see me off at the station."

"And who said we were going to?" asked his father with a subdued edge of hostility. "Neither of us will see you off at the station."

Pierre liked what his father said, for in a way it was an explicit order for his mother not to bid him farewell at the railway station. That suited him, for he was not going to the station anyway.

Suddenly, Christian stood up, stared at his son, and declared, "As you said before, this is your life. You can go to Africa. You can go to hell." He stood for a few moments as if he wanted to add something but he did not. He must have decided not to waste his breath because he never refrained from saying whatever he wanted to say.

Jacqueline, suffocated by the sickening hostility of her husband toward their only offspring, said, "Christian, don't you want to wish Pierre the best of luck? He is leaving France for a long time."

Christian stared at his wife and exclaimed, "Best of luck!" Then he frowned at Pierre. "I can't wish him any luck on something I don't approve of." He strode toward the staircase, leaving them alone.

Jacqueline whispered, almost apologetically, "Pierre, you have to understand what drives your father. He can't comprehend how anyone, particularly his own son, cannot aim for the very top in any career. Not only aim for the top but also have to achieve it. He wanted you to study medicine, you refused, and he was really disappointed. And when you decided to study political science, he expected you to get a master's degree and then a doctorate. He wanted you to be a political science professor or a political thinker and writer."

"You know very well I don't care one iota about what he thinks. He can't impose on me or others his own benchmarks."

Jacqueline had a pensive look on her face. "Your father is an overachiever and he expects those close to him to be overachievers. I know he is not happy that I am still a deputy branch manager at the bank. He can't understand or accept that I am happy and content with my job."

"That is his problem. I am very glad you are happy and content with your job."

"Just take his brother, Charles-Maurice. Your father despises his own brother and they are barely on speaking terms. Why? Because Charles-Maurice, after getting his bachelor's degree in history, decided to become a teacher. Your father thinks his brother is a useless loser. The fact that Charles-Maurice is now a secondary-school headmaster, happily married, and has three lovely children is neither here nor there as far as your father is concerned," said Jacqueline in a low voice.

"So to him, achievement—or rather, overachievement—is more important than happiness?"

"Yes, Pierre. Regrettably so. Your father, deep inside himself, is very insecure. He is an unhappy man despite his distinguished career. His is driven by internal demons of which he might not be consciously aware. He will go to his grave without coming to terms with himself or his nearest and dearest."

"He has got it all wrong then. So in his twilight years he will look back with great regret at how he missed the most precious things in life: love and happiness."

"I don't know if he will ever come to that realization." She sounded both sad and sorry.

"But with people outside the family, he is an excellent listener. A charmer. Don't you think so, *Maman*?"

"I think his most serious weakness is his insatiable hunger for attention and adoration by others. All his overachievement is a desperate reaching out for adoration. With outsiders, he makes everyone think she or he is the center of the universe. And in return he expects glorification and idolization from them. He thinks this is love. Which is not," said Jacqueline, heaving a sigh. She paused, mulling earnestly over something, before adding, "You are my only child and my only true friend. I have to be very open with you. Now you are going to Cameroon and I will be very lonely. However, I don't want you to change your plans. I want you to live your life the way you want to live it. Otherwise, I will be failing you as my son and failing myself as a mother, Pierre."

Pierre knew she was not going to be lonely for long; after taking care of the three sluts who, he was certain, had caused his mother immense anguish, he might resurface in three months, or at most, six. "*Maman*, I promise you, if I don't like it in Cameroon I will be back in a maximum of six months. I think you can tolerate my absence for such a short period."

His mother smiled and seemed a bit relieved. "I hope that will be the case." A smile brightened her face briefly. "You never know. I might join you in Cameroon."

Pierre beamed and held her hand tightly as he chuckled. "That would be a great idea. And just leave this beast in France." They both laughed.

"Are you sure you don't want me to bid you farewell at the station?" asked Jacqueline. "I don't care about what your father said."

"I know. But I don't want you to leave your work to come to the station."

After a few moments, his mother cautioned him, "Take care of yourself. Don't let yourself get an infectious or horrible African disease."

He could see tears welling in her eyes. Gently wiping her tears, he pleaded, "*Maman*, please don't do that. Your Pierre is a grown-up man and is as tough and resilient as any Dillon."

"Unfortunately, I don't have the Dillons' resilience. I have inherited the fragility of the Rollins. Most members of my maternal family, the Rollins, are sensitive and easily breakable," she said, and stood up.

"You are not breakable. You are stronger than you think you are."

With a smile, she said, "If you say so, then I am stronger than I think I am."

He wanted their conversation to end on a light note. So he said in a genial vein, "At least you and I have inherited our thick hair from the Dillons."

"No, not the Dillons. The Rollins are the ones who gave us thick hair."

"I didn't know that. So it is the Rollins, bless them." Then he said tenderly, "I have to go now, *Maman*."

"I know you are a sensible and resourceful man. You are capable of turning your Cameroon venture into a very rewarding experience."

"Thanks, *Maman*. Just wish me the best of luck."

Jacqueline's maternal instinct told her that her son was seeking something more than a simple wish for luck, but she couldn't put her finger on it. She found herself saying, "I am proud of you. I am very proud of you, *mon* Pierre."

Then he left home, and cycled to the abandoned apartment. As he rode, irrepressible certitude about the success of his criminal plan filled his heart. His heart and mind were devoid of fear, worry, and uncertainty. As he approached the apartment building, the headlight of the bicycle shone on a cat with three kittens ambling across the dark street. He swerved his bicycle with agility and avoided hitting the poor creatures. He was deeply pleased with himself.

# CHAPTER 11

Next morning, Pierre awoke in his new bed, and could hear pigeons cooing. He peered through the outer window's slants. He saw two pearl-gray pigeons dancing and cooing sweetly on the ledge of the window, unfettered by any concern. I have delightful company, he reflected. There was one small egg in an old nest.

He went into the spacious living room, in a buoyant mood, and decided to do his morning 200 push-ups before having anything to eat or drink. Putting an Ella Fitzgerald's CD on the compact set, he started his grueling exercise as he listened to her melting voice and moving tunes. I need my morning and evening push-ups to maintain my physical alertness and mental harmony, he told himself. After he finished his exercise, he took a shower then ate two croissants, and made himself a mug of black coffee.

As he settled on the couch, sipping his coffee, the large, framed photo of Martine's paternal grandfather on the wall opposite caught his eyes. As he stared up at it, he could detect behind the pince-nez a fierce predatory instinct in the old man's eyes.

That did not equate with the wonderful characteristics Martine had ascribed to her grandfather. It certainly takes the eye of a stranger—an outsider—to detect the hidden characteristics and inclinations to which family members are blind, he thought.

Did granddad Aubert have a murky side that he had masterfully concealed from his family until he died? Pierre wondered. It seems everyone has a dark side that he or she masks as long as possible—or forever: his own father, Christian; Granddad Aubert; Christian's three mistresses; Dr. Isabelle Bourdin; and he himself, Pierre Boucher, aka Jean-Claude Marchand.

He went into the bedroom, picked up the seven-hundred-and-fifty-something-page *Don Quixote*, and returned to the couch, putting under his head one of the new, orange-yellowish cushions he had bought three days ago. A short introduction pointed out that Cervantes was a devout Catholic who'd had a colorful life. He was a member of a cardinal's household, a diplomat, a soldier, a prisoner, a junior government official, and a struggling writer. Cervantes' solemn yet tongue-in-cheek style captivated him.

Time flew as he became engrossed in *Don Quixote*, but one hour before Martine's promised visit, he closed the book and stood up. He lit two kerosene lamps, putting one on the small table next to the right arm of the couch, and the other one on the dining table. At five minutes to eight, he descended the staircase to the small foyer with a flashlight. Just two minutes later Martine opened the main door carrying a plastic bag with some Chinese takeaway. They kissed passionately, like any new lovers. Inside the apartment, Martine put the bag on the marble table, and then glanced around the living room—in her elegant, richly yellow dress. "Oh, oh, I can't believe it," she screamed. "You have done a terrific job." She walked around the living room to take in more of what Jean-Claude had accomplished, and then gazed at him. "My father will be very pleased when I tell him about it." She put her hands over her mouth and her eyes twinkled as she marveled at the amazing state of the living room. "Wow! Wow! You have even cleaned the hallway, the stairs, and the landings. I hope you haven't broken your back, Jean-Claude."

"I think my back has become stronger, Martine." He focused the beam of the flashlight on Martine's grandfather. "I did not forget to clean the frame and glass of the photo of this great Aubert."

Martine seized Jean-Claude's face and gave him a long kiss. "You have done an awesome job, darling." Martine surveyed the living room again, now softly lit by kerosene lamps. "And you have bought new cushions and table covers."

Pierre turned off the flashlight, and walked to the dining table to open a bottle of wine, and Martine settled on the couch. She crossed her comely legs and picked up Cervantes' book. "You are reading *Don Quixote*. It is a fascinating book. I have read it twice."

Jean-Claude, still busy opening the bottle at the dining table, said, "It is a more than fascinating book, Martine." Then he brought two glasses of red wine, gave one to Martine, and settled next to her on the couch. He clicked his glass against hers. "I have decided to read *Don Quixote, The Red and the Black*, and *War and Peace*."

"That is a very good selection," Martine said. She sipped her wine, dwelling on its taste. "I like this wine."

"It's a merlot. I thought you would like it."

Martine flicked through *Don Quixote*, and started reading the introduction. In her old copy at home, there was no introduction, and she found this one interesting and well researched.

"Let's drink first and eat later, Martine."

"Fine with me," she replied and held up her glass for a refill.

After hot and passionate petting on the couch, Jean-Claude took a kerosene lamp, and gently led Martine to the bedroom and undressed her slowly, the way she always undressed herself. The lamp's light gave the bedroom a romantic aura, coating Martine's naked and supple body with a magical golden color. The seductive scent of her feminine perfume permeated the room, flooding it with arousing sensuality.

As Martine abandoned herself to her unbridled carnal moans, Jean-Claude whispered in mock deadpan, "Martine, please restrain your voice and moans so as not to disturb the pigeons sleeping on the window ledge."

She sweetly slapped his shoulder. "What a teaser!"

"Can you coo, darling?"

She laughed. "I can't coo." He joined in her laughter, before raising her shapely legs onto his shoulders.

Martine was wild with lusty passion, moaning loudly and leaving scratches on his back. He gently bit her shoulders and arms, and she encouraged him, "Harder, harder, please." Except for the erotic wobbling of her flushed breasts and erect nipples, her whole body was immobilized by his tight squeeze of frenzied indulgence. When she climaxed, her nostrils flared and her whole body flailed in intense waves of gratification before she surrendered to a calming sensation of stillness. Heavenly tranquility replaced the waves of ecstasy, washing her body, soul, and spirit. She mused that this was sex in a different dimension—in a metaphysical realm. All of the sex I experienced before Jean-Claude was amateurish and pathetic, she thought.

They silently embraced affectionately for some time before dressing and going into the living room. As they sat at the dining table for their green salad and Chinese-food meal, Martine commented, "It must be very quiet here by night."

"It's also very quiet during the day. The night is sometimes disturbed by dog and cat fights."

"I think short spells of solitude could be both relaxing and stimulating," she said.

"That is true. However, I find the cooing of the pigeons gives me a strange sense of nostalgia that is somehow soothing. I can't exactly describe it. It could be existential nostalgia."

Martine giggled at the term 'existential nostalgia'. "How many pigeons are giving you existential nostalgia?"

"There is a pair of pearl-gray pigeons nesting on the outer ledge of the bedroom window and an all-white pair in what looks like a newer nest on the kitchen window ledge."

"So you have nice company." She liked Jean-Claude's delight at having pigeons for company. Few people would pay attention to pigeons nesting on their window ledges. There is something special about this young man, she thought. She chided herself for the fact that, so far, she wanted to see more and more of him for the breathtaking sex he served her without fail. But he is certainly more than a sex machine, she mused. He is great fun, full of insights, and has novel takes on things.

As they partook of cheese and crackers, Martine glanced at her wristwatch. "I had better go, Jean-Claude."

"Martine, thank you for a great evening."

"*C'est mon plaisir,*" she said.

As they walked to the door, Jean-Claude remembered the flashlight that he wanted to give her to keep. "Just a minute, Martine." He stepped back and took it from the marble table. "I want you to keep it in your car. So whenever you come after dark you can find your way up the stairs."

"Oh, thanks." She took the flashlight with a smile.

They descended the stairs, guided by the beam of Pierre's large flashlight. When he opened the door, he said, "I will watch you until you drive off safely."

Martine kissed him again. "I enjoyed every minute of our evening."

"Let's do it as often as possible, Martine."

"Why not?" she responded enthusiastically.

"*Bonne nuit*, Martine."

Before walking to her car across the road, she waved her hand and said, "Happy dreams with your sweet pigeons."

As he lay on his bed in the dark bedroom, he told himself, I must execute Brigitte Villard without delay—before her husband returns from his Asia business trip. I know I could kill her even if he was in the city, but I would rather do it while he is away, for I have great respect for the man.

# CHAPTER 12

On three successive nights, Pierre carried his murder kit to the Villards' opulent house to kill Brigitte Villard. He always entered through the small gate at the back of the house. On the first night, Brigitte was out of the house—her BMW coupé was not in the garage. He waited for more than two hours, and then left. The next attempt was aborted. Though Brigitte was at home, the ultramodern security system in the house made it impossible for anyone to break in without setting off an alarm that would alert the nearest police station.

On the third night, observing that Brigitte was out in her BMW, Pierre hid in the Villards' front yard and stayed put until she returned. As she emerged from her car in the garage, he shot her with three bullets from behind, one in the back of her head, one in the neck, and the third in the upper part of her body. Then he returned to the apartment on rue Karl Marx. As he ascended the stairs to his apartment, he felt a strong sense of relief that Brigitte had not seen who had snuffed out her life. Her final moments would have been filled with immense horror and profound sadness if she had realized that it was Pierre Boucher, the son of her close friend, Jacqueline, and her secret lover, Christian, who had shot her.

To Pierre it was a matter of retribution, and in the dictionary of retribution, the words mercy and pity do not exist, he told himself.

The next morning in the Villards' large residence, the alarm clock rang loudly at six o'clock in the bedroom of the childless Italian couple, Elisa and Antonio Moretti, employed by the Villards as cook/housekeeper and gardener respectively. Elisa stopped the alarm and immediately climbed out of bed. With difficulty, Antonio sat up on the edge of the double bed to preempt any scolding from his wife. He rubbed his wrinkled face, took a deep breath, straightened his old back, and then stretched his hands forward and backward a number of times, before he went to the bathroom and rinsed his mouth three times with an Italian red wine that he believed was more effective than any toothpaste. They dressed and had a heavy breakfast, as usual, to face another long day of work. They left their one-bedroom villa, just four meters from the main house, at six fifty-seven. Elisa opened the back door of the Villards' large kitchen by entering a six-digit combination to deactivate the security system in that part of the house.

In his blue overalls and old gray beret, with a cigarette stuck in his mouth, Antonio headed toward the garage, where he kept his gardening equipment in a small closet, thinking about what he had to do before his midday lunch break. He decided to work in the backyard first. He crossed the front of the main house, with the large front yard to his left, and reached in his pocket for the small black remote control to open the white garage door. As he raised his head, he noticed that the garage door was open and he assumed that Mrs. Villard had forgotten to close it. Antonio crushed his cigarette with his right boot as he put back the garage remote control into his trouser pocket. When he stepped into the garage, he froze in horror. Mrs. Villard's body, facedown, was on the floor between the BMW and the Volvo. There was a lot of blood on her dress and on the floor; the blood was mostly dry and had a red-brown color. The shock made him dizzy, and the foul smell of congealed blood filled his nostrils. For a few moments, he stood in a state of mental and physical paralysis. Then he found himself racing to the kitchen. His beret fell to the ground. In the kitchen, Elisa, with a large knife in her hand, looked at her husband, and yelled, "Antonio, are you all right? What is wrong with you?"

"Mrs. Villard's been murdered. Somebody killed her—in the garage." His face was as pale as that of a corpse.

"Are you out of your mind, Antonio?" Elisa yelled again.

"Call the police, Elisa. Just call the police," he said loudly as he flopped onto a kitchen chair and put his hand to his chest, where he felt acute pain.

Elisa's hand was trembling as she dialed the police emergency number, 112, and nervously announced, "There has been a murder at the Villards' house."

A middle-aged woman responded in a gentle tone, "Please calm down and give me your name."

"I am the cook, Elisa Moretti." Then she gave the dispatcher the address of the Villards' house, 14 rue Moulin Rouge. The woman told her emphatically that nobody should go near the crime scene and nobody in the house should leave. When Antonio asked for some cognac, Elisa filled a glass for him, sternly telling him to compose himself.

Within seven minutes, a patrol car carrying two officers arrived at the mansion. Two minutes later, another patrol car screeched to a halt outside the mansion. At once, the four officers proceeded to secure the crime scene and the mansion; one officer stood at the large front gate and another guarded the small gate in the back. Five minutes later, the Forensic Laboratory ambulance arrived. The police forensic pathologist, Dr. Jacques Thomas, was right behind it in his own car, accompanied by two of his assistants.

While the morning shift of the Criminal Investigation Department usually started at eight o'clock, the head of CID, Chief Inspector Gerald Dupré, was at his desk before seven every day. Once he was told of the shocking murder, he phoned Senior Inspector Henri Laporte and formally assigned him to lead the investigation. Laporte immediately drove to the Villards' opulent mansion, arriving one minute after Dr. Thomas did. Laporte knew that the body would not be moved to the morgue before the arrival of his boss, Gerald Dupré, and Dupré always wanted the media to be kept at bay. Accordingly, he instructed the officer stationed at the large main gate to close it and not to allow anyone to enter the premises except those involved in the investigation.

In his office, the bald Chief Inspector Dupré sent a text message about the murder to the police commissioner; he did not want to disturb him at this early hour with a telephone call. As he was leaving his office to go to the murder site, the commissioner phoned him. "Good morning, Gerald." Before Dupré could reply, the commissioner added, "This is incredible. This is a big tragedy."

"Yes, Robert. It is a devastating bolt from the blue."

The commissioner, Robert Garnier, who was a close friend of the Villards, volunteered to personally convey the grim news to Jean-Paul Villard in Manila, and advise the mayor of the tragedy. "I will also tell the mayor that we should keep the examining magistrate, André Milo, away from this case as much as possible. Of course, Gerald, you know Milo is either depressed or drunk. We don't want him to mess up an investigation of this magnitude. Unfortunately, the other examining magistrate, Pierre-Yves Durant, who is a cooperative true professional, is on leave. We have to await his return from leave."

"That is a wise idea, Robert," commented Dupré. "By the way, I'll issue a press release by six this evening. We owe it to our citizens before the media starts poisoning them with outlandish fabrications. I will e-mail it to you by five for your approval."

"Very good. Very good, Gerald. Please keep me promptly posted about any developments."

"Certainly, Robert. And rest assured we will apprehend this depraved perpetrator."

"Thanks, Gerald. I am sure you and your people will do an excellent job. The perpetrator has no chance of escaping justice." Garnier always trusted Dupré's professionalism and tenacity. He also admired Dupré's ability to outwardly curb his abundant drive and passionate intensity.

Dupré loosened his tie and massaged his bald head. It occurred to him to phone his old friend, Charles Lefevre, who was the CEO of Villard's group of companies in the city, to let him know the sad news and attempt to glean any pertinent facts about the backgrounds of the victim, her husband, and those in her circle. Charles answered, but it was obvious he had been awakened by the call. "Charles, sorry to phone you so early," Dupré started in a low voice.

Charles yawned and sighed. "No problem, Gerald. It must be something important. Otherwise, I will kill you."

"Charles, I regret to say it is devastating news."

"What are talking about, Gerald?"

"Mrs. Brigitte Villard was found murdered at her home."

"You mean our Brigitte Villard?" Charles asked incredulously.

"Yes, Charles. It is shocking and saddening. However, I wanted to let you know before you hear it over the radio or on TV."

"What has the world come to, Gerald?"

"Let's face it. We live in a mad, mad world."

"I just can't believe it."

Dupré, who never minced words, particularly with his close friends, went directly to the heart of the matter. "Tell me if there are any skeletons in the lives of Jean-Paul, Brigitte, or Jean-Paul's daughter and son." Charles assured him there wasn't even a dark speck in the personal and professional lives of Jean-Paul; his son, Daniel, who was managing the Villards' Asian hotel chain from Manila; and his daughter, Aimée, who was managing a resoundingly successful software company in Bangalore, India. He added that Brigitte and Jean-Paul had no child from their marriage, a fact that Dupré already knew.

"What about Brigitte, Charles?"

In a wavering voice, Charles replied, "I have heard something disturbing about her, but of course I have not been interested in verifying it because it was none of my business. However, it could be just a rumor. You know what I mean."

"Charles, in our work, most rumors turn out to be true."

"I hope this rumor turns out to be false. I heard from a friend who lives in an apartment building at 231 boulevard Charles de Gaulle that Brigitte has a furnished apartment on the fourth floor of the same building. She is using—no, was using it as a love nest." As Lefevre spoke, Dupré jotted down the address and remained silent. Lefevre continued, "She was meeting on a weekly basis an important-looking, middle-aged man there. The concierge told my friend that Brigitte and this man usually meet during the day, and they spend two or three hours in the apartment."

"Does your friend know the name of this man?"

"No, Gerald. But he said that he had seen him a number of times. He seemed to be a distinguished character with a haughty bearing. She usually arrived ten or fifteen minutes before the arrival of her lover."

"So we don't have a name for this gentleman or lover?"

"I think your best bet would be the concierge."

"Charles, let me ask you bluntly. Is this friend of yours a reliable person?"

"Unfortunately, he is very reliable person, Gerald."

"Anything else that might help us in the investigation?"

"No, Gerald. But if anything crops up, I will let you know immediately. Now I have to contact Jean-Paul in Manila and convey this tragic news to him."

"Robert Garnier said he would phone Jean-Paul and give him the grim the news."

"I see."

"Many thanks to you, Charles." Dupré ended the call, locked his drawers, and picked up his car key.

When he arrived at the crime scene, he parked his car next to the forensic pathologist's ambulance in front of the Villards' mansion. Looking at the high pink brick walls, he thought that a lot of people could not afford to build such expensive walls. As he walked in with one hand in his pocket, he was awestruck by the grandeur and beauty of the front yard. This is not big money, but big money with refined taste, he thought. He walked toward his staff working in the garage, and noticed four men on their knees combing the grass in the front yard, centimeter by centimeter, searching for any piece of evidence. He was pleased that everyone was wearing gloves, even the photographers. Inspector Fauchet and Dr. Thomas stepped out of the garage to brief him.

"So, what do we have, gentlemen?" Dupré directed his question to both Fauchet and Thomas, as the sun glistened on his bald head.

Dr. Thomas responded first. "She received three bullets; each one of them could have been fatal, in my tentative opinion. One in the back of the head, one in the neck, and the third on the upper part of her back. So it is a case of a brutal overkill."

Dupré's eyes told Thomas to carry on. "We found her face down, but after completing our work on the back, we turned her body over. After we completed our forensic work, we covered her with a plastic sheet." Dr. Thomas adjusted his thick glasses with the back of his gloved hand.

Dupré now looked at Fauchet. "Any preliminary guess, Dominique?"

"It looks like a professional job," ventured Fauchet. "Money is not the motive because the victim is wearing very valuable jewelry, which was not touched. A contract killer or someone with a military or law-enforcement background. He used a silencer."

"A silencer!" interjected Dupré.

"Yes. Because none of the people in the house heard any sound of a report."

Dupré gazed at Dr. Thomas, who cleared his throat, and said, "I tend to agree that it was a professional job."

"A professional job?" wondered Dupré. We don't have contract killers in our city, he told himself. He paused, reflecting. "What type of casings?"

"They look like those of .22-caliber bullets," replied Fauchet.

Thomas said, "I am sure we will find the three bullets lodged in her body during the autopsy."

"Do you think a contract killer would use .22-caliber bullets?" asked Dupré.

Fauchet responded, "Normally, no. A contract killer would use a more powerful caliber."

Dr. Thomas interposed, "Dominique, I beg to disagree with that. I know of many cases where professional killers used .22-caliber bullets. In fact, from close range, a .22-caliber bullet is absolutely lethal. When it penetrates the skull, it causes havoc because it zigzags and in most cases will not exit after all the internal devastation it creates. That's why the three bullets are still in Mrs. Villard's body."

Dupré, who followed Thomas's words attentively and agreed with his argument, said, "Whether the killer is a professional or not, Dominique, please assign Detective Calley to form a team immediately. I want them to collect and analyze the names of all persons who checked into all hotels and pensions in the last three days and those who checked out last evening and this morning."

Fauchet used his cellphone to convey the chief inspector's instruction to Detective Calley who assured him he would start immediately on the task.

"Thanks, Dominique. Please let Henri know about this," said Dupré. "Where is the videographer?"

"He is working inside the house now," replied Fauchet. "One of the two dogs led us to the backyard and we found that possibly the murderer stood for some time on the grass on his way out. We videotaped and photographed the area. Then the dog led us to the back of the house but it lost the scent outside the alley. It just kept going left and right on the sidewalk. However, we found three shoe prints on the soil at the back of the house. Two of them are not clear but the third one is very clear, and we made a very good casting of it. The shoe size is forty-four."

"Good," interposed Dupré.

Fauchet continued, "We found two large, green, garbage containers at the back of the house, and Henri ordered that they be taken to the lab and their contents be gone through meticulously. Even a tiny item in them could prove to be of significance."

Dupré returned to the weapon, "A .22-caliber! What kind of pistol could it be, Dominique?"

"My best guess: it is a Beretta, a semiautomatic Beretta. But it is just a guess, Gerald."

"The ballistics people will identify it," said Dupré. Then he addressed Thomas. "What about the time of the murder?"

"Tentatively, I would say between eleven and midnight. Let us say eleven to one in the morning because the rigor mortis is complete. It normally takes about six to seven hours."

Dupré asked for gloves and put them on, then entered the garage. He knelt and removed the sheet from the upper part of the body. The dress was clotted with blood. The blank, deathly look in Brigitte's wide-open, blue eyes filled him with compassion. He noticed they had put transparent plastic bags over her hands and tied them with rubber bands. He assumed they had done the same to her feet. However, in his mind's eye, he was sure that Brigitte and her killer did not come into contact, so they would not find any traces of the killer under her well-manicured fingernails. He covered her face with the sheet and stood up. Human depravity knows no limits, he thought. Evil was still unfathomable to him despite his long career in law enforcement.

"Where is Henri?" Dupré asked Fauchet.

"He is inside the house taking statements from the Italian couple, the Morettis, and a young German woman named Anna Marr, who is living with the Villards. The fingerprint people are also working inside the house after completing their work in the garage, on the four cars, the external sides of windows and doors, and the table and six chairs behind the shrubbery." Dominique paused before hastily adding, "By the way, one of the dogs picked up a scent leading to a garden table behind that shrubbery, but we failed to find clear fingerprints on the table or the six chairs."

Dupré reflected. "So the killer was wearing gloves as he waited behind the shrubbery for Mrs. Villard's return."

"That is what I have deduced also, Gerald."

Now Dr. Thomas approached them. "We have completed our work in the garage. The body, the cars, the walls, the floor, and the door leading into the house from the garage. My team has taken blood samples, mouth swabs, and head hairs from the Italian couple and the Villards' German guest. We have bagged and marked thirteen hairs we found in the garage. Can we take the body for the post-mortem, Gerald?"

"Yes, you can. When do you want to start the autopsy?"

Thomas looked at his watch and paused, reflecting, then stated, "At twelve sharp."

Dupré addressed Fauchet. "Please ask Detective Paul Moreau to be there at quarter to twelve."

Promptly, Fauchet phoned Detective Moreau and gave him the chief inspector's instructions. Moreau, who hated attending autopsies, nonetheless assured Fauchet he would be there twenty or thirty minutes before noon.

"Thanks, Dominique," said Dupré. Then he asked Dr. Thomas, "When can we have your preliminary report, Jacques?"

"Tomorrow morning. Before noon, I hope. However, the final report will not be ready for five to seven days."

"Good. Very good. Many thanks, Jacques." Dupré admired Jacques' professionalism and the way he treated the bodies he autopsied, with respect, solemnity and dignity.

Dupré, Thomas, and Fauchet watched two of Thomas's men put Brigitte's body in a gray body bag and zip it shut. The sound of the zipper somehow tugged at Dupré's heartstrings. How brutal and unpredictable life could be, he thought. He turned to Fauchet. "Dominique, for the next three days I want police guarding the front and back of the house twenty-four hours a day."

"It will be arranged," Fauchet jotted that in his large brown notebook.

Then Dupré decided to go inside the house and have a word with Senior Inspector Henri Laporte. As he glanced around the magnificent reception hall, a sense of dejection and sorrow assailed him. Why would anyone snuff out the life of a beautiful, refined, and gracious woman like Brigitte and deprive her of all this splendor? He found himself saying silently, Brigitte, we will hunt your killer or killers and bring them to justice whatever it may take. It doesn't matter if you had a lover or a string of lovers. Then it dawned on him that the killer was not necessarily a man. He made a mental note to raise this point with Henri and Dominique later. Though he instinctively excluded her husband and his two children as suspects, they had to interview them upon their return to France. He would also interview Jean-Paul's ex-wife and his brother, Valery, both of whom lived in other cities.

He could hear Henri talking to someone in the dining room, but the conversation was subdued and he could hear only a few words from a male voice and a female voice. He decided to enter the room. Laporte was talking to a young, statuesque, blonde woman. They were seated opposite each other at one end of the long dining table. Laporte had a writing pad in front of him and a small tape recorder between him and the young woman.

When Laporte saw Dupré, he stood up and made the necessary introductions. Anna Marr tried to stand up, but Dupré hastened to say, "Please remain seated." Then he added, "I will take the senior inspector into the reception room for a few moments. Would you stay here, please?"

Anna nodded and clasped her large hands together, resting them on the table.

Dupré led Laporte to the other end of the reception hall; clearly, he did not want the German woman to be within earshot. Then he said in a low voice, "Two things, Henri. First, I have come to know that the deceased had a love nest at 231 boulevard Charles de Gaulle, on the fourth floor. I don't want anyone else to know about this. If the media get a whiff of it, they will turn it into a nasty, sensational scandal. I want you personally to go and extract the name of this unknown Don Juan from the concierge. And warn him never to reveal we talked to him. He should never reveal the name of this Don Juan to anyone else. Tell him he will be arrested for obstruction of an investigation if he utters a single word to any soul."

"I'll have to do that after I complete this interview and prepare for a one-to-two hour meeting with the staff who will be working on the investigation."

"No problem with that. The other thing, I want you to draft a press release by five so that I can e-mail it to the commissioner for his comments. I intend to put it on the Internet at six. Then the media can spread it all over France, and the world, if they want."

"I will have it ready before five, Gerald," Laporte confirmed with a slight nod.

"Good. Before I came here, I spoke to the commissioner, who assured me he would support us fully in this case. He made it clear to me that we can leave out the examining magistrate, André Milo, for the time being. I suppose he will advise the mayor of that. I don't know why Milo has not been asked to pull himself together or be sacked," said Dupré, with some distaste.

"This is for the powers-to-be to decide, Gerald," responded Laporte with a faint smile.

"Where is the fingerprint team?"

"They are upstairs. They first covered the ground floor. Though I don't think the killer entered the main house, we have to be very meticulous about everything in the event the case goes to court. We don't want a defense lawyer to come up with a convoluted theory and claim that the real murderer had entered the house and we failed to search for his fingerprints."

"Yes. We have to play it by the book, Henri. Now I'll leave you with the German girl."

Outside the main house, Dupré peeled off the plastic gloves, inserted them into his jacket pocket, and walked to his car, parked outside the mansion.

Dupré was open to all theories. His team would eliminate them one by one, until the field was narrowed to one or two logical theories. The very best forensic science and technology was at their disposal, but old-fashioned detective work would be indispensable. It was with diligence, probing, analysis, sifting, and intuition that they would apprehend the perpetrator.

However, Dupré knew that some crimes remain unsolved despite the best efforts of the police. Two such cases still rankled him occasionally. One was the rape and murder of two female French nursing students in their shared apartment a few years ago. The other, which took place a few weeks after that double murder, was the fatal stabbing of five Algerian men as they slept in their cramped room in the old industrial city. The photos of the hapless bodies of the young Frenchwomen and the young Algerians were etched in his mind, and from time to time, they flickered across his vision.

He always consoled himself with the fact that at the time of these two horrific cases, he was just an inspector and was not assigned to work with either of the two investigative teams. But now he was the head of the CID and he would not leave a murder case unsolved. The late Chief Inspector Bernard Marty—bless his soul—went to his grave disappointed and embittered by his failure to solve those two cases. I don't want to go to my grave without solving Mrs. Villard's murder or any other murder, Dupré told himself.

He parked his car in his designated slot behind the two-story forensic laboratory and walked, in deep contemplation, toward the eight-story police headquarters building. He threw the plastic gloves into a green trash can as he walked to his office.

At his desk, Henri Laporte started making amendments to the first draft of the police communiqué. Then he hammered out the second draft and decided to do the third and final draft after his return from the building on boulevard Charles de Gaulle where Mrs. Villard had maintained a secret love nest. Concierges know much more about the lives and secrets of their buildings' occupants than the occupants think or suspect, he reflected. He sent an e-mail to all of the detectives and officers whom he would lead in the investigation, asking them to meet at two in conference room 3.

Unbeknown to the man leading the hunt for the murderer and the murderer, they were both listening, at the same time, to the first radio broadcast about the murder—Gerald Dupré in his office, and Pierre Boucher in the apartment. And almost simultaneously, both switched off their respective radios when the murder news item came to an end.

At once Dupré phoned Laporte who was about to leave his office.

"Yes, Gerald," Laporte responded.

"Henri, the news of the murder is already on the radio. I presume it will be on TV within minutes."

"Anything of significance, Gerald?"

"They said it was a professional job. How dare they jump to such a conclusion?"

"Gerald, this is the media. The media will investigate the murder, tarnish the image of the victim, accuse a number of people and prosecute them before the case goes to court."

"And they hinted in the radio broadcast that it could be one of Jean-Paul's business enemies. The man has no business or personal enemies, as far as I know," said Dupré with blatant annoyance.

"Gerald, we should not be concerned with the media circus and their untamed hounds," said Laporte and added, "Now I am leaving for that secret mission, Gerald."

"This is a taboo subject, an absolute taboo, Henri," Dupré cautioned.

"I know, Gerald."

Pierre who heard the news while lying on the couch, mused, so they think the murder was committed by a professional killer. Good for them, he told himself. He wondered how his father would be reacting to Brigitte's murder. Shocked? Certainly. Heartbroken? Doubtful. He reckoned his mother, Jacqueline, despite her painful knowledge of the affair between her husband and Brigitte, would be more anguished and crushed by Brigitte's demise than his father.

He decided to follow the news of the murder on his radio/CD set, and the two leading local newspapers: *Le Quotidien* and *Le Matin*. He glanced at the compact radio/CD player on the ceramic floor next to the couch, and then resumed reading Cervantes's *Don Quixote*.

# CHAPTER 13

Around noon, Dupré went to the restroom to freshen up and when he returned to his office, he found a large manila envelope marked in big, blue letters: Chief Inspector's Copies. Opening it, he found some sixty photos from the crime scene. As he was studying them, his personal cellphone, for which few people had the number, rang. The man on the other end exclaimed in a hoarse, smoker's voice, "What the hell is going on, Big Chief?" It was Claude Fournier, the senior editor of *Le Quotidien*.

"Easy, easy, Claude. Have I done anything wrong?" asked Dupré. However, he was delighted to hear Claude's voice. Claude was not only a very close friend but he had helped Dupré to solve the Duval case with astonishing speed, and that had been instrumental in clinching his promotion to chief inspector when the highly strung Chief Inspector Bernard Marty's deteriorating heart forced him to retire.

"Of course, old man. There has been a mega murder and you haven't even given me a call!"

"Claude, you can imagine how busy we are in the early stages of the investigation of this grotesque crime. I am still stunned by what happened."

"You're stunned! Old man, you wouldn't be stunned if the apocalypse suddenly erupted in your office. So please cut the crap and fill me in."

"I can't give you all the facts, such as the type and caliber of the murder weapon. But I can give you a few important facts." He paused and looked at the photos in front him. "I can e-mail you three photos from the crime scene. You should consider that a big scoop because none of the media people was allowed into the Villards' mansion."

"Now we're talking. Forward the photos to me as soon as possible. But give me a few facts that will not jeopardize your investigation."

"OK. The forensic pathologist estimated that the murder was committed between eleven last night and one this morning."

"What else?"

"The autopsy is still going on. Dr. Jacques Thomas is conducting it. I think you know him."

"Yes, I—" Fournier started coughing uncontrollably. Dupré remained silent while Fournier continued hacking for a minute or two. Finally, Fournier managed to speak normally. "What else, Gerald?"

"The commissioner, Robert Garnier, has assured me no funds will be spared to apprehend this monster. And we will not leave a stone unturned to bring the perpetrator to justice. I have canceled all scheduled leaves in the CID. Senior Inspector Henri Laporte is leading the investigation under my supervision. He is a laid-back man, soft-spoken, but he possesses a highly analytical and incisive mind."

"Gerald, the reporter I have assigned to this story has already drafted some lines about you and the commissioner with what I could describe as glowing bullshit. So are you suggesting that she gives the same treatment to Laporte?"

"Affirmative. I want the public to know that there are capable hands working on the case, Claude."

"I will tell her that. So we have Poirot, Holmes and Maigret working on the case." Fournier chuckled and immediately started coughing.

"I know it is pointless to tell you to stop smoking, old man. You are a hopeless case."

"Stop preaching at me, old man. Any other tidbits about the case?"

"We have already established a team of detectives to check the names and identities of all persons who stayed in all the hotels and pensions in the city during the last three days and in particular, those who checked out last evening or this morning."

"Good point. What else?"

"The forensic technicians are sifting through two public garbage containers found behind the house." He decided not to tell Claude about the hairs collected in the garage or the shoe-print found behind the house.

"Where exactly did the murder occur?"

"In the Villards' mansion garage. It is a four-car garage."

"The murderer used how many bullets?"

"Three bullets. But I want you to simply say 'with more than one bullet', Claude."

"Gerald, you know very well we will never quote you on this."

"You had better not quote me unless I tell you to in no uncertain terms. Otherwise, I will kill you and your reporter. However, Mrs. Villard was taken by surprise. It seems the killer was waiting for her inside her front yard."

"I think I will be satisfied with this for the time being, Gerald."

"I can't believe my ears!" They both laughed heartily, and Fournier started coughing.

"Gerald, I have assigned this case to a very bright, self-driven, young investigative journalist. Her name is Denise Lambert. She is twenty-nine years old. I want her to liaise with you. I feel confident she could provide you with useful information from her many sources."

"It will be quid pro quo. Sometimes we will want her to write certain information or disinformation, Claude."

"Of course, Gerald. So if you don't mind, I will give her your personal phone number and e-mail address."

"No problem. But please impress upon her the need to be extremely discreet. And under no circumstances should she give my personal telephone number to any other soul."

"Rest assured, Gerald. She has been a journalist for seven years. She is highly professional and ethical."

"Tell her that whenever she comes to see me, she should use the back door of the HQ—never the main entrance on avenue Victor Hugo."

"I will do that, old man."

"Good. And send me her e-mail address and cellphone number. Or ask her to do so, Claude. By the way, I will release a press communiqué at six this evening on our website."

"I will advise Denise of that."

"Fine, Claude."

Teasingly, Claude said, "I didn't tell you Denise Lambert's greatest asset."

Dupré instinctively expected Fournier to say something cheeky so he remained silent. After a long pause, Claude announced, "Denise has a stunning olive complexion, old man."

"Fuck off, dirty old man." They both chuckled and ended their conversation.

Half an hour later, Senior Inspector Laporte came into Dupré's office carrying a piece of paper. He took a chair in front of Dupré's desk. "Gerald, this is the name and land and cellphone numbers of Mrs. Villard's secret lover." He leaned forward and handed the paper to his boss. Dupré, stroking his bald head, looked at the paper, then asked, "Dr. Christian Boucher?"

"Yes, Gerald. The famous heart surgeon."

"You and I need to talk to him urgently and privately. This is a very delicate matter, Henri. I will think about a discreet place to meet him, away from his house and our offices."

"It is extremely delicate. Jean-Paul Villard is the epitome of refinement and eminence at the same time."

"You couldn't be more right. The man has donated about thirty cars to the police force over the years. We have to protect his reputation. But we have to interview this son of a bitch, Dr. Boucher. I will call him later and set up a meeting with him at a private venue."

"Good. I will send you the press release by four thirty. Now I have to go to my meeting with the staff who will be working with me on the investigation. We need to review what we have so far, agree on a strategy, and assign specific tasks to specific individuals or teams. I expect it to end by three thirty or four o'clock."

Shortly after seven in the evening, Chief Inspector Dupré phoned Dr. Christian Boucher on his cellphone number. Christian and his wife, Jacqueline, were having their evening meal. Christian, who did not recognize the number on his phone screen, remained silent and put the instrument close to his ear.

"Could I speak to Dr. Christian Boucher?" asked Dupré in a polite tone.

"Yes. Who is speaking?"

"Gerald Dupré."

"Gerald Dupré?" asked Boucher in an annoyed voice.

"I am the head of the CID. Chief Inspector Dupré."

"I am having dinner right now. Is it something urgent?"

"I would classify it as urgent and important."

Christian Boucher felt a lump in his throat yet managed to say, "Just a minute." He stood up and walked with his cellphone to the living room.

Left alone, Jacqueline took a swig of her vodka. The name Gerald Dupré rang a bell. She searched her mind and remembered that the name had been mentioned today on TV and radio broadcasts about Brigitte Villard's murder. Oh, he is the head of the CID! Could it be that they have discovered the filthy affair between my husband and Brigitte? she wondered. Dupré had been described in the news broadcasts as a brilliant detective. If he had discovered Brigitte and Christian's affair in less than twelve hours, then perhaps he is a super detective, she reflected.

In the privacy of the living room, Christian said on his cellphone, "Yes, Chief Inspector, what can I do for you?"

"I am sorry for interrupting your dinner. This is about the murder of Mrs. Brigitte Villard."

Boucher, feeling some alarm creeping into his mind, asked, "Do you want me to come to your office?"

"Oh, no, Dr. Boucher. I don't want you to come to my office, and I don't want to come to your hospital or invade the privacy of your home. It is too delicate for that."

Christian, telling himself to maintain his composure, said in a tremulous tone, "I do appreciate that, Chief Inspector. So where do you us want to meet?"

"How about the Oxford Pub on avenue Talleyrand? It's not far from your hospital and it's not frequented by many French. Its patrons are mainly young Brits, Americans, and Canadians. You see what I mean?"

"Yes, I do. And I know the Oxford Pub."

"Good. How about meeting there tomorrow morning anytime between ten and twelve?"

Christian paused, somewhat bewildered, but he had to give a time for this ominous secret meeting. "Is eleven o'clock OK with you, Chief Inspector?"

"Eleven o'clock is fine with me, Dr. Boucher. And have a good evening."

"You too, Chief Inspector," Christian said, wondering how he could have a good evening after this call. In his mind, the writing was on the wall, large and clear. The delicate matter was evidently his affair with Brigitte. The fact that the police had so swiftly discovered it stunned him. Then he told himself that perhaps they had not discovered it. Perhaps it was just a rumor they had stumbled upon, and they expected him to cave in without resistance. They ought to know better than that. He was not a man who could easily be intimidated. If his wife and his closest friend, Jean-Paul, came to know about the affair, how would they react? He didn't want to think about that. What would happen to his social and professional standing if the media came to know about it? His fall from grace would be monumental. He decided to take a sleeping pill before going to bed to keep these dreadful musings at bay. Otherwise, he would not sleep a wink all night, he reflected.

Had Brigitte been careless enough to commit their affair to a diary? Is it possible that the police had traced the many cellphone calls they exchanged? He was sure he and Brigitte had never communicated by e-mail. Therefore, it could not be something on her laptop or PC. He took a few deep breaths, ran his fingers through his hair, and decided to banish all these horrific apprehensions from his mind, telling himself that things might never take the catastrophic direction that he thought they would. As he returned to the dining room and settled in his chair, he looked at his plate and thought, 'I have lost my appetite and I can't finish my meal.' He urged himself to act normally and not to avert his eyes from his wife.

Jacqueline could see that his face was pale. He looked as though he had seen a ghost. Nevertheless, she was determined to tell him somehow that she knew the caller was the head of the CID. As he raised his glass of red wine, she asked innocently, pretending it was a casual question, "What was it, Christian?"

"Oh, nothing important." He looked her in the eye.

"It must be important. I heard you say Gerald Dupré."

"It has nothing to do with you, Jacqueline," he responded sharply.

Fortified by the three glasses of vodkas she had already downed, she pressed on. "Your face is so pale. There must be something wrong."

"Don't talk nonsense." His tone was harsh and dismissive.

"Please tell me, Christian. Is there anything wrong?"

"No, no, and no. Stop pestering me." He gulped some wine and stood up. He decided to go to the living room and have a tumbler of malt. Before he left the dining room, Jacqueline hastened to ask, "This Gerald Dupré, isn't he the head of the CID?"

Christian stopped in his tracks, turned toward her, and gave her a menacing look. "How do you know?"

"All today's radio and TV broadcasts about Brigitte's murder said that Gerald Dupré is the head of the CID."

"And so what? Are you implying something?" he yelled.

"I am not implying anything. You are my husband and I am concerned about your welfare."

"Damn it. I am old enough to take care of my own welfare. I don't want you ever to be concerned about my welfare." He raised a threatening finger toward her. "You had better take care of your own welfare."

"Fine, Christian." She was pleased that she had made it clear to him that she knew who Gerald Dupré was.

He stared at her, detecting mischief in her eyes, and that infuriated him more. "Stop pestering me. Just stop pestering me," he shouted and left the dining room.

Jacqueline fell silent, telling herself that she had made her point.

As she reflected that they would be sleeping in the same bed, she felt repugnance filling her heart. She thought that the most nauseating and revolting experience in life is to sleep every night next to a man you despise, hate, and fear.

She shuddered in disgust.

# CHAPTER 14

Early the next morning, Chief Inspector Dupré, wearing a dark-blue suit and a matching shirt and tie, sat in his office reading the lead story by a staff reporter of *Le Quotidien,* whom he assumed to be Denise Lambert. It filled a quarter of the front page, including a photo of the Villards' house from the outside; and about half of page six, where there was a photo showing him talking to Inspector Fauchet and Dr. Thomas in front of the Villards' garage. So Claude and Denise had used two of three photos he had e-mailed to Claude yesterday, he reflected. He was enormously impressed by the coherence of the article and gratified, like a small boy, by the glowing words about him and his staff.

Then he picked up *Le Matin.* Its lead article was also about the murder case, but it had no photos and no facts beyond those given in the police press release last evening. Yet it was more than double the length of *Le Quotidien's* article. It was filled with background information about Jean-Paul Villard and his wealth, and an outright attack on the police CID. It blatantly said the magnitude of the case was above and beyond the capabilities of the local CID team, headed by Chief Inspector Gerald Dupré. It gave many details of the Duval case, which, the paper concluded, was an easy, open-and-shut case. It said a layman could have solved the Duval case, but the Villard case would be extremely difficult to crack because it was the work of a professional killer. *Le Matin* did not forget to attack the police commissioner, Robert Garnier.

This is irresponsible journalism at its worst, he reflected. In disgust, Dupré folded *Le Matin* and threw it in the trash can as though it was the stinking carcass of a filthy animal.

It was seven in the morning now and he knew that his detectives working the eight-to-four shift would be in their offices by seven thirty or eight o'clock. So he sent an e-mail to Senior Inspector Laporte to come and see him once he arrived for work. Then he turned his attention to six reports on other cases: one rape, one attempted rape, three muggings, and one case of domestic violence with serious bodily injury. His immediate subordinates had decided to seek his guidance on these cases. He hoped to finish reading them and jot down appropriate comments and instructions before his detectives came in. Then it would all be about Brigitte Villard's murder.

He'd read with an attentive eye four of the reports and was immersed in the fifth when Senior Inspector Henri Laporte walked in holding a copy of *Le Quotidien*. "Good morning, Gerald."

Dupré stacked the six reports on his right. "Hi, Henri. Have you read *Le Quotidien's* lead article?"

"Yes, it is an excellent article."

"Have you read *Le Matin's* lead article?"

"Gerald, I don't read *Le Matin*. It is gutter journalism. So I leave it to young Detective Calley to read it and provide me with clippings that have a bearing on our work."

"Well, I read it. It is a heap of filth. *Le Matin* always depicts any public official as a moron with zero IQ. I know how to teach its editors a lesson."

"I am not surprised. I am not surprised at all." Laporte, sitting in a chair at Dupré's desk, raised the folded *Le Quotidien* in his large hand. "*Le Quotidien's* article is balanced and impressive."

"It's nice that the reporter made us all sound like super detectives."

Laporte chuckled. "He made you sound like Sherlock Holmes and Jules Maigret put together, though assisted by super sleuths. And Robert Garnier was painted like a demigod."

Dupré leaned back in his chair and fell silent for a few moments as he rubbed his head. "Henri, we have to deliver on Mrs. Villard's case or we will be a laughing stock," he said in a solemn tone.

"I have no doubt we can and will deliver, Gerald, though the situation looks very murky right now." Laporte delivered his words in his usual upbeat but calm manner.

"I like your optimism, Henri. But we don't have any forensic evidence of value: no fingerprints, no semen, no saliva, and no skin matchups. The killer made sure not to leave any clue. We have only the bullets, the cast of the footprint from behind the Villards' house, and the few hairs found in the garage. I am sure the killer did not come too close to Mrs. Villard." Dupré paused and then looked earnestly at Laporte. "I want you to join me at eleven o'clock to interview Dr. Boucher at the Oxford Pub. When I phoned him last evening, he tried to sound unruffled but he failed. I could detect he was quite shaken."

"I will join you. But now I have to prepare for the ten o'clock briefing for the inspectors, senior detectives, and detectives working with me on Mrs. Villard's case."

"Please postpone it until two. I want to give them a few motivational words before you start the meeting."

"It is good of you, Gerald, to spare the time to encourage and energize the troops."

"So, please, let your team know that the meeting will be at two in the main conference room."

Laporte stood up and picked up his copy of *Le Quotidien*. "I think we'll have to leave here by ten twenty. The traffic is unpredictable," said Laporte.

"Since you will be doing the driving, you just tell me when to leave," responded Dupré with a smile. "I will be talking to Claude Fournier to thank him for the splendid article."

Laporte, who was now standing at the door, asked, "You know Fournier well?"

"Not well. Very well. You could say too well. I was the best man at his wedding, and he was the best man at mine." Dupré chuckled. "And that is why both our marriages ended in divorce. He calls it the Dupré curse and I call it the Fournier curse." Laporte grinned pleasantly as Dupré went on, "You know, Claude could easily be a senior editor at a national paper but he simply loves this city. He is a hopeless workaholic like me. I think that is why our marriages failed."

Laporte left and Dupré looked at the vase with its seven roses on his small meeting table. His live-in partner, Charlotte Fontaine, renewed them every week. Charlotte had been a high-class escort girl in Geneva, where she'd used the professional name, Vicky. She was born and brought up in Dijon in a well-to-do and respected family. When she was eighteen, she rebelled against her strict parents and ran away to work as a prostitute in Paris before moving to Geneva to work for a high-class escort agency, which catered to millionaires, successful professionals, top diplomats, and visiting ministers. Dupré met her in Dijon while he was attending a police conference. She had come on a holiday to visit her family, who had finally accepted her work as a fait accompli. Her uncle, Senior Inspector Antoine Fontaine, a friend of Dupré, was attending the same conference and invited Dupré for a family dinner. He and Charlotte simply hit it off; their chemistry clicked in a perfect way. In no time, Dupré was disarmed by her jovial manner more than her glamorous looks. It was a serendipitous dinner, Dupré believed. It came in the wake of his acrimonious divorce. Claude Fournier had praised him for his courage to have a former escort as a live-in partner, and he knew Dupré had the guts to marry her if he and Charlotte decided to do so.

Charlotte Fontaine had brought tranquility, affection, and pleasure to his domestic life, Dupré reflected. Unlike his ex-wife, who was a professional nagger, Charlotte never complained about the long and unpredictable hours of his job. It is certainly far better to live with an ex-professional prostitute than with a born professional nagger, he thought. Charlotte filled her days painting watercolors, and she was good at it. The first thing she did when she moved in with him was to spruce up his wardrobe. Dupré immensely admired her relaxed and attentive listening, something he had never experienced with his ex-wife, Annette, who had a seven-to-ten-second attention span.

Now he looked at the copy of *Le Quotidien* on his desk, and sent an e-mail to Senior Inspector Laporte asking him to instruct the archiving section to keep press cuttings on Mrs. Villard's case from local, national and international newspapers and magazines, including the trashy *Le Matin*.

Dressed in an elegant blue suit, a matching tie, and a white shirt, Dr. Christian Boucher, in a gloomy mood of oppressive apprehension, arrived at the Oxford Pub some twenty minutes before the agreed-upon time of his meeting with Chief Inspector Dupré. He admitted to himself that it was decent of the chief inspector to talk to him in this pub, rather than in his house or at the police HQ. He glanced around the pub and chose a corner table at the far end of the large place. There were twenty to thirty young people—mainly English-speaking— idling away their time in the pub instead of working or attending their lectures or French lessons. Fortunately, they occupied tables at the front of the pub, some distance from the table he chose. As Dupré said, the patrons were mostly Brits and Americans; there were only a few French people dragged in by their rowdy

Anglo-Saxon friends. The décor, the furniture, and the ambience were decidedly British, he reflected.

He raised his hand for the young, blonde, English girl wearing a white T-shirt and a short, black skirt with a small red-and-green-checkered apron tied at her waist. He wondered whether the impending meeting with Dupré would be a friendly conversation or an interrogation.

"Good morning, sir," said the bubbly waitress, who had a lovely, mischievous smile, and wore no makeup. The freckles on her face probably made her look younger than her true age, thought Boucher. He ordered a double vodka with four cubes of ice, and a bottle of soda water. He decided against whiskey, reasoning that vodka would not be smelled by others when he returned to the hospital. Within a minute, the girl brought him the vodka and ice, a bottle of soda, and a bowl of assorted nuts on a small, round, wooden tray. She put the glass, the soda bottle, and the nuts in front of him and placed three white, paper napkins on the table. She smiled. "Do you want anything else, monsieur?"

"No thanks, mademoiselle." She gave him a lovely smile, and walked away with youthful energy. He filled the vodka glass almost up to the brim with soda water. The ice cubes clinked against the glass as he took a swig of his drink. He liked the taste and thought about his wife's love of, or addiction to, vodka.

Within a few minutes, he had drained the glass. It imbued him with a sense of boldness and a readiness to handle the chief inspector. So he asked the young English woman to serve him the same order again. She brought him his vodka and soda and left him to his own thoughts, which oscillated between apprehension and defiance, between helplessness and certitude. He glanced at his expensive wristwatch; it showed five minutes to eleven. The chief inspector would appear any moment.

He took a sip from his drink and stared at the pub's door. Within a few moments, two tall, important-looking men in full suits walked through the door. One of them was bald and stocky, and the other had thick hair that was well trimmed on the sides. The bald man glanced around the place, and seeing that Boucher was the only person sitting alone, walked confidently toward him. The other gentleman, who was obviously self-possessed, followed quietly behind the bald man. Boucher did not like that; he was expecting Gerald Dupré to be on his own. He was certain that was the impression he had gathered from their phone conversation last evening. He was irked, and that put him in an obstinate mind-set.

"Good morning, Dr. Boucher," said the bald man. "I am Gerald Dupré." Christian Boucher stood up as Dupré continued, "And this is Senior Inspector Henri Laporte."

"Pleased to meet you, Dr. Boucher," said Laporte.

"Me too, Mr. Laporte."

They shook hands and then settled on the wooden chairs.

"Would you care for a drink, gentlemen?" asked Boucher.

The two detectives gently turned down the offer.

Dupré clasped his hands and rested them on the table. "You will appreciate, doctor, that we need to talk to everyone in the social circle of the late Mrs. Villard."

"Yes, I do understand that," responded Boucher.

"It doesn't mean that everyone we talk to is a suspect. And even if one is a suspect, it would be very helpful if he or she is candid enough to give us full answers so we can eliminate him or her from the list of suspects."

"This is very logical, Mr. Dupré," allowed Boucher.

"So, Dr. Boucher, can you describe to us your relationship with Brigitte Villard?" asked Laporte in his affable manner.

Boucher looked at the two officers as steadily as he could. "Jean-Paul and Brigitte have always been very close family friends."

Dupré looked annoyed. "Doctor, we want you to focus on your relationship with Brigitte Villard. Not Jean-Paul."

"Brigitte was a dear friend of my wife and me. Our friendship goes back ten or eleven years," said Boucher evasively.

Laporte sensed that Dupré would be irritated by such evasions and would prematurely try to nail the doctor, so he glanced at his boss, signaling to him to go easy on the doctor. Dupré accepted that and let Laporte address Boucher.

Laporte quietly said, "Dr. Boucher, we already know this. It has been confirmed to us by a number of sources. We want you to throw more light on the nature of your relations with Brigitte."

"The normal relationship between family friends," said the doctor, taking a sip from his vodka glass to calm his nerves.

Dupré interposed, "Are you sure, Dr. Boucher?"

"I am very sure." Boucher felt his chest tightening.

"So it was never anything more than that?" asked Dupré.

"Absolutely not."

Dupré was annoyed by the doctor's pompous response. "Are you saying there was no intimate or romantic element in your relationship with Mrs. Villard?"

"Who gave you such an unthinkable idea, Chief Inspector?" Boucher was obviously losing his nerve despite the vodka he had consumed.

Dupré said, "Are you denying any romantic liaison between the two of you?"

"There is nothing to deny, Chief Inspector."

"For the last time, Dr. Boucher, are you absolutely sure you did not have any sexual relationship with the deceased?" Dupré asked brusquely.

Boucher reckoned the two officers were relying on hearsay but nothing solid; they were simply trying to bluff him and intimidate him into revealing his clandestine, intimate relationship with Brigitte. "Absolutely. So this is the end of it as far as I am concerned, gentlemen," blurted Boucher.

Dupré was pissed off and decided to go on the attack. "What about apartment 402 on the fourth floor at 231 avenue Charles de Gaulle?"

The two officers saw Boucher wince, yet he managed to ask assertively, "What about it?"

"The apartment in which you and the deceased met weekly for the last four years or so," Dupré said. "The apartment was owned by Mrs. Villard."

Boucher looked as though he was struck by a tidal wave. To steady himself he took his drink and drained it in one go. As he tried to put the empty glass on the table, the two officers saw his hand quiver, pathetically. Dupré and Laporte remained silent so that Boucher could consider his only two options: to tell the truth or continue lying. The doctor searched his mind for a way out but concluded there was none. He had to cave in.

He averted his eyes, stared at the young waitress as she stood next to the bar chatting with a young barman, and then he sighed. "OK, gentlemen. What do you want from me?"

"The full and unvarnished truth so we can eliminate you from our list of suspects," Laporte assured him in a calm tone.

"You mean I am a suspect?"

"Everyone who had a relationship with the victim and is concealing information is a suspect with a capital 'S', Boucher." Dupré's voice was low and soft. It sounded to Christian Boucher like the hissing of a rattlesnake pretending to be civil.

Boucher was unnerved and shaken but he knew now that he had to come clean. "Yes, we were lovers." He looked pitifully ashamed.

"We already know that, Boucher. We have witnesses to confirm that. You are not telling us anything new. We have important questions and we expect honest answers. Do you get me, Boucher?" asked Dupré.

Boucher felt humiliated by being forced to capitulate. He tried to put on a façade of self-control but he sensed the discerning eyes of the two detectives could see through his guise. He said with some reluctance, "I do get you, Chief Inspector."

"That is good, Boucher. Was there any falling out or any acrimonious incident between the two of you during your four-year love affair?"

Dr. Boucher clasped his hands firmly in front of him. "No, we were on the very best of terms until she was brutally murdered, Chief Inspector."

"How can we verify that, doctor?" retorted Dupré.

"You can take my word, unless you can find something or someone who could contradict it."

"Your word is not good enough because you lied to us, doctor. You lied to us, and once a liar, always a liar," growled Dupré as he gazed into the eyes of the doctor, who was dumbfounded by the flagrant and demeaning insult. The last speck of his panache evaporated. He felt the same helplessness and degradation he had felt when he had been verbally attacked by his parents as a child and a teen. Nonetheless, Boucher was surprised that the chief inspector, despite his aggressive tone and degrading words, was not shouting or talking loudly; he delivered his insults in a low voice, as though he did not want anyone other than them to hear him. Dupré had inserted the dagger deep in the doctor's heart and twisted it, yet he ensured that the cruel act did not attract attention or emit any sound. This was a feat that Boucher, the prominent surgeon, knew he could never emulate.

Laporte, who could see some sweat on the doctor's forehead, decided to intervene so that they could ask questions without rubbing Boucher's nose in the dirt. "We will take your word, Dr. Boucher."

"Thank you. I appreciate that, Mr. Laporte."

"We have a few questions. You are free to answer them or refuse. But your honest answers will be very helpful to us in solving this heinous murder." Laporte's tone seemed soothing compared to Dupré's hissing.

Dr. Boucher cleared his throat. "By all means. I am ready to answer all of your questions to the best of my knowledge."

"Good. Thank you," Laporte replied calmly. "Could you tell us where you were on the night of the murder from ten in the evening until one in the morning?"

"I was at home from six thirty in the evening until eight thirty the next morning."

"Your wife can verify that?" asked Dupré.

"Chief Inspector Dupré, there is no need to involve my wife in this. I don't think our marriage could survive the exposure of my affair with Brigitte."

Dupré fixed Boucher with a look that the doctor felt was cunning and stern, though this was not the chief inspector's intention. "We are not going to reveal to her your affair or your love nest, Boucher. Rest assured."

"Still, the moment you ask her to verify where I was on the night of the murder, she will start having serious suspicions." He looked at Dupré in a pleading way. "My wife is not in a stable emotional state. Even a slight hint of the affair would make her disintegrate. I am not worried about what she would do to me but what she might do to herself."

"OK. We may not need to talk to her at all if you cooperate with us fully. I have another question."

"Yes, Chief Inspector." Boucher felt ashamed that he sounded so acquiescent.

"Do you have any other lover or mistress?" asked Dupré in a quiet tone.

Boucher looked unsettled. "What has this got to do with Brigitte's murder, Mr. Dupré?"

"It has a lot to do with it, Dr. Boucher. We have to pursue every possibility. If you have another mistress, we cannot rule out the possibility that she might have decided to eliminate Brigitte out of sheer jealousy. This happens every day all over the world."

"I have no other mistress." Boucher rolled and twisted his tie, and Dupré thought he was lying but decided not to add further insult to injury.

"Neither recently nor some time ago? Say in the last five years?"

Boucher mustered the courage to pick up a napkin and wipe the sweat from his forehead. "Since I married, I have never had any mistress other than Brigitte." The fact that the two detectives were not taking notes gave him some sense of relief.

"Are you sure of that?"

"Absolutely, Chief Inspector," responded Boucher emphatically.

"Did you have a fling with a female doctor, a nurse, an employee, or a patient in the last five years?"

"No, Mr. Dupré. I think it is highly unethical for any doctor to have intimate or romantic relationships with women working under him, let alone his patients."

"And you are one hundred percent sure of that?" Dupré continued.

Christian Boucher was annoyed by Dupré's style of questioning but he had to bear it. "One hundred percent."

"How many children do you have?"

"Only one grown son."

"Is he working?"

"No. He is a university student. But he dropped out of his master's studies and went to Cameroon to work with a humanitarian organization in an administrative position."

"When did he go to Cameroon?"

"About a month ago," replied Christian Boucher.

"And you agreed to his abandoning his studies and traveling to Cameroon?" asked Dupré.

"No, Chief Inspector. He is a very stubborn idealist. He is of the opinion that Europeans robbed Africa of immense wealth during the colonial era and left it destitute and in shambles. It is his adamant view that now it is the moral responsibility of Europeans to help Africa in all possible ways. He thinks he can make a contribution, however small, as restitution to Africa and Africans. He is a hopeless idealist."

"That is commendable. Highly commendable, Dr. Boucher," responded Dupré. He looked at Laporte to allow him to put across any other questions to Christian Boucher.

Laporte paused before saying, "Let me assure you again, Dr. Boucher, that we will keep all of this between the three of us. We know that if the affair were leaked, it would cause an immense rupture in your friendship with Jean-Paul Villard, and would cause you serious marital problems. I don't think we will gain anything by harming any innocent person. And we don't want to cause you any harm."

Boucher wiped the sweat that had again formed on his forehead, and, with great relief, said, "Many thanks. I do appreciate that, gentlemen."

Laporte continued, "Fine. But I have a few more questions." Boucher seemed apprehensive but remained silent. "How would you describe the relationship between Brigitte and her husband?"

"It was an excellent relationship. They loved and adored each other. They had a very happy and solid marriage."

"So they had no marital problems?"

"As far as I know, they had no problems in their marriage."

"How about Jean-Paul's former wife? Do you know or suspect that she had any bitter feelings for Jean-Paul or Brigitte?" asked Laporte.

"No, Emmanuelle is happily remarried and has three kids from her second marriage. Jean-Paul, true to his nature, handled the divorce in an amicable manner. They have remained very good friends." Boucher kept talking as though he wanted to avert any demeaning question or comment from Dupré. "When they divorced, he bought her an expensive apartment in Paris and a country villa. He also deposited in her bank account, at the time, the equivalent in francs of two million euros of today's money."

Dupré interrupted him. "This says a lot about Jean-Paul's character."

"Yes, it does. He is a truly magnanimous man, Mr. Dupré."

"As far as you know, did Brigitte or Jean-Paul have any enemies?" asked Laporte.

"I don't think so. The two of them were blessed with charming, sincere, caring, and generous personalities."

"Can you recall if any one, male or female, had a grudge against Jean-Paul or Brigitte?"

"I can assure you, Mr. Laporte, nobody had any grudge against them. And it is against their nature to bear a grudge against anyone. This is to the best of my knowledge." Boucher paused, racking his brains, before adding, "The very idea of their having an enemy is farfetched, I don't—"

Dupré interrupted him. "Do you suspect Brigitte had other lovers?"

"I don't think so. But, honestly, I couldn't vouch for something like this with categorical certainty, Mr. Dupré."

"What about Jean-Paul?"

"I don't think so. He truly adored his wife, Mr. Dupré."

"But his wife adored him and still had an affair with you. And I presume you and your wife adore each other, yet you had a long, clandestine affair with Brigitte Villard."

Boucher felt demeaned by Dupré's coarseness. "I must admit I made a very bad judgment by having an affair. Knowing

Jean-Paul as I do, he would not make such a bad judgment. He has neither the inclination nor the time to do so."

"Have you ever known or suspected Jean-Paul of having any dubious business deals?"

"Jean-Paul is certainly above that. I can assure you I have never known or suspected he was involved in dubious or crooked deals. He amassed his huge wealth by risk taking, integrity, hard work, innovation and creating strategic partnerships. He believes that both competition and cooperation have their place in creating wealth and employment opportunities and advancing innovation, for businesses and countries if utilized shrewdly. You have to know when to compete and when to cooperate. He thinks that most politicians and policy makers, all over the world, seem oblivious to this simple yet profound paradigm."

Dupré, who listened to Boucher's exposé on Villard's business success recipe with exaggerated patience, looked at Laporte. "Do you have any further questions for Dr. Boucher, Henri?"

"No. But maybe the doctor has questions for us."

The two law-enforcement officers looked at Boucher, who hesitated before asking, "Are we going to keep this between the three of us permanently?"

Laporte sensed the nervous man needed reassurance. "It will and should always remain confidential, as far as we are concerned."

Boucher found himself saying, in an imploring tone, "I take it that it will remain 100 hundred percent permanently confidential."

Dupré allowed himself a small smile. "I would say 99 percent. I don't think there is anything that could be permanently 100 percent confidential. The 1 percent risk could come from your side, Dr. Boucher."

The three men chuckled and stood up. Each of the two detectives gave his card to Boucher, and Dupré emphasized, "Doctor, if you remember anything that could help us in our investigation, please don't hesitate to get in touch with Senior Inspector Laporte or me."

Boucher nodded. "For sure. This monster should be brought to justice by all means."

They shook hands and the two police officers left Christian Boucher alone. Outside, in glorious sunlight, Laporte said, "Gerald, we obviously underestimated the insecurities of this prominent and pompous surgeon."

Dupré nodded. "He is as pompous and insecure as the editors of *Le Matin*."

"I didn't sense that he was proud of what his son is doing in Africa, Gerald."

"Boucher to my mind is the type of person who thinks he is above all others, lesser mortals, like his son, the Africans, you and me. Perhaps even his wife and his late mistress. He is an egocentric who thinks the world owes him a lot. This is my impression from this meeting. However, I might be wrong."

Then they braved the maddening traffic congestion on avenue Talleyrand, a task more vexing than interrogating someone like the vain Dr. Boucher or even a heartless psychotic serial killer.

Inside the Oxford Pub, Christian Boucher, his vanity and dignity fatally wounded, ordered his third double vodka and soda. As he nursed his drink, he brooded over the disgrace he had been subjected to by Chief Inspector Dupré. A sense of shame enveloped him. I have never been insulted without hitting back in double measure, he told himself.

Musing about sex with his wife, Jacqueline, he knew that for the last seven or eight years, their sexual life had been devoid of affection and tenderness. He was always the one who initiated sex because she had apparently lost all interest. Though she did not enjoy it, she never denied him his conjugal rights; she was a handy and safe sexual outlet for him. He felt sorely sad for himself and Jacqueline that neither of them even pretended there was any love or warmth in their arid intimate life. Sometimes, while having intercourse with his compliant wife, he felt compassion for her.

He settled the bill and thanked the young bubbly waitress, leaving her a 20 percent tip. As he stood up, he felt his legs carrying him with difficulty; he was tipsy and did his best to walk out of the pub in a composed manner. How, he wondered, could Jacqueline consume more than half a bottle of vodka a day yet remain coherent and composed?

As he crossed the avenue in the direction of the hospital, a noticeable dizziness invaded his head. He blamed himself for drinking too much vodka in too short a time. He mulled over the degrading meeting with the two officers, how he had lied, and how he was scolded and insulted for doing that. He wondered how this bastard, Dupré, had so swiftly found out about his clandestine affair with Brigitte; he had thought it was a tight secret known to him and Brigitte only.

While his legs could hardly carry him, Boucher's mind was in overdrive. That idiot, Dupré, was an arrogant and aggressive asshole. Dupré's words rang in his ears and constricted his chest: 'Once a liar, always a liar.' The son of a bitch had growled his insults in a matter-of-fact tone and then ended the interview with a jest. As for Laporte, I think—

Suddenly the deafening sound of a car screeching to a halt sent a shiver down his spine. In his confusion, he instinctively jumped onto the sidewalk. He looked back at the car. At once, he realized that the alertness of the angry driver had saved him from a horrific death or a severe permanent disability. He stood stock still, shaken, dazed, and scared. His mind told him to thank the driver of the metallic-silver sedan, but he remained speechless.

"You bastard, you son-of-a-bitch. You moron!" The infuriated driver yelled, sticking his index finger to his temple, as he looked at Boucher. As Boucher stood speechless, looking at the car, the driver grasped his right elbow with his left hand and raised his right fist three times in the universal 'fuck-you' gesture before driving away. Onlookers seemed to censure Boucher, eyeing him with different degrees of reproach and condemnation.

He thanked God that he had not been run over by the car. As he started walking toward the hospital, a wave of internal heat engulfed him; he felt suffocated and thought about taking off his jacket but decided against it. Was it the vodka, the humiliation by Dupré, or the scare of the near-miss car accident? Or a combination? He couldn't tell. He forced himself to put one foot briskly in front of the other to reach the haven of his office.

Despite his conviction that the police would keep his scandalous affair strictly confidential—not for his sake but for that of Jean-Paul Villard—he was, in fact, in a very precarious situation, he thought as he walked into the hospital. Still dissecting the meeting, it dawned on him that the two officers seemed reasonable and responsible despite the rudeness of Dupré. And what about Jacqueline and Pierre? He was not sure how his wife and son would react to this explosive scandal if even a whiff of it reached them. He felt relieved that his son, Pierre, was in Africa helping the Cameroonians, for his reaction could be extremely insolent, volatile and unpredictable. A voice inside his mind even wished that Pierre would meet his end in Africa, just as his maternal uncle, Marcel Dillon, had. Damn the Dillons! They are a wild bunch of stubborn, conceited, and vindictive individuals. Eight years ago, a first cousin of Jacqueline, François Dillon, who lived in Rennes, shot to death his wife and her lover. He was sentenced to ten years imprisonment. While the community in Rennes considered that a very lenient sentence, the Dillons believed that François had done the right thing and he should not have been sent to prison. The Dillons, with their Dark Ages mentality, thought he was a brave hero.

Suddenly, he felt ashamed of himself for contemplating the death of his only son. How mean and base of me to entertain such a callous idea, he told himself.

I had naively thought my affair with Brigitte was an impen-etrable secret, he mused. Nevertheless, who could have antici-pated that Brigitte would be murdered? Who could have imagined such a sudden end, an end that came like lightning striking from a calm and cloudless sky? He recalled the words of his late, authoritarian mother: 'You can't choose your path but you can choose how to travel the path God chooses for you.' He had never subscribed to that idea, considering it the delusion of a very religious and perpetually angry woman. Now a trace of doubt crept into his mind about his rejection of that wisdom—though he never considered his mother a wise creature. Do I have to maneuver through this quandary, this path that I did not choose? He pondered for some time his most effective course of action. Finally, he decided that the best strategy was to do nothing and throw himself at the mercy of the two police officers. My mother was wrong. And I was wrong. Evidently, sometimes you cannot choose your path or choose how to travel it.

Inside his office, he removed his jacket and tie, discon-nected his office telephone, put his cellphone on silent mode, and set a small alarm clock on his desk for four o'clock. He opened a desk drawer, took one tablet of a sedative, and swal-lowed it without water before he flopped onto the office sofa. He massaged his forehead and temples, rested his hands on his chest, and closed his eyes. I need a long nap, he told himself. I am lucky to have returned to the hospital in one piece.

His nap was neither pleasant nor serene. A few minutes after he entered the realm of sleep, his mind was crowded with the unsettling faces of the degrading chief inspector, the obscene car driver, and his abusive dead mother and father. They alternated in rebuking and belittling him. He sensed they were united in their revulsion at his inferiority, ignominy, and cowardice.

# CHAPTER 15

The day after the meeting at the Oxford Pub between Dupré, Laporte, and Boucher—of which Pierre was unaware—the alarm clock awakened Pierre at eight, and he swiftly silenced it. He threw the bedcover to one side and lay in bed for a few minutes thinking about the day ahead, the highlight of which would be a lunchtime visit by Martine. He yawned and stood up, and then pulled aside the old, blue-patterned curtains. Sunlight filled the room. He could not hear the pigeons cooing, so he peeped through the slanted bars of the outer, wooden shutters. The two pearl-gray pigeons were not there. He could see the small egg in the nest. Obviously, the pigeons were on a mission to search for food, he thought.

In the bathroom, he took a long shower as usual, dried himself, put on blue boxer shorts, then shaved and splashed some of his invigorating aftershave on his face.

He looked into the mirror. He was very pleased with his face, and very pleased with himself. Suddenly he found himself addressing an imaginary audience in a clear and command-ing voice. 'We erroneously attribute whatever happens to us to fate. This is a shameful and disgraceful abdication of our responsibility and our free will. We must realize that our free will can confront fate and reshape and create our own destiny.' He considered that though his listeners had appreciated the significance of his brilliant wisdom, they needed further illumination, so he raised his voice and added, 'Free will is the true mark of an independent and daring human being. Without free will, we are nothing more than robots, helplessly letting fate take us to abject destinies which we will, when it is too late, loathe, lament, and regret.' The response of his grateful audience was enthusiastic and gratifying. So he delivered his captivating words again, but in a more deliberate and persuasive tone.

When he finished, there was a long, standing ovation. He bowed his head three times, reciprocating his audience's resounding appreciation with profound humility. Tears welled in his eyes, and he let them run down his face before wiping them away with his right hand. Then he put his hand to his tongue; the tears tasted warm and salty.

He was perplexed by his spontaneous speech in front of the mirror; he wondered if he really needed to address an imaginary audience or simply needed to talk to himself.

He went into the kitchen and made himself a mug of black coffee, which he took to the bedroom, and as he dressed, he sipped from it now and then. The coffee was good and hot. He liked it. He put on a sleeveless cotton undershirt, a green-and-brown-checked, long-sleeved shirt, and blue jeans. As he sat on the edge of the bed to lace his shoes, he reminded himself to put the size-forty-four shoes he had worn for Mrs. Villard's murder into a paper bag and dump it somewhere away from the rue Karl Marx building. For the Nicole Gautier murder, he would use a pair of new jogging shoes—size forty-six.

He fetched a paper bag from the bedroom next to the kitchen, where he stored empty bags and cartons, and deposited in it the shoes he had used in Mrs. Villard's murder. Then he recalled from yesterday's radio news the name of the chief inspector at the CID: Gerald Dupré. Neither Dupré, his staff, nor their forensic laboratory, which was described on the radio as sophisticated and ultramodern, will unravel my three murders, he assured himself. With Brigitte Villard's murder, they are already out of their depth. They will be in deeper water when I eliminate Nicole Gautier. When I dispose of Monique Roget, they will be forced to seek assistance from Paris. And the city residents will be clamoring for the removal of Chief Inspector Gerald Dupré.

How could the police solve these murders with his modus operandi: taking the victim by surprise, leaving no fingerprints or other evidence of value except the size and type of the bullets, never coming into contact with the victim, and using a different pair of shoes for each murder? Pierre had researched the exchange principle of the Frenchman, Edmond Locard, which asserts that when a killer comes in contact with his or her victim, a transfer of evidence is bound to take place; the killer leaves some evidence on the victim or at the crime scene, and the victim carries some evidence from the killer and the place where the crime was committed. Locard's exchange principle is the basis on which police and forensic experts everywhere investigate murders. Pierre believed that with his modus operandi, Locard's principle, as sound as it may be, will be of no use to the police. He would render it irrelevant.

Pierre was sure the police would be bogged down with interviewing hundreds of innocent people, following endless dead-end leads, cramming their computers with useless data, and amassing vast piles of paperwork and photographs. Yet they would remain as far away from him as Mars is from Earth.

He decided to bide his time before he killed Nicole Gautier, at least until the dust had settled on Brigitte Villard's murder. He would let the police waste more energy and resources barking up many wrong trees. For some time, he dwelled on his battle with the police. Then he reminded himself that the real battle was between him and his narcissistic and diabolic father. For all intents and purposes, the police did not factor into this familial war.

In a somber, contemplative mood, Pierre asked himself why people bring children into this world only to debase them, abuse them, and subjugate them. It is all about obedience to authority and the mores of the family and society. They love their children as long as they are obedient; any disobedience is considered to be an unforgivable threat to the family, its harmony, and its façade of perfection, as well as a threat to society and its mores and tranquility. If he ever married and brought children into this chaotic world, he would treat them with the utmost respect, unconditional love, and boundless tolerance. Otherwise, why should he bring another soul into this convoluted world? For most people, it is all about a few minutes of sexual gratification. They never foresee or are prepared for the challenging emotional and moral responsibility of nurturing a child into an independent spirit and a free soul. Isn't that a crime? It is the worst crime. The worst part of it is that everyone claims and brags that he or she loves his or her children. They simply do not know what real love is, Pierre reflected.

As for marriage, Pierre concurred with his late uncle, Marcel Dillon, that marriage is not a natural institution but a social one, which most of the time precipitates a lot of misery and sorrow. It is a relationship entered into when dopamine is flooding one's brain and the bride and groom are envisioning a life of enduring love and happiness. But when the dopamine ebbs within a few months and vanishes in a few years, it often leaves the marriage partners, or at least one of them, staring at the bleakness and emptiness of the shambles of a union they had thought would remain rosy until death did them part.

Pierre mused that when the Russian literary giant, Tolstoy, wrote that all happy families resemble each other, he was oblivious of the fact that most seemingly happy families might not actually be happy, and truly happy families are the exception that proves that most families are unhappy. Tolstoy's own marriage was a telling example of the depletion of dopamine: he fell in love with his young, sweet wife; they proceeded to produce thirteen children; and then he and his wife drifted apart and were at loggerheads for more than a decade before their marriage descended into an out-and-out war. At the age of eighty-two, the great Russian author secretly escaped from his sprawling dacha at dawn with one of his daughters and his physician. They traveled aimlessly by train until his ill health forced him to seek refuge in a small cottage, offered by a kind stationmaster; and he died in that forlorn railway station at Astapovo.

Pierre picked up the paper bag containing the black shoes he had used in committing Brigitte's murder. In the kitchen, he put his food scraps in a large, strong, plastic bag. As he cycled nearer the edge of the city, he dumped both bags in a large, green, steel garbage container. Then he cycled to La Librairie Stendhal, parked his bike on the opposite sidewalk, and entered the bookshop. When Martine saw him, she gestured with a slight head tilt, indicating to him to go into her office.

A minute or so later, Martine entered the office and locked the door. She sucked his lip, and said, "Let us have a quickie." He nodded, and already aroused by her daring request he started opening his trousers. She lowered her black trousers and red, tight panties before bending over the desk, with its invoices and printouts, and held the other edge of the desk with her hands. He firmly gripped her hips, before starting making love to her—briskly and passionately. They both managed to muffle their feverish moans, despite their vigorous and swift sex. Martine was giddy with gratification; she found it intensely thrilling and animated. Once Jean-Claude stepped back and started zipping his trousers, she pulled up her panties and trousers. She turned toward him, gave him an appreciative peck, and whispered, "Sometimes a quickie is immensely exciting, darling."

"Yes, darling. It could be very exhilarating."

"This was more than exhilarating, Jean-Claude," she assured him as she tucked her turquoise silk shirt in her black trousers.

She unlocked the door, leaving it closed. Then she gave him the third cellphone she had charged for him. He took the one in his pocket and asked her to recharge it.

"What do you want me to buy for lunch?" asked Martine.

"You don't need to buy anything. I will buy two grilled chickens."

"In that case, I will bring a few bottles of wine and a six-pack of beer," responded Martine.

"Martine, I have a large stock of red wine. Just bring some beer if you want," he said before adding, "So see you at one, darling. I have to go now."

As he left, he told himself that he should stop or curtail his visits to La Librairie Stendhal, for he would be unnecessarily exposing himself to the risk of being seen by someone who knew him.

He went outside to the corner of La Librairie Stendhal, turned left, and walked down the street. In one shop, he bought six boxes of tissues. Then he went into a small brasserie for two takeout grilled chickens. Back at the rue Karl Marx apartment, he put the food parcel in the kitchen, placed four of the tissue boxes on one of the kitchen shelves, and took the other two to the marble table. He glanced at his watch; the time was eleven forty-five. The next news broadcast would be at twelve. He returned to the kitchen, made himself a mug of black coffee, took it to the couch, then switched on the radio and lowered its volume.

Two minutes before twelve, Pierre raised the volume of the radio, eager to capture any new developments in the murder case. The newscaster announced that Jean-Paul Villard and his son, Daniel, had arrived in the city three hours ago in Villard's private jet, and that Jean-Paul's daughter, Aimée Lambert-Villard, would be arriving in Paris with her husband and two children this evening. The police were interviewing friends and acquaintances of the family as well as some current and former employees of the different Villard companies in the city.

Pierre was delighted that the police were wasting their time interviewing people who had nothing to do with the murder. He reckoned it would take them weeks and weeks to interview all these innocent people. He switched off the radio and opened *Don Quixote*. He was engrossed in the fantastic adventures of *Don Quixote*, when he heard courtly knocks on the door. He put the book on the small table next to the couch and stood up. It was Martine, carrying a large, yellow, plastic bag. She beamed. They exchanged gentle kisses, and then Pierre closed the door and locked it, immediately wondering why he bothered with the lock. There was no need for it—no one would intrude in this abandoned building.

Martine deposited the yellow plastic bag on the dining table. She took out three newspapers and declared, "I have brought three bottles of red wine and a six-pack of beer." She put the newspapers on the round, marble table.

"I will make you drink those three bottles of wine," Pierre said, deadpan.

"Are you planning to rape me?"

"It never occurred to me. But I think it's a good idea."

"So you like the idea, Jean-Claude?" She grinned sweetly.

"Martine, I would never rape you without your permission."

Martine laughed. "That would be the most dignified and refined rape, Jean-Claude. Anyhow, if I drink four cans of beer, you won't need my permission. But do it gently and affectionately, please."

"I always do it affectionately though not always gently. It depends on the needs of my partner, Martine," he said with a twinkle. "Now, what would you like to drink, wine or beer?"

"Beer, please." She stood up, brought the three newspapers from the table, and settled back on the couch, putting the papers next to her.

Jean-Claude opened two cans of beer, which were still cold, and joined Martine on the couch. Sitting close to her, a wave of tenderness enveloped him, and he asked himself how could he deceive Martine who oozed innocence from every pore in her being? A tenderness that almost brought him to the verge of disclosing to her his true identity. But I have no intention of harming her or even bruising her sensibilities, he mused. Isn't smooth and harmless duplicity sometimes necessary for human relations and bonding whether in work, friendship, love, or marriage?

She took a long sip from her beer, as though she was very thirsty. "The taste is very nice. It is Dutch beer," she commented.

"I like it too. It was good of you to bring some beer for a change."

She took another sip from her can. "I have brought you *Le Quotidien*, *Le Figaro*, and Le *Matin*."

"I'll read the newspapers later. Now I just want to enjoy your company."

She continued, oblivious of his remark, "Today, *Le Quotidien* has another well-written article on the murder."

"I will certainly read their article. I liked their article yesterday. It was factual, well researched, and not too long. Yesterday, *Le Matin* had a very long story on the murder, yet it didn't say anything of substance about the case," he commented, before adding, "The story was aimed mainly at frightening the community."

"But this is what *Le Matin's* readers want. Salacious scandals. Wild speculation. Outright fear-mongering."

"I think the police are facing a very difficult murder case, Martine."

"I agree, Jean-Claude. Apparently, they have no adequate forensic evidence as *Le Quotidien* is saying today."

"They may never be able to solve it if they have no adequate forensic evidence."

"No, Jean-Claude. The fact that they know the weapon is a .22-caliber semiautomatic Beretta could be sufficient for them to hunt down the murderer. However, it will take them a lot of effort and time to apprehend him. They have to trace every registered Beretta. Of course, it might be a Beretta not in the national police database. Yet, my own hunch is that they will ultimately catch him."

Jean-Claude took a sip from his beer and paused. "Why do you think it is a he and not a she?"

There was surprise in Martine's large, green eyes. "It never occurred to me that Brigitte's murderer could be a woman."

"It is just a possibility. One can't rule out such a possibility, Martine."

"With insufficient forensic evidence, the police need a lot of luck, regardless of whether it is a she or a he."

Jean-Claude found himself saying, "I wish them lots of luck."

He rose from the couch and announced, "I will switch to wine." As he walked toward the kitchen, he stopped and turned to her. "Before I forget, Martine. Could you please ask your father to give me a list of, say, five must-read novels according to his taste. They should not include French works and not *Don Quixote* and *War and Peace*. I want more books to read as I am about to finish *Don Quixote*, then I will immediately start reading *The Red and the Black* and *War and Peace*."

"If you want a list of one hundred must-read novels, he could do it without much sweat."

"I have no doubt about that. But let's start with five," he responded.

In the kitchen, he filled a glass with red wine and opened a can of beer. Then he joined Martine on the couch, and handed her the can of beer. Sitting next to her, he felt at once proud and elated to have an intelligent and stunning woman like Martine as a companion. Her dazzling green eyes alone made her a goddess, he reflected. He took a gulp of his wine and said, "Right. Let me prepare the food."

He disappeared into the kitchen for some time, and in the meantime, Martine browsed *Le Figaro*. Then Jean-Claude emerged from the kitchen with two plates of chicken with sliced tomatoes and carrots. He went back and brought out a basket of sliced baguette and a plate of *fromage blanc* and *fromage bleu*. After placing them on the dining table, he rubbed his hands a few times and pretending he was a butler, he bowed and declared in a polished tone, "Food is served, Your Grace."

After they finished their meal, they returned to the couch, and Martine set the newspapers on the small table to the left of the couch. She wanted to say something but Jean-Claude held her face with his hands, kissed her ear, and then moved to her scar and lips. As he sucked her lower lip, Martine's desire was kindled. She undressed in her orderly manner, before she stretched on the couch, opened her legs, bent her knees, and put her hands under her head—burning with desire and flushed with anticipation. Her nude, lithe, and curvaceous body intensified Pierre's desire, who joined her in his full nakedness on the couch. As Martine gave a loud moan and shrieked with sensual gratification, Jean-Claude screamed mockingly, "You are disturbing the pigeons, Martine."

"Fuck you and fuck your pigeons," she yelled back. She surprised herself because they never used the word 'fuck' at home.

"You can't take a joke," he said casually.

"Fuck you. Fuck your pigeons," she yelled again.

Jean-Claude was pleased with her yelling. He laughed and fell on top of her.

"Damn it. Why have you stopped?"

"I haven't stopped. But please stop disturbing the pigeons," he continued teasing her.

She chuckled and mimicked him, "But please stop disturbing the pigeons."

They both laughed, and then Martine playfully punched his shoulder. "You're the one who is disturbing the pigeons, Jean-Claude."

"All right. I think both of us are disturbing the pigeons."

"How do you know? Maybe they're enjoying it."

"Maybe, Martine."

"Maybe they are fed up with the sounds of dogs copulating every night, Jean-Claude. We are giving them a different variety of noises."

"Darling, human beings create a lot of commotion when copulating. No animal can beat them at that."

"Say 'making love', not 'copulating'." She gave him a mock scolding look.

"Right, Martine. Making love," he replied in a deliberately soft voice.

When they both climaxed, they lay side by side on the couch, enjoying their shared warmth, tenderness, and affection. Martine closed her eyes and let herself savor the rapture of her deep sexual and spiritual fulfillment. But after a few moments of blissful silence, Jean-Claude whispered, "Somehow the way you yelled 'fuck you and fuck your pigeons' gave me the impression that deep down you have a free spirit of a streetwise woman, Martine. But you are holding yourself back by trying to be too proper or *de rigueur*."

She put her hand playfully around his neck as if she wanted to strangle him. "A streetwise woman! You mean a hooker? Fuck you, Jean-Claude. And fuck you again."

He grinned. "Calling a woman 'streetwise' doesn't mean she is a hooker, Martine. To my mind, it simply means she is skillful and shrewd and not afraid of taking risks and making mistakes."

"Thanks for reassuring me."

"Martine, in sex you can say anything or do anything or use any position as long as it is safe and comfortable. Don't inhibit yourself or your partner."

"I think the more I know you, my streetwise guru, the more inhibitions I will shed."

"I don't want you to be influenced by me or anyone else. Your emancipation should come from within. From your own free will, Martine."

"I will. I will," responded Martine with a sweet smile, and stood up. "I have to go back to work." Then she went into the bathroom. When she returned to the living room, fully dressed, she found Jean-Claude in his boxer shorts and nursing his glass of wine.

He accompanied her down the stairs barefoot, and they kissed passionately in the lobby. As Martine drove to the bookshop, she reflected that she had been leading not only a sheltered social life but also a sex life devoid of sexual experimentation and adventure. As Jean-Claude said, I should boost my self-confidence and free will, and enjoy life to the maximum, she told herself. She resolved to show Jean-Claude that she was not afraid to try new things in love making—without any inhibitions.

After Martine left, Pierre—aka Jean-Claude—locked the main door and ascended the stairs to the apartment. Inside the apartment, he decided to have a shower, read the papers, and then return to *Don Quixote.*

That night he went to bed content with himself, Martine, and the world. In the depth of his sleep, he had an unsettling dream. A nebulous, naked figure opened the main door of the building, closed the door, and ascended the stairs. Then Pierre realized it was an angry man. As the naked man stood at the door of the apartment and turned the knob, Pierre rebuked himself in the dream for leaving the door unlocked. When the man entered the apartment, Pierre realized he was the muscular man who had rescued him from drowning almost twenty years ago when his father threw him into the swimming pool, telling him to sink or swim, and for long horrific moments, he had felt he was going to die. The man had pulled Pierre from the pool, insulted Pierre's father, and was intent on having a bloody brawl with him, but his father had chickened out. Now as the man walked into the sitting room toward the bedroom in a menacing manner, Pierre could see he had an erection.

In the dream, Pierre struggled in horror for a few moments to wake up and confront the belligerent man who was about to leap into his bed. Pierre emitted a thunderous howl and woke up, sitting up with his two fists clenched, ready to fight. With his left fist still clenched, he reached with his right hand for the flashlight. He swept the beam of light across the bedroom. There was intruder in the room. He expelled a large sigh and put his head back on the pillow. He switched off the flashlight, deciding to resume his sleep. In the darkness, he reasoned that the dream was bizarre and meaningless because he had never seen a sexually aroused naked man. Never, he told himself.

With his eyes still open, a memory suddenly sprang from the deep recesses of his mind. Yes, he had seen a sexually aroused naked man. It was his father. The night after the swimming pool incident, he had awakened in the middle of the night, and was scared to be alone in his bedroom. So he ran in his pajamas to his parents' room to snuggle next to his mother. Now he could vividly recall that the two bedside lamps were on; his naked father was shoving his body briskly and violently between the legs of his naked mother; his mother was groaning and moaning. The four-year-old Pierre's fear surged and he jumped into the bed, screaming and pleading, "*Maman! Maman!*" Dad was hurting *Maman*, he had thought.

His father jumped resentfully from the bed, while his mother covered her body with a purple cotton sheet and remained silent and motionless. As Pierre tried to cuddle with his mother, she hid her face firmly with the bed sheet. She did not respond to his pleading. His father was furious; he yelled angrily at Pierre, "Go to your room at once." Then he grabbed Pierre's tiny arm, pulled him from the bed, and brusquely pushed him to the door, shouting at him, "Damn it. Go to your room, you brat." Then he banged the door shut on Pierre's young, frightened face.

Outside the door, Pierre had stood scared and bewildered, with tears drenching his face. He heard his mother shouting, "How dare you treat him like that! That's beastly of you!"

His father snapped, "You ought to teach him some manners."

Then his mother retorted, "Who ought to have some manners, a four-year-old boy or a thirty-something adult?"

His father yelled, "Don't you ever insult me!" With that, Pierre ran to his room, perplexed and shaken, and lay on his small bed sobbing. With his young terrorized eyes roaming the room with dreadful apprehension, he covered his face with his blanket as though it would prevent any lurking creature from attacking him, for his fertile imagination filled the room with dangerous creatures ready to pounce on him. He closed his eyes as his body shivered with fear.

Within minutes, his mother, wearing her nightgown, entered his room carrying a bed sheet, a pillow, a blanket, and an alarm clock. She put them on the carpet, then kissed his cheek, brushed away his tears, and stroked his hair. "Pierre, there is nothing to fear. Mommy is with you." She tenderly patted his chest and purred, "I will be with you until you go back to sleep. My Pierre, you are sweet and brave."

He felt secure and his fears evaporated. In all innocence, he asked his mother, "Why was Daddy beating you?"

She smiled and softly assured him that they were just playing.

"*Maman*, I saw him hitting and hitting you," he replied.

"No, Pierre. We were simply playing. When you grow up you will understand how sometimes grown-ups play like this." Her tone was convincing. After a while, she arranged her bed sheet and pillow on the carpet next to his bed and lay down on them. She kept purring soothingly, "My sweet and brave Pierre," until he fell asleep.

Now in the darkness of the Auberts' apartment, he was surprised that his father had not even attempted to hide his erection. His own father! How crude and repugnant!

Deciphering the functioning of human memory is a daunting if not impossible task, he admitted to himself. How could such a sickening incident be expunged for so long from his memory, yet he could still evocatively recall different smells, trifling incidents, and insignificant statements from his childhood, some with nostalgia, some with disgust, and some with indifference? Then, suddenly, this disturbing incident springs into his mind with stunning force and vivid detail.

He wondered how he had forgotten this revolting incident. Was it his immense distress and confusion at the time that shoved it to the lowest depths of his memory? Or was it because it had happened just a few hours after the immensely traumatic near-drowning incident in the swimming pool, with its intense, primal fear? Though the two incidents occurred on the same day, he had never forgotten the swimming pool experience; yet his seeing his parents making love and the disgraceful reaction of his father remained submerged for a very long time.

He considered it a moot point because the subconscious is an untamed, mysterious, and unfathomable creature—it has its own logic and laws. However, he thought, now most people attribute everything to the subconscious. They cheat on their partners, rob banks, fail exams, explode in anger—and they simply blame their subconscious. He believed that Freud was a pseudoscientist because he had no concrete and scientific proof of his theories. But people had turned him into a pseudo prophet, a prophet with no divine revelation. Just sham revelations by a modern shaman.

He reflected that people have surrendered their free will to Freud's baseless and shaky tenets. Freud gave them a religion that doesn't demand contrition, repentance, or personal accountability. Pierre considered Freud to be a brilliant shaman who laced all of his utterances with scientific jargon. And like any shaman who's worth his salt, he was correct once in a while—a point here and a point there. Yet Pierre admitted that Freud was more influential than other sages, seers, and gurus. He was undoubtedly the most successful and erudite shaman, and he could remain so for a long time.

Then Pierre gradually slipped into a peaceful and deep sleep, like the placid and tranquil child that he had never been.

# CHAPTER 16

As Pierre bided his time before moving to execute Mrs. Nicole Gautier, a mother of two sons, he followed the news of the investigation of the murder of Mrs. Brigitte Villard with keen interest. He kept up with the muddled and hit-or-miss efforts of the police that, he thought, would never lead them to him.

The police had so far interviewed Jean-Paul Villard, his brother, his son, his daughter, his ex-wife, his son-in-law, and some of the incumbent and former managers of his companies. Villard had announced a one-hundred-thousand-euro reward for anyone who provided information that led to the apprehension and conviction of the murderer. The police commissioner, Robert Garnier, gave an interview to *Le Quotidien* in which he expressed his satisfaction with the progress of the investigation and reiterated his unfailing support for the local police and his firm conviction that the police would eventually apprehend the culprit.

*Le Quotidien* revealed that the police had been receiving eccentric calls and misleading information and tips from the public. Within seven days of the discovery of Brigitte's body, four men and one woman went individually and of their own accord to the police and confessed to the murder. Two of them demanded the reward money before they gave their false confessions. The police interviewed them and in each case found that the confessor had no idea what had really taken place. The reporter quoted a police spokesperson saying that it's normal to have some unhinged people confessing that they were the perpetrators, particularly in such a big case, and the police usually interviewed them even if they were visibly disturbed.

In one edition of *Le Quotidien*, there was a sidebar to the main investigation story about an eighteen-year-old school dropout who went to the police with strong evidence against his father, a former army sergeant. He told the police that his father had a large collection of guns and three silencers, and that on the night of the murder he left home shortly after seven in the evening and returned after one in the morning. The teenager demanded the reward, and the police told him it would be his once a court convicted his father. At dawn the next day, the police raided the family's house, confiscated the father's collection of guns and ammunition, and arrested the father, Mr. Roger Calvet. To the disappointment of the police, the guns did not include a Beretta pistol, and at the time of the murder, Mr. Calvet had been enjoying a leisurely dinner with two former army comrades at a restaurant, Chez Rochette. The police contacted the two friends while Calvet was in detention, and they both separately corroborated his alibi. It turned out that the school dropout resented his disciplinarian father and wanted him to go to jail for a long time—if possible, for the rest of his life.

Pierre was baffled by the fact that *Le Quotidien's* staff reporter had such detailed information about this incident and other incidents while *Le Matin*, so far, had not published any meaningful details pertaining to the investigation, though it spilled by far more ink on the case than *Le Quotidien*.

The city's two leading local papers gave Brigitte's funeral full coverage. Each printed a large, somber photo on its front page. Jean-Paul Villard stood in the middle; on his left were Brigitte's old mother; Jean-Paul's daughter, Aimeé, wearing dark glasses; then Pierre's mother and father. On Jean-Paul's right stood the mayor; the police commissioner; Jean-Paul's brother, Valéry; then Jean-Paul's son, Daniel. Behind them were the faces of Jean-Paul's upper-crust friends. Pierre was able to identify all of them except a tall woman and a middle-aged man standing next to her. Perhaps they were relatives of Brigitte, he speculated.

As he studied the photo again and again, he was assailed with sadness and remorse. Brigitte did not deserve such an end, he told himself. He tossed the papers against the marble table, then went into the kitchen where he swallowed three gulps from an open bottle of red wine to numb his feeling of remorse.

He stretched out on the couch, and closed his eyes, deciding to banish all thoughts of Brigitte and her murder. He attempted to focus on other persons and things: Cathy Derome, Martine Aubert, his mother, *Don Quixote*. However, an inner voice intruded and declared, "Since you have murdered Brigitte Villard, you cannot spare Nicole Gautier or Monique Roget. You cannot and should not." Is this my double talking to me, he wondered, and reinforcing my determination?

Nicole and Monique would never be spared. Yet it occurred to Pierre that he should have started with murdering Nicole, not Brigitte. He had not given this idea ample consideration; he had simply decided to eliminate the three sluts in the order he had found their names in his mother's secret diary. Brigitte, then Nicole, and finally Monique.

In the following days, Pierre settled into a routine that he did not find boring: reading, writing down notes and quotations in his literary journal—a habit he had started since his final year at school, doing his morning and evening push-ups, and listening to Mozart, Beethoven, Edith Piaf, Duke Ellington, Ella Fitzgerald, and Louis Armstrong. He also followed the news of Brigitte's murder investigation on the radio and in the newspapers, enjoyed the affectionate and stimulating visits by Martine Aubert.

Pierre appreciated the fact that he had a lot of time on his hands, and cherished the liberty of doing things at his own pace. He did not feel isolated or lonely. He loved the taste of this kind of solitude and reflected that everyone might need to get away from the hustle and bustle of hectic, daily life every now and then. One would come out of such a solitary, but not idle, break invigorated. Even calmer and wiser.

Having completed reading *Don Quixote* and *The Red and The Black*, he started reading Tolstoy's *War and Peace*. He discovered that he enormously enjoyed reading great works of fiction, something that he was not aware of during his school and university years.

Martine came to the rue Karl Marx apartment four or five times a week during her lunch breaks. On Saturday evenings, she usually stayed from eight until midnight or one in the morning. Martine, with her new resolve to be adventurous in sex, boldly asked for different positions in love making. She also initiated the exciting practice of having some of their meals while they were stark naked. Besides having food and sex, he and Martine laughed, commented on the media coverage of the murder, drank wine, teased each other, talked about her work, and discussed what he was reading at the time. He also enjoyed her tidbits about her father and Françoise Lépine. Martine was undoubtedly very fond of both of them. He guessed they provided a strong and special kind of emotional support to her.

However, it was evident and immensely gratifying to him that he and Martine were firmly gravitating toward each other, bonding affectionately and warmly, and that their minds, spirits, and souls were merging closer and closer. He was providing her with emotional fulfillment that was different from what her father and Françoise provided her. Martine was also giving him immense emotional gratification, which soothed his painful breakup with Catherine Derome. It seemed to him that he would soon bury his relationship with Catherine Derome somewhere in the vast bank of his memory. Still, he wished her well and hoped she would accomplish her ambitious political aspirations.

Despite all of the enjoyable diversions in Pierre's daily routine and the affectionate company of Martine, he sometimes found himself delivering his short but profound speech with great intensity to his imaginary audience in front of the bathroom mirror. There were little variations in the words he used in the speech. Sometimes he added a new thought here and there. Nonetheless, the logic and substance of what seemed to him a splendid speech remained intact. He couldn't find a rational reason for delivering his speech, but he felt immense gratification in delivering it, and enormous relief after delivering it to the nonexistent, rapturous, and entranced audience. Though he assured himself he was not mad or unhinged, he found the strong and spontaneous urge to deliver the speech an aberration.

One evening, he decided to survey the vicinity of the Gautiers' house. He had been to it a number of times as a dinner guest with his parents. The house was, of course, nothing like the Villards' mansion. It was something like Pierre's family house but its furniture was a notch or two above that of his family. Nicole Gautier owned a successful beauty salon in the city center. Her husband, Dr. Georges Gautier, was a professor of philosophy at the university. Pierre thought his parents could afford to buy similar furniture, but he knew his parents' miserable marriage had encased them in an emotional inertia. They had no interest in mundane things like sprucing up their house's décor or furniture.

The Gautiers' two-story house at 27 rue Bizet faced a small public garden, Parc du Prince. After Pierre parked his bicycle at a reasonable distance from the house, he sauntered to the end of the small park and back. He noticed that there was almost no traffic on the quiet street. It was dimly lit by a few streetlights that gave off a dull, yellow light. Now he looked at this watch: it was five past eight. The two-story houses that flanked the Gautiers' house were quiet and mostly dark—some completely dark. However, in one of the houses, a restive dog was barking. It fell silent. Then it started barking loudly again for a minute or two before falling quiet again, and the street became quiet and still.

Pierre patiently gazed at the entrance to the Gautiers' house.

Since it was a surveillance mission, Pierre had not brought his murder kit with him. He stayed stealthily near his bicycle. Within a few minutes, he saw a black Citroën leaving the Gautiers' house with a woman in the driver's seat. It was Nicole. Her car was moving fast. He got on his bike and followed the car, which turned left onto the street and then turned right at the end of the park. He biked with all his force, but when he turned right at the corner of the park, he couldn't see the car. It had disappeared into the traffic on avenue Kléber. He returned to his apartment, telling himself he should have biked at a faster pace.

The next evening, after doing his two hundred push-ups, washing, and drinking a small bottle of water, he put on the new, size 46, navy-blue jogging shoes he had bought to use in the murder of Nicole Gautier. He biked to the small park in front of the Gautiers' residence. He was carrying his murder kit in the various pockets of his trousers and black leather jacket.

When he reached rue Bizet, it was two minutes past eight. This time he parked his bike closer to the Gautiers' house but not in front of it. As he waited next to the fifty- or sixty-centimeter-high cement wall of the park, he looked at the trees inside it. The park was completely and eerily dark. The municipality either neglected to illuminate it or did not have enough funds to do so, he thought. There were trees and shrubs in the park—now all dark and silent. A cat, a squirrel, or some other small creature rustled in a shrub inside the park. The dog that had been barking the previous evening was barking again, and then falling quiet for a while, before it barked again. It occurred to Pierre that this agitated dog must be annoying the neighbors. However, it did not distract him from his mission; he was too focused to be distracted by the barking of a restless dog.

Pierre waited patiently in the semidarkness, his eyes fixed on the entrance to the Gautiers' house. The new jogging shoes felt very comfortable, though he had laced them very tightly. An owl hooted somewhere in the dark public garden, startling the restless dog, which barked with intensity for a minute or two before whimpering and then falling silent.

At about eight fifteen, Nicole emerged from her house driving the Citroën. Pierre raced after the car on his bike and managed to stay a few meters behind it as it turned right at the corner of Parc du Prince. He followed closely as it turned right again onto avenue Kléber on the other side of the park. However, Nicole sped away, leaving Pierre behind, breathless and disappointed.

He returned to his apartment despondent and thinking that he needed a car to execute Nicole. The first thought that came to his mind was renting a car for one day. However, he discarded the idea as being too risky. Using the flashlight, he returned the murder kit items to the cupboard in the bedroom, and locked the cupboard.

He poured himself a glass of red wine, and sat on the couch, sipping it. Rubbing his face, he felt somewhat relaxed, though he was absorbed in finding a car for Nicole Gautier's murder. He looked at his stretched-out legs and he could see that the glowing light of the kerosene lamp gave a gentle sheen to his brand-new, navy-blue jogging shoes. He was confident the police would be confused if they had found his footprints in the dirt behind the Villards' house and then discovered his footprints at the crime scene of Nicole's murder. They would be faced with different shoe-sizes. For his third murder, that of Monique Roget, he would don a pair of black sports shoes, with different tread design on the soles, that he had been using for more than ten months.

The thought of buying a secondhand car presented itself; he dismissed it at once as being risky and impractical.

How about Martine's car? Should he ask her to lend it to him for one or two days? He hesitated, as he felt that might expose the trustful and thoughtful Martine to enormous risk. That would be a gross betrayal of her. Yet, he thought, how could he eliminate Nicole, using his bike? He considered the option of hiding near the corner of the park at which Nicole usually turned to the right and shoot at her two or three times.

That was, he perceived, highly risky for two reasons. First, since Nicole's car would be moving rapidly as he had seen it doing so twice, his shots might not be accurate, and even if he managed to shoot her two or three times, there was no guarantee the shots would be fatal. Secondly, if Nicole's car veered to the left or right, or crashed into a car ahead of it, the chances of his escaping unnoticed by pedestrians or other drivers would be very slim, if not nonexistent.

He took a gulp from his red wine, stretched out on the couch, and gazed at the antique pendulum clock with its everlasting time of four seventeen. After careful and long reflection, he managed to convince himself that borrowing Martine's car would not expose her to any risk as long as he could execute Nicole with stealth and meticulousness. If he found murdering Nicole risky, he would abort it; then he could borrow Martine's car another time. However, the wine he had consumed intensified his confidence; he would execute Nicole the first time he used Martine's car. He picked up his cellphone and dialed Martine's number.

He told her he wanted to borrow her car to have a final, nostalgic, farewell tour of her great city before leaving for Ethiopia. "I was told a few days ago that my departure would be in three or four weeks. But this evening they phoned me saying I could be asked to leave earlier, Martine," he said. "So I am in a state of limbo, darling." She did not hesitate in telling him to come tomorrow morning to take the car. When he suggested he would come at closing time and drive her home, she assured him that Françoise would do that. They blew each other a few hot kisses before ending the call.

The next morning, after having a light breakfast with black coffee, he decided to skip his morning push-ups and walk to La Librairie Stendhal. It took him longer than he expected; he arrived shortly after eleven. He collected the keys from Martine and drove her gray Peugeot to a gas station. He filled the tank and paid in cash. The obese man who collected the money surveyed the car, and commented, "This is a well-maintained car." He brushed the sweat from his forehead with a red handkerchief and assured Pierre that it would give him at least seven years of trouble-free service.

Pierre drove the car to rue Karl Marx and parked it in a side alley on the opposite side of his building to keep it out of sight and away from his building. He went up to his apartment and drank a small bottle of water in the kitchen before he picked up *War and Peace*. He read for more than an hour, stretched out on the couch. At three in the afternoon, he made himself a tuna sandwich and washed it down with a glass of red wine.

He took *War and Peace* into the bedroom and read for a while. Then he decided to take a nap and set the alarm for five thirty. After the refreshing nap, he did his evening two hundred push-ups, showered, and put on a dark-brown shirt and dark-blue jeans. He sat at the edge of the bed and laced the new navy-blue jogging shoes tightly, feeling determined and ready for action. Glancing at his watch—it was six twenty—he decided to drive to Nicole Gautier's street at seven five or ten. At once, he started distributing the parts of his murder kit in the pockets of his black leather jacket carefully and unhurriedly. He double-checked the six cartridges in the Beretta.

In the living room, he lit the kerosene lamp and placed it on the marble table, then went into the kitchen and drank a small bottle of water. He walked to the couch, sat down, and smoked two cigarettes with gusto. He glanced at his wrist-watch once again. It was five minutes past seven. Retrieving his leather jacket with its deadly contents, he decided not to turn off the kerosene lamp. He left the apartment building and found that darkness had descended upon the city. Deciding not to put on his leather jacket right now, he put it on the front passenger seat, reversed the car from the alley into rue Karl Marx, and drove to the small park on rue Bizet, arriving at seven thirty-five. Now he had almost forty minutes to kill before Mrs. Gautier would emerge for her nightly sortie.

He drove around the dark park three times. Suddenly it dawned on him that he could wait next to the park on avenue Kléber instead of parallel parking on the dimly illuminated rue Bizet in front of the Gautiers' house. The avenue and the rue were separated by Parc du Prince. He was positive that Nicole would turn right onto avenue Kléber roughly at eight eighteen or eight twenty if she left her house around eight fifteen as usual.

Therefore, that is what he did. He decided not to put on his leather jacket yet. The minutes passed slowly and heavily as Pierre kept the engine running with the car lights off, and kept his eyes fully alert for the black Citroën and Nicole Gautier. The noisy, heavy traffic did not muddle his concentration.

One of the scenarios he imagined was that Nicole was meeting a lover in an apartment or hotel room. He would wait as long as it took her to emerge from that hotel or apartment building. He would follow her and shoot her before she started her car engine. Alternatively, he could shoot her as she tried to enter her car. If he found these two options too risky or not practical, he would follow her and maneuver his car abreast of hers, or as close as possible, and then shoot three or four times through the window of her Citroën. Yet the thought that he should not take unnecessary risks lest he put Martine's car in a police chase or even investigation, never left his mind.

Other scenarios played in his mind. However, he was adamant that he would kill her tonight. Tonight, Nicole. Not tomorrow. He waited in the car with his eyes on the left side mirror.

Suddenly, he saw the black Citroën merging into the traffic on avenue Kléber. He put on the lights of the Peugeot and carefully eased it into the traffic. She drove fast. Obviously, she was in a lustful hurry, he concluded. However, a red traffic light forced her to stop. Pierre could see there were three cars between the black Citroën and the gray Peugeot. He thought that was a safe distance between them; he did not want his car to be immediately behind hers because she might spot him.

When the sign turned green, Nicole turned to the left, and Pierre followed her. They drove for about seven minutes with only one light-colored Fiat between their two cars. Then Nicole parked her car with its lights on next to a taxi, which had its lights off. Pierre had no option but to pass Nicole's car. He managed to stop about fifteen meters ahead of her car. He could hear Nicole making three loud and urgent honks. Pierre, who could see her car in the rearview mirror, was intrigued. What was going on? All the scenarios he had considered plausible now seemed doubtful. He told himself to be patient. After all, Nicole might be taking someone to a love nest in an apartment building. Of course, she could afford to have more than one love nest. With her alleged sexual overdrive, she might need more than one love nest, he mused.

A lanky young man in his late twenties or early thirties, wearing a dark, checkered shirt and darker trousers, climbed from the taxi driver's seat, walked to the Citroën, and settled in the passenger seat. At once, Nicole started driving, and Pierre followed her at a good distance.

He kept driving behind the Citroën for about half an hour and then he saw it entering Le Jardin Anglais, a very spacious public garden with four large entrances. Pierre recalled that when he was a child his mother used to bring him here to see the white swans and feed the ducks in a large, man-made lake.

Now he parked the Peugeot outside the garden, and decided to give Nicole and the young man a few minutes before following them into the park on foot. He glanced at the car's clock; it was nine seventeen. He switched off the engine and the lights, picked up his leather jacket, climbed out of the car, and locked it. He put on his jacket then his black gloves before cautiously strolling into the park. He walked a few steps and stopped to put on his mask before venturing further into the park. There were chirping sounds of crickets and the muffled rustling of leaves and tree branches. He took in the breezy air, saturated with the smell of grass and trees.

After a few more steps, he could see the Citroën, with its lights switched off, in the semidarkness of the park. He walked a few more steps then stood stock-still; he swallowed with a knife-edge tenseness as he attached the silencer to the Beretta. He forced himself to stay put and looked around; as his eyes adjusted to the light level, he could see dense trees, shrubs, and flowerbeds. He estimated that the swan lake was three or four hundred meters from the spot where he waited. He inhaled deeply a number of times before walking agilely toward the car, adrenaline pumping through his body.

About ten meters away from the car, he could hear it rattling in rhythmic jolts. As he held the small flashlight in his left hand and the pistol with its silencer in his right one, he advanced slowly and stealthily toward the sound of vigorous copulation.

Silently, he moved up like a tiger about to pounce upon an unsuspecting prey. There was no doubt in his mind that he had to kill both Nicole and her lover. Of course, the man was innocent and had nothing to do with Pierre's plans, but his cruel luck had put him in the wrong place at the wrong time. Pierre assumed the man was a taxi driver—a most unfortunate taxi driver.

When he was about two meters from the car, he could hear a surge in the sound of Nicole's unbridled sexual moans and groans in the back seat. He decided not to get any closer to the car, as he was always mindful of Locard's exchange principle: every contact leaves a trace. Switching on his flashlight, he directed its beam through the rear passenger window, which was rolled down. Nicole was fully naked, her ample white breasts popping with abandon, and her body rising and falling on the man under her. When the light fell on her face she gave a wild scream, and instantaneously Pierre lodged two bullets in her face. One penetrated her forehead and the other one lodged below her left eye. Her body hit the car door behind her and then bounced forward on the naked body of the taxi driver, who was trying to scramble from his vulnerable and constricted position. He managed to raise his head but he was still constrained by Nicole's body. Pierre pumped two bullets into the back of his head, which immediately fell back on the back seat. The report of the bullets was muted by Uncle Marcel's effective silencer.

There was a high and tortured gurgling sound. Pierre could not determine whether it was from Nicole or her lover. Most probably from both, he assumed. He reflected that the two lovers would not suffer a lot because they would die within a minute or two. The thought tempered his sense of guilt.

He thought about lodging another bullet in Nicole's blood-drenched head, which rested now on the chest of the hapless taxi driver, but he decided to refrain. That was unnecessary. Somehow, Pierre was relieved that the two bullets had missed Nicole's eyes. He turned the beam of the flashlight to the front seats and saw their clothes piled on both of them. He noticed that the windows in the front were rolled up but both back windows were rolled down. As he switched off the flashlight and inserted it into the left pocket of his unzipped leather jacket, the foul smell of blood mixed with cordite pervaded the air near the car.

Before he walked away, he looked around. There was no sign of any human being. Evidently, the birds, the ducks, and the swans were having their nightly rest. The only sounds he could hear were of some hidden but active insects and rodents.

As he walked, unhurriedly, toward the park entrance, he decided to keep the silencer on the Beretta until he climbed into the Peugeot, because he was determined to shoot anyone who would cross his path, there and then. He decided to remove his head mask inside the car, lest a single strand, or more, of his hair dropped on the ground. In a tree to his right, a bird flapped its wings in the darkness and then settled in its place. Pierre was unruffled by this sudden noise. A few meters from the exit of the park, he removed his thin, leather gloves and held them as he proceeded to the Peugeot, telling himself not to hurry, not to panic. Before climbing into the car, he inserted his gloves in a pocket of the leather jacket.

Inside the car, he took off his leather jacket and mask, and placed them on the floor in front of the passenger seat, then detached the silencer and put it and the pistol under the leather jacket. He exhaled a number of times before he started the car. As he drove to his apartment, he thought about the two dead, naked bodies. Whoever discovers them will be shaken to his very core. He wondered if the police would call this a double murder and the work of a professional. As far as he was concerned, on the scale of professionalism, this reached the full thirty centimeters of the ruler.

When he reached rue Karl Marx, he parked Martine's car in its original place in the side alley. He inserted the pistol and silencer in two pockets of the leather jacket, then gathered his face mask and jacket, got out, and locked the car.

Inside the building, he turned on the flashlight, and with its sharp beam, he ascended the stairs. He felt drained and somewhat detached; he did not want to think about the two entangled, dead bodies. When he opened the door of the apartment, the living room was bright with the light of the kerosene lamp on the marble table. He locked the door and strode into the bedroom, where he carefully placed on the bed the face mask and the leather jacket with its murder kit.

He took the flashlight to the kitchen and fetched a bottle of red wine and a glass. As he settled on the couch, he flipped off the flashlight and placed it on the side table.

He took a gulp of the red wine. A job well done, he reflected. The police will find four bullets of the same caliber and make as the three that killed Brigitte Villard; and perhaps, if they are thorough, different shoe prints—with different make and size. That is all. Nothing else. Chief Inspector Dupré and all of his highly trained staff would be more baffled. No help from Paris could extricate them from their quandary. Pierre reflected that if Dr. Edmond Locard were alive, he would not be able to shed much light on the two murders. Or, rather, the three murders.

Pierre assured himself that his well-planned and well-executed murders would remain unsolved, notwithstanding all the police effort and expertise. They would be just a few additions to the hundreds of unsolved killings in France and the thousands of unsolved murders around the world. That did not mean law enforcement professionals were not doing their best, he thought, but it meant that some murderers were more cunning and ingenious— like him. With unmistakable contentment, he took another gulp of wine and looked at his new jogging shoes. He had to get rid of them first thing in the morning. Fetching a strong paper bag from the bedroom next to the kitchen, he sat on the couch, removed the shoes, and before depositing them in the bag, he inspected the soles and removed a green leaf that was stuck to one of them. With a lighter, he burned the leaf over an ashtray, and the little bit of smoke wafted upward and soon disappeared. It left a slight smell of smoke, but that soon dissipated too.

He went to the kitchen for three chocolate biscuits to eat before he retired to his bedroom. Then he heard the loud, ferocious snarling of dogs fighting in the empty lot outside the kitchen window. He wondered if this dog-eat-dog fighting was over a new bitch, or if a new dominant dog had stormed the nightly orgies and the usual group was trying to prevent him from disrupting their orderly and settled arrangements.

As he stretched out on his bed in his pajamas, he decided to lay low for at least a week or ten days before going after his father's third mistress, the youthful and stunning Monique Roget. The face of Nicole, a second or two before he shot her, sprang into his mind with striking vividness; her eyes, with the beam of the flashlight focused on them, displayed intense primal horror and hopeless resignation. They were the eyes of an animal, unexpectedly caught in a powerful trap, realizing there was no chance of escape. At that moment, he had pitied her, so he had shot her instantly to put an end to her agonizing horror and to quell the sense of pity he felt.

Before he drifted into a calm and long sleep, he felt sad and sorry for killing the unfortunate taxi driver, but that had been the only avenue open to him.

Next morning, after doing his morning push-ups, showering, and dressing, he took the paper bag with the jogging shoes and went to Martine's car in the side alley. He circled around the car twice to make sure there were no dents or scratches on the body. Then he inspected the tires for leaves or any other possible traces of Le Jardin Anglais, although he had parked the car outside the park. He also meticulously searched for any traces on the two front seats, the floor of the car, the dashboard, the accelerator, and the brake. He found two yellowish leaves on the floor in front of the driver's seat. He pocketed the two leaves with the intention of burning them later. When he was satisfied that everything was in order, he drove toward Le Coq Rouge Café, which stood at the very end of the inhabitable area—nearest to the abandoned area where Pierre took refuge. It was frequented by laborers and people down on their luck. After reaching the café, he turned left and searched for a large garbage container, as he had decided not to use the same garbage container in which he had dumped the shoes he used in Brigitte's murder. After a few minutes, he found one and threw the bag with the new jogging shoes into it.

Shortly afterward, he parked the car opposite Martine's bookshop. It was past ten in the morning. He entered the bookshop and glanced around but he could not see Martine, so he walked to her office and gently knocked on the door. He heard her call, "Come in, please." He found her with a pile of computer printouts and a large number of bills in front of her.

He deposited the car keys on the desk before they embraced, and then hotly kissed and fondled each other. Before leaving her, he mischievously cautioned her, "Don't spoil those precious green eyes by checking too much data." Then he thanked her for letting him use her car for his nostalgic tour. She blew him a kiss as he turned to the door.

Outside the bookshop, he decided to walk to his apartment and skip his evening push-ups. On his way, he picked up three shirts and two pairs of trousers from a shabby dry cleaner. It was the only dry cleaner in the vicinity. When he entered the apartment, he took the two leaves out of his pocket, burned them over the kitchen sink, opened the tap over the ashes, and dispensed with the last thing that linked him to Le Jardin Anglais. As he closed the tap, he found himself saying, "Chief Inspector Dupré, it is nothing personal, so best of luck. You need buckets and buckets of good luck."

# CHAPTER 17

Chief Inspector Gerald Dupré was at his desk by six twenty in the morning, feeling tired and sulky. He had not slept well last night, and a cold shower and the two cups of espresso he had consumed at home had not alleviated his weariness. Yesterday, he had received two sobering knocks.

He recalled yesterday's disappointing morning meeting with Dr. Emeline Napier, head of the Forensic Department. Three of her subordinates had accompanied her: Dr. Jacques Thomas, head pathologist; Dr. Juliane Dalmain, senior materials specialist; and Mr. Arthur Cabbell, senior ballistics specialist. Dupré had always admired Emeline's technical thoroughness, her willingness to cooperate, and her upbeat spirit. She had been raising two daughters and two sons on her own after her lawyer husband committed suicide six years ago; there had been no indication that he was depressed, let alone suicidal. However, Emeline had taken the devastating tragedy in stride and carried on with her life in an admirable way.

In the meeting, Dr. Napier gave Dupré and Laporte copies of two reports: one on the ballistics results and the other on the thirteen hairs retrieved from the Villards' residence. Then she asked Arthur Cabbell to go through his report. He gave a ten-slide presentation showing many types of weapons before focusing on the different types of Berettas and where they were produced, expounding on their specifications, and finally concluding that the weapon used in the murder of Mrs. Villard was a .22-caliber semiautomatic Beretta produced in Italy between 1972 and 1976. Then, after a seven-slide explanation of different types of bullets, he pronounced the bullets were a Winchester type manufactured in the United States between 1980 and 1985.

Then Dr. Juliane Dalmain presented a few slides, using a laser pointer to show different types of shoe prints and then showing the size-forty-four shoe print found behind the Villards' residence in red. She also showed photos of different size-forty-four shoe brands. She determined that that specific shoe print was made by a shoe brand manufactured in China for a French company. Emeline interjected, "Of course, no one can ascertain whether this shoe print belongs to the murderer or to someone else." With a sardonic smile, she added, "It is for you, Gerald and Henri, to establish this."

Dalmain then turned to the thirteen hairs found at the crime scene and explained in a short slide presentation that five were cat hair, four came from Antonio Moretti, one belonged to Jean-Paul Villard, and the remaining three belonged to the victim, Brigitte Villard. Dupré looked as disappointed as

Laporte did, which prompted Emeline to say, "Keep smiling, Gerald and Henri. Just keep smiling. We are still at the beginning of an investigation that might be long and demanding."

Then last evening, Dupré had sustained another disappointment, but he had told himself that he was not a person who would get demoralized by setbacks. He recalled that he and Laporte had scrutinized all the color photos taken by the police photographer at Brigitte Villard's funeral, since some killers attend the funerals of their victims. Then Laporte had shown the thirty-six photos to Jean-Paul Villard, his son, daughter, and brother, and they all pinpointed two faces they did not recognize. One of the two figures was a tall woman who appeared in seven of the photos. In six of these, a middle-aged man stood next to her in the last row at the cemetery. Laporte had circled their faces in the seven photos. They both looked somber and sad. In two of the photos, the couple appeared to be talking to each other. Now the two faces revisited his mind, causing him palpable disillusionment.

Dupré had been optimistic, though cautiously so, that this could be a lead when Laporte told him none of the Villard family members could recognize either the man or the woman. And he had asked Inspector Fauchet to assign one of his detectives to trace the enigmatic couple and bring them in for questioning.

And around six o'clock last evening, the young journalist, Denise Lambert, of *Le Quotidien*, who had been assigned by Fournier to liaise discreetly with Dupré, had showed up in Dupré's office—with her smooth and lively olive complexion—to seek his views on her article for today's edition and she dashed Dupré's hopes. When Dupré allowed her to look at the photos while he read her article, her attention was drawn to the circled faces in some of the photos.

After Dupré expressed his satisfaction with the draft article, Denise held up one of the seven photos and commented, "I hope Antoinette and Gerard are not suspects."

Dupré did a double take. "What do you mean, Denise?"

"These are Antoinette Torres and Gerard Blanchet."

"Do you know them?" he asked, staring at her.

"Yes. They manage an organization for the homeless called 'The Shelter.'"

Dupré wanted to know more, but his next question to Denise was, "Are you sure?"

"I'm very sure, Gerald. About a year ago I wrote an article about their organization."

"What brought them to Mrs. Villard's funeral?"

"I don't know, Gerald. But I am inclined to think Mrs. Villard was one of their secret donors." She shrugged her shoulders. "Just a guess."

"Do you remember the address of this Shelter organization?"

Denise had paused, staring up at the ceiling, before announcing, "Yes, I do remember it. It is 67 rue Charles Floquet."

Dupré's optimism had faltered on what had seemed to be a very promising lead. "Thanks, Denise, for this information."

"No problem, Gerald. Thanks for all your assistance." She inserted her papers into her briefcase and stood up. "Good night, Gerald."

"A very good night to you, Denise. Tell the old man not to change a word in the article."

After Denise left, Dupré had asked Fauchet to send a police car to bring Blanchet and Torres to the police HQ. When they walked in, they looked shaken. Dupré and Fauchet interviewed them in Dupré's office. They explained that they had attended Brigitte Villard's funeral to pay their respects because she had supported their organization for many years, donating twenty thousand euros annually. Moreover, she had been generous with her time and ideas, though she had refused to serve on the board of trustees.

Dupré and Fauchet thanked them, but what had promised to be a very strong lead had crumbled.

This morning, Dupré decided to read a report by one of his detectives on a vicious rape case and another about a stabbing in a dark alley next to a nightclub before preparing a brief report for his meeting with the commissioner at thirteen hundred hours. There was a review-and-coordination meeting at ten with the detectives involved in the Brigitte Villard murder investigation, but he would leave that to Henri Laporte.

Dupré decided to be frank with the commissioner and tell him that so far they did not see any light at the end of the tunnel, but they would be tenacious and thorough. He jotted some points in his diary and intended to add other issues to discuss at the meeting.

Unknown to Dupré, at the time he was reading the two reports, retired Admiral Philippe Dordain, his daughter, Chantal Barryre, and her four-year-old daughter Camille, were having a leisurely breakfast. Chantal's husband, Fabien Barryre, was in Russia on a business trip. Admiral Dordain, who was fit and healthy for a man of seventy-three, though he suffered from occasional bouts of gout, doted on his granddaughter and had come from Marseilles to spend two weeks with his daughter's family. After breakfast, he put on a light, beige jacket, picked up his elegant walking stick, and inserted his pipe into his jacket pocket. He left the house for his daily after-breakfast stroll in the large Le Jardin Anglais, which was just across the street from the Barryres' house. It was a sunny morning with a slight chill in the air. Dordain liked this garden, which was exquisitely landscaped with lots of different species of trees, flowers, and shrubs, and benches tucked into groves for those who wanted to rest or have an intimate conversation. This part of France was subtropical; hence, some tropical trees could grow here, and some of the park's flora reminded him of the Caribbean and Southeast Asia.

He strolled inside the public garden for a minute or so, and was about to take out his pipe and his tin of special tobacco, when his observant naval eye was drawn to a black Citroen, glittering in the sun. It looked abandoned and that intrigued him, so he decided to have a closer look at it. When he was a few steps from the black car, he glanced at its interior, then went closer, and had the shock of his life.

He had never seen anything so horrifying in his long naval career. A dead, naked woman on top of a dead, naked man. He could see a lot of congealed, darkish blood. Petrified, he stepped away from the car, and walked briskly, leaning heavily on his walking stick. "Oh my God. Oh my God," he repeated to himself. The horror he had seen made him feel that there was a dark, invisible cloud pressing over the entire park. The admiral abhorred all evil and he'd always believed that mankind was a cruel and vicious species. Yet he could not fathom how a human being could be so monstrous and wicked as to snuff out the lives of two innocent people making love in a car.

The admiral rested his weight on his walking stick, took out his cellphone, and dialed 112, then asked in a commanding voice, "Is this the police?"

"Yes, sir. What can I do for you?" a middle-aged woman asked.

"I want to report a double murder."

"A double murder?"

"Yes, madame."

"Would you please give me your name?" she asked in a professional manner.

"I am retired Admiral Philippe Dordain."

The policewoman's tone instantly became deferential. "Where is the location, Admiral?"

"It is the southern entrance of Le Jardin Anglais, madame."

"Could you please wait until the police arrive, Admiral?"

"Of course, madame."

The admiral put the phone in his jacket pocket and walked to the park entrance to await the arrival of the police. He looked at his large wristwatch; the time was eight twenty-three. When he saw a slim, young woman and an elderly couple, perhaps her parents, jogging on a track about twenty meters away from the car, he worried that the Citroën would attract their attention. However, they kept jogging. The admiral's shock was intensified by the fact that his daughter and her husband had moved to this city to have a family, arguing that it was one of the safest cities in France in which to bring up children.

At the CID's headquarters, Inspector Fauchet knocked on Chief Inspector Dupré's door and entered without waiting for permission. Dupré was not a man of formalities. As Fauchet, wearing a brown suit and matching necktie, walked in, Dupré immediately sensed solemnity mixed with excitement in his eyes. He stopped reading a report, stared at Fauchet, and asked, "What is it, Dominique?"

"A gentleman who said he is a retired admiral, Admiral Dordain, just spoke to Marie Gaspard and told her he'd found two dead bodies in Le Jardin Anglais." Fauchet firmly clasped his hands in front of him in an attempt to tone down his excitement. Dupré seized the news like a barracuda and frowned. His weariness immediately vanished. "What! Two dead bodies in Le Jardin Anglais? The park covers twelve square kilometers. Which part of it, Dominique?"

"He said near the southern entrance of the park. I have already sent six men to secure the crime scene. I also told

Dr. Thomas to send an ambulance and take his forensic team there immediately."

"What about the photographer and videographer?" asked Dupré, standing up, ready to rush to Le Jardin Anglais, but he decided to alert the commissioner first.

"They are on their way, Gerald. I have also alerted Henri, who is on his way, too."

"That's fine. Please send some police dogs and their handlers."

"I will do that, Gerald."

"Have some detectives do a thorough, hands-and-knees search for at least one hundred meters around the crime scene, Dominique."

"I will do that, Gerald."

"Now I want you to hurry to Le Jardin Anglais. Please, Dominique, no police sirens or lights. I don't want the media to be there ahead of us."

"I understand." Fauchet was worried about the enormous workload that would be added on top of the Villard's murder investigation. If this is the work of the same killer, then we will not be running in different directions, he thought. If it is a different killer, we'll be swamped.

He left Dupré's office hurriedly, and Dupré phoned the commissioner. The call was brief and somber. The commissioner expressed his concern that they might have a serial killer prowling the city. Dupré calmly countered that it might not be a serial killer; at least, there was no reason to think so yet. Nonetheless, as Dupré drove to Le Jardin Anglais, he felt in his heart of hearts that what the commissioner feared might prove to be true. Could the murderer be the same person who killed Brigitte Villard? he wondered. He assured himself that the police would crack these cases regardless of how long it took and despite the fact that their resources would be stretched to the limit. Two years ago, the powers that be had brutally down-sized his department with no apparent justification and despite his protests that a city with half a million people needed a larger force, not a smaller one. Not a 'leaner and cost- effective force' as they had justified their folly.

Before he climbed out of his car in front of the southern entrance of Le Jardin Anglais, he adjusted his expensive, new, blue-and-red necktie. Charlotte had bought it for him just a week ago. He was eager to see this Admiral Dordain. Dupré found the forensic ambulance outside the park and the forensic evidence-retrieval vehicle inside the park, about twenty meters away from the black Citroën. The police crime-scene tape was in place, extending from the park entrance and covering an area within about a fifty-meter radius in all directions from the Citroën. When Dupré walked into the park, he observed that none of the investigative team, dog handlers, or forensic specialists was idle. He could hear sparrows and finches chirp-ing in the trees. Police officers strictly kept curious bystanders away from the crime scene.

Fauchet, with his no-nonsense and hands-on style, was directing the investigative team like a slave driver. Dr. Tho-mas and his forensic team were already engrossed in their work. Dupré spotted Senior Inspector Laporte talking to a distinguished-looking, elderly man who was leaning on an elegant black walking stick. That must be the admiral, Dupré told himself. Then he swept the scene with his sharp, detective's eyes. The tall trees and the shrubbery could provide handy hiding places, particularly at night. People who strolled or picnicked in the park usually left by six or seven in the evening. Dupré knew there were a number of lovers' lanes in this large park, and plenty of sick voyeurs lurked around lovers, but the police never concerned themselves with such activities.

He asked one of Dr. Thomas's team to fetch him a pair of rubber gloves. Holding the gloves in his left hand, he approached Laporte and the elderly gentleman, who had thin, white hair and prominent, thick, salt-and-pepper eyebrows. Laporte, in a light gray suit, nodded at Dupré and said, "This is Admiral Philippe Dordain." Then, gesturing with his hand toward Dupré, he added, "This is Chief Inspector Gerald Dupré, the head of the CID."

"Pleased to meet you, Chief Inspector," said Admiral Dordain.

"Pleased to meet you too," responded Dupré, shaking hands with the admiral. Then he pleasantly asked, "Am I to address you as Admiral or Your Excellency?"

The admiral chuckled. "I like 'Your Excellency' but I have never been addressed as such. Just call me Philippe."

Dupré smiled and put on his rubber gloves. "Right, Philippe, could you tell us how you happened to discover the two victims?"

"I was having a stroll, which I usually do after having breakfast. I had walked for a short distance when I noticed the black car, and I thought it odd to abandon an expensive car inside a public park. I decided to have a closer look at it. Just an old seaman's instinctive curiosity. I was shocked by what I discovered." Dordain spoke in a clear and unhurried way. His face was composed; his eyes were frank, relaxed, and forthcoming, reflecting the contentment of a man who seemed to have achieved all he had aspired to, a man who had seen a lot in his life.

"What did you see?" inquired Dupré.

"A naked woman on top of a naked man, murdered in the back seat of the car. It was obvious that a shotgun killed the two of them. Then I immediately contacted the police emergency number."

"The Admiral lives in Marseilles," interjected Laporte. "He is visiting his daughter and her family here."

"I visit my daughter's family in your pleasant city every year. I have always enjoyed coming here. But I think today I got more than I bargained for."

"You couldn't be more right, Philippe. Could you please give us your cellphone number?" asked Dupré.

The admiral recited the number, which both Dupré and Laporte saved on their cellphones.

"Many thanks. We may need to talk to you in the coming days, either at your daughter's house or at the police headquarters, whichever is convenient for you."

"You can call me anytime. I don't mind coming to your headquarters. I would love to see how you run your operations, Gerald."

"It will be our pleasure, Philippe."

Then Laporte asked the admiral a few questions and jotted his responses in a police notebook. Finally, he thanked him sincerely.

Dupré smiled. "We shouldn't keep you any longer from your daughter and granddaughter, Admiral."

Dupré, as he stood next to Laporte, reflected that if Brigitte Villard's murder had sent shock waves through the community, this double murder would cause a massive explosion of panic throughout the city.

Dr. Thomas approached them, and said, "Our photographer took many shots of the car, inside and outside, and of the two dead bodies from all conceivable angles before we started sifting for forensic evidence, Gerald," said Dr. Thomas in his usual, soft-spoken manner.

"Thanks, Jacques," responded Dupré, who knew that the CID's own photographer and videographer were also present.

"I think we would finish our work here in less than an hour. We will let you know before we move the bodies," said Thomas.

"Henri will give you the green light, Jacques," stated Dupré.

Then Dupré and Laporte left Thomas to carry on with his tasks, and walked out of the area cordoned off by the crime-scene tape. They strolled on the grass, looking for anything suspicious. Nothing looked out of place.

Inspector Fauchet, who had searched the dead woman's clothes and handbag as well as the dead man's clothes, retrieved their ID cards and cellphones. He strode to Dupré and Laporte and announced, "The dead woman's name is Nicole Gautier, and the dead man's name is Alexander Dimitrov. She was the owner of a beauty salon and he was a taxi driver."

"First a billionaire's wife and now we are dealing with a taxi driver and a beauty salon owner!" Dupré brushed his bald head with his gloved hand. "Could you please, Dominique, find the cellphone numbers of the spouses or next of kin of the two victims? We must contact them before they receive the tragic news from the media. Also ask them to come to the General Hospital as soon as they can to formally identify the deceased."

"Of course, Gerald."

Laporte and Dupré left Fauchet and walked over to Dr. Thomas, who was supervising the bagging and tagging of evidence by his staff. Dupré saw Dr. Thomas's young assistant, Dr. Sonia Girard, with her jumble of brown hair. She was wearing a light-blue shirt and gray trousers and was crouched near the Citroën's open back door, inspecting the head of the male victim with evident concentration. Dupré, and his senior staff, always preferred to deal with the soft-spoken, self-effacing, and sometimes hesitant Dr. Thomas. He and his senior officers avoided dealing with Sonia— who was expected to replace Thomas within five to seven years when he retired—because she carried herself with imperial haughtiness, as if she was the custodian of all the secrets of the universe and was not ready to reveal any of them to lesser mortals. Perhaps she came from a family with negligible social skills, or perhaps she suffered from an undiagnosed avoidant personality disorder, Dupré thought. He was determined to deploy different means to help her gradually come out of her ivory tower, and hopefully foster a much-needed rapport with the CID staff.

Dupré gently gestured to Thomas, who approached them in a somber mood. "When do you intend to perform the autopsies, Jacques?" asked Dupré.

Dr. Thomas consulted his watch before saying, "At twelve. We will perform them at the same time. One will be done by Dr. Pernet, and the other by Dr. Lecoq. But, of course, under my supervision."

"When can we have a preliminary report?" asked Dupré.

Dr. Thomas hesitated before responding, "I would say tomorrow afternoon. Around two or three in the afternoon, Gerald." Thomas knew that although the cause of death was loud and clear, Dupré always wanted full and thorough autopsies so that no judge or defense lawyer could claim that they had left some questions unanswered, such as, what was the victim's last meal and when did he or she consume it? Or who was involved in the transfer of each item of evidence? And what was the exact sequence in the transfer chain from the crime scene? Dupré always insisted on leaving no room for loopholes, even in rape or bodily violence cases. And this was a double murder case.

Dupré said, "Fine," and then looked at Laporte. "You need to send two of your men, each to attend one of the autopsies."

"I'll send Detective Planter and Detective Bissot," replied Laporte.

"Tell them to be there before twelve, please."

"At once," said Laporte, and immediately phoned Planter and then Bissot, telling them to attend the autopsies and that they should be at the General Hospital by eleven forty-five at the latest.

Dupré, Thomas, and Laporte walked around to satisfy themselves that everyone was focused on the job. Seeing a young woman making a cast of a shoe print, Dupré stated, "I see you have found shoe prints." He looked at Laporte and Thomas.

Laporte replied, "Yes. They are taking casts of different shoe prints, even those that are not clear. However, one of the technicians said the predominant shoe prints are from jogging or tennis shoes."

"So they are different from the shoe prints you found behind the Villard house?"

"Yes, they are different. And they are one or two sizes larger than the ones found in Brigitte Villard's case, Gerald."

"Do we have a different murderer here?" asked Dupré.

"We can't assume that. Not for the time being."

Laporte and Dupré exchanged knowing glances. Thomas crossed his arms. The three men, each with rubber-gloved hands, stood silently, stupefied by this savage, double murder coming so soon after that of Mrs. Villard. Dupré gave Thomas a solemn look. "Can you give us a guesstimate of the time of the murders, Jacques?"

Dr. Thomas pondered, averted his eyes, and hesitated before saying, "The rigor mortis is absolutely complete in the two bodies. Therefore, I presume the murder took place before midnight. Roughly, I would say between nine and eleven o'clock last night."

Dupré massaged his head with the back of his gloved hand. "Can we get a closer look at the two bodies now?"

"Yes. We have already dusted the car for fingerprints and gathered, bagged and tagged everything of forensic value outside and inside the car," Dr. Thomas said, gesturing with his hand to indicate that they could approach the car.

In the meantime, Inspector Fauchet assigned a large contingent of officers the laborious task of a crawling-search for any possible evidence inside the area cordoned by the crime-scene tape, and up to a hundred meters outside the cordoned area. He also arranged for a truck to tow the Citroën to the Forensic Laboratory garage once Laporte authorized it.

Dupré and Laporte approached the Citroën, with its four doors now wide open; they were repulsed by the horrific sight of the two victims on top of each other, locked together in the embrace of death. The dead man's motionless left arm dangled from the back seat, and his hairy leg rested on the floor of the car in a pool of red-brown blood. On top of him, the woman's head rested on his chest; it was facing and abutting the leather of the back seat. Her left arm was underneath her, and her right arm was awkwardly placed on the shoulder of her partner.

They stared down at the two dead bodies for a while; it was a nauseating and grotesque scene. Then they moved to the back door on the other side. Here the scene was utterly indecent, vile and lewd. The woman's vulva jutted between her sprawled buttocks. After the first look, Dupré averted his eyes. "Henri, this is grossly obscene. This is the work of an outrageous barbarian." He felt not only disgust but also indignation—utter and overwhelming indignation.

Laporte, who was leaning forward with his hands on his knees, had his eyes fixed on the vicious and obscene position of the two bodies, and did not respond to Dupré's remarks. He was assailed by intense pity and compassion, rather than disgust. With his hands still on his knees, he closed his eyes and a surreal feeling blurred his senses for a moment or two; it left him hoping that the woman might suddenly leap to life and cover her stark nakedness. In this fleeting, surreal, hope against hope, he imagined the woman could tell them who the killer was, or at least give them a clue or two about the brutal murderer. Realizing the absurdity of his thought, he straightened himself and stepped away from the car. He vowed to himself that they would make the murderer pay for his inhumanity.

Dupré, still affected by the repulsive and indecent scenes, spoke in a calm, almost dull voice, "Henri, make sure that the photographer makes only two sets of all his shots. One set for you and Dominique, and one set for me."

"I will tell him no one else should see the photos."

Dupré said, "Yes, please." Then he sighed and adjusted his necktie with his gloved hands. "My gut feeling, Henri, is that this is the work of the same person or persons who killed Brigitte Villard, though I don't see any immediate, strong connection between the three murders."

"My gut feeling is the same. There might be a connection, though we don't see it now. Maybe he deliberately used two pairs of shoes with different sizes to confuse us. Let's get all the facts and analyze them first. Then we may find a connection."

Before he left the crime scene, Dupré thanked Dr. Thomas and told him that Inspector Fauchet would stay, with some of his assistants, until everybody left.

# CHAPTER 18

As Dupré sat in his office, he gazed at the seven roses with their different, deep colors, in the elegant, white, porcelain vase on the small meeting table. This was one of the graceful touches that Charlotte had brought into his life. Yet his mind was churning hypotheses, theories, possibilities, and alternatives like an automatic machine gun. It was stopped by a knock on his door.

Laporte entered Dupré's office, seated himself on a chair at the desk, and told his boss that the husband and wife of the two victims had been given the tragic news, and they would present themselves for the formal identification of their respective spouses before the autopsies.

Dupré thanked Laporte and added, "Before I forget, Henri, I want you to prepare a brief communiqué on the double murder by five o'clock so that I can read it to the commissioner before we release it on our website at six or seven, at the latest." He paused, and then added, "Please include something reassuring to the community, Henri."

Laporte nodded emphatically. "I will do my best. But people will be beyond reassurance once they hear about this heinous, double murder."

"I know. They will be alarmed, and some will panic. But without an official police communiqué, they will be up in arms against us. However, I am sure our friend Claude Fournier will sustain *Le Quotidien's* support for us. And we certainly need it."

"For how long, Gerald?"

"For as long as *Le Matin* keeps lashing at us, Henri. Claude is not a fair-weather friend. And he is supporting us in a proper and professional manner," commented Dupré. "Who are the spouses of the two victims?"

"The female victim's husband is Professor Georges Gautier, a professor of philosophy at the university. The male victim's wife is Suzanne Dimitrov, a waitress at a local upscale restaurant."

"A professor's wife fornicating with a taxi driver and murdered in a lovers' lane in flagrante delicto in her expensive car!" exclaimed Dupré. "This is going to make the editors of *Le Matin* dance in their offices. I wouldn't be surprised if they publish a series of special editions and supplements filled with lewd and outrageous fabrications." Then he rubbed his bald head with his right hand and turned his eyes to his left to stare out the large window in his office. He sighed in exasperation and decided that after Laporte left, he would phone Denise Lambert of *Le Quotidien* and ask her to come to his office so he could give her some facts—but not all the facts—and one or two photos for her article in tomorrow's edition. He wanted to disseminate some information to the public that he would not include in his official communiqué. And he also wanted to leave the reporters and editors of *Le Matin* high and dry— bereft of any worthy facts or details. Covering his face with his palms, he exhaled a few times and then placed his hands on his desk. "Thanks, Henri. I shouldn't take more of your time. Now you have three murders on your plate."

Laporte stood up and smiled. "They are on your plate, boss."

"It's the same plate, Henri," Dupré declared and gave Laporte a broad smile.

It occurred to Dupré to send the commissioner an e-mail instead of talking to him on the phone so that he could read it and reread it. The e-mail turned out to be a lengthy report on the victims, how they were killed, their spouses, the two scheduled autopsies, and the CID detectives who would supervise and take photos and notes at the autopsies. It also said the investigative and forensic teams had completed their work at the crime scene, the Citroën had been towed to the forensic garage, and the preliminary report on the autopsies would be ready tomorrow afternoon. He included almost everything. After typing 'best regards' and his name, he read the lengthy e-mail again before sending it. He reflected that it was a comprehensive and meaty e-mail, and the commissioner would need to read it more than once to grasp all of its contents. Keep him posted, keep him busy, Dupré mused.

He phoned Henri Laporte, asking him when he was going to hold his meeting with the detectives he'd chosen to work on the three cases. Laporte was going to brief them about the double murder, seek their views on the strategy he was going to adopt in handling the investigation of the three murders, and assign specific tasks to specific individuals or teams. Laporte said the meeting would start at three o'clock that afternoon. Dupré said he would address the detectives for five to ten minutes to emphasize the importance of the investigation and try to galvanize their enthusiasm and commitment, and then he would leave Laporte to chair the meeting. He jotted down the three o'clock meeting on his yellow 'To Do Today' pad.

Then he dialed Denise Lambert of *Le Quotidien*. "Hi, Gerald." Her voice was sweet and enthusiastic.

"I want you to come to my office at two sharp, Denise."

"What is this about?"

Dupré injected a strong trace of authority in his voice, "Don't ask. Just present yourself at my office at two."

Denise said apologetically, "Sorry for asking. It was dumb of me."

"You know you are not dumb."

"Thanks, Gerald. I'll be there, as ordered, at two," she replied in a pleasant voice.

"See you then."

"*Certainement*, Gerald."

Dupré was determined to give her and *Le Quotidien* a scoop. However, he would not give Denise all of the facts. At one thirty, Laporte opened Dupré's door in his gentle way and entered, carrying four large, manila envelopes, each marked: Le Jardin Anglais Double Murder Photos, and numbered one, two, three, and four, explaining that envelopes one and two contained photos taken by the police photographer, and numbers three and four contained shots taken by the forensic team photographer.

"This is your set, Gerald."

"Thanks, Henri."

"So see you at three, Gerald." Laporte wanted to make sure the chief inspector did not change his plan to address the meeting.

"I will be there, Henri." Dupré admired Laporte's readiness to listen to and seriously consider any idea or suggestion, even from the most junior detective. Moreover, he never allowed any inspector or detective to shoot down or deride others' ideas, however silly or wild they might seem.

"Thanks, Gerald," Laporte said as he walked out of the office.

Dupré opened one of the envelopes and found more than thirty color photos. Scrutinizing the photos carefully, he found most of them obscene and repulsive. He stacked the photos in the other envelopes, studied them, and then selected two photos to give to Denise: one of police cars parked outside the park, showing the crime-scene tape along the park entrance; and the other, a panoramic view of the forensic and investigative teams attending to their diverse tasks. Neither showed the Citroën. He was satisfied that these two photos were safe and prudent for an article on the double murder. Claude and Denise should be grateful to have them, he reflected.

Contemplating what he should say at the beginning of the three o'clock meeting with Laporte and his staff, he put a blank sheet of paper in front of him. He immediately scribbled four points. Then he pondered for some time before adding three others. After racking his brain, as he gently drummed his green-ink, ball-point pen on the sheet of paper, he penned some additional points. He put numbers in front of each and found that he had fifteen points. He read the points and decided they were more than sufficient; however, he deemed six of them to be very important, and decided that if he talked about them for about ten minutes, he should exclude the remaining points from his address. He had no intention to delay them from their task. Then he turned his attention to responding to some thirty e-mails. After a while, he put his palms to his face, rubbing it slowly, and then decided to go to the restroom to reenergize himself.

When he returned, refreshed and energetic, he found Denise, with her usually discerning and subdued make-up, sitting in a chair at his desk. She was dressed in an elegant, gray-striped business suit and a white shirt. Her black briefcase was on the floor. She stood up, and they shook hands.

"Thanks for coming, Denise."

With a sweet smile, she asked, "How could I refuse a summons from you, Chief Inspector?"

Dupré sat in his leather chair behind his desk and Denise resumed her chair and put her spiral-bound writing pad and a pen on the desk.

"You look more like a businesswoman than a journalist, Denise."

Playfully, she asked, "Do you have any business ideas for me?"

"Start a trucking business. Or a catering business. You'll be obscenely rich within a few years instead of spending your life running around day and night searching for sources, interviewing people, researching, verifying, writing and rewriting drafts, and meeting deadlines."

Denise chuckled. "You always have abundant ideas and wisdom, Gerald."

"Don't flatter me. You are deft in making well-placed and well-timed compliments, which is a great asset in any career, particularly journalism," he said, smiling at her. "Now let's talk about this double murder."

"A double murder?" asked Denise with intense eagerness. "I'm glad that nobody in the media has any inkling of it yet." Gazing into the chief inspector's eyes, Denise seemed as delighted as a young child who'd just been given a box of her favorite candy.

"I can assure you before you leave my office the news will be on the radio and TV broadcasts. But as usual they are bound to twist some facts and come up with wrong inferences. Advertently or inadvertently."

"Tell me all the facts, please." It was a spontaneous plea.

"I will tell you some facts and I will tell you what not to mention in your article. Is that clear?" asked Dupré in an authoritative tone.

"It is clear. Loud and clear."

Dupré picked up the two photos he had selected to give her. "Here are two photos to go with your article."

Studying the two photos carefully, Denise asked, "Do you have other photos, Gerald?"

"I have more than one hundred photos, but they are not for publication. You should consider yourself lucky to have those two. Nobody in the media has any such photos. Even these two photos might make someone in the media suspect there is collusion between the police and *Le Quotidien*."

"I see what you mean. I think they will be sufficient for the first article. Can I keep them?"

"You can make copies of them, publish them, then return the originals to me within a few days," said Dupré in a conversational tone.

"Many thanks, Gerald. So what about the murder?" she asked and raised her pen over her writing pad.

"Where should I start?" Dupré's question was posed to himself rather than to Denise.

She hastened to say, "Anywhere. Then I will organize the information."

"This morning, a retired admiral was having a stroll in Le Jardin Anglais when he discovered the naked bodies of a man and a woman, shot dead in the woman's car."

"Were they both married?"

"Sadly, yes. They were killed while they were making love. Please make sure you don't mention this fact. At least for tomorrow's edition. Let's spare their spouses the embarrassment for a day or two."

"What are their names, Gerald?"

"The woman's name is Nicole Gautier. She owned a beauty salon in the city center. She was married to Professor Georges Gautier. A professor of philosophy at the university. The name of the murdered man is Alexander Dimitrov. He was a taxi driver." Dupré spoke slowly to let Denise capture his words, for he knew she did not use shorthand. "His wife is a waitress in a restaurant. Her name is Suzanne Dimitrov. Of course, you can do your own research on the surviving spouses for your article."

"This is dramatic! It is breathtaking!" Denise could hardly conceal her enthusiasm. "When did the double murder take place?"

"Dr. Thomas's guesstimate is between nine and eleven last night."

"Please let me be clear about this, were they murdered in flagrante delicto?"

"The answer is yes, but I don't want you to mention that in your article  tomorrow," he said, then pointed his index finger at her. "Denise, I don't want you to write a sensational article. Leave that for *Le Matin*. I expect from you a decent and factual article."

"You have my solemn promise, Gerald. You know we don't go for sensationalism."

"I have to see your draft this evening and then I will decide, Denise," he said earnestly.

"Gerald, I will e-mail you the final draft by seven for your approval. You can delete any sentence or part you deem sensational or inappropriate."

"You shouldn't think I doubt your ethics, Denise."

"Thanks, Gerald. This is gratifying."

Dupré paused, reflecting before stating, "The two autopsies are being conducted right now, each by a different forensic pathologist under the supervision of Dr. Jacques Thomas, and each one is attended by one of our experienced detectives."

Denise scribbled this information, and asked, "What type of weapon was used?"

"The weapon used seems to be a .22-caliber semiautomatic Beretta. However, we have to wait for the ballistics results to confirm that. If you mention this in a direct way, the local community will be unnecessarily terrified and scared. I want you to write that some source or sources speculated that the weapon was a semiautomatic shotgun. Don't mention the caliber and don't relate it to Mrs. Villard's murder."

Eager to reassure the chief inspector, she rushed to say, "I promise to do that."

"What else do you want to know?" asked the chief inspector as he leaned back in his chair.

"How many bullets did each victim receive?"

"Each was killed by two bullets." He felt pleased with himself that he had not shown Denise the obscene and repulsive photos of the two victims.

"The bullets were lodged in which parts of the two victims?"

"I don't want to tell you that now. If I tell you, even a reader with a zero IQ may conclude they were caught in an intimate position. For the time being, I want the readers to know that they were murdered in Le Jardin Anglais. Just leave the readers to guess whether they were having an evening stroll or something else. You are not to mention the fact that they were murdered in Mrs. Gautier's Citroën. You can postpone that for a day or two."

"That is fine with me." Denise nodded. She quickly checked what she had written down so far, and then inquired, "What is the name of this admiral?"

"Retired Admiral Philippe Dordain, who lives in Marseilles and is visiting his daughter and her family here. It would be nice if you write a few uplifting words about the admiral and his career to add some spice to his visit to our city. You can Google his biography," replied Dupré.

"I will do that," she said then asked, "When do you expect the preliminary autopsy reports?"

"Tomorrow afternoon," answered Dupré, glancing at his wristwatch. He decided to give Denise about ten minutes before he terminated the meeting.

"And the final report?"

"Hopefully, in a week or ten days. Dr. Thomas is a meticulous forensic pathologist and, consequently, as slow as a tortoise." Dupré chuckled and added, "Don't you ever publish that. Anyway, I admire his thoroughness because whatever we do during any investigation, however small, will be put under the merciless legal microscopes when the case goes to court."

Denise laughed. "You are absolutely right."

"I'll issue a press release this evening, hopefully at 6 p.m."

"That's great," Denise hastened to say, "Because I'll quote parts of it in my article."

"You must make sure you e-mail me your article by seven, Denise. And I promise to send you my comments before eight."

"That's fantastic. I am deeply, deeply grateful to you, Gerald."

"I am also grateful to you. I hope my friend, Claude, is grateful to us."

"Of course he is. He always reminds me to keep this relationship hush-hush. He doesn't want anyone else at the paper to know about it."

That brought a smile to the inspector's face. "He has always been good at keeping everything hush-hush. He's a great man."

"You too, Gerald. You are a truly great man," said Denise in an effusive but genuine manner.

"Don't bullshit me, Denise," he said teasingly. "I am too old to be bullshitted."

"Gerald, I'm not bullshitting you."

Dupré chuckled, "You journalists can bullshit anyone. The devil and every angel."

Denise laughed heartily. "The world would not function effectively without some bullshitting—it lubricates all human interactions. However, nowadays it's called 'positive stroking.'"

"Positive stroking!" he exclaimed. "I like that. I think I'm an expert in giving generous, positive strokes, particularly to my staff." He had always prided himself on his style in dealing with his troops, regardless of their rank.

"That is a primal characteristic in a great leader." Denise's face glowed with the positive stroke she had just dealt the chief inspector.

Dupré brushed his face with his palm. "Now, Denise, I have to prepare myself for an important meeting. However, if you have any questions or you need any extra detail, you can call me on my cellphone."

Denise slid the two photos and her writing pad into her small briefcase and stood up. "Many thanks, Gerald."

As she walked out, Dupré mused that with her slim and tall figure, she could be a first-class model, especially for women's business suits. At seven minutes to three, he left his office to go to the briefing meeting.

# CHAPTER 19

The press release hit the police website at 6 p.m. and was immediately broadcast by the local TV and radio stations. Within half an hour, the police dispatch center received a phone call from a Mr. Pierre-Yves Gamelin. He wanted to speak urgently to an officer working on the investigation of the double murder. Officer Yves Taponier transferred the call to Senior Inspector Henri Laporte.

"This is Senior Inspector Laporte," responded Laporte in an even tone.

"I am Pierre-Yves Gamelin." There was a hint of a tremor in his voice.

"Yes, Mr. Gamelin. I understand you want to talk to someone involved in the investigation of the double murder."

"Yes, sir. Last night I saw a dark-blue Renault parked very close to the southern entrance of Le Jardin Anglais at seven forty-five in the evening. I was taking my daily stroll after my supper."

"What is your profession, Mr. Gamelin?"

"I am a mathematics teacher at the Lycée Zola," Gamelin replied in a timid tone.

"Go ahead, Mr. Gamelin. Tell me exactly what you saw." Laporte put a writing pad in front of him and jotted down the name of the caller, his profession, and the date and time of the call, though he knew that all calls to the police are automatically recorded.

"I first saw the car at seven forty-five. It was unoccupied. When I was returning home from my walk about eighty thirty, the Renault was still there and I saw two men coming out of the park and acting suspiciously. They looked around and seemed to be in a big hurry. When I was several meters away from the car, one of them threw something in the back seat, and they raced away at high speed."

Thinking that this could be an important lead, Laporte said, "Mr. Gamelin, could you come to CID headquarters at 48 avenue Victor Hugo? Or would you prefer that we come to your house to take all the details?"

"I am ready to come to your headquarters, sir." Gamelin, who was a bachelor, was ashamed of his small, messy, and cluttered apartment.

"Do you have any means of transport, Mr. Gamelin?"

"I have a car and I could be with you within twenty to thirty minutes."

"This is very considerate of you, Mr. Gamelin. When you arrive, ask for Henri Laporte. My office is on the second floor."

"I will start for your office immediately, sir."

"Many thanks, Mr. Gamelin. I'll be waiting for you."

Immediately, Laporte phoned Dr. Jacques Thomas and asked him if it was possible the double murder could have taken place before nine last evening, since he had stated at the crime scene that the time frame was between nine and eleven. "Would it be possible that it had happened before nine o'clock, Jacques?"

"What I mentioned to you in Le Jardin Anglais was just a guesstimate, Henri. I would not have any squabble about extending the time frame back to eight o'clock. But by tomorrow I would be able to give a more definitive time frame."

"Many thanks, Jacques."

In the meantime, Dupré was busy with his PC. Denise had kept her promise, as usual, and had e-mailed her draft article to him. He liked it and was pleased she did not divulge what he had told her not to disclose. In his e-mail reply, he asked Denise to include some nice words about the standoffish assistant of Dr. Thomas, Dr. Sonia Girard, as a much-needed positive stroke. It was his hope that a few glowing words about Sonia Girard might diminish, however slightly, her remoteness from lesser mortals. In fact, he was planning to invite Sonia with Thomas and his wife, Laporte and his wife, and Emeline Napier for dinner with him and Charlotte.

When Pierre-Yves Gamelin, a slim, middle-aged man with unkempt, graying hair, was ushered into Laporte's office by the uniformed officer, Yves Taponier, Laporte stood up and gave Gamelin a serene smile and a warm handshake. He gestured to a chair in front of his desk and Gamelin sat down in a reserved manner. He reminded Laporte of one of his high school history teachers. He'd been timid and awkward, and the pupils had taken advantage of that in mischievous and cruel ways.

After Gamelin had repeated what he had told Laporte on the phone, Laporte asked him in a civil tone, "Are you 100 percent sure of the timing, Mr. Gamelin?"

Gamelin swallowed nervously. "As for the time I saw the dark-blue Renault outside the southern entrance of Le Jardin Anglais, it could have been between seven forty and seven fifty. Therefore, I reckon it was seven forty-five. I am not 100 percent certain about the exact minute, but I am sure of the time frame because I started my stroll at seven thirty. Usually it takes me about ten to twelve minutes to reach the southern entrance of the park."

"Good. That's fine. What about the eight thirty sighting of the two men?"

"I am certain of that. I was returning home from my stroll when I saw the two men acting suspiciously and then racing away in the car. I looked at my wristwatch under a streetlamp. According to my watch, it was exactly eight thirty, Mr. Laporte."

"Let me ask you another question, Mr. Gamelin. Do you think it is possible the two men had been in the park for some time before you saw their Renault at seven forty-five?"

"I am inclined to think so, Mr. Laporte."

Laporte noticed that Gamelin kept his hands clasped on his lap and although he spoke in a hesitant voice, his words were clear. But there were no hand movements, no gesticulations, and no highs or lows in his tone. He wished Gamelin would relax. "The Renault was definitely dark blue, Mr. Gamelin?"

"Yes, Mr. Laporte. I passed very closely to it and with the streetlight I saw the color very clearly."

"Which model, Mr. Gamelin?"

"I am not good when it comes to car models or years. However, it was a sedan. Maybe three to five years old. Definitely not a new car but in a very good condition."

"Do you remember the plate numbers or a few of them, Mr. Gamelin?"

"No. It did not occur to me to look at the plate numbers until the car disappeared."

"Did you notice anything about the body of the car, such as a dent, a scratch, or broken glass in its lights or windows?"

"No. There wasn't any damage on the body of the car."

"Now, Mr. Gamelin, let's talk about the two men. Were they French or foreigners?"

"They were white. I think they were both French."

"Did you catch any words from them, or their accent?"

"A few but they were indistinct, Mr. Laporte. Because when they came out of the park, I was twenty or thirty meters away from them. I was walking toward them, which was my normal route back home, and they were talking to each other. I could detect from the few, indistinct words that I caught that they had French accents. They were looking left and right in a very suspicious way."

"Could you describe them?"

"Yes. The man who drove the car was a tall, slim, young man, in his late twenties or early thirties. The other man was somewhat fat and short. I would say he seemed to be in his mid or late forties. His hair was disheveled. The younger man's hair was closely cropped—the haircut usually associated with men in the armed forces. I had the impression that he was the one giving orders." Gamelin paused and Laporte remained silent. Then Gamelin added, "As I said, both of them were white and most probably French."

"Was either of the two men wearing a face mask?"

"No. I am sure neither of them was wearing a face mask."

"Was either of them wearing gloves?"

"No," said Gamelin. Then, with a hint of doubt in his voice, he added, "I don't think so." He paused again, racking his memory. "I am sure neither of them had gloves on his hands."

"Anything else you can recall about the two men, Mr. Gamelin?"

Gamelin paused, trying to organize what he intended to say. Laporte kept silent as he gazed amicably at Gamelin. "Yes. Their shirts were not tucked into their trousers. And I saw the young man holding what seemed like a stick or a flashlight, about twenty centimeters long. He quickly threw this thing on the back seat. Then he exchanged a few words with the older man, who looked very shifty and kept looking in all directions nervously. Then the young man climbed into the driver's seat. It seemed to me he ordered the older man to get into the car. And the older man briskly climbed into the passenger seat and closed the door. Then the car screeched away at top speed and disappeared in a few moments."

Laporte asked in a conversational tone, "Could this thing the young man threw on the back seat be a pistol if it was not a stick or a flashlight?"

"I'm not sure. But that did not cross my mind, Mr. Laporte."

"Don't you think it's unusual for two suspicious men to have a twenty-centimeter-long stick in a public park at night?"

Gamelin hesitated before admitting, "Yes. I fully agree with that. But it did not occur to me that it could be a pistol or a gun."

"Why not?"

"I don't think one would throw a pistol so hurriedly and carelessly into a car. It could go off if thrown in such a manner."

"What you have said is an assumption, Mr. Gamelin. Do you have some experience with pistols or guns?"

"Never. However, the young man was not holding it like a pistol. I have seen a lot of movies and TV shows and I have seen how pistols or guns are usually handled."

"Could your assumption be wrong, Mr. Gamelin?"

"I must admit it could be wrong. I have zero knowledge about weapons. So my assumption could be completely mis taken, Mr. Laporte."

"Did you see the color of this small object, Mr. Gamelin?"

"Yes. It was black," he replied and then hastened to give a more exact recollection. "It was blackish."

Gamelin's slow pace enabled Laporte to take unhurried notes.

"How about your estimate that it was about twenty cen-timeters long. Could it have been shorter or longer than that?"

Gamelin seemed a bit confused. "It could be. But I think I am good at estimating the length of objects and I wasn't that far away from the two men and the car at that point."

"Fine, Mr. Gamelin. If we ask you to help a police artist to draw the faces of the two men or at least the face of one of them, could you do it?'

"I don't think so. In fact, I was about twenty meters away from them when the young man entered the car. And I was about twelve or fifteen meters away from them when they raced away."

"Is there anything else you can recall from your encounter with the two suspicious men?"

Gamelin racked his memory for some time before saying, "No. I don't think so."

"Anyway, many thanks for coming forward with this important information. We highly appreciate that, Mr. Gamelin."

"No problem. No problem, Senior Inspector. It is my duty as a citizen to come forward with this suspicious and somewhat bizarre incident taking place on the night of the double murder."

"That's really commendable," said Laporte, standing up. Gamelin followed suit and Laporte handed him his card. "If you recall any other detail, however insignificant it might seem to you, please do not hesitate to call me. If I am not in, ask for Inspector Dominique Fauchet."

"If I remember anything, I will immediately contact you."

"Thank you for taking the initiative to contact us, Mr. Gamelin."

Laporte, left alone, stretched his arms a few times before resting them on his desk. He glanced around his office. Closing his eyes, he felt exhausted and decided to go home to give his wife at least one or two hours of quality time before they fell asleep. His kids would be dreaming in their sleep by now, he thought.

Glancing at the large wall clock, he saw that it was eight thirty nine. He decided to send an e-mail to the head of the IT team and then call it a day. He copied the e-mail to Dupré and Fauchet. In the e-mail, he asked the IT team leader to produce a list of all the dark-blue Renaults licensed to individuals, firms, organizations, and car rental companies in the last five years, and giving the names, addresses, phone numbers, and nationalities of the owners, as well as the cars' models and years of production. He ended the e-mail by asking for electronic copies to be sent to the Chief Inspector, Inspector Fauchet, and himself; and three hard copies to be delivered to Inspector Dominique Fauchet by eleven o'clock the next morning.

# CHAPTER 20

The next morning, Chief Inspector Dupré was at his desk by six thirty. He felt energetic after six hours of sleep; he was out of bed at 5 a.m. and out of the house by 6 a.m. as usual, leaving Charlotte still asleep. Before starting anything, he made himself a hot cup of black coffee in the second-floor kitchenette, not far from his office. Back at his desk, he took a few sips of the coffee, and then picked up *Le Quotidien* and read the front-page article on the double murder, by 'A Special Reporter', i.e. Denise Lambert. He was pleased that she had inserted a glowing paragraph about Dr. Sonia Girard. She described her, in a very serious tone, as a brilliant rising star in the world of forensic pathology. She also gave the title of Sonia's doctorate thesis and described it as seminal. Denise is a born bullshitter, he mused.

Then he decided to call Henri Laporte and Dominique Fauchet in for a meeting. It was eight fifteen when the three of them sat at the small meeting table in Dupré's office. Dupré sat with his back to the window, and Laporte and Fauchet sat facing him across the table, with Charlotte's elegant porcelain vase of roses, chosen with refined discernment, between them. In front of each of them lay a writing pad and a pen. The faint fragrance of the seven roses in the vase permeated the whole office, arousing a sense of finesse and sweetness.

Dupré said in an earnest tone, "Gentlemen, we have three murders to investigate. The three of us should focus on strategy and on significant leads and turns of events. So I want you to delegate as much as possible to your subordinates, otherwise we will not be able to see the wood for the trees."

Laporte and Fauchet nodded their agreement.

"Now I want you to raise any matters of concern in the investigation," Dupré said. He looked at his two subordinates, and then added, "It seems Dr. Thomas will not be able to give us his preliminary report on the two autopsies before this evening, though he promised yesterday to submit it earlier than that."

"We shouldn't push him," counseled Laporte.

"I have no intention of pushing him. We don't want to interfere with his modus operandi. He is a charming man but an annoying perfectionist."

"By the way," said Laporte, "I called him about the time frame of the double murder, and he advised me it could have happened before nine. You remember he told us at the crime scene that the time frame was between nine and eleven. Because the man who came forward last evening was categorical that he had seen two men leaving Le Jardin Anglais at eight thirty. They were acting suspiciously and raced away in a dark-blue Renault."

Fauchet enthusiastically announced, "Most probably these are the murderers."

"Hold your horses, Dominique. We can't be that sure," Laporte stated calmly, and then he gave them what transpired during the interview with Mr. Gamelin.

"This could be the lead that takes us to this cunning murderer, or murderers," insisted Fauchet.

Laporte cautioned, "Let's not be too optimistic, Dominique."

"Point taken, Henri. I'll lead the team sifting through all this information. Once I receive the hard copies, we will start contacting French, male owners of dark-blue Renaults," declared Fauchet.

Dupré, who was not happy with the suggestion, gazed at Fauchet. "Dominique, do not involve yourself in such a laborious job. Please ask Senior Detective Coderre to form a small team and let him handle this time-consuming task."

"Fine, Gerald. I will ask Coderre to do that," responded Fauchet, jotting a note to himself on the pad in front of him. Nevertheless, he told himself he would keep a close eye on the progress made by Coderre's team. This could prove to be the solid lead they had been seeking. It could turn out to be the breakthrough that would lead to the apprehension of the murderer or murderers. His enthusiasm unabated, Fauchet asked Laporte, "Did Gamelin give a good description of the object they threw on the back seat before racing away in their Renault?"

"He gave a hazy description of it. He said it was about twenty centimeters long, and of a blackish color. Gamelin assumed it was a stick or a flashlight."

"This sounds very odd," interposed Dupré. "Two men act-ing suspiciously and then racing away after throwing a small stick in their car back-seat! It could have been a pistol, Henri."

"I specifically asked him if it could have been a pistol. He replied that that thought had not crossed his mind and admit-ted that he could be mistaken in assuming it was a stick. He told me he thought it was unrealistic to throw a pistol care-lessly into a car. I don't think it occurred to him that the pistol might not have had any bullets or that its safety mechanism could have been activated. However, he admitted he has zero knowledge when it comes to weapons." Laporte paused briefly. "You will find all of what he told me in the transcript I have asked Christine Fould to produce from my notes and give each of you a copy."

"It can't have been a stick," Fauchet declared. "It defies all logic to take a twenty-centimeter-long stick to a public park when it is dark." Then he sarcastically added, "Were they pick-ing mushrooms? I don't think one can pick mushrooms in the dark."

"It could have been a flashlight," opined Dupré. "The park has a number of lovers' lanes. Perhaps they were stalking lov-ers in action and they needed the flashlight from time to time to find their way among the many trees, shrubs, brambles, and dense groves in the park."

"Voyeurs?" asked Fauchet. Without waiting for an answer, he said, "That's possible. It is possible they saw the murderer shooting the two victims and they decided to run for dear life. Do you remember that inept voyeur, Abdul Kareem

Chadeed—the Moroccan who was beaten on three occasions when he came too close to lovers in Le Jardin Anglais? The last time he was beaten almost to death by two homosexuals." He paused for breath and then asked, "Should we pay Mr. Chadeed an unexpected visit? He is always active at night in lovers' lanes."

Calmly, Laporte answered, "Maybe later. If all avenues lead us to a dead end, we would then visit Mr. Chadeed, Dominique. You know he is a compulsive liar. He will not tell us anything factual unless we torture him. But we never use torture."

"Could it be a vibrator, not a stick, or a flashlight?" Fauchet ventured to ask.

"A black vibrator?" asked Dupré. "Just like a black tulip. Have you ever seen a black vibrator?"

Fauchet pressed his lips together. "No, I haven't seen one. But I've read that now there are black, pink, yellow, and green multipurpose, modern vibrators on the market."

Dupré smiled gently and asked, "For heaven's sake! Why would a couple, heterosexual or homosexual, take a vibrator, regardless of its color, into a lovers' lane? The sound of a vibrator would attract hordes of voyeurs."

"Gerald, some of the latest, ultramodern ones are advertised as being almost noiseless, even at their highest speed," responded Fauchet. "I wouldn't be surprised if, with the rapid progress of technology, they come up with inbuilt silencers for vibrators."

The three investigators laughed. Dupré said in jest, "I am told that people who use vibrators find the sound of a vibrator exciting and arousing."

"I always thought so," responded Fauchet. "So what's the point of manufacturing a soundless vibrator?"

Both Dupré and Laporte admired Fauchet's audacity to think aloud and his willingness to ask suspects awkward questions—questions that, at the time, do not seem to be well thought out. But what was positive about his style was that he usually posed his awkward questions at the right time, rather than waiting for the perfect questions, asked too late.

Dupré with his masterful and low-key joviality, said in deadpan, "You know, the two of you make a great investigative team. One with an overtly dirty mind and the other with a covertly dirty mind."

Laporte chuckled but decided not to respond. He said in a sedate manner, "As far as I know, a lot of pistols and guns come in black, but even if the two men had a black vibrator, let's trace them. Even if they were not the killers, they could have seen the black Citroën and perhaps the murderer or murderers. They could still provide us with some useful information."

With his hands clasped on top of his writing pad, Dupré nodded and looked at Fauchet for his reaction, as the calming scent of the roses filled his nostrils.

"I agree that these two men must be traced and interrogated," affirmed Fauchet.

"How about your investigation-progress meeting, Henri?" inquired Dupré.

"I am holding it at nine o'clock."

"Fine, Henri. So I could have a summary of the key points sometime today?"

"Let's say by one o'clock. Senior Detective Hugo, as usual, will be taking notes and will send the three of us an e-mail of the main points. Hugo is very good at zooming in on the pertinent points. In fact, I have assigned him to supervise all the documentation of this investigation. What do you think, Gerald?"

"Henri, I never interfere in how you deploy your staff." Dupré paused, then asked, "What about the progress made by the team tracing the Beretta owners in the city?"

Laporte replied, "There are 1,093 individuals who own Berettas here. They have spoken to about 140 so far."

"Henri, I do remember your point that the killer is most probably a young man, which I am inclined to agree with. So I would suggest they start with Beretta owners who are between twenty-one and thirty. Then, those from thirty-one to forty, and so on. How about that?"

"That's a good idea, Gerald. I wonder why this idea did not occur to me or the team." Laporte scribbled the suggestion in his notebook.

Fauchet stated, "Of course, there is a possibility that the Beretta used in the murders is not registered in the database."

"Nonetheless, Dominique, we have to go through this laborious exercise," said Laporte.

Then Dupré said, "I want the two of you together to interview Professor Gautier and Mrs. Dimitrov today at their homes. Do not bring them here at this point in time. As you know, interviewing someone at home will provide you with pertinent details that could prove to be very useful to the investigation."

"We will do that the moment the meeting is over," said Laporte.

Fauchet inquired, "Do you think we need to take one of our psychologists with us in case the spouses are badly traumatized?"

"Let's first see if either needs counseling and get their approval to have one of our police psychologists talk to them," said Laporte.

"Fine," agreed Dupré. He mused that Laporte and Fauchet complemented each other. Without explicitly knowing it, they formed the proverbial team of good cop and bad cop. Of course, Laporte was the good cop: calm, urbane, and soft-spoken. But his laid-back style was immensely deceptive because he had a highly incisive, analytical mind and the ability to see the forest as well as the trees. On the other hand, Fauchet was confrontational, combative with suspects, and always ready to jump to conclusions. Yet he was industrious, persistent, and surprisingly systematic in gathering and preserving evidence. Fauchet's major shortcoming, reflected Dupré, is that he dealt with his subordinates in the same brusque way he used with suspects, so he was not well liked among his staff. Some of them hated his guts.

After a pause, Dupré said, "I want the reports of your interviews with Dimitrov and Gautier on my desk before eight this evening."

Laporte and Fauchet exchanged glances as if questioning the feasibility of that deadline. Then Fauchet said, "Agreed."

Laporte nodded. "Once we finish the meeting, say by ten thirty or eleven, we will drive to Mrs. Dimitrov's residence," advised Laporte. "Dominique, please call the two spouses and tell them we would come to their residences to interview them."

"I will do that immediately," said Fauchet.

With his elbows on the table, Dupré said in a somber tone, "I don't want to demoralize you or myself, but it seems we are hunting a ghost—a demonic and cunning ghost who leaves no significant evidence of his wicked crimes. However, we are going to apprehend this ghost." Then he stood up, indicating the meeting was over.

As he walked to his desk, he anxiously hoped that the team assigned to vet the Renault owners would not end up with a time-consuming fiasco like the team that was assigned to trace the hotels and pensions' clients who checked in and out around the time of Brigitte Villard's murder.

Immediately after their meeting with the detectives assigned to the investigation, Laporte and Fauchet drove to the address of Mrs. Suzanne Dimitrov, arriving at her tiny apartment on the fourth floor of an old, six-story building at eleven fifteen. They had to take the stairs because the elevator was out of order.

Fauchet knocked on the door a few times before she opened it and stepped back, telling them, "Close the door behind you." Laporte obliged and closed the door gently. Though Fauchet had already advised her of their visit, she was still wearing a light-green, cotton robe that had seen better days. Her hair was disheveled, and she wore a brown T-shirt and yellow shorts under the robe, leaving her thighs and unshaven legs exposed. However, her green, flip-flops looked almost brand new.

She sat in an old armchair and gestured for them to sit on an old sofa. Each of them took one end, for Mrs. Dimitrov had carelessly dumped her black two-piece waitress uniform in the middle of the sofa. They immediately noticed, without letting their eyes linger on it, the name "Suzanne" professionally stitched in red on the left breast.

When they settled down, she gave them an obnoxious look. There were no signs of dejection or sadness on her face; rather, she had a devil-may-care look. Then, half-heartedly, she asked them if they wanted anything to drink, and they politely turned down her offer. In the room to their left, there was a wooden dining table with six chairs. It looked like a recent acquisition, not like the old sofa set. On the wall behind Mrs. Dimitrov hung two, outdated, black-and-white photos of Marilyn Monroe and James Dean. What a juvenile taste! Fauchet mused.

Fauchet said, "Mrs. Dimitrov we are all saddened by—"

She interrupted him rudely and lashed out, "Cut out all the crap. Just ask your damned questions. It is not the job of the police to be saddened by a murder. Your job is to ask questions. That is all."

Fauchet was taken aback and Laporte gave him a knowing look, telling him not to overreact. Laporte was not surprised by her vulgar reaction because he had been told that she had identified her husband's body yesterday by saying, "Yes, this bastard was my husband, Alexander Dimitrov," and then spat on his face. She had been promptly forced out of the room. It seemed someone, in the hospital, had had the bad taste to tell her that her husband was murdered while having intercourse with the dead woman in her car, before she was taken in to identify him.

Suzanne picked up a yellow mug, took a sip, and placed it next to a half-empty brandy bottle on a small table near her armchair. Next to the bottle, there was a large, white ashtray, with the brand name of a famous French cigarette embossed on it in dark blue. There were fifteen or sixteen cigarette butts in the ashtray.

A fat, Persian cat with very thick, dark-gray hair streaked with white sat silently not far from Mrs. Dimitrov, gazing brazenly at the two detectives as if warning them not to cross any red lines with his owner. Fauchet rightly guessed it was a tomcat. Suzanne lit a cigarette and puffed on it a number of times before asking in a condescending tone, "What can I do for you, gentlemen?"

Fauchet, having composed himself, said in a matter-of-fact manner, "This is Senior Inspector Henri Laporte. I am Inspector Dominique Fauchet. I spoke to you on the phone."

"Pleased to meet you, inspectors," she said with blatant disdain in her voice.

Unfazed, Laporte looked at her full in the eye, and said in a calm but serious voice, "We have some questions for you. We expect you to cooperate with us to apprehend the murderer of your husband. Let me be very clear with you, if you don't answer our questions here, we will be forced to take you to our headquarters for an intensive interrogation."

"Are you threatening me?" she snapped.

Fauchet interposed, "This is not a threat. This is a promise. A solid promise." His stern tone made her flinch. She puffed at her cigarette and stared at her fat cat without responding.

Laporte gave her ample time before declaring, "Mrs. Dimitrov, you should know that in any murder investigation, the spouse is always the prime suspect."

"Is that so?" she asked with bewilderment.

"I don't think I need to repeat that. Right now, you are at the top of our list of suspects," he said, sensing she was now worried about being dragged to the CID's headquarters.

She took a long drag on her cigarette, exhaled the smoke in two straight streams, and then looked at Laporte. "I have nothing to do with his murder. Yet, I am not sorry at his brutal end. The bastard and the whore who was with him got what they deserved."

Fauchet, undeterred by her rudeness to him and Laporte, blurted, "I'm sure you are still in shock. This is natural, Mrs. Dimitrov."

"I am not in shock and I am no longer Mrs. Dimitrov. I am Suzanne Levasque. I have reverted to my maiden name, Inspector." She spat out the word 'Inspector'.

This bitch has, for no good reason, a blatant antipathy toward me, Fauchet told himself. She is nothing more than white trash. However, he did not want to lash out at her in the presence of Laporte. With difficulty, he suppressed his indignation and decided to let Laporte interview her in his unruffled style. It occurred to him that Alexander Dimitrov had been entitled to cheat on this scum-of-the-earth wife.

Laporte stated in an even tone, "Whether you are Suzanne Dimitrov or Suzanne Levasque is not a matter of concern to us. We want you to help us in investigating this double murder. As far as we are concerned, this is a very serious crime. And you and Professor Gautier are the prime suspects until we have enough evidence to exclude both of you or one of you."

Suzanne retorted, "To me, this is not a crime. This is divine retribution. The bastard had been betraying me and our two-year-old daughter." She averted her gaze from the two officers, picked up the bottle, and poured some brandy into the mug. As she brought the mug to her lips, Laporte and Fauchet noticed a sudden tremor in her hand; a tremor of edginess and fury rather than of fear or anxiety, Fauchet thought. She took a large swallow from the mug.

Laporte and Fauchet remained silent.

Suzanne started talking without looking at the two officers, as if she was delivering a soliloquy. "He was a filthy bastard. I loved him. I married him. I gave him French citizenship. What did he do? He was not faithful. He was not grateful. He failed to appreciate all that I willingly gave him. He betrayed my young daughter and me. Now, she'll be called Natalie Levasque, not Natalie Dimitrov." She paused to light another cigarette, and then took a long drag on it. "I will not attend his funeral or be involved in its arrangements. I will leave that to his fellow Bulgarian thugs. Or maybe the police or the municipality can take care of his burial." She took another long drag before adding, "Maybe the police don't believe in divine punishment and retribution. But this is a pure and unmistakable case of divine justice."

She turned her eyes to Laporte and Fauchet. The slow manner in which she'd delivered her monologue had enabled Fauchet to commit to his notebook every word she uttered. The three of them remained silent until Laporte said in a calm voice, "Suzanne Levasque, you are entitled to see it as divine retribution or extraterrestrial punishment. And perhaps you are right. But we have some questions that you have to answer. We want to apprehend the murderer or murderers before they murder other innocent people."

She did not respond, and Laporte asked her calmly, "Do you understand what I mean, Miss Levasque?"

"Yes, I do," she said, and pulled the sides of her light-green cotton robe over her nude thighs and legs.

"What do you do, Miss Levasque?"

"I'm a waitress at Chez Maurice in the city center. It's a high-class restaurant frequented by executives and other professionals," she said in a tone that signaled she was ready to talk.

Her opening up surprised Fauchet. Was it because Laporte placated her by calling her Suzanne Levasque? he wondered; or had Laporte's threat to take her to headquarters for an intensive interrogation finally penetrated her thick skull? Maybe Laporte's concession that she could be right about divine justice had softened her.

"Where were you between eight in the evening and one in the morning? That is, the night of the murder?" asked Laporte.

"I was at home with my mother, my aunt, and my daughter. I was not working that evening. In fact, my mother spent the night with us, sharing a room with Natalie. My aunt, who lives nearby, left around midnight. I left the apartment at seven-thirty in the morning to go to work, and I received your call about the murder during my morning shift. Thus, I have a solid alibi. You can verify this with my mother and aunt."

"We might talk to them later. The fact that you have such an alibi doesn't mean that you are automatically excluded as a suspect, Miss Levasque. We have to do a lot of digging before we can rule you out as a suspect," Laporte cautioned her.

"What do you mean by that, Senior Inspector?" she asked in a nervous voice tinged with puzzlement.

"You have to leave that to us. Perhaps you planned the murder and at the same time arranged what you now call a solid alibi. We'll find out. That doesn't necessarily mean your mother and aunt were wittingly involved in the plan."

"Why would I arrange the murder of a husband who I naively believed—until the last moment of his fucking life—loved me?" she asked, stubbing out her cigarette with vigorous force in the full ashtray, scattering some butts on the table.

"We don't know yet. But we could find evidence that would remove you from the suspect list," said Laporte. He paused for effect. "Let me assure you, we will conduct a thorough probe. We are completely neutral. Only evidence, facts, and analysis guide us. I should impress upon you that a suspect is not necessarily the killer. Do you get me, Miss Levasque?" Laporte gazed at her and awaited her response.

Mrs. Dimitrov took a large swallow from her brandy mug, frowned as the stiff stuff hit her throat and stomach, and then hastened to state, "I do get you. I will cooperate with you to prove that I have nothing to do with his murder or Mrs. Gautier's. But frankly, I don't care at all whether you apprehend or fail to apprehend their killer."

Laporte disregarded what she said, and asked, "When did you first meet Alexander Dimitrov?"

The fat Persian cat stood up, walked over to Suzanne, and gently rubbed his fluffy body against her legs. She tenderly stroked his back. Then the cat disappeared somewhere in the small apartment, showing no interest in the three human beings engaged in a heated discourse.

"Eight years ago," replied Suzanne. "He was a waiter at Chez Maurice. The same restaurant I am still working in. And I foolishly fell in love with him."

"When did you get married?"

"Six years ago. That was the greatest mistake of my life. The most stupid thing I have ever done." Suzanne looked Laporte in the eye, her hands clasped in her lap.

"How was your married life, Miss Levasque?"

"It was what you could describe as a very happy life. He deluded me by filling our life with laughter, affection, and intimacy. Now it's obvious that was all deception."

"When was your daughter born?" asked Laporte.

"Two years ago. We agreed not to have children for the first three or four years of our marriage."

"Could you say he loved his daughter?"

"I have to admit, he loved her. He doted on her." She paused and her eyebrows tightened in a tense way. "And she loved him. But anyone could deceive a two-year-old child by pretending to love her." She sighed and averted her eyes from the two law-enforcement men. "How about deceiving someone as old as me? I am thirty-three years old and he made me believe he loved me. And I stupidly loved him. However, as it turned out, it was all a gross Bulgarian sham. Only a Bulgarian could be so conniving and deceptive."

"Miss Levasque, we are not interested in your prejudices. So keep your chauvinistic views to yourself," Laporte stated firmly. "Did you ever suspect or actually know your deceased husband indulged in extramarital affairs?"

She stated loudly, "Never. If I had ever suspected or knew anything of the sort, I would have cut off his prick and testicles with a large kitchen knife."

"Did he have any enemies?"

"Not that I know of. He was a friendly, helpful, and a considerate person. I have to admit that everyone who knew the bastard liked him. In fact, he could charm anybody." She paused, reflecting, and then she added, "These are the signs of a sociopath. A perfect, textbook sociopath. Don't you know that, Senior Inspector?"

Laporte decided not to respond to her last condescending remark. However, he thought Mrs. Dimitrov—or Miss Levasque—was talking about her husband as though he was the murderer rather than the victim. "So to the best of your knowledge, he did not have any enemies?" he gently pressed on.

"That's correct. You can question some of his Bulgarian friends. Some of them look seedy and shifty. I can give you a list of six of them, the ones whose strange names I can spell correctly. There are others whose names I can't spell. But these six can lead you to them."

"We appreciate that, Miss Levasque," responded Laporte.

Suzanne briskly stood up and went through a small passage to a room at the back of the apartment.

Fauchet whispered to Laporte, "She is completely nuts. She seems to have a personal vendetta against all Bulgarians, though she loved, married, and lived happily with one who was friendly and considerate."

Laporte whispered back, "She's in shock and lashing out at Bulgarians, herself, her dead husband, and the world."

"And at us," said Fauchet.

"Please ignore all her nonsensical and vulgar remarks, Dominique." Fauchet nodded in agreement, making a great effort to contain his seething anger. He pursed his lips together and passed his pink tongue between them—left, right, left, and right again.

In a few moments, Suzanne returned holding a sheet of paper torn from an exercise book. She handed it to Laporte and said, "I think any one of them could be a suspect. They frequent Le Cafe de Foy on rue Garnet. I have written that on the paper." She sat down in her armchair with a thud.

Laporte thanked her and read the six names written in vigorous fury. He passed the list to Fauchet, who put the date and time at the top and then folded it and inserted it in an inside pocket of his jacket.

"You said he had worked as a waiter at Chez Maurice. When and why did he become a taxi driver?"

"The practice at the restaurant is that all tips are pooled. Management takes 5 percent of all the daily tips and then distributes the rest equally between all the waiters who worked that day. However, two waiters complained to the assistant manager that Alexander did not put all of his tips in the pool, but kept some of them. The assistant manager believed them and sacked him at once. Of course, Alexander denied the accusation and told me that the assistant manager was a chauvinist pig who hated all East Europeans. At the time, I believed him. But now it's obvious that he was stealing some of the tips."

"Then he became a taxi driver?" Laporte prompted her to carry on.

"Not immediately. He was unemployed for almost eight months. Then an old Bulgarian who's a naturalized Frenchman, who seems to be the godfather of the Bulgarians living here, offered him a job at his small cab company. Alexander seemed much happier being a taxi driver than a waiter."

"What is the name of this taxi company?"

She responded immediately but with a hint of disgust, "ITC Taxi Services. Its old owner could be the godfather of the Bulgarian Mafia here."

Laporte gazed into Suzanne's eyes before telling her, "Miss Levasque, there is no Bulgarian Mafia here. Your prejudices are making you imagine things. Let me ask you another question. Do you personally have any enemies?"

"I have a few enemies but not enemies who would go to the extent of harming me or my family. You see, I have an explosive temper, which has caused aggravations from time to time. I have put some people in their proper place. Sometimes in a rude way that I later regret. But I don't consider them as enemies."

"Did you and Alexander fight?"

"No. He never gave me any reason to lash out at him or put him in his place. On the contrary, he was affectionate and obliging to me and Natalie."

"So you would say you had a harmonious marriage."

"A deceptively harmonious marriage." Her tone was filled with bitterness.

The fat cat returned, rubbed his body against Suzanne's legs, and then sat about a meter away from her. The cat resumed his silent and unblinkingly defiant stare at the two officers. He seemed to be as combative as his owner was, thought Fauchet.

"Do you know anyone who owns a dark-blue Renault, Miss Levasque?"

"Yes. There is a Senegalese waitress at Chez Maurice. She has a battered, dark-blue Renault."

"No, we are not talking about an old or battered Renault. We are talking about a Renault in a good condition. And owned by a Frenchman. Not a woman."

"I know two Frenchmen who own Renaults, but their cars are not blue."

Laporte gazed at Suzanne and asked slowly, "Did you know Mrs. Gautier? And if so, how would you describe your relationship with her?"

"I never heard the name of that whore before yesterday."

"You can't judge people you don't even know so harshly. The lady was not a whore," Laporte rebuked her with undisguised disapproval. Surprisingly, she accepted the rebuke without any protest or retort. "Did your husband have a life insurance policy?"

"An insurance policy!" exclaimed Mrs. Dimitrov. "We could hardly make ends meet."

Laporte turned to Fauchet. "Do you have any questions for Miss Levasque?"

"No, not for the time being. Of course, as the investigation progresses I might have a lot of questions for her." Fauchet wanted to emphasize to Mrs. Dimitrov that this interview was a preliminary one; nothing more than an overture.

Suzanne Dimitrov looked at Fauchet with indignation laced with apprehension.

Laporte stood up. "Thank you, Miss Levasque, for bearing with us. However, if you remember anything that might throw some light on this cold-blooded, double murder, please do not hesitate to contact us." He gave her his card. She read it carefully, and then gently placed it on the small table next to her almost empty bottle of brandy. Fauchet was surprised that she did not toss it rudely on the table.

Closing his thick, brown hardcover notebook and inserting his pen in his shirt pocket, Fauchet stood up, and said with a strong hint of sarcasm, "You have been very cooperative, Mrs. Dimitrov."

Miss Levasque remained seated in her armchair. "You are always welcome, Inspector," she said in a scornful tone. Then she looked at him and almost ordered, "Close the door behind you, Inspector Fauchet."

Outside the apartment, Laporte said merrily, "Dominique, I know she wanted you to close the door but I will spare you the trouble. I will close it. She doesn't understand the extent to which she pissed you off. And if you close it, you will shut it with a bang that might bring the whole building down."

As Laporte closed the door gently, Fauchet chuckled. "What a vulgar whore. If she thinks that the death of her husband was divine retribution, I think it was divine salvation for poor Alexander Dimitrov. I am sure his soul is in a much more peaceful and serene place."

They descended to the ground floor in silence and climbed into Fauchet's car. As Fauchet drove, he glanced at Laporte. "What an obscene bitch! What a filthy whore!"

"Before I forget, I want you to assign some detectives to interview the people who are acquainted with Mr. and Mrs. Dimitrov and Professor and Mrs. Gautier. The staff at Chez Maurice, the six Bulgarians, the staff at Nicole Gautier's beauty salon, the owner and the staff at ITC Taxi Services, and some of Professor Gautier's colleagues and students. They have to carry out these interviews as soon as possible, Dominique."

Nodding, Fauchet stated, "It will be done, Henri. But my gut feeling is that these Bulgarians have something to do with the double murder."

Laporte smiled and looked at Fauchet. "Now you're talking like Mrs. Dimitrov, Dominique. Let's get some facts before we talk about gut feelings."

"Right, Henri," said Fauchet. "What did you think about her?"

"I can understand her situation, Dominique. She thought, and rightly so, that she had a perfect marriage and her husband loved her and their little daughter. Then she found herself in the eye of an unexpected and overwhelming tornado that shattered all her illusions."

Fauchet decided not to comment, though he did not agree with Laporte's take on Mrs. Dimitrov. Instead he said, "Now let us see what Professor Gautier will tell us."

# CHAPTER 21

**P**rofessor Georges Gautier, wearing a long-sleeved, white shirt, brown trousers, and brown shoes, led Senior Inspector Henri Laporte and Inspector Dominique Fauchet to a large sitting room with stylish furniture. An exquisite Persian carpet covered the floor. His thick, dark hair was obviously losing its battle with rapidly advancing gray. He looked in good shape except for a small paunch in the lower part of his abdomen. The detectives settled into comfortable armchairs close to each other while Gautier sat on the right end of a sofa, facing them.

In an amenable tone, he answered their questions about his age and the ages of his deceased wife and their two sons. The boys were eight and ten. He stated that he had been at home with them, as usual, at the time of the murders. He explained that his sons had decided, for reasons of their own, not to take a day or two off from school, and he had not tried to dissuade them. In the style of people who are not rushed by the pace of their interlocutors, he answered their questions at length, offering more than the detectives expected. Fauchet, who was taking notes, wrongly assumed that the professor was numbed by the tragic demise of his wife. Laporte, who adeptly studied the man's body language and what his eyes transmitted, concluded that Gautier's style of speech was an ingrained trait.

Though Gautier forgot the usual courtesy of offering them something to drink, he candidly and without the slightest hint of embarrassment stated that his twenty-two-year marriage was not what people would call a conventional marriage, though it had started as one. It had gradually changed over the years. He admitted that Nicole had been his student at the university when they commenced a clandestine sexual relationship. From the very outset, she had had an unrestrained sex drive. Until seven or eight years ago, he'd managed to cope with her insatiable sexual needs.

"Some people label women with strong sex drives as nymphomaniacs," Gautier said. "However, psychologists call it sex addiction, which is a process addiction. Like all addictions, it is very difficult to cure or curb. Some psychologists and psychiatrists believe that sex addiction is more difficult to cure than addiction to alcohol, tobacco, heroin, or other substances.

"A few months after the birth of our younger son, Nicole suddenly embarked on unrestrained sexual adventures. I am not sure if it was something to do with an undiagnosed postnatal depression or some hormonal disturbance. She started with one-night stands with attractive young men but soon descended to full-fledged extramarital affairs. At the beginning, I raised hell with her but soon I realized it was a hopeless battle. I tried to convince her to seek professional help, but she adamantly refused. I consulted on my own some eminent psychologists and psychiatrists, who had different views, yet they agreed that sex addiction needs prolonged talk therapy or psychoanalysis." Gautier paused, searched the eyes of the two silent detectives, and then made a measured gesture with his right hand. "Of course, I could have resorted to divorce but I decided that a divorce, particularly if it turned into an acrimonious battle, would leave deep and permanent scars in the psyche of my two sons." Again, Gautier paused before resuming in his deliberate pace. "The emotional and mental well-being of my children is more important and valuable to me than what people might say or not say about me or my marriage. Nonetheless, I think my marriage was a happy one."

Fauchet thought the professor seemed to be delivering a lecture. An incredible and difficult-to-swallow lecture.

Then Gautier professed that he and his departed wife loved, respected, and cared for each other. Fauchet mused that this was bizarre—very bizarre, indeed. A happy marriage with a wife who opened her legs to any man she fancied? Is this what people call an unconventional marriage? The professor must be an unhinged or an emasculated wimp. Nonetheless, Fauchet used the term "sex addiction" in his notebook instead of 'nymphomania.' He felt it would be inconsiderate to use the latter word at what must be the darkest hour in the life of this candid and urbane man, and it would be tasteless when others in the CID read the transcript, though he had always used the word 'nymphomania'—the word used in the parlance of everyone he knew.

"Can we definitely say your marriage was a happy one?" asked Laporte.

"It really was. It was friendly, affectionate, and happy. It may sound surprising to you, but she had put her heart into it like she did with anything that mattered in her life."

Fauchet interposed, "Do you and your sons get along well together?"

"Very much so. The three of us cherish our strong affinity. I greatly adore them and they genuinely love me. I enjoy their mischievousness and their inquisitive minds."

Fauchet inquired, "Were they well bonded with their mother?"

"To some extent. Not as much as they are bonded with me."

"Do you think they were aware of their mother's behavior and the actual reason for her going out after the family dinner?" asked Fauchet.

"I don't know. Children are usually more intelligent than adults assume. Even if they knew, neither of them ever hinted or insinuated that he was aware of his mother's behavior."

Gautier locked his hands behind his head and stared almost absent-mindedly through the window at the trees in his small yard. "I think the kids knew she loved them. However, there is a difference between knowing that someone loves you and feeling he or she loves you. I think the boys knew that she loved them but perhaps they did not feel she loved them.

She was always busy with her beauty salon during the day and was out in the evenings on her adventures." He paused and added almost to himself, "I never thought she resorted to lovers' lanes. That was absolutely unnecessary. I think it was very reckless of her."

"Professor Gautier, was there any recent conflict or altercation between you and your wife?" asked Laporte.

"Not for almost the last seven years. As I adopted a philosophical attitude toward her affairs, she reciprocated by doing her best to ingratiate herself to me. She did not argue with me or nag me about anything, including my busy teaching and research schedules."

Laporte continued, "Did you have any financial problems? Say in the last five years?"

"We've never experienced financial problems in our marriage. Firstly, my university salary is decent, though not large. Secondly, I have royalties from three books I have authored. Thirdly, Nicole's beauty salon has always generated a very handsome annual profit. We own this house and a country villa near Bordeaux. And we have more than adequate savings for our retirement."

"Are there any insurance policies?"

"Yes. Each of us has a life insurance policy of €250,000."

"So you will be entitled to a quarter of a million euros."

Gautier responded in a professorial voice, "You can say so, Mr. Laporte, though I am not happy about that. Her life was more important to me and to our sons than any insurance money. Human life is priceless."

"Quite right, Professor. I fully agree with that," said Laporte. He leaned back in the armchair in a serene manner. "Excuse me for asking this. Do you know the names of any of the men she had stable or long affairs with?"

"Yes, I do," replied Gautier. "I will go upstairs and bring you her address book." Then he stood up and walked slowly and steadily toward the staircase.

When the two officers were left alone, Fauchet whispered, "Henri, how can a man allow his wife to have an army of lovers and still maintain a friendly and loving relationship with her?"

"Dominique, this is the difference between a civilized man like the professor and someone who is a barbarian, like the two of us."

"I'm glad I've never been interested in philosophers or philosophical views."

"Dominique, could you please keep quiet?" said Laporte without any hint of reproach in his tone.

Fauchet shrugged his shoulders and then gazed at the staircase. A few moments later, Gautier came down holding a slim, rectangular, black address book. He handed it to Laporte, returned to his place on the sofa, and crossed his legs.

Laporte flipped through the address book. Gautier said, "This is her lovers' address book. She always carried her personal and business address book in her handbag. So I presume it will be in your custody as part of the evidence you collected from the crime scene."

Nicole's handwriting was small and the letters slanted to the right. Next to each name, there were one or two telephone numbers. She had written comments next to each name. "Professor, the names are not in alphabetical order and some of them are deleted. And she used first names without family names," Laporte said, searching for an explanation.

Gautier nodded and responded nonchalantly, "Mind you, all of these men are married. However, give me any name and I will tell you who he is."

"Martin?" inquired Laporte.

"Martin is Martin Mounier. He is the owner of a fairly large IT firm here. It has a branch in Toulouse and one in Brussels."

"Jacques?"

"Jacques is Jacques Genet—he's a young dental surgeon here."

Fauchet was writing the full names with a hardly masked disbelief.

"Carlos?"

"He's Carlos Samadja, a French of Spanish origin. He is the major shareholder of Samadja Property Company. His company has branches in other French and European cities."

"Christian?"

"Christian Boucher, the well-known heart surgeon."

Laporte paused and glanced at Fauchet but then he remembered that Fauchet was not aware of Boucher's affair with Mrs. Villard.

"Marcel?"

"Marcel Narbonne. He's a senior investment banker in this city."

"Yves?" Laporte could read the name, although it was crossed out with two bold strokes.

"Yves Chenier. He was an investment banker here. Three years ago, he was transferred to Paris. Sadly, he died of a heart attack after a few months in Paris."

"So that's why his name is crossed out," Laporte said.

Gautier nodded, then said, "You will find other crossed-out names where she had decided to terminate her relationship with them, or they had left the city permanently."

Laporte decided to make a request. "Professor, could we borrow this address book and return it to you later on?"

"Yes, by all means. As long as you return it to me."

"Of course, Professor," Laporte assured him.

"Good. I can give you the surnames of those whose first names she crossed out but who are still living here. These are the ones she had discarded. You have my cellphone number. So you can phone me about these names or anything else."

"Was your wife a member of any society or charity organization, Professor?" inquired Laporte.

"No. She had neither the inclination nor the time to be a member of any society or charity organization," replied Gautier.

"Do you suspect or think that your wife had any possible enemy or someone who had a grudge against her?"

"No. I don't think she had any enemies or people who had grudges against her. That would be against her nature because she was friendly, warm, and very forgiving. Yet she did not tolerate poor customer-service in her salon. Over the years, she sacked a number of low-performing employees as well as some embezzlers. But I find it unthinkable that a sacked employee would go to the extent of killing her."

"Did she have any animosities or fallings-out within her own family?"

"Absolutely none. She had two brothers and one sister, and she had very close and truly affectionate relationships with them. Even her aunts and uncles really loved her. I expect a lot of them will be at her funeral, including some of her cousins, nieces, and nephews. It is a very close-knit family. I think one can say that about few families, Mr. Laporte."

"It must be very hard on all of them." Laporte felt very sympathetic toward the man.

"Very hard, indeed. To say the least. Particularly, for her sister and mother. Nobody expected her to meet such a sudden and brutal end. She was still young." Gautier's eyes brimmed with tears but he swiftly managed to stem them.

"I presume you did not know Alexander Dimitrov."

"I did not know the names of men she had casual sex with."

Laporte, holding the black address book, said, "Professor, our hearts are with you and your family." He paused briefly before adding, "Many thanks for your openness and cooperation. However, we might need to interview you again."

"I stand ready to extend to you all assistance and support. I hope that you apprehend this animal. And soon, before he murders someone else."

"We will do our utmost," muttered Laporte and stood up. Gautier and Fauchet followed suit. Laporte handed Gautier his card. "If you recall anything or you want to inquire about the progress of the investigation, do not hesitate to call Inspector Fauchet or me." Fauchet hurriedly handed his card to the professor.

They shook hands with Gautier and thanked him again. He walked them to the door.

As Fauchet drove back to the station, Laporte flipped through Nicole Gautier's little black book. "I think the next person we should interview is Christian Boucher," he said.

"Who's that?"

Laporte did not answer Fauchet's question. He started reading Nicole's remarks about Christian Boucher aloud, "'Seductive but not skillful. He is arrogant to the point of megalomania. Sex with him is just satisfactory. Nothing special.'" Laporte shook his head in disbelief.

Fauchet smiled. "Not flattering. Not flattering at all."

"There is nothing flattering about this Boucher, Dominique. He was having a long-term affair with Mrs. Villard. Now two of his mistresses are dead. We have to tighten the noose around his neck. I have a gut feeling he is somehow linked to these murders." He filled Fauchet in on the secret meeting at the Oxford Pub between Chief Inspector Dupré, Christian Boucher, and himself. Is Boucher just a womanizer who happened to be the lover of two murdered women? Or was he a seducing sociopath? He wondered. Then he decided, "We'll interview him at his house this evening. We won't phone him in advance."

Fauchet nodded.

"We'll grill him," Laporte said. "But Dominique, we must keep a tight lid on his affair with Mrs. Villard. Nothing about this affair should be put in any document or on a PC. We must protect the reputation of Mr. Villard. We don't want him and his late wife to be fodder for gutter journalism and other sensational media."

"I fully understand that." Fauchet nodded solemnly.

"And if this megalomaniac tries to be difficult, we'll just haul him in for a very long and exhaustive interrogation."

After some moments of silence, Fauchet asked, "Have you read *Le Matin's* article today about Mr. Villard and his business empire? It covered almost two pages."

Laporte stated he didn't read *Le Matin*.

Fauchet said, "You must read this article. The bastards insinuate in it that Brigitte Villard's murder was a Mafia job. They claim there are very active Russian and Romanian mafias in our city."

Laporte commented, "Poor Mrs. Dimitrov believes there is a Bulgarian Mafia operating here. But it seems that even *Le Matin* is not aware of that."

"Unfortunately or fortunately, she doesn't know that *Le Matin* would pay her handsomely for such a scoop," stated Fauchet.

Laporte phoned Gerald Dupré and told him that he and Dominique were going to interview Dr. Boucher at his house, without giving him any advance notice, because they had discovered he had a long-standing affair with Nicole Gautier. Dupré was infuriated. "So the bastard lied to us at the Oxford

Pub when he assured us he had no other mistress. I want you to break him. If you fail drag him to my office and I will grill him personally."

Laporte smiled and said, "I think Dominique is capable of grilling him."

"Henri, let Dominique make the bastard regret every moment he spent fornicating with Mrs. Villard and Mrs. Gautier."

# CHAPTER 22

After giving Christine Fould their interview notes for transcription, Senior Inspector Henri Laporte and Inspector Dominique Fauchet drove in Laporte's car to Dr. Christian Boucher's house, arriving shortly before seven at his two-story villa. Fauchet rang the bell. After a few moments, he rang it again, then a mature, beautiful woman with blue eyes opened the door. She looked at the two men with a faint smile, her eyes conveying ambivalence about whether they were welcome or not welcome. Laporte smiled at her and announced, "This is Inspector Fauchet, and I am Senior Inspector Laporte from the CID, madame."

Despite his friendly smile, Laporte's commanding bearing told her the two men were here on a very serious business. Her face instantly showed concern and bewilderment. She managed to say, "I am Jacqueline Boucher."

"Is Dr. Boucher in?" asked Laporte gently.

"Yes. You want to see him?"

"Yes, madame," responded Laporte.

In the sitting room, she told her husband, who was enjoying his first evening malt while reading *Le Monde*, that there were two gentlemen who wanted to speak to him.

"Who are they?" he inquired, crossing his legs and letting *Le Monde* drop to his lap.

"Senior Inspector Laporte and Inspector Fauchet from the CID," she replied.

A dark cloud of concern descended on his face.

When Boucher came to the door, Fauchet, never mincing words, announced, "This is Senior Inspector Henri Laporte and I am Inspector Dominique Fauchet. We want to talk to you about a very important matter."

Boucher felt a tightening in his chest. "Could we talk about it somewhere else? In a quiet bistro or the Oxford Pub?" There was a hint of imploring in his tone despite his outward composure.

"No, Dr. Boucher. It is either here or at our headquarters. If we take you in for interrogation, the media might get wind of it, and your face will be splashed on the front pages of the papers and broadcast on TV," replied Fauchet.

After a moment of contemplation, Christian said with resignation, "Come in, please." Their rudeness for not phoning him in advance infuriated him.

After each of them settled in an armchair, Laporte said, "Dr. Boucher, we would like you to help us in the investigation of the recent double murder. We have a few questions for you. In fact, we are talking to all of Mrs. Nicole Gautier's friends."

Despite Laporte's mild tone, the moment he mentioned Nicole Gautier, Boucher felt as if a sudden, violent storm was spinning out of control within him. He hoped some malt would abate it. Before reaching for his tumbler, he asked, "Would you care for something to drink, gentlemen?"

The two visitors declined the offer politely. Boucher found himself nodding his head and saying almost to himself, "I see." The least they'll do is to spoil my evening, he reflected. That is, if they don't throw an unexpected hand grenade at me. Suddenly he stood up and muttered, "Excuse me, gentlemen. I will be back in a minute." Boucher strode into the kitchen and found his wife, Jacqueline, putting the final touches on their dinner. She immediately asked him, "Will this take long?"

"How would I know?" he retorted.

"Should I put our dinner back in the oven to keep it warm?" she asked in a nonchalant tone, though she sensed her husband was immensely unsettled by his unexpected visitors.

He ignored her remark and ordered, "Do not interrupt us in the sitting room. You should either remain in the kitchen or go upstairs."

"I'll stay in the kitchen, Christian."

"Fine," he said and hurriedly left the kitchen.

He returned to his unannounced and unwelcome visitors, settled in his armchair, and crossed his legs in a forced, self-possessed manner. Deciding to show them he was not apprehensive about the interview, he asked, "What do you want to ask me about, gentlemen?"

To shake Boucher's obviously feigned façade of composure, Fauchet said sternly, "We want you to tell us about your relationship with the late Nicole Gautier."

Boucher paused for a few moments before saying with all the calm he could muster, "She was a very close family friend, Inspector Fauchet."

Fauchet snapped, "Just like Brigitte Villard?"

Boucher felt the pounding of his heart reaching his fingertips, and trying to stall for a few moments to order his thoughts, took a sip of his malt. "You could say so, Inspector Fauchet."

"We are not talking about the family relationship. We are here to talk about your personal, or should I say *intimate*, relationship with Nicole Gautier. And please don't give us a repeat performance of the Oxford Pub interview." Fauchet was pissed off with Boucher the moment he saw Jacqueline Boucher: the doctor was a cheap man to be cheating on such a beautiful and dignified woman.

At that moment, Jacqueline washed and dried her hands, took a stiff gulp of vodka, and decided to eavesdrop on the conversation taking place in the sitting room. She walked stealthily to the living room adjoining the sitting room and hid herself behind the door between the two rooms.

Boucher firmly clasped his crossed knees with his hands, physically suppressing a quiver in his left hand. "Inspector, can you go directly to the heart of the matter?" he asked in a collected manner.

Fauchet replied bluntly, "Did you have a romantic affair with Nicole Gautier, Dr. Boucher?"

"No, I did not have a romantic relationship with Nicole Gautier," Boucher responded, thinking that Fauchet might be bluffing.

Laporte gave Fauchet a look that Fauchet understood from their long and close working relationship: Laporte wanted him to delay his belligerence to a later stage in the interview, if it proved to be necessary.

"Dr. Boucher, we are not accusing you of anything," Laporte said in a placatory tone. "You are not a suspect in this double murder. We are simply trying to gather information from people who were close to Mrs. Gautier. Just like our questioning you in Mrs. Villard's case. So we want your full cooperation and candor."

Hearing that from her hiding place, Jacqueline was stunned. Her legs could hardly support her. She leaned with her shoulder on the wall. So Christian had been questioned in Brigitte Villard's case and he chose not to tell me. What a conniving beast! Now, two of his mistresses are dead. For a fleeting moment, she thought that he might have had something to do with the two murders, but she quickly banished the idea. Why would he murder two women who gratified his despicable carnal needs? The swiftness with which the police discovered her husband's disgraceful affairs with the two dead women astonished her.

Fauchet, adopting a sedate tone, said, "Dr. Boucher, we just want you to come clean."

Boucher, suspecting that Fauchet was trying to hoodwink him, said, "Let me repeat myself again, gentlemen. I had no romantic relationship with Nicole Gautier at any time."

Laporte glanced at Fauchet, signaling that he could resume his stern questioning.

"You are lying, Dr. Boucher," Fauchet said.

"Don't call me a liar."

"You are a compulsive liar," snapped Fauchet without disguising his frustration. Boucher looked beseechingly at Laporte, hoping he would intervene, but Laporte ignored him. Fauchet pressed on with his assault, "When you were questioned about your sexual affair with Mrs. Villard, you lied through your teeth until you were confronted with irrefutable evidence. We have kept a tight lid on that affair because we don't want to hurt your wife's feelings or Jean-Paul Villard's. They are innocent victims of your duplicity."

Jacqueline, still leaning against the living room wall, felt nauseated. What a swine! What a disgusting and repelling animal! Although she had suspected that her husband was Nicole's lover, she had been telling herself that she did not have a solid proof. Now she knew, beyond a shadow of doubt, the extent of her husband's despicable cheating and betrayal. The rascal had already confessed his affair with Brigitte to the police. She was sick to her stomach. She felt grateful to the police for sparing her and Jean-Paul public humiliation.

Fauchet went on in a loud voice, "And now, Boucher, you are lying about your affair with Mrs. Gautier."

"Could we be civil about this? You don't need to shout, Inspector," pleaded Boucher.

"I'm shouting because I'm sick of your lies. I can't be civil with a compulsive liar, whatever he is and whoever he is. Do you read me, Boucher?" Fauchet's face displayed flagrant contempt.

Boucher's left hand started to tremble and he placed his right hand on top of it. He was mortified and speechless. He stared up at the ceiling, pondering how to react. He lied, of course, but he was not a compulsive liar. He managed to ask, "What evidence do you have that I had an affair with Mrs. Gautier?"

"So you won't be candid with us until we give you some evidence?" asked Fauchet loudly.

"I want material evidence, Inspector."

"We have damning material evidence," declared Fauchet. "Unfortunately for you, Mrs. Gautier, in her own handwriting, committed the names and telephone numbers of her lovers to a studbook—a special address book for her long-standing studs. Your name and telephone numbers are there."

Laporte was not happy with Fauchet's choice of the word "stud." A bit crude, he thought.

"But I told you that my wife and I are close friends of the Gautiers. So what is surprising about having my name and telephone numbers in one of her address books?"

"Boucher, don't play dumb. I told you this is a special address book for her lovers only," Fauchet retorted sharply. "Let me quote her opinion of you." He flipped the pages of his notebook. "Quote. 'Seductive but not skillful. He is arrogant to the point of megalomania.' Unquote. I don't want to read her remarks about your sexual performance because they are obscene and unflattering."

Boucher felt a lump in his throat. The demeaning words of his adorable Nicole were an unbearable, grievous jolt. His immediate reaction was a feeling of betrayal blended with a compelling need to rethink how others saw him. He'd always seen himself as a charming and a friendly person. Then he found a loophole in Fauchet's logic. "Christian? Just Christian? Do you know how many people in France, and even in this city, are called Christian?"

Fauchet's hostility surged thunderously. "You are being—"

Laporte calmly interrupted him. "Just a minute, Dominique." Laporte sometimes went along with Fauchet's go-for-the-jugular style because it was effective with obstinate people, but when it seemed unnecessarily too relentless, he gently put the brakes on him. He turned to Boucher and calmly stated, "Dr. Boucher, I think you will make it easier for us and for yourself if you confess your affair with Mrs. Gautier and then let us pose some questions."

Fauchet leaned forward, still looking at the doctor with open hostility. "We are absolutely certain you had a long, sexual relationship with Mrs. Gautier. In her address book, your office telephone number and your cellphone number follow your name. We have already verified them. So even if there were twenty or thirty million men called Christian in this country, it wouldn't matter." Then, deciding to put the final nail in Boucher's pitiful evasion, he announced, "And for your information, her husband, Professor Gautier, told us it was you and no other Christian. He has always been aware of your clandestine affair with his wife, but in his wisdom, he decided to keep his marriage intact for the sake of his two young sons. And his late wife did not conceal from him the identities of her lovers. It may come as a shock to you that you were not the only man with whom she had a long affair. She had a long list with remarks and grading of each stud in the list. Her evaluation of you is not something to be proud of."

Jacqueline shuddered and her eyes brimmed with tears. She dashed to the kitchen as she started sobbing, lest her husband suddenly popped into the living room. She poured what remained of the vodka into a tall glass. It was not enough. She opened the fridge and took out a chilled bottle of vodka, opened it, and filled her glass. She sat at the kitchen table, wiped her burning tears, and took a gulp of her drink. She was assailed by a morass of excruciating emotions—rage at her husband's betrayal, a scathing sense of degradation, a paralyzing hopelessness, and self-pity. Her husband was subhuman compared to Professor Gautier. While her callous and despicable husband had relentlessly abused her and their only child, Pierre, Professor Gautier had accepted his wife's flagrant infidelities and maintained their marriage for the sake of their children. What a jarring contrast! A contrast between a noble, civilized, and responsible human being, and a brutal, draconian, and heartless animal.

With a crippled heart and a crushed spirit, she let hot tears run down her cheeks as she contemplated the abuse, unfairness, and indignity she had suffered in her marriage. Even if she spent days enumerating the incidents of degradation and humiliation she had stoically lived through, she could not recount them all. She was overwhelmed by searing anger; anger at her sick and sickening husband, anger at an unfair and bleak world, anger at her own idiocy for bottling up her resentment and indignation. And for what? To keep her marriage intact just like the magnanimous Georges Gautier? But she was not Georges Gautier. There are few human beings in the world like Georges Gautier.

Perhaps, she pondered, I have been, in my hellish marriage, as noble and magnanimous as Georges was. However, I know his marriage was not devoid of love and affection like mine has been. Why have I always tried to discount, rationalize, and accommodate the aggravations, slights, and indiscretions by my husband? She asked herself. I know why. I have always deluded myself that I was too proud to be insulted, too proud to be provoked, too proud to stoop to taking an eye for an eye. How stupid I have been! How misguided I have been! Christian has certainly mistaken my tolerance and magnanimity for acquiescence and submissiveness. It's too late now to do anything about it, she thought. I have lost everything of significance in human life: my self-worth, my hope, and my will to live. I am responsible for incarcerating myself in that inescapable abyss.

Nobody else is to blame, she told herself with suffocating bitterness and resentment. I am solely responsible for what has happened to me. I have wasted my life. I have foolishly and submissively squandered my life.

She wiped her tears with both hands and took a sip of vodka. She could not bear life anymore. She had reached an irreversible breaking point. All her being, her bearings, her world had imploded. There was nothing she could clutch onto. Not a single straw. No hope. No future. Nothing. Life isn't worth living anymore, she thought, numb with helplessness.

In the sitting room, Christian Boucher was forced to admit, with servility, that he had had a sexual affair with Nicole Gautier. Now Fauchet decided there was no point in shouting at him, so he asked in a calm tone, "For how long, Dr. Boucher?"

"For six or seven years." Christian heaved a long sigh. Though he was flushed with shame and humiliation, his hand stopped trembling after his capitulation, so he reached for his malt and took a gulp.

"Could you tell us where you were at the time of the murder? That is, between eight o'clock and midnight?"

"I was at home from six twenty or six thirty in the evening until eight thirty the next morning, Mr. Fauchet."

Laporte interposed, "Dr. Boucher, we will take your word. We will not ask your wife for corroboration. That might cause unnecessary aggravation."

"I appreciate that, Mr. Laporte," stated Dr. Boucher with evident relief.

"Did you have any inkling that Nicole Gautier had other lovers?" inquired Fauchet.

"No. In fact, she led me to believe I was her only lover, Mr. Fauchet. But I suspected she indulged in one-night stands with some young men who took her fancy. In a few occasions I observed her chatting up young attractive men who waited in restaurants and parties with brazen disregard for the company she was with."

"Did she mention to you any problem or quarrel with anyone, male or female?"

"I don't recall anything of the sort. You see, she was a very smooth and charming woman. She was not prone to be agitated by aggravations, Mr. Fauchet."

"Did she ever talk to you about any problems in her marriage, Dr. Boucher?"

"Not serious problems. She occasionally complained that her husband had lost interest in having sex with her."

I don't blame him, thought Fauchet. "When you were having your affair, where did you rendezvous?"

"In different hotels and motels. She always insisted on footing the bill. She had two credit cards under an alias, Edith Martel. I don't know how she managed to do that. She was a very audacious and shrewd woman."

"Did she mention any problems with employees at her beauty salon?" Fauchet inquired.

"I don't recall anything of the sort. I had the impression she was friendly with her staff, but she did not tolerate poor performance. She simply sacked any employee who showed laxity or was involved in even petty embezzlement."

"So it is possible she had a string of disgruntled or embittered ex-employees, Dr. Boucher?"

"Yes, but I don't think that any of them would go to the extent of murdering her. To my mind, Mr. Fauchet, that's farfetched."

"Did you know that her husband knew all along about her extramarital affairs?"

"Honestly, this is a complete surprise to me." He paused, reflecting, and then said, "I have always respected Georges. But with this revelation, I am inclined to respect him even more. He is certainly a man above all of us."

Fauchet was not of the same opinion but he kept that to himself. "When was the last time you met Nicole?"

"Last Tuesday. We usually met on Tuesdays between eight thirty and ten thirty in the evening."

"Where did you meet last Tuesday?"

"At the Holiday Inn on rue Garancière."

"You always went to this hotel?"

"No. We went to a lot of hotels and motels, and Nicole made the bookings under her alias, Edith Martel. She preferred three- or four-star hotels. Not posh hotels."

"During the last few months, did you or Nicole suspect that there was anyone following you or stalking you on the way to your rendezvous or at any other time?"

"Never," he replied.

Fauchet nodded amicably. "Let me ask you another important question."

"Yes, Mr. Fauchet?" Christian looked at Fauchet and then Laporte, with restless eyes.

"Have you been having an affair with any other women? That is, other than Brigitte and Nicole?"

Christian pondered the question for some time and decided to be frank. These officers seemed to know a lot about him.

Maybe they already knew about Monique Roget. "Yes, I have. A long-standing affair with a third married woman."

"Could you tell us her name? I am asking this question because there is a possibility, however remote, that this third mistress might have some connection to the murders of Mrs. Gautier and Mrs. Villard." Fauchet leaned back in the armchair, allowing Dr. Boucher some time for reflection.

Boucher emphatically said, "No way. This is too far-fetched." Then he looked at Laporte as if seeking his assent not to give her name. Laporte stated, "You don't have to reveal her name, Dr. Boucher."

Fauchet looked at Laporte and then at Boucher. "Fine, Dr. Boucher. I don't want to scare you. But if she had nothing to do with the murders, there's a possibility that her life could be in jeopardy. It would be prudent to freeze your affair with her for the time being. Say, until we apprehend this murderer. Is that reasonable, Dr. Boucher?"

"Very much reasonable and prudent," Boucher managed to say. These detectives were shrewder than he had thought they were, he reflected.

"In your view, is your third mistress a jealous or vindictive person?"

"Absolutely not. She's not the type of person who would be angry or upset if she knew I had another mistress or mistresses. She loves her husband and their kids. She is a sweet, open-minded, and noble woman."

Fauchet was annoyed that Boucher would describe a woman who is cheating on her husband as noble. He had no problem with calling her sweet and open-minded, but noble seemed to him a glaring contradiction in terms. Perhaps, I have a calcified and obsolete mentality, he mused. He saw everything in black and white; there was no place for much gray. He admitted that gray was a fact of life, yet he believed it should be limited and kept within proper bounds. People who accepted an abundance of gray always perplexed him. He looked at Boucher and asked in a calm tone, "So you are sure no one could have known you had three mistresses at the same time?"

Boucher paused for some time, racking his mind, and then he asserted, "Honestly, gentlemen, I think the fact that two of my mistresses were barbarously murdered is just a very sad and tragic coincidence. It has nothing to do with the fact that they were my lovers."

"Even if they were murdered by the same person?" asked Fauchet.

"Still, I don't see a link to my being their lover. Though the two ladies were part of a large social circle, they had little in common. They had contrasting characters and they were not that close. Come to think of it, Brigitte and Nicole did not warm to each other, yet they did not show even a hint of distaste toward each other."

"How about your wife? Do you think she is aware that you have mistresses?" asked Fauchet in a casual manner.

"Perhaps she suspects I had an affair with Brigitte Villard because some time back, Brigitte phoned me on my cellphone late one evening while I was in the bathroom. I suspect, but I am not sure, my wife read the cellphone number and knew it was Brigitte. But I might be wrong because my wife and Brigitte enjoyed excellent and friendly relations." He ran his hand through his hair. "However, I am sure she doesn't know or even suspect that I had affairs with Nicole Gautier and the other lady. To be fair to my wife, she is not the vindictive type. She is a gentle soul. So the idea that she might be involved in a murder is absolutely unthinkable, Mr. Fauchet."

"I understand you have a son. Do you think he suspects or knows you have a string of mistresses?"

"No way. He was busy with his studies and his own love affairs until he went to Africa," Boucher said and let out a sigh.

"What is his name?"

"Pierre."

"Where is he now?"

"He is in Cameroon, working with a nongovernmental humanitarian organization. He believes that Europe was built with the enormous wealth pillaged from Africa and that Europeans should help Africans as a form of restitution, even with simple acts of humanitarian work. He has lofty and youthful ideas."

"When did he go to Cameroon?"

"Almost two months ago."

"That is, before the first murder?"

"Yes, Mr. Fauchet. Pierre is a pleasant young man but he has a mind of his own. Though I was against the idea of his going to Cameroon, his mother gave it her blessing. And I had to give in. He intends to work for a few years in Africa. In Cameroon first, then perhaps he will move to another African country.

In addition to his so-called restitution to Africans, he believes that the experience will broaden his perspectives."

"I think you are lucky to have a son with such noble ideas, Dr. Boucher," commented Fauchet with sincerity. He felt satisfied with the way he had conducted the interview and was genuinely pleased that the lecherous Boucher had a son worthy of respect and who truly deserved to be described as noble.

Dr. Boucher found himself smiling. "Thank you for the compliment, Mr. Fauchet."

Laporte added, "Your son is to be commended for his concern about the Africans. I endorse his view that the Europeans pillaged enormous wealth from Africa."

Boucher smiled. "It's true. However, I think the Africans should pull themselves together. No external aid or humanitarian work would salvage Africa."

Fauchet looked at Laporte, indicating he had no more questions. Laporte asked, "Dr. Boucher, do you know anything about Mr. Alexander Dimitrov?"

"Absolutely nothing. I'd never heard of him before this heinous crime. I don't know how he came to know Nicole or how long he'd known her." He paused, and then awkwardly asked, "Was he attractive?"

"Very attractive," responded Fauchet.

"That's the type of man Nicole picked for her one-night stands as I suspected. What an unlucky guy. He had to pay with his life for a tryst," said Christian Boucher in a somber tone. "Life can be very cruel and deal any one of us brutal and unexpected blows."

"Dr. Boucher, please excuse us for delaying your dinner. And many thanks for your time and for bearing with us," said Laporte.

Boucher felt a deep sense of relief that this ordeal had ended; his face showed it. "Don't mention it, Mr. Laporte. You are simply doing your job. I will help you in any way possible to capture this criminal who has cold-bloodedly snuffed out the lives of two refined and noble ladies." Then he added as an afterthought, "And the unfortunate Mr. Dimitrov."

"If you remember anything that may help our investigation, please don't hesitate to contact us. You have my card," said Laporte.

"Yes, I do. I won't hesitate to contact you if I recall anything, gentlemen."

At the front door, they shook hands and bade each other good night. As Christian closed the door, it occurred to him that he would not be surprised if the police already knew that his third mistress was Monique Roget, and that they had their rendezvous in an apartment shared by two of Monique's female friends.

He locked the door and returned to his armchair and malt. He found himself unnerved by the interview and wanted some solitude to ruminate on a lot of things. He took a sip of malt and mused about Nicole's recklessness. She'd been shameless, telling her husband about her lovers, recording their names and telephone numbers, and grading them. However, something inside him told him that she was somewhat right in her description of him as arrogant to the point of megalomania.

Though her words astonished him, in his mind's eye he sensed they carried a grain of truth. Nicole had been very astute in evaluating the inner dynamics of people, regardless of their façades. Does everybody see me in that light, he wondered, despite my friendly and charming nature? Does Jacqueline perceive me as a megalomaniac? Is that how my son, Pierre, perceives me?

He mused that he loved Nicole, Brigitte, and Monique—genuinely loved them. Then a question intruded in his mind: did he love Jacqueline? In some ways, he did. He admitted to himself that they had drifted far apart over the years; he was guilty of being verbally, emotionally, and occasionally physically abusive to her. That was very shameful, he admitted. Pierre? He reproached himself for the way he had treated his only son; but that was the way his own parents had treated his younger brother and him—with relentless verbal, emotional, and physical abuse.

But why had his brother, Charles-Maurice, emerged unscathed by the abuse? Charles-Maurice had become an urbane and caring man. He had a wife and family he loved, and they loved him. I have always considered him a loser, he thought, but who is the loser: my younger brother or me? I am, he answered.

Why has Pierre turned out to be not only pleasant and charming but confident and unbreakable despite the abuse I've shamelessly subjected him to since his childhood? Pierre is a son any parent would be enormously proud to have. There must be something seriously convoluted within me, yet despite my intelligence, I have been perpetually blinkered to it.

In the deep recesses of his soul, Christian could hear a voice telling him that his illustrious achievements and his insatiable womanizing were driven by his endless search for the love he never had in childhood.

A heavy and harrowing sense of guilt about the savage and merciless treatment to which he had subjected his wife and their only child over the years clutched at him. Why have I always abused my only son and my wife? It has only served to alienate them. Pierre has become antagonistic and prone to cold-bloodedly trampling on all my views and instructions. With a strange mixture of pride and humility, Christian admitted to himself that Pierre's character was stronger than his was. Though there was no way to undo what had been done, he vowed to treat Pierre with all the respect and dignity he deserved, once he returned from Africa. Christian found himself saying silently, "Forgive me, Pierre. I have put you through hell since you were a child. I love you, Pierre. I do love you."

His very words surprised him. Perhaps there was more than a germ of truth in what Nicole had written about him, he mused. Though he disagreed with the megalomaniac label, he admitted that his character was conflicted and convoluted—as if there were two personalities within him.

With acute despondency, he realized that it had taken the heinous murders of two charming and refined mistresses and

the abject humiliation by the foul and uncouth Inspector Fauchet to make him wake up, and to bring about this startling
yet illuminating paradigm shift in his mind-set. He hoped
that the revelation had not come too late. He pledged to do his
utmost to change himself, mend his ways, and respect his wife
and son. Would they forgive me? Would they believe in the
sincerity of my new behavior? He doubted that, yet he vowed
to keep trying for however long it took. Given the immensity
of the emotional devastation he had caused over the years, it
might take years, if not decades, to regain their trust and love.
I have to commit myself to the daunting process of redress. He
vowed he would immediately start treating Charles-Maurice,
Jacqueline, and Pierre with all the respect and thoughtfulness
they truly deserved.

He stood up, feeling shaken and humble, and decided to go
and see Jacqueline in the kitchen instead of going upstairs to
their bedroom without speaking to her. He would endeavor to
say something nice to her—he'd at least say, 'Good night', in a
tender way. He reflected that Jacqueline had not inherited much
of the Dillons' fighting streak, but she had many of her maternal Rollins' obliging and compliant traits. She was a woman
who truly deserved respect and love. He resolved to start his
crusade of ingratiation at once. Tomorrow, he thought, I will
sit down with her and express my remorse, apologize for my
dismal maltreatment of her, and assure her that we can open a
new and bright page in our lives.

As he walked into the kitchen, Jacqueline looked at him with
eyes blurred by sobbing and alcohol, and asked mischievously

but in a feigned nonchalant tone, "What was the police visit about?"

Christian leaned against the kitchen wall and felt genuinely sympathetic to her. "The two officers asked questions about Nicole Gautier, since she was a family friend." He was about to say that he was going upstairs and he did not want anything to eat, when Jacqueline suddenly jumped up and screamed, "Why are you lying?"

Christian was taken aback, yet he decided to respond in a calm voice, for he had just vowed to treat her with respect and thoughtfulness. "I am not lying, Jacqueline."

"You are nothing but a compulsive liar," she retorted.

"Please don't call me a liar," he requested in a subdued and appeasing tone.

"You are a liar par excellence. You will be shocked to learn that I have known for a long time about your sordid affairs with Brigitte, Nicole, and Monique. One night at Le Club Bellecour, at the reception for the mayor of Lille, you and Monique Roget had the tastelessness and indecency to sneak into the boardroom upstairs to fornicate while her husband and I were downstairs with the rest of the guests. One of the club's employees saw you and she told her aunt, who told me the next day. In my naivety, I did not believe her. But now I do believe her." She paused for breath. "Can you deny it? Of course you can't."

Christian was stunned because all that she said was true, yet he was perplexed as to why she had kept silent about all of this for so long, bottling it up inside. His face was filled with regret and astonishment. I ought to be hugely ashamed that

I have blindly caused my delicate and beautiful wife to suffer beyond human endurance, he told himself.

There was no point in denying her sudden accusation. He remained silent and looked at her with vacant eyes. Then he looked at the half-empty vodka bottle on the table, felt sorry for her, and blamed himself for pushing her to the solace of alcohol. "Jacqueline, I am terribly sorry for that. I do sincerely apologize for many things. Could we open a new chapter? I solemnly promise to treat you with all the respect and love you truly, truly deserve."

She rested one hand on the kitchen table and said in a broken and forlorn tone, "If you think I can believe one word of what you say, you must be very naive. I regret that I have wasted my whole life with you. And it is too late for apologies and a new start."

"Please, Jacqueline, it is never too late. I must admit I have been blinded for a long time to my gross treatment of you, Pierre, and Charles-Maurice. The three of you deserve genuine love and respect."

Though she sensed a pleading tone in his voice, she was adamant that it was too late for regret, forgiveness, and pleading. "Christian, I have always been faithful to you, but you cheated on me with three women and maybe others. Women whose decent husbands have naively trusted you and considered you a true friend. You betrayed me, you betrayed Pierre, and you betrayed your best friends. You are nothing but a fake."

Christian felt insulted and hurt, yet he forced himself to suppress the rage that enveloped him. Be calm, restrain yourself, and let the storm pass. He looked at her with pity, and stated, "I am sorry, Jacqueline, that I have failed you. I am deeply sorry."

"Sorry! What's happened to you? Was it the humiliating treatment by Inspector Fauchet? He was correct in saying you are a compulsive liar. He dragged you through the mud, and you deserved it. You've never said the word 'sorry' in your life and now you suddenly use it. Do you expect me to believe you? No way."

So she had eavesdropped on the humiliating interrogation by Fauchet. He thought that was low and vile but he decided not to blame her for it. Any woman in her circumstances would have done it. "I really mean it, Jacqueline," he said in a conciliatory tone.

"It is too late to say you're sorry. Too late, Christian." Tears welled in her eyes. "You have broken my spirit and crushed my soul. Luckily, you failed to break our only child because Pierre has the Dillons' genes. And no Dillon can be broken or crushed. Thank God my Pierre has a fearless and invincible soul. He is more refined and courageous than you are."

Christian stared at the floor and nodded. She was right. Without raising his head, he said in a mournful tone, "Jacqueline, I know I have not been a good husband or a good father. I promise you I will do my best to mend my ways."

"I don't believe any promises from you. I have had enough. More than enough. From now on, I will sleep in the guest room. It is sickening to sleep next to a man who sleeps with whores—any whore who opens her legs for him."

"Enough. Enough, Jacqueline," Christian said in a commanding voice. He had to put an end to this ugly confrontation.

"I just don't know why God made me marry a depraved man. What have I done to deserve this shambles of a marriage? I was out of my mind when I agreed to marry you." She raised her eyes to the ceiling and seemed to address God earnestly, "What have I done, God? What sin have I committed?"

Christian failed to hold on to his conciliatory tone, and shouted, "Stop talking off the top of your head!" Then he strode to the sitting room in a huff.

Jacqueline, melancholy and heartbroken, struggled to drag herself up the stairs, one step at a time, holding the wooden banister lest she fell down. She entered the guest room, in a dense fog of despair and delirium, switched on the light, and locked the door before walking feebly to the bed, where she collapsed. Her cellphone slid next to her hip. She drifted into a restless and fitful sleep.

In the sitting room, Christian sat in an armchair, clasping his malt tumbler with both hands. He did not feel discouraged by his failure in his first attempt at rapprochement with his wife. I have to give her more time, and more time and then more time, because the psychological harm that I have caused her has been prolonged and atrocious, he told himself.

Then he became lost in a miasma of apprehension and trepidation about what would happen to his reputation in society and medical circles if his infidelities with the wives of his best friends were splashed on the front pages of the local and national newspapers.

He felt certain that his world, at the pinnacle of success and fame, would crash around him. Many friends and colleagues—particularly Jean-Paul—would desert me; and my wife, son, and brother would further shun me. I would be a pariah. A loathed pariah. The idea that he would be stigmatized filled him with horror and consternation. He would be clinging to nothing but shattered dreams, and a defiled persona. I have brought it upon myself, he told himself. I have to face the music in a brave and dignified manner. Yet the price I would be forced to pay could be colossal.

With despair, he reflected that if the floodgates of scandal were unlocked, he would not have the power to stem the deluge.

# CHAPTER 23

J acqueline woke up in the guest room and noticed that the light in the room was on—she had forgotten to switch it off last night. She looked at her wristwatch—it was eighty thirty in the morning—and realized she had slept for more than ten hours. As she stared up blankly at the ceiling, self-pity and condemnation assailed her. Her world was nothing but a numbing confluence of doom and gloom; her interest in living had completely evaporated.

Suddenly she remembered that she should have been in her office by now. But she felt unable to drag herself to work. Nor was she keen to see other human faces. Withdrawal from the world gave her a sense of comfort. Picking up her cellphone, she dialed her boss's number, telling herself this could be the last time she would speak to him. Albert Poitier cheerfully agreed to her request for a day off and told her to take good care of herself.

Feeling thirsty and hungry, she decided to go to the kitchen before Mrs. Maryse Gasnier arrived for work at ten. Opening the fridge, she drank almost half of an orange juice container.

She made herself a cheese sandwich and then took a bottle of vodka from the fridge. Her eyes fell on the set of seven stainless-steel kitchen knives. She gazed at them before choosing the one in the middle.

In the guest room, she put the vodka bottle, the knife, and the sandwich on the left bedside table. Then she remembered her medications. She went to the master bedroom and fetched all of her sleeping pills, tranquilizers, and anti-depressants. Returning to the guest room, she closed the door without locking it. She put the room light off. Though the curtains were drawn, there was enough light for her to see around the room. After carefully putting her medications next to the knife, the sandwich and vodka bottle on the bedside table, she lay on the bed.

Taking one bite of the sandwich, she found it insipid, so she put it back on the table. She reflected that, in the last few days, all food had tasted bland. Opening the vodka bottle, she took a swig and then another swig and felt the alcohol spreading rapidly through her veins. She picked up the knife, gazed intently at it, and then slowly brought its sharp edge to her left wrist with its blue veins. She was overcome by a sense of déjà-vu but she could not comprehend why she had that feeling. Did I commit suicide in a previous life? Or is my mind just deluding me now?

Still, she felt she was reliving something she had experienced before. She sensed that she could not dissociate her body from her mind.

Turning her attention to the knife unblinkingly, she felt its slim and razor-sharp point touching her white wrist—just touching it. She cringed. Should I slash my wrists? She wondered. That would be painful, messy, and abhorrent. That is not the right way to leave this bleak and wretched world. There would be blood all over the bed and the carpet, and that would be repulsive and nauseating. I am not an untidy woman. I will not leave a mess behind me. With some sense of temporary relief, she put the knife next to the sandwich on the bedside table.

The image of her son, Pierre, came to her mind. She decided to write a note to her beloved Pierre. She found a few blue envelopes and some thin, blue-lined sheets of paper and a pen in the drawer of the desk in the guest room. Without trying to put her thoughts in order, she briskly wrote in her thin longhand whatever occurred to her:

*Dearest Pierre,*

*You know how much I love you. In fact, my life without you would have been completely meaningless and pointless. You gave my life meaning, love, and warmth.*
*This is more than a mother can expect from her son. Take good care of yourself for yourself and for my memory.*
*For me, I can't bear it anymore. Don't you ever blame yourself. I blame myself for   letting my despicable husband extinguish my spirit and crush my soul. I am the one to blame, solely and entirely.*
*Forgive me. Forgive me. And forgive me, Pierre.*

*Moreover, pray for my soul. Always pray for my soul, dearest son.*

*Your ever-loving mother,*
*Jacqueline*

She folded the sheet of paper, kissed it as tears welled in her eyes, inserted it into a blue envelope, and sealed it after slowly licking its flap. She addressed it: *My Dearest Pierre.* Not Pierre Boucher. Folding the envelope, she inserted it in another envelope, which she sealed, and then wrote at the top, *To Mrs. Maryse Gasnier*, and underlined the name with a shaky stroke. Below the line, she wrote, *Please keep the envelope inside until Pierre is back from Cameroon. I beseech you not to show it or give it to any other soul. Thanks so much for your great friendship and companionship, Maryse. I have never told you that you are an angel but now I want you to know that you are a true angel. And please pray for me. With love, Jacqueline.*

Rising from the chair, she found her right hand trembling. She walked slowly to the door, bent slightly, and slid part of the envelope under the door. As she stepped toward the bed, she found her lower lip quivering. It occurred to her that she needed a human being to hug her, comfort her, and soothe her, yet she was ashamed to see any human being. She felt like a hopelessly terrified and helpless child. Sitting on the edge of the bed, depressive ruminations churned in her mind, pulling her further and further into the incapacitating vortex of numbing melancholy.

The incident of the man who had rescued Pierre from drowning in the swimming pool when he was three or four pierced her mind with regret. Had she not interceded at the time, the angry and well-built man would have given her husband a bloody hiding. Now it occurred to her that if she had let the man teach her husband a much-needed lesson, the very nature of Christian's relationship with her and Pierre would have been different, completely different, for she knew that deep inside, her husband was a coward. If she had only let that man thrash her husband publicly, Christian never would have recovered from the humiliation. The dynamics of their marriage would have been thoroughly altered to her advantage and Pierre's. She blamed herself for calming down the furious man and letting her husband escape without being taught a public and humbling lesson. It was an opportunity lost, and she blamed herself for that. It was immensely naive of me. It was a colossal mistake by me, just like all my mistakes in this miserable marriage, she thought.

Her life, she thought, was a conglomeration of mistakes, lost opportunities, regrets, and boundless aggravations, all due to her shameful submissiveness. A submissiveness that she deluded herself, for so long, into believing was magnanimity. A submissiveness that precipitated the worst life any human being could have. She had to put an end to it. There was no point in living such a barren, gloomy, and meaningless existence. She had crawled into herself for a long time, and that gave her no consolation. Now she wanted to crawl into something more comforting—into a shell, into oblivion, into the hereafter.

She glanced around the room and thought it was drab, bleak, and as dark as the darkness within her. She lay down on the bed, covered her knees with the end of her skirt, and pulled a duvet on top of her up to her breasts. Turning her head to the table on her left, she gazed at the vodka bottle, the gleaming knife, and her different medications. For a few moments, the stainless steel knife filled her with dread. Focusing on her psychiatric medications, she picked up the sleeping pills and found there were twenty-seven. There were twenty-six tranquilizer pills, eighteen of the antidepressant pills she had used for a long time, and eighteen capsules of the antidepressant that Professor Lacan had prescribed to augment the effect of her old antidepressant. Eighty-nine pills and capsules, she calculated, wondering if they were enough to ensure she would drift into an eternal, blissful sleep. She piled them next to her on the bed, all mixed together, and held the vodka bottle with her now trembling left hand.

Before putting any pill or capsule in her mouth, she said, "Forgive me, Pierre. Forgive me, Pierre." It seemed to her that someone else was uttering these words. Then she closed her eyes and in numbed supplication pleaded, "Forgive me, God. Forgive me, God." She decided not to hesitate any longer. Raising her head slightly, she rapidly took about ten pills and capsules, swallowing them with a gulp of vodka. Within a minute or two, she had swallowed all of the pills and capsules, washing them down with vodka. Impulsively, she screwed the cap of the vodka bottle and placed it on the bedside table next to her with her usual care and orderliness, despite the drowsiness that had started to overcome her. Closing her eyes, she clasped her hands on her stomach under the duvet, and then uttered the words: "Forgive me, Pierre; forgive me Pierre. God knows how much I love you, my dearest darling."

***

Mrs. Gasnier arrived at the Bouchers' house a few minutes before ten and let herself in through the kitchen door. She closed the door and put the key in her battered, black handbag. Standing in front of the of the fridge, she was surprised that Jacqueline had not left any instructions for today's dinner; there was no piece of paper under any of the six small, round, blue, magnetic holders stuck to the top of the fridge. She thought that was odd because Jacqueline, with her usual orderliness, religiously left instructions or suggestions. Perhaps Jacqueline had left for her office in a hurry, she assumed. Opening the fridge, she found two packs of boneless chicken wrapped in thin plastic and decided to make a chicken casserole; she knew the Bouchers always liked it the way she cooked it.

By midday, she had completed the cooking, taking all of the dishes and silverware from the dishwasher and putting them away. With a spoon, she tasted the chicken casserole and pronounced it perfect. At once, she started cleaning the kitchen, and then moved through all the rooms on the ground floor, cleaning them meticulously as she sang parts of old songs, some from her childhood and some from her youth. Shortly before two, she ascended the stairs with her cleaning equipment, estimating she would be able to clean the three bedrooms, the two studies, and the bathrooms by three o'clock because Pierre's room, the guest room, and the two studies did not need a lot of cleaning—just some dusting.

Mrs. Gasnier took great pride in her work and enjoyed working for the Bouchers because of the refined, trusting, and friendly treatment they all sincerely accorded her. She missed Pierre and his mischievous and sweet teasing—and he enjoyed her teasing of him; she admired him for volunteering to do humanitarian work in Africa. However, she thought his mother missed him terribly, for she'd noticed that Jacqueline had become more and more dejected since Pierre had departed for Cameroon. Jacqueline's dejection was very apparent to her whenever they talked on the phone. Mrs. Gasnier detected mounting gloom and flatness in Jacqueline's voice. She wished Pierre would return soon from Cameroon.

After cleaning the master bedroom, she dusted Pierre's room. As she walked toward the guest room with a duster and a vacuum cleaner, she immediately noticed a blue envelope partially pushed under the closed door. Picking it up, she found it addressed to her with a few sentences under her name telling her to give the enclosed envelope to Pierre and not to give it or show it to any other soul. When she read: *And please pray for me. With love, Jacqueline*, she felt a lump in her throat.

Bewilderment and apprehension gripped her; she dropped the vacuum cleaner and duster, folded the envelope, and slipped it inside her bra. With a thumping heart, she opened the door and saw Jacqueline stretched out on the bed with a duvet up to her chest. Then her eyes fell on the nearly empty vodka bottle, the sandwich, the kitchen knife, and the small bottles and boxes of medications on the night table. The worst came to her mind. She was paralyzed for a few moments. The words addressed to her on the envelope resonated in her mind and her panic surged. Then she forced herself to advance to the bed. Jacqueline's eyes were closed and her face was peaceful and tranquil. As she stood a few steps from the bed, she softly said, "Jacqueline. Jacqueline." Her dread intensified and she called loudly, "Jacqueline! Jacqueline!" Her own tone of voice added to her horror.

She mustered the courage to nudge Jacqueline's shoulder. There was no response. She touched Jacqueline's left arm; it was cold. Deathly cold. There was no pulse in Jacqueline's wrist. Then she brought her face very close to Jacqueline's face. She was not breathing.

Maryse felt as though her legs could not bear her. Her world fell apart and she felt a chill running down her spine; she ran downstairs, her hand on her throbbing heart, to retrieve her cellphone in the kitchen. In her panic she howled, "Oh, my God. It can't be true. It can't be true." At once, she phoned Christian Boucher and managed to tell him hysterically that there was something wrong with Jacqueline. He asked her to calm down and said he would rush home, yet Maryse could sense profound apprehension in his voice.

Sitting on a kitchen chair, she sobbed. The kind words Jacqueline had written about her resonated in her mind, and she found herself saying, "Jacqueline, you are the true angel. There is no angel other than you." For a moment she considered putting the envelope in her handbag but dismissed the idea—it was safer in her bra. Then she started praying earnestly for Jacqueline's soul. At the same time, she felt she needed to pray for Pierre and for herself.

With incomprehension rather than dread overwhelming him, Christian Boucher locked the door of his office. At the nurses' counter, he asked a senior nurse to send an ambulance to his house at once. "It's urgent," he shouted, striking the top of the counter with his palm. When he reached his house, he found the ambulance already in front of it. Two paramedics and a doctor in his medical garb were talking to Mrs. Gasnier at the front door; her face was pale and tears glistened on her cheeks as she held the door wide open. He locked his car and raced behind the men, who were now on their way toward the staircase. Christian and Maryse joined them in the guest room upstairs.

The short, young, and mustached doctor, Dr. Lyon, sat on the edge of the bed and put his stethoscope to Jacqueline's chest. After a few moments, he stood up and faced Dr. Boucher. "I am sorry, Dr. Boucher. There is no pulse and no heartbeat." Nonetheless, her husband double-checked her pulse. The sad reality almost choked him. His first thought was, why would she do such a crazy thing? Were all the medicines prescribed to her by Professor Lacan ineffective?

Then he asked Mrs. Gasnier, "Did you find any suicide note?"

"No, Dr. Boucher," she lied. She had to honor Jacqueline's request not to show or reveal the envelope addressed to Pierre to any other soul.

Christian, unnerved and angry, told himself that this was the ultimate humiliation by Jacqueline. She committed this malicious act to disgrace him; she wanted everyone to hold him responsible for her tragic end; she wanted him to be held in contempt; she wanted him to be seen as a despicable and repugnant husband. She wanted to shame and degrade him from her grave.

Dr. Lyon addressed Dr. Boucher. "I have already contacted the police. We have to await their arrival."

"I see," replied Christian. Then he approached Mrs. Gasnier. "Maryse, please go to the kitchen and calm yourself before the police arrive. They might be asking you some questions."

Wiping her tears with her hand, she nodded and then went downstairs to the kitchen. Her old legs could hardly support her. Fearing she might topple down the stairs, she grasped the smooth, wooden handrail and descended one step at a time. When she sat at the kitchen table, she patted her chest, reassuring herself that Jacqueline's letter to Pierre was still inside her bra. Once again, she reflected that it was the safest place to hide it. The police might decide to search her handbag but they would not search her clothes.

Upstairs, Christian approached the bed and stared down at the empty medication containers and the kitchen knife. As he was about to lift the knife, Dr. Lyon warned him in a sharp tone, "Don't touch it, Dr. Boucher. Don't touch anything, please."

Christian was taken aback by the harsh order from a disrespectful, junior doctor, but he could only obey him.

***

At the CID's headquarters, Chief Inspector Dupré and Senior Inspector Laporte were brainstorming the way forward in the double murder investigation, after Laporte had briefed Dupré about the interview he and Inspector Fauchet had conducted with Boucher at his house last evening.

"It's my gut feeling, Henri, that this Dr. Boucher somehow has something to do with these murders," the chief inspector pronounced.

Laporte politely said, "I don't think we have sufficient evidence to indicate that. I believe him when he says it's a coincidence that two of his mistresses were murdered by an unknown killer."

Dupré sighed. "So we have to wait until his third secret mistress is murdered? Is that what you are saying?"

"I don't know if his third mistress will be murdered."

"I see, Henri." Then Dupré turned to the profile that he'd been developing of the killer: a male in his twenties who had served in the armed forces or worked in law enforcement, and who is suffering, or had suffered, from mental afflictions. Obviously, this profile excluded Dr. Boucher. "Henri, today I want you to see the director of the White Beacon asylum, Dr. Charles LeGarde. I have already talked to him and persuaded him in a very lengthy call to provide us with the names of inmates who've been released in the last two years. Understandably, he refused to cooperate until I told him he would feel very guilty if this serial killer murdered another innocent person. Finally, he agreed to give us the names of the patients, the dates of their release, their addresses, and their professions at the time they were admitted. He insisted that he was doing us a great favor, but he categorically refused to divulge anything about their diagnoses or prognoses."

"I think he is doing us a great favor by providing us with the names, addresses, and professions of the ex-inmates, Gerald."

"Yes, he is. However, I want you to visit him today before he changes his mind. You know, some of these shrinks are as crazy as their patients."

"I'll phone him first and tell him I'll see him today if the list is ready," said Laporte.

"Please phone him as soon as possible."

"I will phone him once I return to my office, Gerald. If the list is ready I will promptly drive to the White Beacon." Laporte found himself enthusiastic about Dupré's profile of the serial killer. He felt it made a lot of sense.

"This list could prove to be extremely helpful. We should focus first on the released patients who have worked in the armed forces and law—"

Before Dupré was able to complete his sentence, Inspector Fauchet barged in and announced, with a hint of relish in his voice, "We just received a call that Mrs. Jacqueline Boucher has committed suicide."

"You mean Dr. Boucher's wife?" exclaimed Dupré, leaning forward.

"Yes, Gerald," Fauchet replied emphatically, knowing this news would get Dupré worked up.

"Now I'm fed up with this son of a bitch. Dominique, I want you to handle this as homicide until proven otherwise. Call Dr. Thomas and his team and take some detectives with you. Don't forget the photographer and video man. Go there immediately and take charge of the situation. Right now, phone Boucher and tell him the body should not be moved to a hospital until you say so. Tell the bastard it's a crime scene."

Fauchet adjusted the top of his trousers and his belt as he walked to his office. He alerted Dr. Thomas, the photographer, and the video specialist to proceed to Dr. Boucher's house on the double, and then instructed six detectives to proceed to the Bouchers' residence.

Then he phoned Dr. Boucher on his cellphone. "Dr. Christian Boucher?" asked Fauchet.

"Yes, this is Dr. Boucher."

"We are very saddened by the tragic demise of your wife, Dr. Boucher."

"Thank you, Inspector Fauchet."

"Please make sure that your wife's body is not taken to any hospital until I decide to release it."

"But Inspector Fauchet, we have a medical team here and an ambulance waiting outside. It is a clear case of suicide."

Fauchet commanded, "It is a crime scene, Dr. Boucher. Our forensic team is on its way to your house."

"What do you mean it's a crime scene, Inspector Fauchet?"

"Listen, Boucher, I have declared it a crime scene. So it is a crime scene. This is not a decision for doctors or nurses." Fauchet's tone left no room for doubt about who was in charge.

There was silence on the other end of the line, and Fauchet asked, "Do you read me?"

"Of course it is up to the police to decide," conceded Boucher in a shaken voice.

"Where is the body?"

"In a bedroom," answered Boucher, irritated by the very voice of the insolent Fauchet.

"I want you and everybody else, including your medical team, to remove yourselves from the bedroom at once. And I mean everybody."

"We'll do that," responded Boucher, who was filled with debasement. This is exactly what Jacqueline really wanted for me, he thought. Humiliation piled over humiliation.

After ending the conversation, Fauchet returned to Dupré's office and reported what had transpired. Dupré was evidently pleased. "That's the right way to treat this heartless monster. I am sure the rascal pushed her to suicide with his scandalous sexual shenanigans."

Laporte calmly commented, "This is a very sad thing. The poor man will be under enormous stress. So, Dominique, treat him with civility."

"Come on, Henri," said Dupré, swiping the air with his right hand. "No civility for a man who's had two of his mistress murdered and a wife who's taken her own life." Then he looked at Fauchet. "Dominique, I want you to bring him here and squeeze him like a lemon."

"Gerald, we should give Boucher some breathing space under the circumstances. Otherwise, we could be accused of harassment," Laporte cautioned in his even-tempered style.

Dupré pondered Laporte's advice. "Thanks, Henri, for your prudent counsel." Then he addressed Fauchet. "Dominique, let's postpone Boucher's interrogation until a more appropriate time. So for the time being take a statement from him."

"OK," said Fauchet, managing to conceal his disappointment. Then he left to drive to Boucher's house.

"Now I need to tell the commissioner about this tragic suicide," said Dupré

Laporte stood up. "I am going to phone Dr. LeGarde right away."

After Laporte closed the door gently, Dupré dialed the cell-phone number of the commissioner, Robert Garnier. Dupré told him about the suicide of Mrs. Boucher. The commissioner was stunned. "How could such a beautiful, intelligent, and cheerful woman commit suicide? I don't understand it, Gerald."

"It is always difficult to understand what drives a seemingly cheerful person to commit suicide, Robert. However, I have already sent our forensic and investigative teams to the Boucher residence to make sure it is a suicide, not a homicide."

"All right, Gerald. I have to call the mayor, who is a close friend of Christian and Jacqueline." Garnier paused before saying, "I am sure this is a very hard blow for Christian. I'll give him a call to give him some support." Then added, "It would be nice, Gerald, if you personally give him a call to express your condolences."

"I will. It must be very devastating to him," responded Dupré, thinking that a phone call would be a fine gesture.

After they concluded their conversation, Dupré immediately called Dr. Boucher and expressed his deep personal sympathy and sorrow. "Everyone in my department shares your sorrow," he added.

"I am sure of that, Chief Inspector," replied Boucher in a feeble voice.

"Of course, the task of telling your son in Cameroon will be difficult. It will come as a great blow to him."

"No doubt, it will be devastating to him. Yet I have to contact him as soon as possible," Boucher lied because he did not intend to contact Pierre, nor did he have an address or a telephone number for him. Now it occurred to him that Pierre's irresponsible decision to go to Cameroon was the main cause behind Jacqueline's suicide. She had had evidently missed him, and her depression had worsened, causing Professor Lacan to increase the dose of one of her two antidepressants just two weeks after Pierre embarked on his senseless and childish mission to save the Cameroonians. The stupid, card-carrying Samaritan had pushed his mother to her grave.

"Dr. Boucher, if there is anything I can do, please do not hesitate to let me know." Dupré was a bit surprised that he was sincere in what he said to Dr. Boucher.

Dupré started wondering if there would be another murder. Would the third and unnamed mistress of Dr. Boucher be the next victim? A nebulous idea made him think there could be a connection between this suicide and the murders of Christian Boucher's two mistresses.

# CHAPTER 24

About an hour before Maryse Gasnier discovered Jacqueline's body, Jean-Claude/Pierre and Martine were enjoying an Indian curry takeout meal in the Auberts' apartment, washing it down with red wine. They had already discussed the two local newspapers' coverage of the double murder. *Le Matin,* which devoted four pages to Nicole Gautier's sex life, unashamedly compared her to Catherine the Great of Russia. And it flagrantly attacked her husband, Professor Georges Gautier, painting him in gross words as an uncaring and irresponsible husband and father and labeling him a cuckold par excellence. Martine was very upset by that and told Jean-Claude that on the contrary Professor Gautier, who happened to be a friend of her father, was a caring, responsible, and refined man who possessed a sharp and brilliant mind.

After their meal, they settled on the couch and turned their attention to the books recommended by Martine's father for Jean-Claude. Martine had brought with her three out of the five books. She assured him, "I have asked our head office in

Paris to send me the other two as soon as possible." Then she took a folded sheet of paper from her right trousers pocket and handed it to Jean-Claude. "Here you are. The list of the five must-read books by none other than Pierre-Yves Aubert," she said with cheerfulness. "By the way, my father would like you to join us for dinner sometime."

"It would be my pleasure," he said with feigned relish. "But let me see when I can have the great honor of meeting him and picking his enormous brain." He was determined not to meet Martine's father for he feared the shrewd old diplomat would easily see through his façade. Pierre feared that Martine's father could be acquainted with his own father. Then he added, "How can I thank you and your father, Martine?" before he started reading the note, which was written in elegant longhand:

1. *Crime and Punishment* by Fyodor Dostoevsky. A must-read masterpiece.

2. *One Hundred Years of Solitude* by Gabriel Garcia Marquez. Hypnotic magic realism by a brilliant and fecund mind.

3. *Heart of Darkness* by Joseph Conrad .This is a novella of about a hundred pages, but they are the most captivating and enduring pages published in the twentieth century.

4. *All the Names* by José de Sousa Saramago. He truly deserved his recent Nobel Prize for Literature.

5. *The Heart of the Matter* by Graham Greene. Greene certainly deserved a Nobel Prize for Literature, but for some dubious reasons, he was unjustly denied it.

*Happy reading.*
*Pierre-Yves.*

Jean-Claude leafed through the three books next to him: *All the Names*, *Heart of Darkness*, and *One Hundred Years of Solitude*. Then he picked up Joseph Conrad's *Heart of Darkness*, a small book in English. "Martine, I have to admit I've never heard of Saramago or Conrad before."

"Saramago is a Portuguese writer who was the first Portuguese to be awarded a Nobel Prize. I think in 1998. I brought you his book in French. However, I got Conrad's book in English because my father said it is better to read it in English."

"That will help improve my English," replied Jean-Claude.

"Conrad is a splendid writer. He was a Pole who wrote in English, though he only started learning English when he was nineteen or twenty. Every book he produced is considered a masterpiece."

"So I might start reading his other books," commented Jean-Claude as he gazed at the cover of the small book.

"I think you will love this book in particular because it deals with the horrible plundering and corruption by Europeans in Africa during colonial times."

In his deadpan, cheerfully flippant style, he stated, "Perhaps Mr. Conrad wrote it for me."

Teasingly, Martine said, "I am sure that Conrad wrote it specifically for you because the two of you share the same views about the white man's immorality in Africa."

Playfully, he nudged her with his shoulder. "Why do you sound doubtful?"

"I'm not doubtful at all, darling," she assured him with a poker-faced expression.

They had more wine before making love on the couch. After they dressed, Martine fetched a comb and hairbrush from the bathroom and started combing and brushing his long hair, which he had not cut since he moved into the apartment. "Even a horny, crazy guru like you should brush his hair from time to time, Jean-Claude," she announced with a smile. As she worked on his hair, Pierre's spirit was imbued with a sense of sensuousness rather than sensuality. It was a sensation of affection and caring coming from a sister he had never had. I do love Martine in more than one way, he reflected. He gently held her left hand and kissed it with tenderness.

Martine left shortly before three, feeling tipsy, gratified, and very content with Jean-Claude's company.

Pierre, left alone, turned to Tolstoy's *War and Peace* with gusto. He did not hear the devastating news of his mother's suicide until ten in the evening, when he tuned in to a local radio station as he stretched on the couch still holding the book. He was stunned into incredulity as the female newscaster repeated the name Jacqueline Boucher in another sentence. It was the first item in the half-hour news program. Before moving to another news item, the woman announced, "She is survived by her husband, Dr. Christian Boucher, and their only son, Pierre Boucher, who is currently in Cameroon. Everyone who knew Mrs. Jacqueline Boucher will be deeply saddened by her premature demise."

He sat bolt upright on the couch and threw the book at the marble table; the book struck the edge of the table and then crashed to the floor, its pages making a whizzing sound until they settled open, almost in the middle of the book. With his hands on his head, Pierre started pacing the room aimlessly and in agitation, like a caged and gravely wounded animal.

His world fell apart. He struggled, emotional ropes pulling him between utter disbelief and the horrifying reality. Slings and arrows of sorrow assaulted him, driving him into hysterical rage.

Revenge, revenge, revenge, he told himself. I would not be a real man if I did not avenge the death of my dear mother—and without delay, if possible before my gentle and beloved mother is committed to earth.

Standing in the middle of the sitting room, with his face raised to the ceiling and fists clenched, he let out a primal scream, "The damned Christian Boucher will pay for this, *Maman*. He drove you to kill yourself." His heart-piercing scream echoed in the room. He felt a gaping gash inside him. The voice of the news broadcaster screeched in his ears. He turned to the radio on the table near the couch and switched it off with a furious and rough movement. The radio/CD player tumbled to the floor with a crash.

Exhaling a heavy and sad sigh, Pierre decided he needed some wine to subdue his desperation. As he walked to the kitchen, he reflected that he should not let his father continue enjoying his life as usual with malt, food, sex, friendships, and a pillar-of-society image for long. His father should be buried soon, perhaps a few days after his wife's burial. He was certain that his bastard of a father would be under the delusion he would continue with his life as though nothing had happened.

He opened a bottle of red wine in the kitchen and took a large gulp, then walked back into the sitting room, wading in a sea of darkness and pain. In the middle of the room, he knelt on the floor and, as he took leave of his senses, he found himself pouring all the wine in the bottle on his head; the wine saturated his brown hair that had grown thick and long, then ran down his face, and drenched his T-shirt. Some of the wine cascaded to his jeans and the floor. He violently threw the empty bottle to one side; it hit the wall and ricocheted to the ceramic floor. It broke into pieces with a sharp sound. He glanced at the broken glass for a moment or two and then started rubbing the wine into his hair with vigorous, rapid strokes. Tears ran down his cheeks and mixed with the wine, and the mixture ran down his face and trickled down his T-shirt.

He whimpered like a beaten and inconsolable creature as he hugged himself, collapsed on the floor, and curled his body tightly into a fetal position. "Why, *Maman*? Why, *Maman*?" he wailed. "I have failed you, *Maman*. I am terribly sorry, *Maman*," he cried in a piercing and wounded voice. He hit his head against the floor a number of times and then pounded it harder until the pain became searing and he sensed he would cause a wound on the side of his head. He didn't mind that, but he told himself he would need to go to a hospital, see a doctor or a nurse. That was unthinkable. He stopped pounding his head against the floor and gazed at the floor in front of him, feeling utterly helpless and abandoned.

"Forgive me, Maman. Please forgive me," he whispered, feeling as though he was actually talking to his mother. Still in his fetal position, he clasped his hands tightly, put them between his two knees and closed his eyes, sensing his world had disintegrated and his personal cosmology had imploded. With a pleading whisper, he asked his mother, "Why did you leave me? Why did you leave your only son, Maman? Your only loving son." He fell silent for a while as his tears kept gushing.

Rolling on his back, he stretched his arms and legs in a spread-eagle position and closed his eyes, as if by doing so the shocking reality would be banished from his consciousness— even for a few fleeting moments. He remained in that position for some time, feeling the wetness on his back as his T-shirt soaked up the wine on the floor beneath him.

Now he was certain that his father would be his next target. Monique Roget would be reprieved. She would be spared. It dawned on him that Brigitte Villard, Nicole Gautier, and Monique Roget were victims of his father's narcissism; they were nothing but hot flesh for his sexual gratification. Nothing but steamy and lewd flesh. They were crutches to shore up his fragile and sick ego. Even his own mother, Jacqueline, had been nothing more than a beautiful, educated, and sophisticated woman to be paraded in his father's social and professional circles, serving to maintain his father's vain façade of respectability and superiority.

After almost an hour, he felt emotionally, spiritually, and physically drained; his thoughts were jumbled, his sensations swung from sadness to loathing, from lamentation to hostility, from helplessness to rage. Finally, he stood up and brought an empty carton from the bedroom that he used as a storeroom and carefully, very carefully deposited in it all the pieces and shards of the shattered wine bottle. He took it back to the bedroom and then strode to the kitchen, fetched a mop, and wiped the wine mixed with his tears from the floor. After returning the mop to the kitchen, he took the kerosene lamp to the bathroom, removed all his clothes, and took a hurried shower to wash the wine from his hair and body.

Putting on his pajamas, he lay down on the bed and turned off the kerosene lamp.

The apartment was engulfed in total darkness and eerie stillness. Suddenly he shouted, shattering the darkness and stillness, "Christian Boucher, your days are numbered. You have brought it upon yourself. I will exact justice swiftly and brutally, for you have caused immeasurable pain to those around you. Christian Boucher, it is an eye for an eye and a tooth for a tooth. Nothing less, nothing more."

It is my responsibility to administer justice, he argued, and I am more than up to it. He sensed he had snatched back his certitude and resolve from the jaws of shock and grief. Nonetheless, he had to bide his time to see what would transpire in the next few days before he could move, with cautiousness and acumen, to eliminate his detestable, despicable, and spineless father. In the darkness and stillness of the night, he vowed not to let himself wallow in grief, vacillation, and impotence. He would grieve for his mother after he executed his father. I am sure this is what she would want me to do, he thought. This is also what Uncle Marcel would want me to do. I will not fail them. I will make them proud of me—wherever they are.

Drained and fatigued, he soon drifted into a fitful sleep crowded with convoluted and disconnected dreams that were vivid in a few parts but blurred in most, though strangely they were neither horrifying nor unsettling. It was as if his subconscious, in its mysterious ways, was trying mercifully to dispose of some of his unbounded agony and fury.

# CHAPTER 25

It was shortly after eight in the morning when Pierre woke up with cramped muscles. He stretched his arms a number of times and yawned. The room was filled with sunlight filtered through the bedroom window and curtains. In a blink, the fact that his mother was dead pierced his mind. He found himself engulfed with cold grief—unlike the raging and shrieking grief he had experienced last night—as if the horrifying fact had now sunk into his mind.

An urge to escape the confinement of the apartment took hold of him; he wanted, desperately, to go out to break his feeling of isolation and anguish. He wanted to read the newspaper coverage of his mother's suicide. He did not want to see Martine—she would immediately spot his dejection and his fluctuation between numbness and agitation. And he did not want to see any other human being. He decided to walk to the vicinity of Le Café Coq Rouge instead of cycling. He knew it would take him longer to walk but he felt he didn't have the stomach to cycle.

Locking the main door of the building, he started walking toward the café. The heavy shroud of stupefaction that oppressed him, neither enfeebled his stride nor impaired his intellect. As he walked with vigor, his mind was churning up ideas. He asserted to himself that human dignity was more important than human life. A human being who has been robbed of his dignity and soul is a walking dead person. To kill in order to defend human dignity is not an abhorrent or indefensible act but a noble one. It is proper and necessary to act decisively. His father had killed his mother as a human being before she physically killed herself. And his father had to pay for that.

He craved a cigarette. When he checked his pockets, he discovered he had forgotten his cigarettes and lighter in the apartment, so he went to a tobacconist not far from the café and bought three packs of cigarettes, a lighter, and a copy of *Le Quotidien* and a copy of *Le Matin*. The front- page headline of *Le Quotidien* read: 'City Shocked, Saddened by Demise of Jacqueline Boucher'. He thought the wording of the headline was decent and sympathetic, and that seemed to cement his resolve to eliminate his father.

He stood on a sidewalk and impatiently started reading the article about his mother's suicide. The article said that the police had handled the case as a homicide until their forensic pathologist determined it was a suicide. All of a sudden, the idea that perhaps his father killed his mother and made it look like a suicide took hold of him. He stopped reading as the idea percolated in his mind. Pathologists could be wrong, negligent, or jump to false conclusions. It was a fact that some of the best pathologists in the world occasionally arrived at grossly mistaken verdicts. Whether his father faked her suicide or she committed suicide was an immaterial point, he assured himself. Either way, he killed her. And either way, I am going to kill him.

The idea of a faked suicide became more and more plausible. Now it seemed a strong possibility. Not farfetched by any means. It was not beyond the depraved mind of my father, he reflected. He decided to phone Martine, doing his best to sound like someone who had a nasty flu. "Hello, Martine," he said in a low voice.

"Good morning, Jean-Claude." Her tone was vibrant as usual.

"How are you today?" he asked, coughing in a low, hoarse voice.

"You don't sound normal. Anything wrong, Jean-Claude?"

He paused and coughed again. "No, nothing serious. But I have come down with a horrible bout of flu, Martine."

"So I'll come over and make you a good soup. I will bring with me some vitamin C, one thousand milligrams. It's very effective."

"I've already got vitamin C and a cough syrup." He coughed again. "I have some tablets for the headache and the slight fever I've been having on and off since yesterday, darling."

"Do you know the best medicine for the flu, darling?"

"Brandy mixed with hot water, lemon juice, and sugar," he said.

"You couldn't be more wrong. It is passionate kissing, darling."

He chuckled then coughed for a few moments. "I like that. I would love to kiss you all day. Yet I am sure with one kiss you would be bedridden for days. And I would feel very guilty if I passed this flu to you and you passed it to your dad and Françoise."

"So when can I see you, darling?" Pierre/Jean-Claude, deep down, genuinely longed to see Martine but not now. He decided to struggle with his sorrow and agony on his own. "To be on the safe side, say after two days, Martine. From my experience, this kind of flu lingers for days with me."

"I am not really convinced but I will accept your medical opinion, Dr. Marchand," she yielded, and chuckled, concealing her disappointment. "So I will see you after two days, darling."

"I love you, Martine," he said with some cheer.

"I love you more than you can imagine, Jean-Claude."

When he returned to the rue Karl Marx apartment, he stretched out on the couch and opened *Le Quotidien*. Its staff reporter wrote that Jacqueline Boucher had left no suicide note. Perhaps, he thought, she wanted his father to grovel in shame and embarrassment without leaving him any explanation; she did not want to dignify him by leaving him a single word; she did not want to acknowledge him. Even a brief note or even a simple word of damnation from her would have given his father some relief, but she had evidently decided to deny him that.

Would my father be remorseful? Certainly not, he answered himself. My father is incapable of remorse and contrition. I am

sure my father will be ashamed and embarrassed by the humiliating publicity of my mother's suicide, but I doubt very much
if he will hold himself responsible for her tragic end. He will
not have even a tiny speck of guilt or sorrow over her death. I
will make him pay for that.

For three days, he could not bring himself to brush his teeth,
shower, do his push-ups, shave, or change his clothes. Occasionally, he nibbled at biscuits or cheese to quell his hunger. Red wine
not only quenched his thirst but also numbed him. Occasionally, he was able by sheer will to keep at bay the voices chattering
in his mind. He silenced them by telling himself he needed his
sangfroid and certitude if he was to eliminate his father with
the necessary stealth and dexterity. And he kept exhorting himself that it was imperative to recapture his normal self-assurance
*tout de suite* so as to interact with Martine Aubert with his usual
affection and humor. Somehow, he felt confident that he would
not give her any sign that could reveal his grief and dejection.

He slept on the couch for three nights, abandoning his comfortable bed in the bedroom. Time yawned and dragged on,
heavily and slowly like a gigantic, old tortoise. While he avidly
followed the radio news broadcasts about the murders and his
mother's suicide, he found his real escape in reading—it was a
comforting balm and a means of distraction from his jumbled
inner voices and clamoring thoughts. He resorted again and
again to *The Ruba'iyat of Omar Khayyam*. Khayyam's wise, profound, and transcendental perspective touched a chord in the
depths of his soul and gushed into his mind, filling him with a
much-needed tranquilizing enlightenment and serenity.

The day he was expecting Martine around one o'clock in the afternoon, he woke up on the couch shortly after seven. He rubbed his eyes and yawned. After a few stretches of his arms, he stood up, walked to the bathroom, washed his face and brushed his teeth, but in his apathy he decided to shower and shave later. Then he settled on the couch, awaiting the nine o'clock news. A sense of dejection assailed him but he decided to fight it resolutely. Otherwise, Martine would see through him within a few minutes.

The broadcast commenced with the news that the funeral of Jacqueline Boucher would be tomorrow at eleven in the morning. Pierre's tears welled up and then he started sobbing like an inconsolable toddler. "*Maman*, I will not even be able to attend your funeral," he murmured. "Forgive me. Forgive me, *Maman*." Rubbing away his tears, his ears caught an interview with a Dr. Alain Gilbert. The newscaster enumerated Gilbert's qualifications and his extensive experience in France and some other countries. She added that he was the founder of a criminology company in Paris called IFIC, and that he had been brought in by *Le Matin* to formulate a profile of the murderer of Brigitte Villard, Nicole Gautier, and Alexander Dimitrov.

After a few questions and answers, Dr. Gilbert went on to explain that he had formulated two tentative profiles for the killer based on the facts and evidence that were so far available to him. He declared that the murderer in his two profiles was a man who resided in this city; he was either a middle-aged man suffering from a severe midlife crisis or a young man who had served in the army or worked for the police and had been suffering from mental instability for some time. If he were the middle-aged man, he would be in a dysfunctional and non-gratifying marriage, and possibly have two or three teenage children. If the perpetrator turned out to be the mentally disturbed younger man, he would be single, never have had a girlfriend, would still be living with his parents, and a loner.

How grossly mistaken, Dr. Gilbert, thought Pierre.

Dr. Gilbert went on, "However, in both profiles this killer is well acquainted with different weapons. He decided to use a small Beretta to confuse the police. He is a very cautious and intelligent man. He has a high IQ but either his psychological makeup or circumstances have impeded him from achieving his full potential for academic qualifications and a high-status job. And he has a profound antipathy to beautiful and well-off women." Then Gilbert explained how a psychopath could be friendly, charming, and even seducing.

Pierre switched off the radio, thinking that if the police used anything from this nonsensical rubbish, then he would be safe. It occurred to him that with Dr. Gilbert's two profiles, he could resurface and declare that he had returned from Cameroon to attend his mother's funeral tomorrow. Yet he realized that he had to commit the most justifiable murder one or two days after that, so he would have to remain in his rue Karl Marx hideout. He anxiously hoped the police would use Gilbert's utterly misleading profiles. It occurred to him that Dr. Gilbert's outstanding credentials would somehow make the police take at least some aspects of his two muddled profiles into consideration.

As he was showering, a strange question intruded into his mind: how could I be the biological son of such a barbaric animal? Yet he immediately argued, I do not think my mother ever had a relationship out of wedlock; that would have been against her nature and upbringing. Sadly and indisputably, I am the biological offspring of the demonic Christian Boucher.

Now he was more determined to give his father a dressing-down before executing him. He would also tell his father that he knew it was highly possible that he had murdered his mother with some kind of medical or chemical substance and made it look like a suicide.

After he shaved, he splashed his face with a lot of aftershave. In the bedroom, he put on clean underwear, a light-blue shirt, and dark-blue jeans. He went into the kitchen, made himself a mug of black coffee, and took it with him to the couch. Then he decided to phone Martine. He started by asking, "How are you, Martine?"

She cheerfully replied, "I fine, Darling. How about you?"

"I am excited about seeing you?"

"Me too," she said and chuckled. "Last night we had dinner at home with two of my father's friends. They are both philosophers. Of course, my father always says he is not a philosopher. I was fascinated by their heated discussion over the definition of an 'intellectual'. Who is an intellectual and who is not an intellectual? Françoise and I were amused to see three great minds clashing over what we thought should have been settled a long time ago. Finally, my father, in his warm way, asked

Françoise for her definition. When she answered, in a serious tone, that an intellectual is anyone who decides he is an intellectual, the three men burst out laughing, not in a mocking way but in an amused manner. At that point they were intoxicated enough to agree it was a sound definition."

"So they did not agree on a clear definition of who is an intellectual?"

"No. I think Françoise's definition gave each of them a way out of his pedantic and unbending position. When Françoise and I excused ourselves, to give them the opportunity to exchange obscene or risqué jokes, one of the two philosophers flattered Françoise by earnestly thanking her for solving a complex issue with a simple and brilliant stroke."

"I am very much inclined to agree with Françoise's definition," he said and laughed. "I hope you are coming at one, Martine?"

"Of course, darling. How can I forget a rendezvous with my one-and-only Jean-Claude? I will bring today's newspapers." Then she asked, "For lunch, do you have any preference?"

"Anything you choose, but I want a good green salad with it, Martine."

"It will be done. À bientôt, darling."

Pierre turned his attention to *War and Peace*. He kept reading attentively until Martine arrived shortly after one. A few moments after Martine entered the apartment and put two bags on the dining table, Pierre steered her to the couch and started unbuttoning her purple silk shirt; he gently removed it and carefully draped it on a chair at the dining table—always aware that she handled her clothes with meticulousness whenever she undressed.

"I thought you were hungry, not horny, Jean-Claude," she teased him.

"I am both hungry and horny, but you have always advised me to put my priorities in the right order."

She continued teasing him, "You have three priorities. Copulation, copulation, and copulation."

"Those are our three shared priorities, Martine," he said, and started sucking her protruding and seductive lower lip.

They made love passionately and vigorously on the couch. As if they were starving for sex, they indulged their lust with abandonment and zest. When they both climaxed, Jean-Claude squeezed Martine between the back of the couch and his body, tenderly kissing her scar and closed eyes, and softly sucking her nipples and lips. They remained silent with their eyes closed and their legs entwined, listening to each other's quiet breathing. In their stark nakedness, they were enveloped in deep tenderness, and affectionate warmth. Jean-Claude's sadness and anger seemed to have evaporated, for he felt immensely buoyed by Martine's gratifying intimacy and sexual audacity.

After some time, they put on their clothes, set the food on the dining table, and sat opposite each other. After they enjoyed their meal, she moved to the couch.

He took *Le Quotidien* and *Le Matin* from the round, marble table, leaving behind *Le Monde*, and joined Martine on the couch. She took *Le Matin* from his hand, and said, "Just listen to this nonsense. I read it in my office and it made me laugh."

She read the headlines. "'Renowned Profiler Narrows Suspect Pool, Killer Will Strike Again.'"

"*Le Matin* wants to boost its circulation by scaring people."

"Of course, Jean-Claude. Now the sales of locks and bolts have shot up by more than 100 percent. They will continue to rise as long as *Le Matin* keeps at it." Then she continued reading aloud, "'Our local police force has neither a professional profiler nor the capability to deal with the psychopath prowling our peaceful city with impunity. That is why our civic duty made it obligatory to resort to the expertise of Dr. Alain Gilbert to help the police in stopping this unprecedented mayhem.'" She stopped reading, and Jean-Claude, who found the way she read articulate and fascinatingly feminine, indicated to her to carry on.

"Now listen to this. Obviously, Dr. Gilbert wants to protect his professional reputation. 'These two profiles are based on the meager facts and evidence available to me at this point in time. The police have denied me access to all the facts and evidence in their possession, claiming that they could not divulge any pertinent facts and evidence while they are conducting an investigation. However, if the police give me access to what they hold, the profile would be more accurate and helpful. In fact, it could be a completely different profile.'"

"He's giving himself a lot of cushions to fall back on if his two profiles prove to be completely wrong and misleading," commented Jean-Claude.

"Of course," said Martine. Then she continued reading, "'In the profile of the married man, the fact that his targets are beautiful and sophisticated women indicates that his wife is homely and banal. In the profile of the young man, it indicates that he is also obsessed with beautiful and sophisticated women. So in both profiles, we have an individual with a fixation on the glamorous characteristics of women like Mrs. Brigitte Villard and Mrs. Nicole Gautier.'" Martine stopped reading and looked at Jean-Claude next to her on the couch. "What psychological humbug!" she exclaimed. Then she turned her eyes back to Le Matin, and read, "'The killer in either profiles chooses his glamorous victims at random. He observes them in upscale shopping malls or other public places, and once he decides on a particular woman, he stalks her with extreme caution, studies her daily routine, habits, and the routes she usually uses to her residence or workplace.'"

Jean-Claude put his hand on Martine's arm, and interposed, "Martine, this is psychological hyperbole."

"Of course," she said, then read three more paragraphs of the profile, before exclaiming, "How about that, Jean-Claude!"

"It sounds like very solid and scientific rubbish. But to the average reader, it will seem irrefutable and powerfully convincing."

"Still, with Le Matin's sustained fear-mongering crusade, a lot of women will barricade themselves in their homes at night whether they are glamorous or not."

"I'm sure this Dr. Gilbert is aware of Le Matin's disgraceful reputation. So he is in it for the money. He will pocket thirty or fifty thousand euros and fly back to Paris."

Martine glanced at her wristwatch, folded *Le Matin*, and stood up. "Anyway, you have to read *Le Quotidien*." Then she declared apologetically, "I think I'd better go to work, darling."

Jean-Claude looked up at her enchanting green eyes. "Honestly, I don't want you to go, but your work is more important than keeping me company."

She softly slapped his cheek. "Don't say that. Your company is more precious to me than you can imagine."

He embraced her and smiled. "I know that, Martine," he said and kissed her tenderly. Then he warned her, "Be very careful. According to Dr. Gilbert's criteria, you are a perfect target for this killer."

She laughed, "I am neither well-off nor glamorous."

"You are more than glamorous. I suspect the murderer might be intimidated by your stunning glamour and keep away from you."

Jean-Claude descended with her to the lobby on the ground floor. At the main door, they cuddled and kissed ardently for some time. When Martine left, Pierre returned to the apartment, closed the door, and settled on the couch.

He was neither euphoric nor dysphoric, but felt very contented and his internal volcano had somewhat abated; yet he was not yet firmly astride the saddle of mental clarity and emotional certitude. Somehow, he felt confident he would regain his certitude before he went to eliminate his father and avenge his mother's death.

# CHAPTER 26

The day after his mother had been committed to her last resting place, Pierre woke up shortly after nine and pulled the bedcovers over his face, intending to snooze for a few more minutes. For a few moments, his mind was in a realm of blankness, hovering between wakefulness and drowsiness. Then the thought that his mother was now under the earth forcefully sprang into his consciousness, sending him into a whirl of sadness, grief, and self-blame. He stayed in bed wallowing in his depressive thoughts, with tears running down his face. As he wiped them with the cuff of his pajamas sleeve, they continued to well up again, more than before.

His mother's proper place was not two meters under the ground, he thought. But what can I do? Nothing, was the heart-wrenching answer. Nothing. His heart raced and his mind seemed to be momentarily shut off. Though I cannot bring her back to life, I will avenge her by sending my father to his grave, two meters under the ground.

Suddenly, he felt a pang of remorse over the killing of Brigitte Villard, Nicole Gautier, and Alexander Dimitrov.

If only he had murdered his father at the outset, all these killings could have been avoided. But yet again, he reminded
himself that he had always believed that executing his father
was inconceivable.

Feeling a suffocating compulsion to go out, he brushed
his teeth and put on a T-shirt and trousers. Outside, he cycled
aimlessly around the old abandoned buildings. After more
than ten minutes of this senseless cycling in the vicinity of his
building, he cycled to the shops in the proximity of Le Coq
Rouge Café. He bought *Le Quotidien*, *Le Matin*, a dozen fresh
eggs, eight croissants, and two baguettes from shops near the
café. Then he gave the laundry seven items for washing and
ironing, and collected six ironed pieces, before cycling back to
the apartment.

Sitting on the couch, he picked up *Le Quotidien* and gazed
at his mother's photo. It broke his heart. Pressing his lips against
the photo, kissing it, he felt his eyes brimming with tears. He
kissed the photo a number of times, wiped his tears with his
hand, and made a mental note to clip the photo and article
as a keepsake. He felt consoled when he read that his uncle,
Charles-Maurice, his wife and their children had come from
Poitiers to attend the funeral.

Then he moved to other news and articles, skimming over
them almost absent-mindedly. In *Le Matin,* his attention was
arrested by a list of twelve measures that women should adopt
to protect themselves 'since Dr. Gilbert did not preclude the
possibility of the killer striking again, and the police are irre-
deemably bogged down.' The measures ranged from putting

safety locks on all doors and installing an electronic security system—if one could afford it—to acquiring a trained guard dog and never venturing into a lovers' lane after dark. What is this nonsense? Pierre thought. *Le Matin's* editors are nothing but mean-spirited fear-mongers. Their twelve scary commandments will terrify not only women but also men and children. They made it sound as if Jack the Ripper and Ted Bundy had arisen from their graves and joined forces to visit this city with a spectacular, blood-curdling duet rampage.

Not to be outdone by *Le Matin, Le Quotidien* had brought in a more heavyweight expert, Professor Roland Brault, currently a professor of criminology and forensic psychiatry at the University of Lyon, and previously a professor of criminology at the University of Munich in Germany. On its front page, *Le Quotidien* allotted about a quarter of the space to explain the professor's credentials and his worldwide experience. It quoted him professing that criminal profiling is not infallible and not 100 percent accurate, but it gives law-enforcement agencies a sense of direction that helps them to formulate viable strategies, and focuses their attention on a specific pool of suspects. He explained that a serial killer is someone who murders three or more people over a period of more than one month.

The whole of page six was devoted to an interview with him and his photo, which showed a humble-looking man with thick eyeglasses and a warm smile. Pierre thought the professor looked dependable, trustworthy, and reassuring. Brault asserted that the failure to apprehend a sociopath or a psychopath in any case did not mean that the police had not exerted strenuous effort. "For instance, in the United States, where about eighteen thousand murders are committed annually, 20 percent to 30 percent of the murders remain unsolved despite the cutting-edge forensic technology and the efficacious investigative training in that country," he stated.

Brault pointed out that, while serial killers generally could be split into organized and disorganized ones, there were four types: the visionary, the hedonistic, the mission-oriented, and the urge-to-control type, though a lot of serial murderers have a combination of some features of these four categories. He concluded the interview by saying he would not rush to formulate a profile of the murderer because it could be misleading to the police. It seemed to Pierre that the gist of Professor Brault's interview was that people should not blame the police if this murderer was not apprehended. In effect, the professor was not only giving the police some breathing space but also letting them off the hook in advance. Pierre reflected that the local police would be more amenable to cooperating with Professor Brault. He wondered if *Le Quotidien's* editors had advised the professor to adopt this agreeable stance or if it was the man's natural temperament.

He put the two papers to his left on the couch and phoned Martine. "How are you, darling?"

"I am great, darling."

Then Pierre forced himself to tell Martine, with a well-feigned sense of disappointment, "I am sorry to tell you that this weekend I have to be in Paris." He was not going to consume any alcohol before he executed his father. And if Martine came for their usual Saturday rendezvous, alcohol would certainly be part of their evening. He had already decided to murder his father in the early hours of Sunday. He wondered if his father used alcohol daily as some form of self-medication for his inner turmoil fostered by his split personality—his true, twisted, Dr. Jekyll-and-Mr. Hyde identity.

"Why on earth?" Martine asked with obvious disappointment.

"I was summoned for an urgent meeting with ADPA in Paris. I will take the morning train to Paris this Friday and meet them in the afternoon on administrative matters. Then I will attend two orientation sessions on Saturday, which are mandatory before I can fly to Ethiopia."

"You mean you are leaving tomorrow morning?" asked Martine, her voice dropping with despondency.

"Unfortunately, I have no way to delay it. They phoned me yesterday, saying they are desperately short of administrative staff in Kenya and Uganda, but particularly so in Ethiopia."

Martine yielded, for she believed work was work even if it was in a nongovernmental charity organization. "I will miss our Saturday date, Jean-Claude."

"*C'est la vie*, darling." His tone conveyed a sense of resignation, but it was deftly feigned. "I will return on Sunday afternoon or evening."

"So you will be leaving soon for Ethiopia?" she asked.

"It seems so. They will be telling me in Paris when I should fly to Ethiopia."

"Well, you will be doing something noble, helping the needy and the dispossessed." She paused and then added, "I am proud of you, Jean-Claude."

"I am immensely grateful to you for providing me with a sanctuary from my mother. With her sickening self-centeredness, she doesn't believe in helping others."

"It will be an enriching experience for you, Jean-Claude."

"I'm sure this mission will give my life some meaning."

"I would have loved to join you in your African mission. But you know I can't leave my father."

"I do understand, Martine, but I will miss you hugely."

"How long do you intend to stay in Ethiopia?"

"Frankly, I don't know. It depends on the situation there. It could be one year, two years, or more."

He sounded convincing to Martine despite his lack of precision. "But you must keep in touch, Jean-Claude."

"Of course, darling."

"I love you more than you can imagine, Jean-Claude. Take care of yourself in Paris."

"I will. Take care of yourself until I return, darling."

After ending the call, Pierre's mind was in a state of overdrive. However, what was clear in his mind was that he ought to slip out of France immediately after eliminating his father. He would not be using the names Pierre Boucher or Jean-Claude Marchand, but the name in the passport arranged for him by Uncle Marcel: Martin Gerard Lavoie.

On Saturday morning, he woke up around nine o'clock, and remained in bed for some moments listening to the cooing of the two pigeons nesting on the outer ledge of the bedroom window. Then a perverse sense of satisfaction flooded him as he reflected that he was ready for the deadly night visit to his family house. He killed the hours by alternating between reading Georges Simenon's *My Friend Maigret* and repeating his harsh routine of doing two-hundred push-ups. He told himself to refrain from consuming any alcohol lest it impaired his mental and physical agility for tonight's lethal mission.

He reflected that when the police discovered the dead body of his father, they would simply intensify their efforts and deal with the murder as a frustrating extra workload. However, Dr. Alain Gilbert would be confounded and embarrassed. It would not be the murder of a beautiful and well-off woman but a middle-aged man. Would *Le Matin* drop Dr. Gilbert and bring in another renowned profiler, or would it stick with Gilbert and ask him to revise his profile? Whatever decision the editors make, he thought, they will keep up their vicious attack on the police.

However, he was well aware that staying here until Tuesday morning could multiply the chances of being apprehended by the police. But his abundant self-confidence made him think the police had no clue about where he was. If they had investigated him, he was almost sure that they would believe he was in Cameroon. He also wanted to have a final rendezvous with his beloved Martine, especially after eliminating his father. Moreover, he was eager to see the press coverage of his father's murder before slipping out of France.

Shortly after eight thirty in the evening he decided to take a nap in the bedroom. The alarm went off precisely at 10:00

p.m. He shut it off, reached for the flashlight on the bedside table, and switched it on. He washed his face in the bathroom before going into the living room, where he lit the kerosene lamp next to the couch. He felt cocksure as he strode to the kitchen to make himself a mug of strong, black coffee. He put the flashlight on the kitchen counter and ate a boiled egg and a croissant while the water boiled.

Switching off the flashlight, he walked to the couch, sat down, and placed the coffee mug on the floor near his bare feet. He lit a cigarette, took two long drags on it, and then glanced around the living room. A sense of wistfulness washed over him; he would soon vacate this large and cozy sanctuary; he would soon be leaving the enchanting and affectionate Martine Aubert. He would be going away from his beautiful city where he had been born and brought up, leaving so many sweet and fond memories, notwithstanding the abuse he had suffered since his childhood.

He contemplated with affection all the people and places he had to leave behind. Still, he had not decided where he would be going. Africa? Latin America? Or another European country? Yet he was confident he would reach the right decision once he had executed his father, for he always prided himself on his skill in making decisions, and on the ingenuity of his free will, which had never failed him.

He mused over whether Martine would find herself a new lover while he was away from France. Would she be married to someone else by the time he returned to France? Though he was the person who had helped her to banish her inhibitions and reclaim her self-esteem, he should not interfere with her free will to seek friendship or intimacy with any other man, or with the way she wanted to shape her life. Humanity, he reflected, would be in a much better state if most, if not all, human beings jettisoned the shackles of religion, traditions, and the outdated and stifling ideas about how to control their children, their friends, their lovers, and their spouses under an erroneous conception of love.

At eleven thirty, he stood up. The moment for action has arrived, he told himself. Calmly he picked up the lamp and took it into the bedroom, where he put on a dark brown shirt, black trousers, black socks, and black shoes. He put on his leather jacket, and with complete detachment, distributed his execution implements in its various pockets, making sure that the key ring for his family house was in the pocket of his shirt, with no cigarettes, lighter, or cellphone to clog it. Finally, he picked up his small flashlight, and inserted it in the inside, left pocket of the jacket.

He picked up the kerosene lamp and returned it to the small table in the living room, deciding not to turn it off. Descending the stairs, Pierre took his bicycle outside, and locked the main door. As he cycled toward his family house, with the bike's headlight lighting his path, he avoided going through the city center to be on the safe side, though that added ten or fifteen minutes to the journey. So, taking side streets, he cycled steadily and unhurriedly.

When he reached the house, he parked his bicycle in the paved back alley that Mrs. Gasnier usually used. Holding the bicycle, he soundlessly lowered the kickstand. Before opening the small, rear gate of the property, he put on his black gloves and his black mask with its small slits for the eyes; not to hide his face from his father but to make sure no hair from his head would fall anywhere in the house. Once inside, he closed the gate noiselessly, and walked slowly toward the kitchen door. The house was eerily still and dark. Taking the key ring from his shirt pocket, he let himself into the dark kitchen; without a sound or even a click, he closed the kitchen door. He stood in the darkness for about two minutes, listening patiently. There wasn't any sound in the house.

Still in the kitchen, he switched on the flashlight and took in all the parts of the kitchen, which brought to his mind fond memories, and that instigated a surge of rage within him. He could hear himself breathing. Grasping the Beretta in his right hand, he carefully attached the silencer to it. With the flashlight in his left hand, he stepped into the corridor leading to the staircase, the sitting room, and the living room. From where he stood in the corridor, he could see some light in the living room. He did not need the beam of the flashlight, so he switched it off and inserted it in a pocket of his leather jacket.

Then he slowly stepped toward the living room. It occurred to him that it was possible that his father had fallen asleep drunk in an armchair or a couch in the living room. So, he thought, I have to give him the humiliating and final dressing-down in the living room before shooting him. The idea of executing his father in the living room seemed to diminish the forcefulness of the scenario he had played many times in his head. Yet he strode with enraged vigor into the living room, ready for the lethal confrontation. But there was nobody there. Then he walked into the sitting room. His father was not there either. So it will be the bedroom scenario, after all. He realized that the light from the lamp in the living room spread to the lower part of the staircase. He did not need to switch on his flashlight to reach the upper floor.

Very cautiously, with his hand firmly holding the Beretta with its silencer, he ascended the carpeted stairs. He stood stock still in front of his father's bedroom and remained silent; he could hear someone snoring with a horrid noise. With his gloved left hand, he turned the door handle, swung the door open, and swiftly switched on the bedroom light.

A shocking and enraging scene met his eyes. His blood boiled. There was a naked woman fast asleep on her side next to his father. A yellow bed sheet loosely covered her upper back, leaving her white, voluptuous legs, thighs, and buttocks exposed. His father had a matching yellow bed sheet covering his legs and abdomen— just below his naked, hairy chest. Pierre could not see the woman's face since her head, with its thick, golden hair, was turned toward the right wall of the room, with her back to his father, who slept on his back. Pierre forgot about all the insults and rebukes he had planned to subject his father to before executing him.

With mounting fury, Pierre walked toward the bed, but deliberately stood at a distance from it, and shot his father twice in the face. One bullet lodged in his forehead and the other in his right eye. His father's head jolted up and fell back on the pillow while his arms stretched out with reflexive force before powerfully landing back, his left arm striking the woman. As his head fell back, his father emitted a deep, croaking sound. Blood gushed from his wounds, drenching his face and soaking the pillow. The woman, startled awake, turned to her right and for a few moments seemed confused and uncomprehending, before she began to scream in a heartbreaking panic. She jumped out of the bed, holding the yellow sheet to cover her nudity. In her terror, she dashed to the corner near her side of the bed.

She shrieked in primal horror, "No, no, no please." Then she collapsed to her knees and held the yellow sheet up to her shoulders to cover herself.

"Shut up, you bitch, or I will kill you," Pierre ordered her.

"Please, not me! Not me!" she shrieked in a heart-wrenching voice.

"I said shut up. I don't want to hear any screaming. Do you understand?"

"Yes, I understand, sir," she answered in a faltering voice, put her right hand to her mouth, and supported her trembling body by resting her left hand on the thick, lagoon-blue carpet.

"Let's have a calm conversation or I will execute you."

She instinctively raised her hands, pleading in supplication and panic, and the bed sheet fell, exposing her large and youthful breasts with their pinkish-brown nipples.

"Please, not me. I have nothing to do with him."

"You are in bed with him and you have nothing to do with him? What nonsense!" exclaimed Pierre and stepped toward her.

She raised the bed sheet to her breasts, but instantly it fell down again as she raised her hand, and lamented pathetically, "I am sorry, sir. I am so sorry. Honestly, I have nothing to do with him."

"Don't talk nonsense, you whore," Pierre said in a low, commanding voice. "Stop talking nonsense."

She put her hands on her head and started wailing, "Forgive me, sir. I am so sorry. Please spare my life, please." She dropped her hands and beseeched him in desperation, "I do beg you. I do beg you, sir."

Despite his burning fury, Pierre felt a pang of compassion for her—another victim of his father's insatiable lust. He found himself for a few moments debating whether to end her life or spare it, but quickly decided he was not going to leave a living witness, particularly a trashy and despicable woman who had the bad taste to sleep with a man just a few days after he buried his wife. There was no doubt in his mind that she was aware of this fact, but in her sordid lust she had disregarded it. Neither of them could restrain their animal carnality even for a week or two.

"What's your name?" he calmly asked her.

She managed to reply, "Catherine, sir."

"What's your full name?"

"Dr. Catherine Rolle, sir."

"So you're a doctor?"

"Yes. I'm doing an internship here in heart surgery."

"Under this bastard?" he spat the words with disgust.

"Yes, sir."

"How old are you, Dr. Rolle?" asked Pierre as he lowered the pistol down to his right side.

"Twenty-nine, sir," she said and gasped for air before adding, "I know it's wrong of me to be here."

"Was Boucher your boss?"

"Yes, sir." Her trembling abated yet her face remained a collage of primal fear and helplessness.

"He seduced you, Catherine?"

"Yes, sir," she paused, sobbing. "He made it clear that I had to sleep with him or forget about my internship."

"I am not surprised. He was a lecherous animal. But are you telling me the truth or just making it up, Dr. Rolle?"

In her confusion and panic, she erroneously sensed there was a hint of sarcasm in his tone and that fueled her dread. "Honest to God, sir," she screamed.

He raised his gloved left hand to where his mouth was under the mask, indicating to her to hush up. She nodded her head repeatedly.

"This dead beast was as old as your father. Why didn't you report him to the ethics committee?"

She shuddered with dread and paused before responding, "All members of the ethics committee are as unethical as Dr. Boucher, sir. If I had complained, all of them would have sided with him. And my career would have been ruined forever."

He believed her. "I am really sorry for you, Catherine," he said with sincerity. For a moment, the sight of tears cascading down her face and mixing with the mucus that dribbled from her nose made him feel compassion for her.

"Thank you," she hastened to say, nodding. She hoped that this man, with his calm and melodious voice, would spare her life. "I swear to God I will not tell the police or anyone anything about you. I think you did the right thing by killing him."

Pierre ignored what she said, and asked, "Don't you know that this dead animal's wife was buried just a few days ago?"

She sobbed and gasped for air, and nodded her head as the words choked in her throat. As Pierre continued staring down at her, she managed to say, "Yes. And I am deeply sorry for that. But I had no choice. I could not say no to Dr. Boucher." Instinctively, she brushed the tears and mucus with the bed sheet and then covered her nakedness.

Pierre decided not to drag on the conversation; he had to leave as soon as possible. "Cover your eyes, Catherine," he ordered her in a calm tone. As she closed her eyes, she felt immensely vulnerable, so she swiftly opened them again.

"I said close your eyes," Pierre commanded and raised his semiautomatic pistol toward her face. "Close your eyes until I leave the room."

Her body quivered, though he could detect a glimmer of doubtful hope in her eyes before she firmly closed them. Taking seven steps backward, he lodged a bullet in the middle of her forehead. She made a groaning sound as her head hit the wall behind her. Then she collapsed to the floor, exposing her smooth and curvaceous, white back. Pierre took another step away from her and gazed at the thick coils of her golden hair as it tumbled forward to the carpet. She was certainly more beautiful than Brigitte Villard and Nicole Gautier had been.

She was as beautiful as Monique Roget, he told himself. He shot her again in the middle of her skull. Her naked body tilted to the right and crumpled to the carpeted floor, with the yellow bed sheet under her. Crimson blood started inundating the bed sheet and the thick carpet.

Pierre looked at his shoes and trousers to check if there was any blood on them. There was none. He gazed at her dead body and found himself muttering, "I am sorry, Dr. Catherine Rolle. I am so sorry. But with your own free will, you decided to sleep with this animal tonight."

He turned and walked to the other side of the bed, where his father was motionless and gone. His blood had soaked a large part of the bed. After gazing for some time at his father's bloody and fractured face, he calmly addressed his father's corpse. "This is retribution. This is justice. And you brought it upon yourself, you bastard."

Stepping back away from the bed, he raised the pistol and aimed it at the left side of the chest, releasing a bullet into the dead man's heart. This is the coup de grâce, he said to himself. Silently, he stared at the two dead bodies with their blood still spreading underneath them and around them. Then he gazed at the corpse of his father and said venomously, "This is from me, from my dead mother, and from my late Uncle Marcel." Then he added silently, "In fact, from all the Dillons and the Rollins."

He switched off the bedroom light, closed the door, and started descending the stairs, enormously satisfied with himself. I have done what I should have been done a long time ago, he told himself. If I had first killed the rascal instead of killing Brigitte and Nicole, my mother would have been still alive. Regret over this fact enveloped him with scathing pain and self-blame. He could have executed him instead of executing Brigitte Villard, and gotten away with it. However, he had never thought of killing his father. Not that it had not crossed his mind, but it had seemed too outrageous at the time.

He returned to the living room and glanced around it. An idea cropped up in his mind. He walked into the sitting room, opened the front door of the house, and slowly pulled it, leaving it ajar; he wanted the police to think that Dr. Boucher had been negligent enough to leave his door unlocked. It occurred to him that on Monday, Mrs. Gasnier would in all innocence close the main door, do her cooking, and clean the ground floor before going upstairs and be confronted with the shock of her life—a shock that would eclipse the shock she had experienced when she found his mother dead in the guest room. He hoped that Mrs. Gasnier would not have a heart attack or completely lose her mind on Monday.

After locking the back door of the kitchen, he walked unhurriedly to the small gate at the rear of the property. Closing the back gate, he detached the silencer from the Beretta, inserted each one in its designated pocket of the leather jacket, and then removed his mask and gloves.

As he cycled back to rue Karl Marx, he thought what a coincidence it was that his father's ill-fated sex slave was named 'Catherine' and his own ex-girlfriend's name was 'Catherine'. Life is of full of coincidences, he somewhat reluctantly admitted. The way he met Martine Aubert was a coincidence— a mere coincidence. But that had turned out to be to his advantage. No, to the advantage of both of them, he reasoned.

Back in the apartment, he took the kerosene lamp from the living room into the bedroom where he calmly deposited all the parts of his murder kit in his large briefcase, which he then locked and placed back in the cupboard. He looked at the alarm clock next to the bed: it was two fifteen in the morning. Within a few minutes, he was in his pajamas and lying on the bed. He turned off the kerosene lamp. With his mission successfully accomplished—without a hitch—he felt overwhelmingly proud of himself, yet truly sad and remorseful for killing the young Dr. Rolle.

In the darkness, the idea that he should have killed his father much earlier returned to haunt his mind. If he had done that, then his mother, Brigitte, Nicole, Alexander Dimitrov, and Catherine Rolle would have been alive. But alas, how could I have known? he asked himself. How could I have known how things would unravel, twisting my free-will decisions and creating unforeseen and bizarre dynamics of their own?

If he had known what he was now fully and painfully aware of, he would not have needed this apartment—this sanctuary provided by Martine Aubert. Perhaps he would have rented a small flat in a nearby town, which was his original plan; executed his father; and resurfaced after some time, declaring that he had returned from Cameroon to stand by his mother and share her grief over the loss of his father.

Before he drifted into sleep, a germ of doubt about the soundness of his concept of free will and his firm conviction about it slipped into his mind. If he had known what he now knew, things would have been utterly different. Not only would he not have needed the refuge Martine had generously offered him, he would not have found himself forced to slip out of France to Cameroon, Ethiopia, Brazil, Italy or South Africa.

As he slept, the seed of doubt about free will planted itself in his subconscious without the acquiescence of his conscious mind.

# CHAPTER 27

Pierre awoke around eleven on Sunday morning but stayed in bed, letting his mind revisit what had happened about ten hours earlier. He regretted that the presence of Catherine Rolle had prevented him from heaping savage insults on his father before shooting him—and had prevented his father from knowing who had snuffed out his life and made him pay the ultimate price for the prolonged degradation and hurt he had inflicted on his family.

Remorse over killing Dr. Rolle lingered in his heart. She was an unfortunate, star-crossed innocent who had been forced by his father into being a sex slave. To some people, the relationship between his father and the young Dr. Rolle would be categorized as consensual sex; but Pierre considered it worse than rape—it was sexual slavery. If the powerless Dr. Rolle had had the guts to lodge a complaint against his lecherous father, the unethical ethics committee would have sided with their highly esteemed colleague and wrecked her career.

In his pajamas, he went to the kitchen to make himself some black coffee. While the water boiled, he wolfed down two croissants. Settling with his coffee on the couch, he felt subdued and somber. He decided that tomorrow, Monday, when Martine came for lunch, he would tell her he would be leaving for Paris on Tuesday and flying to Addis Ababa on Wednesday. For some time, he considered which French city he should go to first from here, and from where he would leave France. If he went to Marseilles, he could take a ship to Morocco or Tunisia, and then fly to Cameroon or Ethiopia. What about going to Paris and then flying to any African country? he asked himself. His gut feeling was that these two options were fraught with risk. He also rejected the idea of going to Brazil, which he had considered a safe haven where he could stay under the radar for years. But it would be a long journey, and the Brazilians spoke Portuguese. Swiftly, he also discarded Italy, Spain, and Greece.

Then he reminded himself that he had to dispose of his murder kit this evening. And he decided the best place to get rid of it was the other side of the river, the eastern side adjacent to the old, derelict, and abandoned industrial area inhabited by destitute immigrants, dispossessed French, and some other have-nots. Most people couldn't muster the courage to venture into the area after dark—perhaps not even the police.

Pierre's soul was imbued with gratitude and warmth toward the Auberts as he gazed at the framed, black-and-white photo of Martine's grandfather on the wall opposite him. The long-departed man looked at him with fixed eyes, not straying from him for a split second. Suddenly, it occurred to him that those eyes had witnessed all of his departures to and returns from his murderous missions, all the sex and lively companionship he had had with his granddaughter, all his push-ups, and all his moments of melancholy and moments of elation. All and everything except his silent musings.

As he sipped his coffee, the question of where to go returned to his mind. It suddenly dawned on him that the best course of action was to go to Switzerland and fly from Geneva to Johannesburg. In his mind, it was settled there and then. Therefore, it shall be South Africa. Not Cameroon, Ethiopia, Italy, or Brazil. When he arrived in Johannesburg, he would locate Bill Miller, the CEO of Cromwell Operations Management Corporation, COMCO, and the friend of his late maternal uncle, Marcel Dillon. He might join COMCO, yet he ruled out working with them as a combat mercenary, that is an operations management consultant. He was absolutely adamant that he would never kill any human being again. He had done enough killing—more than what he had planned to do.

If all that Uncle Marcel had told him about Bill Miller was true, he felt confident that Miller would welcome Marcel's nephew with open arms, though he would be known as Martin Lavoie, not Pierre Boucher. He would tell Miller that he was the son of Marcel's other and younger sister, Marianne. In fact, Aunt Marianne had died three months before her twelfth birthday in a botched-up appendectomy. He felt very confident he could convince Miller to give him a job in one of COMCO's departments of public relations, client relationship, or business development, which Marcel had mentioned that COMCO had.

I am not going to talk to Bill Miller from a position of weakness. If he doesn't offer me a position I deem suitable, I will simply walk out on him. That would prove that Miller was a fair-weather friend of Uncle Marcel. In that case, I will seriously search for a good NGO involved in humanitarian work. It would fit my purposes if such an NGO, regardless of its nationality, operates in Cameroon or Ethiopia. Alternatively, any other African country would do. Engaging in humanitarian work, he reflected, could be an atonement and redemption for murdering Alexander Dimitrov and Catherine Rolle. That thought somewhat assuaged his sense of culpability and guilt.

Now his sense of tranquility was augmented by the quiet stillness that usually enveloped the city on Sundays.

At ten to nine in the evening, he put on his leather jacket—with the murder kit items in different pockets—and biked to the old bridge connecting the two parts of the city, holding in his left hand a plastic bag containing the pair of shoes he wore for the double murder at his family's house. The bridge had been built almost a century ago and the locals called it the 'Old Bridge', though its official name was the Forest Bridge. The new bridge, built fifteen years ago, was about nine kilometers to the north. He was apprehensive, with justification, that he might be seen disposing of his murder kit, though he had carried out his murders with efficiency and success. The bridge was deserted. Obviously, people were savoring their last weekend hours at home before facing their Monday blues.

After crossing the bridge, he turned right toward the old residential area inhabited by poor immigrants, Gypsies, and down-and-out French. As he biked for some time, he occasionally and casually looked around. He was relieved that there was nobody around. The whole place was enveloped in thick silence. He disposed of the pair of shoes first, then his murder kit, item by item, cycling for some forty or fifty meters before tossing the next item into the calm and dark river with all his force. Finally, he folded his old black jacket and threw it in the middle of the river. Having done that, he felt an immense sense of deliverance. He decided to cycle from this godforsaken area to the railway station to purchase a one-way ticket to Geneva.

As he entered the large station hall, he was sure, however, that with his hair now long and thick nobody would recognize him. He saw a few people milling around the place. He consulted a train timetable and found that the first express train to Geneva on Tuesday was at eight fifteen in the morning. He entered the spacious ticket office and found only two employees working; on each of the other eight ticket windows, there were CLOSED signs. One of the staff manning the two operating windows was an elderly man with a Salvador Dali moustache, who seemed to be so bored he did not even make the effort to look at Pierre. The other staff member was a skinny, very young-looking woman wearing a casual, flowery dress, which left her shoulders exposed. He approached the young woman, who smiled at him from behind the thick window glass that had a small circle dotted with tiny openings to help customers communicate with the staff. She was plain but had a sunny face.

She smiled. "Good evening, sir."

"Good evening, mademoiselle" Pierre responded with a smile. "I want a one-way ticket to Geneva on Tuesday morning on the eight-fifteen train."

"Do you want a first-class or second-class ticket?"

"Second-class, please," he replied, looking intently at her angular shoulders as she entered some data in a small machine and produced the ticket for a reserved seat. He paid in cash, and with a broad smile, she gave him his change and the ticket. Pierre smiled back and left.

As he cycled to the apartment, he told himself not to arrive at the station on Tuesday before eight o'clock in the morning. It would be better if he showed up at the station a few minutes after eight to reduce the chances of being seen by someone who happened to know him.

*** 

Next day Martine arrived shortly before one in the afternoon, carrying the latest editions of the two local newspapers, green salad, chicken curry, and two bottles of red wine. As Jean-Claude kissed her, he was overcome by mournfulness over the fact that he was leaving her, and might not see her for years, or forever. Why should I be forced by circumstances to abandon such a beautiful, lively, trusting, and loving person, he asked himself with a sad and heavy heart.

After putting the two bags on the dining table, Martine gave him a mischievous look, and declared, "Let's get our priorities right, darling." Then she held his hand and led him to the bedroom. They started making love tenderly, but soon Martine's passion became unbridled. While Martine was making love in an abandoned and vocal way, Jean-Claude's enjoyment was somewhat somber and tinged with a sense of loss.

As they embraced each other after their long and gratifying lovemaking, she sensed he was doleful, and his mind was somewhere far away. "Anything wrong, darling?" she softly inquired and kissed his cheek tenderly.

Jean-Claude paused, pondering what to say to her. He kissed her lips before responding, "Yes, darling. What is wrong is that I will be leaving tomorrow for Paris. And I will fly to Addis Ababa on Wednesday."

"I will miss you enormously, Jean-Claude." She sounded sad and genuine, but in a matter-of-fact way.

"I don't want to leave you, Martine. It will break my heart."

"It will break my heart too. I don't want you to leave. But I don't want you to change such a major life decision for my sake. That would be very selfish of me." She kissed his cheek fondly in a consoling way.

He replied in a choked voice, "Martine, our relationship is the best thing that has ever happened in my life. You are the true love of my life." Martine could sense that his words were deeply heartfelt, and that made her heart bleed.

She clasped his hand in a comforting gesture. "You are the love of my life. You are the first man I've ever loved, Jean-Claude," she whispered as tears swelled in her eyes.

He found himself saying in a dejected tone, "I just wonder if you will wait for me until I return to France." It surprised him that he said that in an unaffected way, though he knew it was a far-fetched dream. Returning to her as whom? Pierre Boucher? Jean-Claude Marchand? Or Martin Lavoie?

"I will. I promise to wait for you however long you stay in Africa. And I will stand by you in your future political career."

Stabs of guilt and turmoil pierced his composure simultaneously. He closed his eyes and fell silent, as though he did not want to speak before mulling over his emotional quandary. Whenever he returned to France and attempted to resume their relationship, she would discover his duplicity and deception. She would swiftly conclude he was the person behind the five murders. It behooved him not to continue to lie to her. He should discreetly slip out of her life, and let her retain a fond memory of a loving and tender relationship with someone called Jean-Claude Marchand. He kissed her scar, her temple, and her ear softly, then said in a low voice, "Please, don't make such a promise. It will simply impede your enjoyment of life for years."

"What do you mean by that?" she asked, gazing into his eyes.

"I mean, let's just agree that we'll resume our relationship whenever I return to France. In the meantime, you have to be free to enjoy your life without promises or fetters. It would be very selfish of me to ask you not to do that."

Martine pondered his words and then searched his eyes as if to ascertain how serious he was. "Do you really mean it?" she asked in a whisper. It was a pained question.

"Yes, Martine. Love and selfishness can't coexist in a genuine and wholesome relationship."

She did not respond for some time. Then, as if something deep in her mind told her not to turn this into a melodrama, she grinned and asked in a mischievous tone, "How far do you want me to go in my enjoyment of life?"

He replied in a tone that was caring and solemn at the same time, "Enjoy yourself to the maximum. Life is too short to be wasted in withdrawing from others. Your life is too precious to be wasted that way, Martine." He paused, expecting Martine to respond, but she remained silent, dwelling on his words. Pulling her closer to him, he whispered, "If you happen to fall in love with a man worthy of you, someone who happens to be better than me, you shouldn't wait for me."

"I don't think I will find a man better than you." She pushed the bed sheet away, propped her head on her arm, turned to him in her nakedness, and gazed into his eyes. "I don't want to find another man, Jean-Claude. I won't be looking for a better man."

He grinned, raised his head, and planted a hot kiss on her lips. "You never know, darling. Life is full of surprises. Sometimes pleasant and amazing. So if you happen to fall in love with another man, I will understand."

"Let's not talk about this, please. It breaks my heart." There was a trace of scolding in her tone, yet she started sobbing.

As his internal emotional tug of war continued, feeling like a physical force pushing him in two directions, his eyes filled with tears. It was an emotional dichotomy that he wanted to avoid: hurting her feelings or deluding her.

"I love you so much. And with love, one can stand any separation whether in time or distance, Jean-Claude." She was sincere, but oblivious of his internal emotional predicament, still assuming it would be a separation of two or three years.

Martine brushed her tears, delicately wiped his tears with her slender fingers, and stroked his shoulder in a reassuring gesture. She stood up and looked at his nude body on the bed. She smiled at him and tenderly said, "Let's not spend our last date crying." She found his tears and sensitivity genuinely endearing. This is the type of man I could wait for for many years. I won't find another man so loveable, so confident, and so unafraid of exposing his softer side, his vulnerabilities, she thought. She sensed that she loved him even more deeply that she had before. She went into the bathroom.

Pierre climbed out of bed. I'm sure I will find a way to be back in her life, he reflected. While I don't want to hurt her feelings, I am determined not to dupe her, either. I'll think of some tenable explanation for why I told her my name was Jean-Claude Marchand. He felt confident that he would, one day, find a plausible way into her life, for he now knew he sincerely loved her. He put on his clothes and headed to the kitchen to heat up the food. Before putting the curry in a large pan, he gulped a glass of wine.

He set the table and brought out the salad, chicken curry, and rice; he filled two glasses with red wine. As they started their last meal together, it occurred to him that Martine was now capable of walking her own path. She was now a truly audacious woman, who had reclaimed her self-esteem from the jaws of inhibitions, restrains, and fears. The thought that she could now travel her own road gladdened him—regardless of the consequences to their relationship. She was not the same

Martine who had stopped him at her bookshop when he tried to steal a German book.

Anyway, he reflected, their relationship was fraught with so many unknowns, which he could not control, nor did he want to control. Her new boldness assured him that she would act according to her free will. And he was pleased with that. He felt happy for her. I ought to be happy for the two of us, he told himself.

"By the way, Jean-Claude, when you send me your address in Ethiopia, I'll send you the remaining two books on my father's list. Or any other books you want."

He sensed that Martine was handling the situation in a much more sensible way than he was. "That's thoughtful of you, Martine." He wondered if he should send her his address in South Africa. Then he decided that this was one of the many issues he would try to resolve when he arrived in Johannesburg. He assured himself he was always capable of working out any problem, however difficult it might seem here and now.

As they ate their meal, each of them consumed three glasses of wine with fervor, as if they wanted to banish the idea of the inevitable long separation. Martine told him that she would delay her departure to the bookshop as long as possible. "I want to be drunk, not just tipsy. I wonder what my staff will think about that." She chuckled and topped up the two glasses with wine. So Jean-Claude went into the kitchen and opened another bottle. He sat down and told her, "I want to be drunk too. I want to blunt my sadness at leaving my Martine."

After finishing their meal, they made love for the last time on the couch. Then Jean-Claude rolled over, next to her, and started sobbing. Martine gently wiped his tears, fondly kissed his eyes, lips and cheeks, and patiently managed to calm him down. She cuddled him tenderly, embracing him tightly and affectionately. The knowledge that they would soon be apart, and for a long time, imbued them with deeper fondness and tenderness toward each other. They remained silent and cheerless, enveloped in a somber sense of profound nostalgia. It made them embrace each other firmly for a long time, attempting to forestall the imminent, painful moment of their inevitable separation.

They savored the sensuous animalistic warmth that radiated from their youthful naked bodies for some time. Then Jean-Claude stood up and put on his clothes. Leaving Martine to dress in her unhurried way, he went to the kitchen and returned with two glasses filled with red wine, and placed them on the table next to the couch. Martine joined him on the couch. They clinked their glasses and then Martine raised her glass and asked, "Will the angels always be by the side of my Jean-Claude in Africa?"

"I'm sure I'll need a lot of angels but more importantly I want my Martine to keep me in her mind and soul."

Martine nodded. "You are already deep in my soul. And you will always be on my mind, day and night." Then they downed their wine and kissed.

"Isn't life cruel, Martine?" he asked. He reflected that life sometimes could be grossly cruel and merciless, like an enraged elephant trampling on the nests of ants and other tiny, power-less creatures.

"Of course it's cruel sometimes, but we have to take it in our stride," she replied.

He admired her brave outlook. "That's the right spirit, Martine."

"You taught me that. I owe it to you."

"No, Martine. Nobody can be taught such a courageous spirit. It is something innate in you," he said, looking into her radiant, green eyes. I will really miss these large, lush, and exotic green eyes, he reflected. For years? Or forever? He asked himself with mournfulness.

She squeezed his hand. "Even if it is something innate, it lay dormant for a long time until you awakened it in me." Then she grabbed his face and kissed him feverishly for some time, leaving his lips tingling, before she announced with palpable sadness in her voice, "I have go now, darling." She stood up and decided to inject a pleasant note before her departure. "I don't know if I am going to drive to the bookshop or end up some-where else. I am really drunk," she said, slurring her words a bit and giggling with delight.

"If you want, I can drive you to the bookshop, darling," said Jean-Claude, standing up.

"You are as drunk as me. I'll brave it on my own, darling. I don't want the two of us to die in a car crash. So let's reduce the risk. If there is a car crash, I will be the only casualty," she said with a broad smile on her face, which was flushed red with the wine she had consumed.

Jean-Claude laughed. "I'm sure there will be no car crash and you will arrive safely."

She chuckled and momentarily rested her hand on his shoulder for balance. "That is what I intend to do," she said. Then she remembered something. "Do you want me to take you to the railway station tomorrow morning?"

"That's very thoughtful of you, darling. But I don't want us to sob and cry in front of hundreds of travelers. Moreover, you have your job to look after."

"It is not a big deal. I can come and take you to the station."

"Martine, you have been more than generous with me. Why should I give you the trouble of taking me to the station?"

"You deserve more than that, darling."

"By the way, you can come and collect the keys any time. I will leave them in an envelope on the marble table. And don't forget to take all the wine bottles, books, kerosene lamps, and everything else in the apartment."

"I will do that."

"You won't find the bicycle because I promised a waiter in a nearby café to leave it for him. He will come to collect it from the railway station." He was telling her a lie but he thought it a white lie.

"That is a very nice gesture for the waiter, Jean-Claude."

They descended to the foyer in a doleful mood. Before saying their good-byes, they cuddled and kissed. Jean-Claude's tears ran down his cheeks and Martine brushed them affectionately with her hand. He found himself holding her hand and kissing it fondly.

Martine gave him a tender kiss that meant more than any good-bye. Then she opened the door and made her way to her car, doing her best to walk with steady steps. Pierre thought that she was not terribly drunk and felt confident she would reach her bookshop safely. He remained in front of the open door and watched her drive away. They waved to each other with deep sorrow and sentimentality.

Pierre ascended the stairs to the third floor slowly and with a dejected heart. As he closed the door of the apartment, tears ran profusely down his face. He fell on the couch, facedown, and sobbed his heart out. It occurred to him that he was crying due to an agonizing cluster of issues with intertwined feelings of anxiety, sadness, and guilt: leaving his lovely Martine, the deception with which he had shrouded their relationship, the death of his angelic mother, leaving his beloved France for an unknown place and future, and the needless murders of the innocent Alexander Dimitrov and Catherine Rolle.

In an attempt to subdue the predicament of his clashing emotions, he drank more red wine. When he was totally intoxicated, he drifted into a long sleep on the couch. It was shortly after nine when he awoke, in the thick darkness of the room, in the clutches of a severe hangover. His head was throbbing with pain.

Lighting the kerosene lamp on the side table, he shuffled to the kitchen, where he rapidly drank two small bottles of water, quenching his thirst and giving him some relief from the hangover. He thought he needed some aspirin tablets but he remembered he had none. Then he made himself a mug of strong, black coffee, heaping into it three spoons of sugar and stirring it patiently. He hoped it would ease the hangover.

He took the coffee to the couch, glanced at his wristwatch in the light of the kerosene lamp. It was nine forty-eight. What about the murder of his father and the young Catherine Rolle? he wondered. He took a few sips of the hot, strong, and sweet coffee, then fetched the radio and switched it on. A male voice announced that the police commissioner would hold a press conference at ten o'clock, which the radio station would broadcast live. The news gripped Pierre's attention, and his excitement grew by the minute. Inwardly, he was wriggling with impatience and agitation as he sipped his coffee. With six minutes to go, he raised the volume.

Finally, a broadcaster announced that Mr. Robert Garnier, the police commissioner, would start the press conference with a brief statement before fielding some questions from the media.

Garnier's voice was grave and commanding. "Fellow citizens, I stand in front of you with a sad heart and somber mind to announce that today two innocent citizens were found murdered: the prominent heart surgeon, Dr. Christian Boucher, and Dr. Catherine Rolle, a brilliant intern at Jeanne d'Arc Hospital. The preliminary police investigation leads us to believe that these most vile and wanton murders are the work of the same killer who, in the last few weeks, took the lives of three other innocent members of our community." Pierre did not miss the fact that Garnier avoided calling his father's and Rolle's murders a double murder.

Garnier declared that there was a vicious and wicked serial killer prowling the peaceful city and though he did not want people to panic, he urged everyone to be cautious. The commissioner's voice was compelling but calming and reassuring, and Pierre reflected that he would come across as very impressive on television. He imagined that most of the city's inhabitants would be transfixed in front of their TV sets.

The commissioner announced three immediate measures. One, the Mayor had authorized a €150,000 reward for information leading to the apprehension and conviction of the murderer; two, the authorities had retained the services of Professor Roland Brault, the preeminent forensic psychiatrist and criminologist, to work with the police on formulating a profile of this ruthless serial killer; and three, in addition to the patrol cars attending to routine policing duties, starting this evening the police would double the number of cars cruising the city from six in the evening until six in the morning, searching every street, alley, square, and public garden. Then he added, "Do whatever you think is necessary to ensure your safety. I cannot overstress the fact that small and simple measures could make an enormous difference. If you see anyone acting suspiciously, I urge you to dial 112 immediately. It is a twenty-four/seven service. And it does not matter if your suspicion proves to be wrong.

"Our police force is working diligently day and night to apprehend this ruthless and brutal murderer. I can assure you we will not rest until this beast is brought to justice. I have great trust in our abilities and capabilities, the forensic technology at our disposal, and the great commitment and dedication of the men and women on our police force.

"Nonetheless, I must emphasize that the police need your full cooperation and assistance. If we all stand together, the chances of apprehending this serial killer will increase significantly. We should not let this monster murder another innocent person in our peaceful, hard-working, and decent society. We should not let him terrorize us."

The commissioner paused, obviously for effect, thought Pierre, before adding, "Our thoughts and our hearts are with the mourning families of the victims of this heartless murderer. Their loss is our loss, their grief is our grief, and their bereavement is our bereavement." Pierre mused that Robert Garnier was an orator par excellence, if not a born actor.

Then the commissioner took questions from newspaper, radio, and TV reporters. However, he dodged most of them by giving responses such as: "I can't go into detail on that at this point in time."; "Since the investigation is ongoing, I can't divulge the manner and circumstances of the two last murders."; and "The police will reveal that at the appropriate time." Pierre switched off the radio, knowing that the commissioner would not give away any specifics.

Taking the lamp into the bedroom, Pierre started packing all that he needed to take for his long journey, including his laptop, which he had not used since he had moved into this apartment. After putting everything in his large briefcase and small suitcase, he double-checked all the items carefully, putting his new passport and train ticket on top of the items in the briefcase.

Having satisfied himself that everything was in order, he set the alarm for six o'clock in the morning. He undressed, took a shower, dried himself, brushed his teeth, and went to bed— tired and haggard. Now he felt his hangover had dissipated.

Putting off the kerosene lamp, he rested his head comfortably on the pillow. In the pitch darkness, he experienced the immense resentment he still felt for his father for the many times he had accused his mother of turning their only son, Pierre, into a sissy. Now his father, rotting in hell, would know that his son was never a sissy. Then he recalled, with stinging bitterness, the few times that his father had declared that he wished they'd never brought Pierre into the world. One such utterance is enough to leave a gaping wound in the psyche of any child, he reflected. He recalled that every time his father had said that, he had silently wished that Christian Boucher were not his father.

# CHAPTER 28

At six o'clock on Tuesday morning, Pierre was aroused by the alarm clock, which he immediately shut off. He climbed out of bed with a sense of urgency. All the final touches to his luggage and the apartment were done briskly and without much thinking. Then he collected all the newspapers and magazines in the living room and the bedroom, piled them in an orderly way on the dining table.

Having satisfied himself that everything in the apartment was neatly in order, he returned to the bedroom, took an envelope, and scribbled, "*For my Martine. Hugs and kisses. I shall love you forever and ever. J.-C.*" He inserted the two keys to the apartment and the building into the envelope, sealed it, and placed it on the marble table. He returned to the bedroom, where he put on a blue necktie and a dark-gray suit, placed one of his cellphones in the breast pocket, and then slid three thousand euros into the right inside pocket of the jacket. About seven fifteen, he was ready. He had enough time to catch the train a few minutes before its departure, he told himself. Taking the briefcase and the suitcase into the living room, he glanced around with tender reminiscence. He stared at the photo of Martine's grandfather and found himself saying to the old man, "Thank you for your nice company. And farewell."

Closing the apartment door, he descended to the ground floor with the briefcase and suitcase. He strapped the two cases to the rear bicycle rack, wheeled the bicycle outside, and closed the front door. He cycled toward the railway station in his elegant suit. When he was about a ten-minute walk from the station, he dismounted, and parked the bicycle in a cycle rack in front of some shops that were still closed. He decided to leave it unlocked, knowing that someone would steal it within a few hours. Carrying his two cases, he started walking toward the station. At three minutes past eight, he reached the bustling station, bought *Le Quotidien* and *Le Matin*, two wrapped croissants and a hot cappuccino in a closed paper cup then proceeded to Platform 3. He was relieved that he did not see anyone he knew, and that the few police officers wandering in the station did not even give him a glance. If the police and the public had swallowed either or both of Dr. Gilbert's profiles of the serial killer, which had been widely publicized by *Le Matin* and the local radio and TV stations, they would not be on the lookout for a young man with a very thick and long hair, he reflected. They would be searching for either a middle-aged man with a closely or decently cropped hair or a young man with a crew cut.

He stepped into a second-class car, placed his coffee, croissants and newspapers on the small table in front of his seat, put the suitcase on an overhead rack, and settled in his reserved seat—next to a window—putting the briefcase on the empty seat next to him. Glancing around the car, he could see that most of the seats were empty.

As the express train pulled away from the platform promptly at 8:15 a.m., a wave of nostalgia enveloped him. He found himself silently saying, "Good-bye my adorable Martine; good-bye my lovely city; good-bye my great country." This was followed by a sincere promise to himself: When I return to France, I will demolish the ice wall between Uncle Charles-Maurice and me—an ice wall that was pettily built by my soon-to-be-buried father, who with his snobbishness and heartlessness, shamelessly looked down on his own brother.

For some time, he peered through the window at the rapidly changing scenery to his left. Then he picked up *Le Quotidien* and found that it had an inside four-page spread on the murder of his father and Catherine Rolle, in addition to half of the front page. On the front page, there was a large photo of the Police Commissioner, Robert Garnier, addressing last evening's press conference with more than a dozen of microphones on the podium in front of him. The headline read, "No Effort to Be Spared to Apprehend Serial Killer." Pierre read the front page and then moved to pages four, five, six, and seven. The photos of his father and Catherine Rolle were printed on page four. Pierre thought Dr. Rolle's photo did not do justice to her stunning beauty. She had been much prettier cowering in the corner of his parents' bedroom. On page six, there was a photo of Professor Roland Brault at the top of an article detailing some of the cases he had helped to solve in France and other countries.

*Le Quotidien's* coverage was factual and proper. However, Pierre was surprised by the newspaper's assertion that the intended victim was the stunningly beautiful Dr. Catherine Rolle—not Dr. Christian Boucher! Therefore, his father was considered to be a collateral victim! Does this mean even the responsible *Le Quotidien* have swallowed Dr. Gilbert's grossly misleading profile of the murderer? he wondered. He put down *Le Quotidien,* ate his two croissants, and sipped from his cappuccino, before he picked up *Le Matin.* He found it had devoted twelve pages to the double murder.

Its front-page headline screamed, "We Always Said It Was a Serial Killer." On the front page, the paper bluntly insisted that the murder of the two doctors in Dr. Boucher's bedroom was a scandal of large proportions in the medical circles in the city. And since the young Dr. Rolle was doing her internship under the old, lecherous Dr. Boucher, it demanded a full public investigation into the ethics of medical doctors in our city, and added that the double murder had shattered the façade of respectability of the medical profession in our society across the country. The photos of the two victims appeared on the front page. *Le Matin* claimed that sources close to the investigation revealed that the attractive young intern and the 'wolfish old heart consultant' were murdered while they were making love, just like Nicole Gautier and Alexander Dimitrov had been, and asserted that the two doctors had been so carried away with lust that they had left the front door of the Bouchers' house unlocked.

Pierre was not surprised by *Le Matin's* assertion that the intended target was Catherine Rolle, whom it described as stunning and glamorous, and not Christian Boucher. Of course, it was upholding the misleading idea of its advisor, Dr. Alain Gilbert. *Le Matin* added that Dr. Gilbert pointed out that the serial killer had been stalking Dr. Rolle for some time and, on the night of the murder, followed her Renault to Dr. Boucher's house.

However, Pierre relished the two columns *Le Matin* devoted to a merciless attack on his father. It claimed that three doctors who had known Boucher very closely, but wanted to remain anonymous, described him as a man with no conscience, no morals, and no ethics. It added that Boucher had the reprehensible taste to have sex with one of his mentees in the conjugal bed he had shared, for decades, with his beautiful and refined wife just a few days after he had buried her. Pierre reread those columns and found every word in them very much justified.

But he regretted that his father's reputation was shattered after he had died; he had always wanted it to crumble when he was alive. At least, that had been Pierre's original plan; indeed, it was his first main scenario.

Staring out the window, Pierre thought it was ridiculous that the two papers claimed that the intended victim was the young Dr. Rolle, adopting Dr. Alain Gilbert's theory about the type of victims the serial killer targeted. Nobody will ever know that it was I who deliberately left the door ajar, Pierre reflected. How could one bogus expert, despite his illustrious credentials, derail the media and, consequently, public opinion, and probably the police and the examining magistrate? With this contaminated string of pseudo-deductions, Pierre had a sneaking feeling that the examining magistrate and the court judges would fall prey to Gilbert's hypothesis because his faulty hypothesis had been transformed by the media into a perception, and perception in the human mind is always an undisputable fact. So *Le Matin*, which had exploited Gilbert's muddled profiles of the murderer to boost its circulation, had elevated his profiles to a collective and irrefutable truth in the eyes of the public and the authorities.

What does this mean? wondered Pierre. Does it mean I am not linked and might never be linked to the murder of my father or to the other murders? Well and good, he told himself. Could it mean I can return to France within two or three months and no one will be the wiser? Is it possible that the murders will remain unsolved forever? He would have to follow the developments of the investigation through any available media sources in Geneva and Johannesburg.

Folding the two newspapers, he opened his briefcase and put them on top of its contents. When his eyes fell on Joseph Conrad's *Heart of Darkness*, he picked it up and closed the briefcase.

After reading about ten pages, Pierre was enthralled. The book's blurb said it was a story within a story narrated by a seaman called Marlow. The story was about a European ivory trader, Kurtz, who was transformed by his African experience into a delusional creature. Pierre found Conrad's style dense, every sentence splendidly crafted; and the story hypnotic and riveting, though he struggled with some of the English words. As usual, he started underlining passages and scribbling comments in French in the margins of the book. It occurred to him that he should reread this book in Africa due to its captivating brilliance. Having underlined a profoundly moving sentence, he read it three times: 'The conquest of the earth, which mostly means taking it away from those who have a different complexion or flatter noses than ourselves, it is not a pretty thing when you look into it too much.' How telling and how penetrating, reflected Pierre.

He raised his eyes from the book and stared through the window at the swiftly changing landscape as the train rattled its way to Geneva at high velocity. Then he returned to the book. He had about twenty pages left when the train arrived at its destination. He closed the book and returned it to his briefcase.

The Geneva railway station was crowded. He disembarked with his two cases and managed to book a room for three days at a four-star hotel, which the middle-aged woman at the hotel reservation desk told him was reasonably priced, and only a five-minute walk to the city center. After changing one thousand euros into Swiss francs, he took a taxi to Hotel Cleopatra, a six-story building. At the reception counter, he was allotted a smoking room—Room 407—on the fourth floor. A polite, young, black man, in a black suit with a red tie, told him there was one restaurant, one bar, and one cafeteria in the hotel, all on the ground floor, and that breakfast was served from six thirty until ten thirty in the cafeteria. He pointed a large finger toward its location. Pierre registered under his new name, Martin Lavoie.

The room was neat and clean, but Pierre thought it was too small for a four-star hotel. There were two single beds, a number of brochures, a room-service menu, two small bottles of mineral water, and two glasses. The color scheme was light beige with brownish curtains. Over the two beds, there were two framed prints of enlarged tulips in light red, yellow, and pink, which complemented the color scheme of the room. Martin/Pierre opened a cupboard with sliding doors and found a small safe-deposit box. Overall, he liked the room. He took off his jacket and necktie, draped them on one of the chairs, and then walked to the window. He could see the roofs of two- and three-story buildings behind the hotel.

He felt exhausted yet relieved that he was away from France and away from the police investigation and the stepped-up night patrols. He removed his belt and shoes and slumped onto the bed nearer the window. Though he did not intend to nap, he soon drifted into sleep.

Shortly after seven in the evening, he awoke, feeling fully rested. He dressed and went down to the reception and enquired about any nearby barber. The receptionist told him there was one in the basement. In the basement he found a small shop selling newspapers, maps, sweets, T-shirts and assorted caps, and a small flower shop in a row with two hair dressing saloons, one for ladies and one for men. When Pierre entered the barber shop, the young and slim barber was busy trimming his nails with his teeth. He jumped from his seat when he saw Pierre. The young barber, who had shifty eyes and a pronounced facial tic on the left corner of his lips, cut Pierre's long and thick hair silently yet with obvious care and dexterity. Pierre was pleased with the result. Now back to the original Pierre, he told himself as he looked at his face in the large mirror.

He returned to his room and took a long, warm shower. He decided not to go out, and retrieved Conrad's *Heart of Darkness* from his briefcase to finish the remaining few pages of the book. Before commencing reading, he dialed room service and ordered a club sandwich and a bottle of red wine, which were delivered to his room after he had completed reading the book.

He devoured the club sandwich as he was almost starving, washing it with three glasses of red wine. After putting the food tray outside the room, he took out his literary journal and scribbled his thoughts about Conrad's book, jotting down a few quotations that had struck a chord with him.

Reflecting upon his journey to South Africa, he had a sense of thrilling elation about it rather than of foreboding or apprehension. Even if my African adventure turns out to be a mistake or a disappointment, I am still young and I can chalk it up to experience. I have to make mistakes—big mistakes; I should not be afraid of making mistakes, particularly at my age. They are the only path to learning in the school of life. He assured himself that he was crafty enough to turn any situation to his advantage and resilient enough to withstand any setback. Then he pressed the wake-up call button on the phone and requested a wake-up call at seven in the morning.

Next morning, he was awakened by a pleasant, female voice on the phone at seven. As he left the room to go to breakfast in a blue suit with a red-and-blue necktie, he saw a middle-aged woman pushing a housekeeping cart, so he placed the Do Not Disturb card on the doorknob. He did not want anyone to enter his room with the tens of thousands of euros in the small safe, even though it was locked. It occurred to him to buy a new briefcase of a reasonable size and get rid of his bulky one.

After having his breakfast and three cups of coffee in the hotel cafeteria on the ground floor, he returned to his room, took the money from the small safe, and deposited it in his briefcase, which he took with him in the elevator to the hotel lobby. He strode to the concierge counter and inquired about the locations of the nearest banks. The affable concierge, whose skin sagged under his eyes and at the bottom of his cheeks, produced a foldable color map of Geneva, made a cross with a black pen on the location of the hotel, and drew a line along a few streets leading from the hotel to four banks, which he circled in black. He smiled, revealing a set of teeth with two front ones missing, one on the top and one on the bottom. "It is a five-to-ten-minute walk, sir."

Martin/Pierre thanked the concierge, put the map in his jacket pocket, and strode out of the hotel in a businesslike gait. The morning was delightful, sunny, and mild. A few light-blue clouds dotted the distant sky.

He adjusted his necktie and walked on with a swagger. As he entered the first bank circled in the concierge's map, he took a queue ticket from a dispensing machine near the entrance, then walked over to a row of six comfortable blue chairs and sat in the first one.

Now Martin stared up at an electronic screen showing the ticket number on the right in red and the customer-service desk number on the left in blue. The bank was spacious and luxurious, with ultramodern but comfortable and appealing furniture, counters, and customer-service desks. After a few minutes, his ticket number, forty-two, blinked on the electronic board next to desk number five. He picked up his briefcase and strode confidently to the customer-service desk. He noticed that the six desks were not crammed against each other; there was ample space between them, thus allowing clients to discuss their transactions discreetly. This is a bank one could trust, he mused.

As he sat in one of the two comfortable blue chairs at the desk, a young woman in a white, silk shirt with a pleasant air about her but a plain face, smiled and said, "Good morning, sir."

"Good morning, Germaine." He had read her name on a small, white plastic nameplate on the desk: Germaine de Remusat.

"And your name?" she asked with a broad smile.

"Martin Gerard Lavoie." He handed her his passport and his queue ticket.

She put the ticket to one side, and then looked at a few pages of his passport, closed it, and placed it in front of her. "What can I do for you, Mr. Lavoie?"

"First of all, can you call me Martin so that I can call you Germaine?" asked Pierre with a disarming smile.

She smiled back and announced, "I don't mind, Martin." She liked his cheerful and direct approach.

"I want to open a call deposit account at your bank."

"That's great. You have selected the best bank in Europe," she asserted. "In which currency?"

"I have seventy thousand euros. I want them converted to Swiss francs."

"Splendid," she said and handed him a one-page form to complete. When he came to the address box, he wrote, Cromwell Operations Management Consulting Corporation, Johannesburg, South Africa—and in the e-mail address box: mg.lavoie@gmail.com.

Germaine checked the form entries. "Is there any post office box number for this corporation in Johannesburg, Martin?"

"Yes. But I don't remember it. If you can give me your business card I will e-mail you the full postal address once I am in Johannesburg, Germaine."

She handed him her card, which said she was a senior customer relations officer. A very slim and elegant card, thought Martin Lavoie, aka Pierre Boucher, Jean-Claude Marchand.

"That will be fine," she said. "Anyway, we normally send our clients monthly statements through our Internet banking system."

"That would be fine with me."

"However, you have to have your secret banking telephone number in case you want to inquire about the status of your account. To do that, you dial the toll-free number in the brochure I will give you. For security purposes, they will ask you a few questions and then you create your own banking telephone number," Germaine explained patiently, then stood up and walked to a photocopying machine with his passport. He could see she was wearing a dark-blue skirt that hugged her supple buttocks in an erotic way. The tight skirt shifted from one buttock to the other with each step she took. Her legs were slim, well-shaped, and provocative. Despite her plain face, she is an attractive woman, he decided.

She returned to her seat and entered some data into her PC. "I do apologize, but we have to wait for a few minutes before we can get your account number."

"No problem. Take your time, Germaine."

"Thanks, Martin."

"While we are waiting, could you tell me where to find the nearest travel agency?" asked Martin.

"Oh, yes. Just cross the street, walk for about fifteen meters, and you will find a large travel agency, Global Travelers' Agency. Or just GTA."

"I have another question, Germaine. Where can I find the best steak in Geneva?"

Germaine glanced at the ceiling, pondering, before responding, "I would confidently suggest Le Café Royale. It is not far from here. Just a few minutes' walk."

Pierre took out his Geneva map. Germaine consulted it for a moment, then used a red pen to mark Le Café Royale, and drew arrows leading from the bank to the café. He was looking at her searchingly rather than at the map. She was wearing a nice and subtle perfume, he thought as its scent intermittently reached his nose.

"Thank you, Germaine," he said and looked at the red arrows that she had made.

"I hope you enjoy it. If you don't like it, I will reimburse you the cost of the meal," she said with a sweet laugh.

"You are a lady with excellent taste. So I am sure I will enjoy it."

She did not comment on what he said. She thought he was a handsome young man with a melodious voice. After a few moments she gave him a printed sheet of paper and asked him to go to till number ten. He walked to the till and handed the money to a cashier, who gave him a receipt, and then he returned to Ms. de Remusat, who handed him his passport. "Of course, you need a checkbook and, I presume, one or two credit cards, Martin."

"I would like to have two credit cards, Germaine."

"Your checkbook will be ready within one hour. The credit cards will be ready tomorrow morning before eleven o'clock." She held her hands together and tilted them to her right in a way that Pierre found strikingly feminine.

"In that case, I will collect the checkbook and the credit cards tomorrow morning."

"Good. So see you tomorrow. Enjoy your Le Café Royale steak." She extended her hand to him with a sunny smile. "And thank you for doing business with us."

Pierre stood up, shook her hand firmly, and inserted the receipt in his jacket pocket. "I enjoyed doing business with you," he said, smiling. "You are pleasant, efficient, and attractive, Germaine."

Her smile widened in a delightful way. "Many thanks, Martin. So see you tomorrow."

He left the bank, crossed the street, and headed to GTA. Inside the travel agency, he booked a one-way, economy seat on a Swiss Air flight to Johannesburg on Friday. He asked for an aisle seat and then asked the obese and intense young man to book him a room at a three- or four-star hotel in Johannesburg not far from the city center. The young man, all business, recommended a four-star Holiday Inn that was about a ten-minute walk from the city center. He looked up at Pierre for approval.

Pierre nodded. "Make the hotel booking for ten nights," said Pierre, telling himself he would decide later whether to extend his stay at the Holiday Inn or move to another hotel.

He paid in cash, and the travel agent gave him, with his fleshy hand, the ticket and a printed copy of his hotel reservation. Then the agent said in his infantile voice, "Your flight takeoff time is at ten in the morning. So it is advisable to be at the airport by eight thirty at the latest, Mr. Lavoie."

"Eight thirty is a decent time," replied Pierre as he inserted the ticket and the hotel reservation in a pocket of his briefcase and closed it.

"Have a nice flight, Mr. Lavoie." The travel agent gave him a forced ghost of a smile. "And thanks for dealing with GTA."

Pierre decided to walk to Le Café Royale and enjoy the pleasant weather. He reached the café in twenty minutes. He treated himself to two mugs of superb German beer, and found the Steak Café Royale unrivaled—he decided to recommend it to any friend of his who would be visiting Geneva. After settling the bill, and leaving a generous tip, he left the café feeling grateful to Germaine de Remusat for her splendid advice. He took a taxi back to the hotel, where he found the room cleaned, the bed made. After he removed his jacket and tie, he went into the bathroom and washed his face.

After drying his face slowly with a small, white towel, he looked at his reflection in the mirror and he was gripped by an urge to deliver his free-will speech to his always spellbound but nonexistent audience. He uttered a few words from the speech, which was etched in his memory, but immediately stopped himself and looked contemplatively at his face. With self-reproach, he told himself, I have to stop this nonsense. Perhaps delivering this absurd speech served to comfort me, to numb my existential angst, to subdue my inner demons. All were the product of the brutal and relentless emotional and verbal abuse by my father but he has already departed this world. Why should I continue with this absurd and nonsensical speech?

Pierre stretched out on his bed and, with the remote control in his hand, switched on a French channel; he waited for almost ten minutes for the news broadcast. The lead story stunned him. It announced that a thirty-two-year-old man, Valery Jupet, had been arrested on the instruction of the examining magistrate, Pierre-Yves Durant. Valery Jupet was accused of committing the five murders. Jupet, who still lived at home with his businessman father, his mother, and a younger brother, had worked in the army for six years before his service had been terminated due to some psychological maladies. Since his discharge from the army, he had been an on-and-off inmate at the White Beacon mental institution. The police had raided the Jupets' house and seized seven pistols, two silencers, and three rifles, including a .22-caliber Beretta that had been recently used.

Valery's father, André Jupet, who appeared on TV shocked and outraged, claimed that his son had the habit of doing target practice in the hills east of the city to release some of the stress of his psychological problems. Martin/Pierre recalled that his late Uncle Marcel had taught him how to use a Beretta and a Kalashnikov in that same area.

While the police commissioner, Robert Garnier, applauded the diligence of Chief Inspector Gerald Dupré and his highly trained and committed staff, André Jupet accused the police of conducting a contemptible witch-hunt. He had retained a top lawyer, Avocat Alain Pomier, to defend his son against this travesty of justice and the incompetence of the police and the examining magistrate. André Jupet told TV and newspaper reporters in an angry and hurt tone, "My son is a gentle soul. He could not and would not kill a bird, let alone another human being. His problems started when he joined the army. Before joining the army, he was normal and had never experienced any mental illnesses. I don't know what they did to him in the army. They destroyed him then sacked him for the mental afflictions they had caused him. They never cared about him after that." He paused for breath and then added, "It was a very unfortunate day when Valery joined the army. I lament the fact that the idea of his joining the army was mine, for he had wanted to train to be a chef. As he was an oversensitive person, I had thought that a military career would strengthen him. It was a very serious blunder that I will regret for the rest of my life." André's voice choked as he added, "Nonetheless, I have great confidence in our justice system. Justice will ultimately prevail and Valery will be set free."

Pierre's eyes were glued to the TV screen, though he did not hear what was said after the incredible lead story. How cruel! How unfair! He found himself in strong disagreement with the trust that Valery's father had in the justice system. Durant is biased, Dupré and his commissioner are biased, he told himself. They'd worked hard to deliver to the public and the judicial apparatus, with its horrendously unquestioning judges, a false perpetrator; any individual would have served their purposes. Poor Valery Jupet unluckily met their criteria for the serial killer: a young man with a record of mental illness who had served in the army; who owned a number of weapons; and who still lived with his parents. He met the full criteria in Alain Gilbert's second profile of the serial killer.

How sad, Pierre thought. Jupet is another collateral victim of my 'so-well-thought-out plan.' What plan! It just unraveled in every possible way. Where are my free-will decisions? Fate contrived to twist everything I planned and trounce my free will.

It was fate that landed Jupet in deep trouble. Now poor Jupet will be saddled with agonizing pain on top of his long, mental misery. Pierre was assailed with enormous guilt and sadness. He knew that the justice system would grind as slowly as a frail snail before it reached a verdict on Jupet's innocence or guilt. Martin felt sick to his stomach. He felt the scales of justice were heavily weighed against Jupet. The bastards would find him guilty as charged. Of course, the public and the media would be relieved and even delighted if Jupet was convicted. The masses, just like Durant and Dupré, are simply clamoring for a scapegoat, and the ill-starred Jupet is the right scapegoat as far as they are concerned. Most probably, the court will concur with their false and disgraceful conclusions. That much-acclaimed moron, Dr. Alain Gilbert had kicked off this cruel travesty of justice. How could anyone trust someone, however prominent and experienced in the field of criminology, who puts forward two profiles. I am sure if Gilbert had suggested three or four profiles, *Le Matin* would have jumped at them and fed them with fervor to the scared public, the embarrassed police, and the injudicious examining magistrate.

Even if—and it's a big if—Jupet is ultimately acquitted, he will be stigmatized for the rest of his life, Pierre thought. Fate had dealt him a crushing blow and put a burdensome cross on his shoulders. Pierre cursed Valery's father, André Jupet, for he had brought this catastrophe upon his son; he had rashly interfered in his son's career choice and aspirations. Instead of letting him walk his own path and become a chef, he'd shortsightedly pushed him to join the army to squash his sensitive spirit. André Jupet should blame himself, not the army, reflected Pierre.

He switched off the TV and despondently put his hand over his eyes as if to block out the misery of Valery Jupet and his own sense of guilt and incredulity. He rebuked himself: I never expected that my rage against my father would lead me to leave a string of innocent victims; had I known that so much horrific damage would be caused by what I had considered at the time to be a well-thought-out plan, I simply would have eliminated my father—and only my father—at the very outset.

Pierre decided to go downstairs to the bar to numb his sadness with a few drinks. I might also find some nice company to distract me from my despondency, he thought. With Jupet's arrest, he was scot-free in the eyes of the police and judicial systems, yet he loathed being beyond suspicion at the expense of an unhinged and innocent man.

In the bar, in his outgoing style, he approached an elegantly dressed African in his late forties, introduced himself, and struck up a conversation with him. The African told Martin Lavoie that his name was Ahmedo Diali. He had intelligent and prominent eyes and smooth, black skin, smooth as silk. Diali informed Martin that he worked in Geneva at the United Nations' International Labor Organization, ILO. He was a Senegalese who spoke excellent French.

Martin warmed to Ahmedo Diali, for he found him charming, knowledgeable, and frank, though he tended to think carefully about any question before replying in his soft voice. He was drinking Bloody Marys, while Martin stuck to Scotch on the rocks. Ahmedo was very pleased when Martin told him he was going to Ethiopia to work with a humanitarian NGO, ADPA.

Diali was a very forthcoming conversationalist. Without prompting, he told Martin he was living in Geneva while his uneducated wife was living with their four sons in Dakar. And Martin proved to be an excellent listener. He did not argue but kept the dialogue flowing smoothly.

Diali enlightened Lavoie about the horrific extent of corruption in Africa and how it was abetted by the West; how beautiful Ethiopia and Ethiopian women are; and how a few Third World countries have labor policies that were ahead of the ILO's bench marks. But sadly they were not enforced. Diali then expounded on the concept of governance, how democracy is malfunctioning in some of the so called 'civilized countries' because of poor governance, then expressed his conviction that governance is more important than democracy—a contention that Martin was not in full agreement with. However, Martin was seduced by Ahmedo's thesis that governance is needed at the organizational, national, regional and international levels if the peoples of the world are to achieve real social justice through effective economic and social development, democracy, capitalism, and commercial, technological and financial globalization. And that people should take governance in their hands and force their governments to be more transparent, and compel their politicians to stop being consenting captives to the corporate world. It sounded to Martin like a 'Marxist-Capitalist' manifesto, though Ahmedo's soft voice and sharp intellect made it a viable one.

Martin/Pierre enjoyed two pleasant hours with his African interlocutor before retiring to his room on the fourth floor. Immediately after returning to his room, he ordered a club sandwich from room service but no wine, since he had had four double Scotches while he conversed with Ahmedo Diali at the bar. After eating his club sandwich, he asked for a wake-up call at seven the next morning, then switched off the light.

The faces of poor Valery Jupet and his shocked father, André, vividly intruded in his mind in the darkness, keeping him awake for some time. The words of André Jupet resonated in his ears: 'I don't know what they did to him in the army.' Pierre was intrigued by this question. What did they do to Valery Jupet in the army? he wondered. Though he regretted as much as Valery's father the unwise decision to force the sensitive Valery to join the army instead of working his way to becoming a chef, he thought that André deserved to regret his interference in his son's career choice for the rest of his life. No father who respected his son would do that; and no strong son would allow his father to interfere in his major, or even minor, life choices.

The cruel and unfounded accusation of Valery Jupet preoccupied Martin/Pierre for some time before he managed to sleep.

# CHAPTER 29

The next morning after enjoying a hearty breakfast at the hotel, Pierre walked to the bank, carrying his large briefcase. As the weather was sunny and mild, he enjoyed his leisurely stroll. Germaine de Remusat was delighted to see him. She gave him his checkbook in a white envelope, and each of the two credit cards in separate envelopes, advising him to put his signature on the back of each credit card as soon as possible.

"Thank you, Germaine, for suggesting Le Café Royale yesterday. It was the best steak I've ever had."

"I am glad you enjoyed it, Martin," she said with a broad smile and a twinkle in her eyes. "So I don't have to pay you for what the meal cost you!"

"No. Not at all," said Martin and stood up. "Whenever I come to Geneva, I will make sure that I come to see you, Germaine."

Martin left the bank and decided to wander around, taking in the flavor and atmosphere of the city. After strolling aimlessly for half an hour, he went looking for a more compact and presentable briefcase. In the window of one shop his eyes fell on an elegant, dark-gray briefcase. He immediately liked it, bought it, and paid in cash.

As he walked out with his old and new briefcases, he thought about poor Valery Jupet, mentally ill and erroneously accused of crimes he did not commit. Can I do anything to prove his innocence? No way, he answered himself. He earnestly wished he were able to save Valery from the barbarous claws of the judicial system. If the case went to court, Pierre knew that it would be a daunting task for Avocat Pomier, or any other defense lawyer, to exonerate the unlucky Valery Jupet. The court, just like the scared masses, would be looking for retribution, and Jupet would be humiliated and described as a heartless, depraved monster. He would be convicted and sent to prison for a long time or to a mental institution for the rest of his miserable life. While the citizens and the media had already, fallaciously, delivered their verdict on Valery in base and obscene language, the court would sum up the same fallacious verdict in dignified and lofty legal parlance. The only difference between the scared masses and the misguided court would be in the terminology—not in brainpower and not in mercy.

Then he took a taxi to the hotel, and went up to his room with his briefcases. He took off his tie and jacket, draping them on a chair, and then carefully transferred the contents of his old briefcase into his brand new briefcase. He decided to give his old briefcase to the concierge the next morning or simply leave it in the room to be taken by one of the chambermaids. Then he picked up Saramago's *All the Names*, and took the elevator down to the hotel's bar. He sat at a window table and ordered a double Scotch with four cubes of ice. He found Saramago's dispensing with punctuation and his long sentences a challenge but he kept reading and soon he was beguiled and unconsciously flowing with the very strange story of a junior clerk, Senhor José, who worked in the city's Central Registry, checking births, marriages, and deaths. Martin found the epigraph thought provoking: 'You know the name you were given, you do not know the name you have.' In my case, Senhor Saramago, I have three names: Pierre Boucher, Jean-Claude Marchand, and Martin Lavoie, and I feel they are all real. Yet I admit that I could have another name that I don't know about. But, on balance, would it really matter if I had been named Robert Garnier, Pierre-Yves Aubert, or Valery Jupet, and I was brought up under the brutal abuse of my father, whether he was called Boucher, Garnier, Aubert, or Jupet? To my mind, a name is just like a brand name or a product bar code; it wouldn't have mattered. Senhor Saramago, a name is simply an identification tag given randomly, at the whim of the parents or the parents' close friends, to each individual among the multitudes of Homo sapiens.

After having another Scotch on the rocks, he closed his book and took the elevator to his room. It occurred to him to watch the French national TV channel to find out if there had been any developments in the case of the star-crossed Valery Jupet. There was a program featuring a panel of commentators debating the need for internationally agreed-upon standards to govern the global financial sector, which was plagued by huge scandals stemming from the corrupt corporate cultures of some of the biggest banks in the world and the rampant crony capitalism between big businesses and politicians. He found the discussion interesting and followed it avidly. He mused that they should have invited Ahmedo Diali to join the debate.

As the clock approached eight in the evening, he sat on the edge of his bed, with his eyes fixed on the TV screen. The news broadcast came on at eight o'clock, and the lead story stunned Pierre. It came as an unexpected knockout.

The broadcaster announced that Valery Jupet had been found dead in his solitary cell at six o'clock that morning; he had punctured an artery in his left wrist with a ball-point pen and had bled to death. He added that this was not the first time Valery Jupet had tried to commit suicide; he had tried to kill himself on three occasions before but failed. This time he succeeded. He went on, "After thirteen hours of interrogation, his interrogators were able to snatch a full confession from him. He confessed to the five murders but he claimed he could not remember how, where, and why he had committed them. At some point during the interrogation, he hid a slim, ball-point pen—one of many on the interrogation table—in the pocket of his prison garb".

Jupet's prominent lawyer, Alain Pomier, who appeared in an expensive, blue, double-breasted suit on the front steps of a high-rise building with a middle-aged woman in a black business suit standing behind him, launched a stinging and aggressive attack on what he called the 'draconian powers that be'. He lambasted them for their unacceptable method of interrogation, which subjected his psychologically sick and now deceased client to inhumane and brutal strain until he gave them all what they wanted. "This is an unacceptable confession because it was obtained under extreme duress," he declared.

Then he said, jabbing the air with his index finger, any normal person—let alone a man with serious mental problems—subjected to unrelenting yelling and intimidation by different teams of interrogators would give in to the demands of such brutal Spanish inquisitors within six to eight hours. "No court of law would accept a confession extracted through sadistic intimidation. A confession obtained under brutish duress is not worth the paper it was written on or the tapes it was recorded on. Though my client died due to police incompetence, hubris, and lack of supervision, I am determined to prove he did not commit these crimes. It is my duty to clear his name and restore to his grieving family their dignity. Nothing short of that. The first thing I will do is to ensure that the videotapes of this inhumane interrogation are released—willingly or through a judicial order. I want every French citizen to know that she or he is not immune to such barbaric interrogation. And I hope the examining magistrate and the police will not tamper with these tapes."

Avocat Pomier declared he would ask an independent ballistics lab to ascertain whether the bullets used in the five crimes came from Jupet's Beretta. He was certain that the bullets collected from the bodies of the victims were fired from another

Beretta, not from Valery Jupet's Beretta. Moreover, he would prove that the authorities had not only conspired to falsely accuse and arrest Valery Jupet, but also caused his death. "I am determined to hold them responsible," said Pomier, adjusted his expensive necktie, and added, "The examining magistrate and the police should feel ashamed when we prove that Jupet had tight alibis when these crimes were committed. Regularly his mother ensured that he took his sleeping pills by ten in the evening. He went to bed by ten thirty or eleven and always woke up around seven the next morning. A more damaging fact to the farce of the examining magistrate and the police is that when Mrs. Gautier and Mr. Dimitrov were murdered in Le Jardin Anglais, Valery Jupet was spending two weeks with his paternal grandparents in Rouen. How could he have managed to commit these crimes here while he was in Rouen? I want the examining magistrate to explain this riddle." He paused then raised his voice, "It was a naive and disgraceful frame-up of an innocent man. It is my intention to force the examining magistrate and the police to admit their guilt. They will be held guilty in the court of French public opinion. They should be subjected to the maximum disciplinary penalties by their superiors, or I will take their superiors to task. If the examining magistrate and the police commissioner think this case is closed, they could not be more wrong. Mark my words: It will not be closed until Valery Jupet is vindicated and his name cleared. I shall not rest until those responsible for his tragic end are dragged through the mud. Have a great day, ladies and gentlemen." With that, Pomier turned around and entered the building followed by the middle-aged woman, ignoring the questions that some of the jostling reporters shouted at him.

Pierre found Pomier very impressive and very combative; he found himself supportive of him. If there is any lawyer who could prove Jupet's innocence, it is Alain Pomier, he reflected. His heart was with Jupet, his bereaved family, and Pomier. And justice—true justice. If there was such a thing.

Then Valery's father, André Jupet, appeared on camera in front of his upscale house, wearing a white shirt and brown trousers, to address a throng of reporters. Though he looked composed, his face was a picture of profound sadness. He held his clasped hands in front of him and spoke in a slow and broken voice. "I have great trust in Avocat Alain Pomier and I am confident he will clear the name of my son, beyond any shred of doubt. My son did not commit these horrendous murders. The authorities subjected him to inhumane interrogation although they knew he was mentally and psychologically vulnerable." He paused, combing his white hair with his left hand, and then resumed in his broken voice, "The army destroyed my son, and now the examining magistrate and the police killed him. Our family wants an investigation into why my son was left unsupervised in a solitary cell when they knew he had attempted suicide three times before. We want to get to the bottom of this. Was it a wicked act or a matter of gross negligence by the authorities? We want to know how Valery was allowed by experienced professionals to take a ball-point pen from their table and hide it. It can't be ruled out that they saw him doing that and decided to turn a blind eye, with the malicious intention that he kills himself so the case could be closed. I suspect they wanted victory at any cost."

He halted and stared blankly at the reporters, before adding, "We want the authorities to give us explanations. A lot of explanations. I believe Avocat Pomier will force them to give us these explanations. He will make our local authorities the laughing stock of France." The grieving father paused for long moments, then abruptly said, "I ask you to respect our privacy at this time of darkness. If you have any questions, please address them to the office of Avocat Pomier. That is all. And thank you." With that, he entered his house and closed its large and exquisitely made door.

When the newscaster moved to another news item, Pierre switched off the TV. He looked blankly at the black screen for a long time, his jaw resting on the palm of his right hand, as though his brain was not functioning. When he managed to gather his wits, he let out a deep sigh of bafflement. This is fate, pure and unadulterated, he said to himself. It had led poor Valery to his grave and dealt his family a cruel and staggering blow.

Pierre thought if there was anyone to blame, it was Dr. Alain Gilbert, for he had planted the idea that the killer was a young man with psychological afflictions, who had worked in the armed forces or law enforcement agencies, and still lived with his parents. The public and, sadly, the authorities had swallowed that profile wholesale.

The police and the examining magistrate were as guilty as Dr. Gilbert was. Where was their professionalism? Where was their gray matter? Where was Professor Ronald Brault, who was retained to advise the police? They were disastrously influenced by Gilbert's psychological nonsense. Consequently they were derailed, and arrested a disturbed and innocent man. Then negligently, or perhaps deliberately, they allowed him to kill himself.

What a travesty of justice! It is what many people call fate. There is no other explanation, he concluded. Certainly, Jupet did not do anything to merit such a cruel end. The helpless man was trapped. No free-will action by him would have helped him to wriggle out of the quicksand of the prosecutorial system.

Pierre asked to be given a wake-up call at six the next morning. He brushed his teeth, put on his pajamas, and lay down to sleep after switching off the lamp on the bedside table. During his sleep, he had a blurred dream in which he saw two faceless men and a woman but he sensed that they were Alexander Dimitrov, Valery Jupet, and Catherine Rolle. The three stood talking to each other, but he could not hear what they were talking about, as they stood at some distance from him on rue Karl Marx. It was dark, but he could see the three figures speaking in an intimate way in soft voices. He walked toward them calmly, but they walked away to keep their distance from him. Suddenly he found Martine Aubert standing next to him. She put her hand on his shoulder and whispered, "Have you met Valery Jupet?"

"No, I haven't, Martine," he replied. He could see her green eyes twinkling in the darkness.

She raised her hand and pointed a finger at the three figures. "He is the one in the army uniform. He is one of your collateral victims, Pierre." In his dream, he was surprised that she called him Pierre, not Jean-Claude.

"No, Martine. No, he's not," Pierre insisted in a petrified voice.

"Yes, that's Valery, Pierre," Martine whispered to him. The fact that Martine had discovered his true name frightened him and he felt a lump in his throat.

Then he heard Dr. Catherine Rolle saying to the man in the military uniform, "You can't blame Dr. Alain Gilbert, Valery. Pierre Boucher is the one to blame."

Martine withdrew her hand from his shoulder and whispered, "You see, darling?"

Pierre struggled to make an objection but he lost his voice. As he strove to explain to Martine that what Dr. Rolle said was unfair and false, his voice failed him. Then Martine, Alexander, Catherine, and Valery suddenly vanished, leaving Pierre alone and scared on the dark street.

After a few chilling moments, he managed to wake up. Shaken and dazed, he groped for the bedside light and switched it on. Gradually, he realized he was in a hotel in Geneva and he was on his way to Johannesburg. What he had just experienced was a horrible, illogical, and muddled dream.

It was an unsettling dream, but still a dream, he told himself. Glancing at his watch, he found it was three fifteen in the morning. Feeling thirsty, he drank a small bottle of water near the TV set. It was a dream. It was just a dream, he assured himself before he returned to his bed and switched off the light. Within a few minutes, he slipped into a dreamless sleep until he was startled by the wake-up call at six.

After settling his hotel bill, he took a taxi to the airport with his suitcase and new briefcase. He arrived at the airport at twenty minutes to eight, two hours and twenty minutes ahead of the departure time. Before proceeding to the check-in and immigration counters, he exchanged five thousand euros into US dollars and put them in his briefcase, except for one thousand, which he inserted in his wallet. In the departure lounge, he walked into a crowded café and ordered two croissants and a café au lait. After consuming this light breakfast, he ordered a large, black coffee.

As he sipped the coffee, he recalled the convoluted and petrifying dream; he again dismissed it as a mere dream. In broad daylight, it was easy to dismiss the unsettling dream. Pierre had never attached much significance to dreams, unlike many people, he reflected. It always surprised him that some people dissect their dreams, analyze their fragmented components, and give them menacing or auspicious interpretations and meanings. He considered dreams to be an emotional safety valve that the brain uses to dispense with some coiled feelings or tensions from the chaos of the subconscious, rather than messages to be given undue meanings where there is no meaning. Nor are dreams intimations to be followed or to take action on because of their supposed revelations. Perhaps they could be revelations to prophets, but there are no prophets around in our time. Unless, he reflected, one adopts the logic of the definition of an intellectual that Françoise Lépine gave to Martine's father and his two philosopher friends: 'an intellectual is anyone who decides he is an intellectual'. So anyone who decides he is a prophet, is a prophet; and he can find hidden messages, profound intimations, and divine revelations in his dreams.

His ten o'clock Swiss Air flight to Johannesburg was delayed by fifteen minutes before it took off. Pierre had an aisle seat; and a sturdy, silent Briton in a short-sleeved, white shirt and dark-khaki trousers was sitting beside him, next to the window. Pierre decided he was a Briton because he saw him reading last Sunday's *News of the World*. He recalled Richard Naylor's mother-in-law, Mary McGregor, when he was a guest at the Naylors' home to polish up his English. Despite her love of literature and Shakespeare's plays— particularly *Macbeth*, which she always called the Scottish play— Mary was addicted to reading *News of the World*. The Briton had closely cropped hair and a smart tattoo on his left muscular arm, depicting a dark blue heart bleeding from a black arrow that pierced it.

Pierre thought the well-built Briton looked like the image he had of a mercenary—or an operations management consultant—and wondered why a white mercenary would fly economy class despite the substantial amount of money he earned in his job. The Briton kept peering through the round window and was evidently not interested in striking up a conversation with Martin. Pierre, aka Martin, greeted him in English, "Good morning."

He gave Pierre a terse good morning without looking at him, and then returned to his English newspaper. After some twenty minutes, he folded the paper, placed it between him and the seat arm next to the window, and consulted the onboard movie and music booklet. Then he stuck the headphones in his ears. Pierre was not offended by the Briton's aloofness, for he sensed that the man was preoccupied with gloomy internal thoughts.

Over the aircraft sound system, the first officer welcomed the passengers and assured them the short delay in takeoff would be made up for during the flight, and they would arrive in Johannesburg at the scheduled time. He made his announcement first in English, then in French, and lastly in German.

During the flight, Pierre took his time reading the day's *Le Monde* and *Le Figaro* before watching an American film. It was a good thriller, *The General's Daughter*. He found it absorbing. Then he alternated between ruminating and reading Saramago's *All the Names*.

He knew that he would not be able to go to COMCO and meet Bill Miller until Monday, and he decided to have a relaxing weekend and try to take in some parts of the city on Saturday and Sunday. Maybe he'd continue reading *All the Names*. After consuming a reasonable lunch and two small bottles of French red wine, he went to the bathroom, where he used the toilet, washed his hands and face, and then looked at himself in the small mirror. He was gripped by the urge to deliver his free-will speech to his imaginary audience. He gazed fiercely at his face. "Stop this nonsense. No ridiculous speeches ever again to a nonexistent audience. Never. Ever," he said aloud. He looked into the mirror and silently stated, "No more childish speeches. No more imaginary audiences. No more standing ovations." A firm conviction swept over him that he would never return to his hallucinatory speech. When he returned to his seat, he found the Briton next to the window fast asleep after consuming six cans of beer. So even a mercenary could be knocked out by six beers, he mused.

Finding himself reflecting on destiny, he argued it could be rosy and rewarding, or dark and agonizing. I am thinking about our destiny in this life, before going into what Khayyam called 'the box of oblivion'. In this temporal world, some are handed benevolent destinies; others are saddled with wretched destinies. Is it my destiny to go to Africa and remain there? And to die there? I am not afraid of death. Death, which claimed my angel of a mother and my beloved maternal uncle, is not able to stop me from loving them as long as I live. An inner voice told him: the fact that I loved them, and will always love them, is not due to my free will but because they truly loved me, and I reciprocated their love, boundlessly. Love is never the result of free will, he reflected. It is above and beyond free will.

What free will did Valery Jupet have? Not a bit. Perhaps he was destined from birth to suffer from mental illness because of his genes, his upbringing, or his unwilling joining of the army. He was destined to be accused unfairly of crimes he did not commit, and, more sadly, he was destined to commit suicide in prison. Pierre doubted if Jupet was like him in deluding himself that his decisions and actions emanated from his free will. Maybe Valery Jupet never thought about, let alone adhered to, the concept of free will.

For the last few months, I have been deluded by the illusion that I had turned my first, fortuitous encounter with Martine Aubert to my advantage: I immediately seduced her, she provided me with a sanctuary in her father's abandoned apartment, and we became friends and lovers. Was this a free-will decision by me, as I had duped myself, or a derailment? It was a derailment. If I had stuck to my original plan of renting an apartment in a nearby town, I could have carried out the murders without the need to leave France; I could have surfaced in my city and declared I had returned when I received the tragic news of my mother's demise. Is my traveling now to South Africa to meet Bill Miller the result of my free will or the workings of fate?

Where was my free will then? Where is my free will now?

The odds of probability, he thought, are heavily stacked against free will. He pondered the matter for some time and suddenly realized that human beings, in reality, have no free will. The thought was like a full moon emerging from an eclipse; it was like a blind person suddenly recovering his sight. It was a eureka moment. A cloud had vanished. A shroud had been removed.

The sleeping Briton next to him suddenly straightened up, opened his bloodshot eyes, rubbed them briskly, and then slumped against his seat and continued his slumber. Pierre wondered how this supposed mercenary could consume six beers and not need to go to the toilet. Perhaps mercenaries

are trained to retain their urine for prolonged periods. However, as operations management consultants, they would not call it urine retention but 'fluid retention'. A civilized euphemism—prolonged or sustained fluid retention—as civilized as 'operations management consultant' instead of 'mercenary'. Unexpectedly, Pierre Boucher/Martin Lavoie felt a gradual but increasing affinity with the silent Briton. The man was as well built and trim as his late Uncle Marcel had been. However, he recalled that Marcel never flew economy class after he entered the field of operations management consulting. The Briton's quietness did not disturb Martin and reminded him that Uncle Marcel had been the type of person with whom he could sit silently without feeling any awkwardness or nervousness. Was this a sign of what Marcel used to call *force tranquille*, the ability to remain quiet in the presence of other human beings yet exude to them a sense of being comfortable and comforting, relaxed and relaxing?

Pierre glanced at the sleeping Briton with his cropped hair and tanned complexion for a few moments. If he was a mercenary, was it a choice he had made through free will? I doubt it, he answered himself. For sure, many circumstances had contrived to make him a mercenary, while he misguidedly believed he had been making decisive and free-will choices. Like Uncle Marcel: if the army had not sacked him, he would not have become a mercenary. He would have worked his way up the ranks and retired as a general. People believe mercenaries have no conscience. Whether this is true or false, is conscience something we are naturally born with? Or something we acquire from our family, society, psychological make-up, and our circumstances and experiences? The verdict on such questions is very problematic, he reflected.

He returned to *All the Names* and some words struck a chord with him: 'Don't be afraid, the darkness you're in is no greater than the darkness inside your own body, they are two darknesses separated by a skin—' and 'My dear chap, you have to learn to live with the darkness outside just as you learned to live with the darkness inside.'

I am a person who has already learned to live with the two darknesses, my dear Saramago. This is what my brain, the wiring of which I had little say in, led me to do. Undisputedly, our minds, with their innumerable configurations, affect and determine what we desire and what we will. We will what our brains will and we act on what we erroneously believe to be our will. We assume we are free to will what we will. But actually we are not free to will what we will. Anyone can do what she or he wills, but none can will what she or he wills, he mused.

How could I have missed this simple fact for such a long time?

Relief washed over Pierre when it occurred to him that the murders he had committed were not born of his free will. Were they preordained? Was it fate? Was it the destiny of his victims to meet their end at his hands? It is certainly beyond my comprehension, and beyond the comprehension of all mortals, including sages, philosophers, and prophets.

Though Pierre was still burdened with remorse over killing Alexander Dimitrov and Catherine Rolle, he reflected that it was fate, not their free will, that put them in the wrong place at the wrong time. Fate is an irresistible yet invisible force that can bring down its smashing fist on any one of us, cruelly crushing one's hopes, dreams, and even one's life. Alternatively, its invisible force can benevolently bestow on us healthy genes, great love, and nurturing upbringing. Some people label this force providence; some call it luck, bad or good; some think it is a metaphysical phenomenon. After earnest contemplation, he found himself forced to admit that being good is the outcome of pure good luck, and being bad is the result of sheer bad luck. Just like being either beautiful or ugly. No one has the choice in being ugly or beautiful. It is a matter of unadulterated luck. He reflected that many people, even very intelligent people, are loath to concur with this glaring fact of the human condition.

It occurred to Pierre that no one can outmaneuver fate— even with the best thought-out decisions or plans. The moment one makes a decision at any point in time, he or she at once has excluded many—perhaps innumerable—other options, paths, and directions. This is what management and economics thinkers call 'opportunity cost.' By making a certain choice, one automatically excludes other choices and their related opportunities. The decision made could be the nexus for a trajectory of unalterable repercussions that could be immensely less fortunate than those that could have cascaded from an excluded path. Any significant decision taken would trigger its own dynamics with interwoven actions and ramifications, leading to one's nemesis or salvation.

The pilot asked the passengers to return to their seats and fasten their seat belts because the aircraft would soon be encountering an area of air turbulence. The flight attendants jumped into action, hastily checking that all passengers had their seat belts secured and the seats were in the right position, before they rushed to their jump seats.

A young African woman, wearing a white blouse and a tight, red skirt that accentuated her bulky buttocks in a distasteful way, forcibly shepherded a vocally angry three- or four-year-old girl and a docile, slightly older boy to their seats. Evidently, she had pulled them out of the toilet. The obstinate girl seemed terrified and bewildered. The black woman let go of the boy's hand and smacked the terrorized girl three times on the back of her head—screaming at her repeatedly, "Shut up, you idiot." Pierre was incensed. It touched him as scathingly personal. I have seen it all. I have suffered it all. I have lived it all, he told himself. He felt strong empathy with the powerless girl, abused verbally and physically and in public; an intense urge to stand up and harshly scold the barbaric woman took hold of him, but the jerking and swaying of the aircraft prevented him from leaving his seat.

They experienced a horrifying air turbulence for almost half an hour. Pierre could see through the window that they were in the midst of thick, dark clouds. Inside the aircraft, a dense cloud of apprehension and silence settled upon the passenger, most of whom braced themselves, with different catastrophic scenarios and imaginings, for an inevitable end. The sleeping, drunken man next to him remained unperturbed by the scary, jerky movement of the jumbo jet. Pierre thought this simply confirmed his assumption that this Briton was an operations management consultant.

Pierre's heart went out to the little girl. He reflected that no one could tell the extent of the damage that the gross public humiliation her mother thoughtlessly served her would have on the still-moldable brain wiring of the poor girl. It could have a permanently negative and destructive impact on her psychological makeup that might plague her into adulthood. Not even an army of preeminent neurologists could foretell its repercussions, he mused.

Then the pilot announced that they were out of the turbulence and reassured the passengers that the flight would reach Johannesburg on schedule. At once, some passengers applauded enthusiastically and others laughed joyously. The flight attendants abandoned their jump seats, and some of passengers resumed their chattering.

I am the offspring of a man and a woman who decided to marry, who decided to conceive me, and I was born carrying a mixture of their genes. I was not involved in these critical decisions. I had no choice or voice in them. Furthermore, I was brought up in a certain society, culture, and family with their particular ethos, beliefs, and attitudes. I did not choose to be the only child in my family. If I had had two or three siblings, I could have—perhaps together with them—dealt with my father's bestial abuse with indifference, mockery, or amusement instead of rage and hate. I had little influence on the schools I was made to attend. Above all, I did not determine the values of my society, my schools, and my family. This poor African girl did not choose this cruel and heartless woman as a mother, nor did she choose her family, tribe, or country.

And indeed, what made her obstinate in the first place, unlike her docile elder brother? I am sure she did not choose her temperament.

One's parents could be his best friends or his worst enemies. How would my life have turned out if my mother was my worst enemy, and my father was my best friend? Or if both were good friends to me? My life certainly would have turned out entirely different. If my father had loved me, or at least had not mistreated me, I would have been a different Pierre; I would not have cared if he had a harem, let alone three mistresses. His persistent degradation of me, since my childhood, led me to eliminate him and two of his three mistresses. It was fate that made him my father, and a beast of a father. My retribution was not the product of my free will. Was it preordained? That could be a possibility, but I don't know for certain.

Wasn't all I have done a crystal-clear chain of willful blindness? Not my free will. Isn't what I used to call free will nothing but blind willfulness? Pierre pondered that the blatant reality, which most people do not like to face or admit—perhaps not even ponder— is that we are free to do what we will but we are never free to will what we will.

The meek and dim-witted as well as the brave and the bright-minded are equally vulnerable prey to willful blindness and cannot escape their destiny; whichever path they take, with scant or abundant deliberation, and whether at a double-pronged or multipronged crossroads, takes them willy-nilly to their destiny. Willful and unwillful blindness are part and parcel of the human condition; they are the products of how our emotions and intellect interact consciously and unconsciously—and this is an enigma that is still beyond human comprehension, he told himself.

It distinctly occurred to Pierre that it was his father's despicable behavior toward him and his mother that pushed him to his vicious spree of retribution. My hate and rage against my father led me to take a path with tragic and irreversible consequences. A path I took under the delusion of my free will.

An astounding realization dawned on him. My father loaded the gun, and I pulled the trigger.

My father loaded the gun. And I simply pulled the trigger, again and again.

# ACKNOWLEDGEMENTS

**M**y profound sense of gratitude to Professor ElFatih M. Baraka of Lancaster, U.K., who sustained his earnest moral and practical support of this project from the very outset.

I am immensely grateful to Ms. Alice Umbarak of Stockport, U.K., for her attentive,   insightful, and patient editing of a number of drafts of the story. I am deeply indebted to Mr. Khalid Alzain of London, UK, who provided strong interest and practical advice at different stages of the development of this work.

My thanks also go to many friends and family members who wanted to be apprised of the progress of the story, and proffered their encouragement.

Many thanks to Ms. Ginnie Gale, Publishing Consultant, and the design and editing teams at CreateSpace for their much-appreciated efforts in the production of this work.

However, any mistakes or erroneous ideas are solely mine.

8036549R00261

Printed in Great Britain
by Amazon.co.uk, Ltd.,
Marston Gate.